The Cleaverman

WOL-VRIEY

Burning Bulb
PUBLISHING

The Cleaverman

WOL-VRIEY

Burning Bulb
PUBLISHING

The Cleaverman
By **Wol-vriey**

Burning Bulb Publishing
P.O. Box 4721
Bridgeport, WV 26330-4721
United States of America
www.BurningBulbPublishing.com

Cover designed by Gary Lee Vincent.
Author Photo: Lolade Akinsowon © 2014.

First Edition.

Paperback Edition ISBN: 978-1-948278-20-1

Printed in the United States of America.

This novel is dedicated to the memory of my dearly beloved wife,
Victoria Oluwatoyin Jesuto (1962 – 2019),
a wonderful and beautiful woman who'll be sorely missed.

CHAPTER 1

Nicole

It was raining in Raynham that midsummer Tuesday night. A light drizzle at first, but then the sky filled up with boiling black clouds and it got stormy.

It was after dinner and Nicole Ellsworth was staring out of her living room window at the downpour. "Just eight-thirty and the world looks like midnight," she remarked over her shoulder. "And the damn rain is flooding our front lawn again . . . and the street looks like a river. And everyone's rides look in danger of being floated away to the Boston Harbor."

She shut the drapes and turned to face her guests again. "Sorry, guys, but for the moment you're all trapped here."

The Ellsworths had a spacious living room, with pale walls, dark green carpeting and seemingly mismatched drapes covering the windows. Their house furniture was a mixture of old and new. Most of it came from the couple's antiques shop. Folks unfamiliar with Nicole and Tommy and entering their home for the first time mistakenly assumed that their house was a part of their business, a warehouse where they kept things they didn't need yet. Reinforcing this impression were the stuffed animals and mounted heads, diverse clocks, various curios and odd decorations from around the world that filled their house.

Nicole smiled at her guests. She was a small woman with long dark hair.

Aside from herself and her husband Tommy, there were eight others seated in the living room:

Her good friend Leona Patten was stretched out on a white sofa, chatting to Tommy. Oh Leona! A psychic brunette dressed in a flowing rainbow-striped gown and looking as if she'd taken a wrong turn out of the sixties; or maybe fallen into a time-warp coma during a seventies Led Zeppelin concert and just woken up. Leona, waving a hand that trailed cigarette smoke like exhaust fumes at Nicole's husband and most likely telling him the color of his aura. What was it? Dark like his hair, or blue like his eyes?

Then there were the Whitfield brothers—Carl and Jeffrey—both handsome sandy-haired men in their early thirties. The brothers were rich: their recently deceased father had left them a chemicals company.

Carl Whitfield was a playboy. Tonight he was in company of a curvaceous girl he'd introduced as Susan Riley. Long blonde hair, sparkling blue eyes, long blue earrings; thin lips and thick red lipstick. Her white dress didn't exactly show her thong, but it was so short that she could easily have replaced Sharon Stone in that interrogation scene in *Basic Instinct*. Nicole was certain Susan Riley's breasts were artificial.

"She's an escort," Leona had whispered to Nicole in the kitchen while they'd been clearing away the dinner dishes. "You know how Carl never dates nice girls."

Jeffrey Whitfield was here with his hulk of a boyfriend, Mike Beefcake. Nicole and Tommy had both done double takes when Jeffrey introduced Mike, until Mike had explained that he was a bodybuilder—he owned a gym located downtown along the New State Highway. His real surname was Rossi; the 'Beefcake' moniker was just what he used for bodybuilding competitions. Mike Beefcake looked the part too. In contrast to his boyfriend Jeffrey, who was slight and slightly effeminate, Mr. Beefcake radiated strength and vitality. Though of average height, muscles bulged out his sweater. (He seemed to have a large bulge in his pants also.) One could easily imagine him oiled up and flexing his muscles on a contest stage; a thought which gave Nicole a tiny tingle of regret—*Oh, but he's gay! The pair of 'em are getting married soon!*

Then there was Mike's younger sister Angela. Angela Rossi was a lawyer. She worked with the Bristol County DA's office in Taunton. She was a mousy and awkward dark-haired woman in a beige pantsuit, who with an almost pathetic air of desperation had been trying to engage the dashing Carl Whitfield in conversation all evening. Carl had been politely responsive—Angela was clearly a brilliant woman and all her conversation was witty—but Susan Riley wasn't having any of it. Each time Carl's gaze flickered to Miss Rossi's admittedly ample chest, Susan would find something 'airhead' to do to distract him.

Most recently she'd 'accidentally' spilled the contents of her purse and spent three minutes bent over retrieving their contents, all the while wagging her butt in Carl's face.

Last of their guests were Mitch and Jacqui Mullins, the young couple who lived down their street, Hall Street. Both were in their late twenties. The husband was tall, dark and fattish, the wife small, light and slim. So far tonight the Mullins had been addressing one another in short, terse sentences, as though they'd had a quarrel before leaving home. Mitch had been out of work for a while now, and had apparently begun drinking heavily to compensate. Jacqui was the boss's secretary at Clip, a Taunton nightclub. (The town of Taunton adjoined on Raynham's south boundary.) As generally happened when the wife was the primary breadwinner in a household, there was tension between them.

Or maybe there was more to it than that. Leona had hinted as much. She'd said Jacqui's aura was scarlet and 'unfaithful.' Nicole didn't know what to make of that.

Nicole walked back to join everyone. Dinner was over, and now they all had either coffee or wine. Leona and Carl were both smoking.

Sure, Nicole might not know if Jacqui was cheating on Mitch, but she knew for sure that Mitch did have a drinking problem. That much was becoming increasingly obvious the further the evening progressed, Mitch was on his fourth glass of wine already. His voice was a little slurred and his eyes a little spaced-out. Nicole hoped the young fellow wasn't going to embarrass himself. Then she changed her mind: maybe it would be amusing if he did; it might brighten up the evening a little.

"So, what do we do now?" Nicole's husband Tommy asked her as she sat beside him, Leona folding her legs to make space for her on the couch. He pointed his mug of coffee at the Mullinses. "You two can't walk home in this downpour; you'll be soaked to the skin before you even reach the sidewalk."

"We could chance it," Mitch said. "There's a game on—"

"Forget it," Jacqui said sharply, "I'm not looking to have a mud bath tonight. And you're just gonna get hammered once we get home anyway." Then she smiled at Tommy. "And besides, we're not the only ones stuck here in the rain. Leona's stuck too—"

"Oh, I'm family," Leona said, her airy wave leaving a trail of cigarette smoke. "I sleep here all the time when Paul's out of town in his truck."

"Where's he gone this time?" Tommy asked, scratching his chin.

"Down to Missouri with a load of farm machinery."

Outside the rain kept coming down.

"So what do we do?" Nicole asked her friends. Overhead, she could hear the rain beat like hammers on the roof of their two-story house. The relentlessness of the downpour and the sound of rain splattering the windows with each succeeding violent gust of wind was making her feel uneasy. She looked around at everyone. Jeffrey and Mike, both seated closest to the television were watching *Mad Max* on TCM with the volume turned off. Seated farthest from the television, Carl had just passed a lit cigarette to Susan, who took a drag of it and stared contentedly at poor Angela Rossi, who, after losing the seduction wars for the umpteenth time tonight, had now gotten out her cellphone and was texting someone. Opposite Nicole and Tommy, Jacqui was intently whispering something to Mitch. He was nodding but didn't seem happy about whatever she was telling him. Most likely she was trying to stop him pouring the drinks back.

On Nicole's right, Leona was blowing cigarette smoke past her face while humming. Nicole nestled against Tommy, who draped a beefy protective arm around her shoulder.

"So, any suggestions?" Tommy asked, then added, with pointed stares at Mike and Jeffrey, "And no, you guys—we're *not* watching Mel Gibson on the boob tube."

Mike and Jeffrey continued watching *Mad Max*, so Tommy picked up the remote and turned the TV off.

"Aw, dude!" Jeffrey moaned. "The hell you go and do that for?—that's the best part."

"Yeah," Mike agreed, with a rather unmasculine pout on his large lips.

"Guys, think of something all-inclusive. A way to spend this wet August night when God seems to be trying to flood the earth again."

"We try rebuilding Noah's Ark?" Mitch suggested. "That'll surely pass a few hours."

Jacqui rolled her eyes at Nicole, then gave her a 'See what I have to put up with?' look. Nicole did her best to look sympathetic.

"Won't work, dude," Tommy said. "We ain't gonna have enough wood to build an ark except we dismantle this house. And then what? None of us have pairs of pets to save."

Everyone laughed.

More gusts of wind blew against the house. Lightning flickered through the drapes. A violent thunderclap made everyone jump, then giggle with nervous relief. Nicole, however, seemed unable to lose the icy chills that the faded thunder had spilled all over her as though dipping her in clouds of rotting ice cream.

"Hey, this seems a great night for some scary stories," Mitch said.

"Oh no," Nicole immediately countered. "No no no. Not tonight. This is the sort of night when the damn power suddenly fails and we're gonna be left in the dark with candlelight and start getting frightened by the shadows." She pointed behind Carl and Susan, to where a stuffed brown bear stood watch in a corner. "Like *that* thing over there. So no, no scary stories."

"Hey, stories aren't such a bad idea," Tommy said.

Nicole cringed. "Honey, please."

Tommy shook his head. "And besides, no one else has yet come up with a better idea." He looked around the room. "Or, any other suggestions?"

"Creepy stories are fine," Carl said, with Susan agreeing.

Everyone else also nodded. "So, who goes first?" Tommy asked.

"Hey, Tommy," Leona said through a mouthful of cigarette smoke, "why don't you and Nicole tell us about some of the weirdest things you've bought? You're always telling me about all the spooky stuff you encounter as antique dealers."

Nicole Ellsworth had never thought herself psychic. But at that precise moment, she had a very clear idea that something was about going wrong. Here and now and for all of them. And it wasn't the rain, either. There was just something unusual in the air now, a twist in the natural order of things that had been created by Leona's enquiry. Or maybe the weird ambience was responsible for Leona's question.

"Yeah," Mitch agreed, gesturing around the living room with its varied paraphernalia from around the globe. "You guys have gotta come across some really weird shit for sure." His wife Jacqui nodded and looked interested too.

"Alright, folks," Tommy said with an impresario's expression on his face. "I'll tell you the tale of the Cleaverman."

When Tommy said that, a strange instinct made Nicole grip his thigh hard. Almost like she was trying to stop him from going on, but couldn't voice her dread. As if her intuition was yelling, "Honey, tell them any story except that one!" But maybe she didn't really grip his thigh as hard as she imagined, because Tommy didn't seem to notice her distress. Nor did anyone else in the house apparently.

Jacqui Mullins was already asking: "The Cleaverman? Who's that?"

"It's a strange tale," Tommy said. "See, there's this book we got at a yard sale, that has a legend attached to it . . . Hold on a minute—it's here in the house, I'll go get it."

CHAPTER 2

Just Before . . .

Tommy was back in a few minutes carrying a small hardbound book. Mitch indicated that he'd like to look at it, so Tommy handed it over to him.

"The Book of Summonings," Mitch read off the book's cover. Then he flicked through to the table of contents. "The Harpersfield Demon . . . The Eldritch Witch . . ." He looked up at Tommy. "It's a book of magic spells!"

"*Very dangerous* magic spells," Tommy corrected him with a grim smile. "Apparently, this book is the real deal—everything in it works. Which is why we keep it at home." He extended his hand for the book and Mitch returned it to him. "If you'd kept reading down the page of contents, you'd have come upon the ritual for summoning the Cleaverman."

"So," Mitch asked. "Who is this Cleaverman?"

"He's a supernatural killer. You know, like in the movies—Freddy, Jason, Mike Myers? Can't be killed no matter what you do—he'll keep coming back after you."

"Hey, let's try and summon him," Mitch said, which statement made both Carl Whitfield and Angela Rossi stare at him in dismay. His wife just rolled her eyes again.

"What the hell you wanna do that for, man?" Carl asked. "Tom just said the guy's a serial killer, and you wanna raise him from the dead?"

Mitch shrugged tipsily. "Just might be fun, ya know. Give a spark to this wet evening." He raised and shook his arms in a scary, emphatic gesture and lowered his voice to a low and creepy baritone. "Raising a demon fits in great with the pouring rain outside. All we need is for the lights to go out."

"Mitch, you need to stop drinking," his wife said.

"I ain't had *that* much," Mitch defended himself. "And it's just a suggestion."

"Well, forget it," Carl said. "Dude, Jacqui's right, you do need to quit drinking."

Leona blew smoke and laughed. "Yeah, Mitch. I'm psychic, so trust me on this—the spirit of alcohol is beginning to speak through you."

Mitch managed to look embarrassed.

Susan giggled and then said, "Lighten up, guys, it won't work anyway. What do you expect? That we cut up some virgin"—her eyes lingered on Angela Rossi's Mona Lisa face while she said this, causing the attorney to blush—"and this Cleaverman will actually appear?" She ran slim fingers down Carl's cheeks. "Oh, don't be naïve, darling. I'm not skeptical where the supernatural is concerned—I definitely believe there's things out there we should be wary off—but this would be stretching the limits of credibility."

Mitch was about to agree with her, but Jacqui stamped on his foot. So instead he leaned forward and poured himself another glass of wine from the bottle the Ellsworths had left for he and Jacqui and which he'd commandeered for himself.

Carl's brother Jeffrey, who'd so far said very little this evening, now asked Tommy: "Does one need to do something that drastic? Killing a virgin?"

Nicole shook her head. "No, you just need a few tablespoonfuls of blood. You use that to draw a circle. Then you open the summoning book to the Cleaverman spell, and repeat the rhyme three times."

Outside, the thunderstorm still raged. The night sky was a combat of noise and electric discharge; as if rather than the thunder being the lightning's bosom companion and its auditory representation, both fought for ownership of the heavens. There was no possibility of the Ellsworths' guests departing. No one needed to convince them to stay where they were; the weather outside was too inhospitable and forbidding for them to act otherwise. The night seemed pregnant with possibilities. And maybe those very possibilities were seeding evil in the hearts and minds of those inside this quaint two-story building on Raynham's Hall Street. Though the house lights were on, nasty things seemed to squirm both within and without the house's walls and also *through* those walls as if entering from the world of the dead. Everyone present in Nicole and Tommy Ellsworths' house felt uneasy to some degree. But it was the sort of unease that one usually attributes to too much drink, or too much food, or the need to fart or defecate . . . or in Nicole's case, a threatened migraine.

"A rhyme?" Jeffrey asked. "What rhyme?"

Nicole nodded. "Yeah, something to do with the guy's wife. Anyway, you read it three times and the Cleaverman appears to you."

Susan made a face. "Ugh, that really works?"

"Well it's supposed to," Tommy replied. "Apparently, either no one's ever succeeded in raising him or no one's ever survived to tell the tale of their success."

"This Cleaverman, what's he look like?" Mike asked.

Tommy laughed loudly. "This is why the story's so creepy. The Cleaverman, he's like a ghost, see? Supposed to be all shadowy . . . black smoke and stuff. The only thing about him that you can really make out is his cleaver, which is about two feet long and a foot wide, and it's razor sharp too."

"Ouch," Angela Rossi said. "What in the world does he want with a knife that large?"

Susan shrugged. "To split you down the middle with, I guess."

"That's actually about right," Tommy agreed. "Legend has it that the Cleaverman was actually a butcher who went mad or something."

"Hey, go on, man," Mike told Tommy. "This is a fantastic yarn."

"And, you know what's the creepiest thing of all?" Tommy told them all. "I'll tell you guys—the Cleaverman is supposedly just a mass of smoke. He isn't solid to the touch. Nothing but black gas and shadows . . . And when he speaks, his voice has this scary bass rumble that makes you want to take an intense crap."

"He talks to his victims?"

Tommy nodded. "Yeah, supposedly. The legend has it that he appears and tells you something. And if you don't know the answer, you're dead meat—pardon the pun." He laughed, though a little nervously, as the thunder appeared to punctuate his words. It was clear his own story had unsettled him. "Yeah, imagine that, right? Something like that trying to kill you if you can't answer his riddle?"

"What's the riddle?"

" 'The riddle is the rhyme; the rhyme is the riddle.' That's what the book says he tells you. He says that to you and if you give him the wrong reply . . . he chops you up into little pieces."

"That's very creepy," Angela said. "Just imagine that happening in real life."

"Guys, I still say let's try the ritual," Mitch said. His wife tried to dissuade him, but partly because he'd drunk too much wine, and partly because it was the nature of the night, he shrugged her off. "Let's friggin' do it!"

There was silence from everyone, and then Tommy, no doubt to dissuade Mitch, said, "Well, I guess it's harmless to try, but we're still short of blood, and I sure as hell ain't gonna donate mine." He shook the book at Mitch. "This may all be fun and games to you, but I don't even like getting shots at the clinic. So . . ."

Mitch burped, then stuck his left arm forward. "Alright, man. I'm type O-negative, a universal donor. Take as much red as you like."

CHAPTER 3

Nicole & Leona . . . The Summoning

After that, there was no turning back. Like a group of bored teens experimenting with a Ouija board, everyone was suddenly eager to attempt to raise the Cleaverman.

Angela was the only one who looked put off by the turn of events. But Nicole didn't know if that was because the lawyer girl was scared of blood, or because she felt too educated to involve herself in their primitive behavior.

We are being superstitious after all; and maybe she feels she's too good for that.

Everyone else, however, had an air of expectancy.

"This is fucked up," Leona whispered to Nicole as Tommy cleared the wine bottles off the coffee table. "Stop them—it's *your* house."

Nicole shook her head. "C'mon, psychic girl, let the other kids play with magic too," she replied.

"You don't get it," Leona said. "What we're about doing is wrong. We're all gonna regret doing this."

But Nicole no longer felt worried. "Relax, it's just fun and games to enliven a dull evening." She gestured across the room at Carl's blond girlfriend, who had one arm draped around his shoulders and was whispering something in his ears while doing her best to hide the fact that she was rubbing his crotch at the same time. "Besides, like Sue earlier pointed out—very sensibly, I must add for a woman of her profession—there's absolutely no real chance of us summoning anything."

Leona scowled over at Susan. "That airhead? The only danger she's aware of is catching STIs. Or maybe that a dick's too big and is gonna choke her to death if she tries to deep-throat it. That slut wouldn't recognize a real problem if it was killing her."

11

Nicole laughed. "Do you know I wanted to display this summoning book in the shop—it's certain to fetch a great price—but Tommy utterly refused? He really does believe the book is dangerous."

"Come with me!" Leona leapt up and pulled Nicole after her out of the living room. As if hypnotized by expectation, none of their friends noticed them depart.

Out in the hallway, Leona sighed and gestured wildly with her pale arms while pacing back and forth barefoot. "Listen," she whispered to Nicole. "The problem is . . . see, I can sense that something is wrong here. All the elements are wrong tonight, which in magic terms means that everything is just *right*—perfect for accomplishing evil. Nicole, listen to the damn thunder—and when was the last time you remember seeing this much lightning? Girl, this is the sort of night when malignant spirits roam abroad and—"

"Yes, yes, darling, I know you're psychic and all that, but please give it a rest tonight."

Leona frowned. "So you're not going to stop it?"

Nicole shook her head. "I can't. It's too late to stop it." And it was too late. Peering back into the living room, both women could see that Mitch was kneeling on the floor with his left arm stretched over the drop cloth that Tommy had laid on the coffee table. And big Mike, who—seeing as he owned in a gym, had a little knowledge of medicine—was sterilizing a switchblade in the flame from Carl's lighter.

"This is exactly what I mean," Leona protested in a desperate hushed voice. "It's *not* too late. The way it feels to me is like something *wants us* to summon the Cleaverman . . ." She stared at Leona and her eyes were scared. "Nicole, what if we succeed? What if we do the ritual and actually pull something from the nothingness into this world?"

Nicole felt scared for a moment, but then she shrugged it off. "That's completely ridiculous," she said, then tugged on the sleeve of her friend's dress. "Come on, let's join the others."

"We're all gonna get killed," Leona said.

"Huh?"

"Just a nasty premonition I just had. That tonight we're stirring the pot of our fates, and cooking the brew of our own deaths."

"That's just bad poetry, not a vision of the future. Oh, come on, girl, don't be such a prophet of doom," Nicole said, pulling Leona after her, in the reverse action to that which had brought them out into the hallway.

In the living room, everyone had formed a circle around Mitch and Mike. And just like when they'd left the gathering, no one noticed their return.

Jacqui was licking her lips as Mike dug the knife into her husband's left forearm. To Nicole's mind it looked like the little blonde was enjoying her husband's pain a bit too much, as if she actually wanted to hurt him herself. It appeared as if Leona was right after all and there was a lot wrong with the young couple's relationship.

After making the cut, Mike collected a little blood into a shot glass. Then he bandaged up Mitch's arm.

"Alright, you bloodthirsty curs, we're ready," Mitch said. "Let's do this."

All eyes now turned to stare at Leona.

"Why are you all looking at me?" she asked.

Tommy explained: "You're a psychic. You'll most likely do a better job than the rest of us of summoning the Cleaverman."

Leona shook her head. "That's a *spell* you're about casting—I'm not a witch, I just sense things that are gonna happen."

Tommy was about replying to this, when Jacqui instead asked: "So what do you sense now about the Cleaverman? Is he nearby? Is he waiting to come to us?" Her eyes were bright and filled with innocent wonder. Gone was her earlier displeasure with her husband.

Leona shook her head; her brown hair swirled about her face, alarm filled her gray eyes. "Oh, hell no—you can totally count me out of this. There's no way I'm gonna help you guys raise . . ." She seemed to sag into herself. "Guys, I don't get it. Why is everyone so insistent on this? Guys, this isn't the ghost of your dead mother you're trying to contact here, it's a psycho—"

"She's scared it's gonna succeed," Mitch said drunkenly, then frowned. "Hey, let's do it!" he growled.

"Yeah, let's do it!" Mike yelled in agreement, pumping his fist skyward in a gesture which, if everyone in the room hadn't been seized by the same urgent and inexplicable rush of emotion, would surely have struck someone as being unnatural and manic.

And that was it. Before she could stop them, Leona was moved through the circle of friends towards the coffee table. Some of the hands pulled her; others pushed her. In a few seconds she was holding the cup of blood in one hand and the Ellsworths' summoning book in the other.

"Guys, this isn't a good idea," she protested to the circle of expectant faces.

"Just do it and stop being a party pooper," Nicole whispered in her ear. "This is my damn house, not yours." Now she really didn't get what Leona was being so reluctant about.

"One isn't supposed to touch other people's blood nowadays!" Leona whispered fiercely to Nicole, desperate to escape this undesired task, slurring her words so it sounded to the others as if she was reciting a spell. "Mitch might have AIDS."

"I don't think so," Nicole whispered back. "Jacqui's been sleeping with him for years and she looks nice and healthy. Just cast the damn spell, girl."

"The blood might splatter on me. It might ruin my dress!"

"I'll buy you another one. Promise."

So Leona did it. She dipped her right index finger into the blood and copied the illustration in the book onto the drop cloth. The circle she drew with Mitch's blood was broken at five points where the tips of a pentagram's star might have been. Inside this she drew a 'C' and a crude knife.

Then she straightened up and frowned at them all. "Alright, guys. Now I'm gonna read the rhyme three times, and then there's no going back." She smiled weakly at the others. "We don't stop now and we're all gonna die!"

"Read it!"

So Leona read the Cleaverman rhyme:

"Tell me the name of John Cleaverman's wife,
An Angel Maria he loved all of his life.
Never a nag like Jenny, never one day in strife.
You, my friends, have just one chance to survive:
Answer this riddle or give up your lives."

And something happened. First thing was that the bloody diagram on the drop cloth caught fire.

"Shit!" Mitch gasped, his eyes going wide. Everyone except Leona immediately stepped back and sat down again. And stared at the burning circle.

Leona, however, found that she couldn't move. She stood stuck in place beside the coffee table with her lips seeming to part and close by themselves, quoting the Cleaverman's rhyme, a rhyme that now struck her as very evil. She'd have loved to have torn herself free and fled, but she was powerless to help herself. The words forced themselves from her lips for a second time:

"Tell me the name of John Cleaverman's wife,
An Angel Maria he loved all of his life.
Never a nag like Jenny, never one day in strife.
You, my friends, have just one chance to survive:
Answer this riddle or give up your lives."

Leona felt as if life was being sucked from her body to animate the horrible words. Once more she read out the rhyme. While her lips moved of their own accord, she stared around the room at the others. Everyone was quieter than a mouse desperate to evade a cat. Leona wasn't certain if they were scared to talk, or if the same force that was making her speak was keeping everyone else silent. Her friends were all staring at the fire and at her; and it was now that she realized she was trembling, her entire body vibrating like a plucked violin string.

"Tell me the name of John Cleaverman's wife,
An Angel Maria he loved all of his life.
Never a nag like Jenny, never one day in strife.
You, my friends, have just one chance to survive:
Answer this riddle or give up your lives."

As the final sentence faded into silence, a force grabbed Leona and flung her back across the room and onto the couch. She felt soft trembling arms grab and hold her tight. Someone else yelled "Shit!" and two women shrieked.

Leona sat there as limp as if she was boneless, both scared and exhausted. She felt drained, as though she could sleep for a thousand years, but her eyes were propped open by dread and curiosity.

Because more was happening:

At the moment Leona hit the couch, the flames burning above the coffee table had turned to black smoke. The fire burnt out completely. The smoke, however, hung there in the air, twisting about.

There was something there now. Everyone saw it. A shape, undeniable by them all. The smoke formed the impression of a man. Like soot swirling in air, trying to become a solid but lacking sufficient amount or density of itself to complete its intended transformation. But it was definitely a tall male shape. It was clearly human too, although the nature of its substance introduced distortions in its form, with limbs lengthening and shortening as it wavered in place. Down by the shape's right hip, something long and rectangular glinted like a ghost bride's vanity mirror.

Then it all dispersed. First the shape broke up into smoke again, then the smoke faded.

There was a loud collective sigh of relief from everyone.

"Hey—there was something there," Jeffrey Whitfield said.

"We all saw it, bro," his brother said. "We all saw it."

"I think Leona was right and this *was* a bad idea," Tommy said. Then he forced a smile. "Well, folks, what's important is that it's gone away now and we're all still alive. The legend is that it would hack us all to death."

"Which makes me wonder again why we were all so eager to summon it in the first place," Angela Rossi said, pursing her lips like she was tasting something unpleasant. "Like we were all expressing a shared death wish. And to think that we almost succeeded."

"Yeah," Jeffrey agreed. "But that was really creepy, you know? I ain't never seen anything like that before in my life. I was sure the Cleaverman was gonna appear and chop us all into hamburger patty."

"Me too," Carl said, with Susan nodding her agreement. "I've never felt so relieved before as when I watched that thing vanish."

"Guys," Mitch said, his eyes sobering up just a little, "maybe we should see what the book says about getting rid of this Cleaverman dude. Just in case we need to." He pointed to the spellbook, which had dropped onto the coffee table when Leona had been flung across the living room. Mitch had just realized that the drop cloth on which the fire had burnt was unharmed, although the blood diagram Leona had drawn on it in his blood had vanished. This was one reason for his worried suggestion.

His wife shook her head. "No, we're not having anything more to do with that silly, creepy book tonight."

"Just saying, honey. You know—to be on the safe side?"

Jacqui shook her head. "No. Ugh!—I'm spooked enough as it is."

Mitch burped, then shrugged and filled up his wineglass again. He sat drinking and let the others talk. Almost before he'd swallowed his first mouthful of wine, his gaze had turned 'drunken' again.

After giving him a look of disgust, Jacqui cupped a hand to her ear. "Hey, people, listen: the rain's stopped. Let's all go home."

This was true. All of a sudden there was no thunder or lightning anymore; no noise of the wind flinging the rain against the house walls. The world outside was silent and serene again.

"When did it stop?" Susan asked.

"During the spell," Angela replied her. "It cleared up while Leona was reciting the spell."

Everyone looked over at Leona, who was cradled in Nicole's arms and was trembling.

"Hey, you okay?" Tommy asked her.

She nodded and shook a shaky finger at them. "Guys, I told you that was a bad idea. We shouldn't have done that."

Susan giggled. "It was fun and games, honey. It didn't work though. But I wish it had—I've a good list of people I'd have asked the killer to kill for me."

"It *did* work, Sue," Leona said. "We all saw the Cleaverman appear." She looked around at them all. "C'mon, you guys, don't make light of this. We all saw him."

"Yeah, alright, so he did show up to the party." Susan made a point of looking around the room, then added dismissively, "And then he left again. I guess he thought we'd be too tough for him to take on at once,"—she grinned at Mike—"particularly with muscular Mr. Beefcake here. It sure was a fun way to pass the evening though." She bent over the couch and kissed first Leona's cheek, then Nicole's. "Thanks for the entertainment, darlings. It was first-rate." And then she turned and strode back over to Carl's side. "Time to depart for home, baby."

"Yeah, it is," Carl said.

"You don't understand," Leona told the men staring down at her with concern. "The Cleaverman's not gone yet. He's still around here somewhere."

"He is?" Tommy asked, slightly worried. Then he laughed it off. "Aw, come on, stop joking."

"I'm serious," Leona insisted.

But no one paid any real attention to Leona. Everyone had been too spooked by what they'd seen and didn't want to think about it anymore. They convinced themselves that she was rambling. It was much easier to do that than to seriously consider what they might have unleashed tonight, what might even now be stalking them from the shadows.

And besides, at the moment, Tommy and Nicole Ellsworths' house had a really spooky and repulsive vibe to it. Everyone present felt an intense need to be far away from the place.

The end of the storm gave them all the perfect excuse to leave. Even Leona, who'd initially planned on spending the night with Tommy and Nicole, changed her mind about doing so. Instead she hitched a ride home with Carl and Susan. Jeffrey, Mike, and Angela went in the second car. Mitch and Jacqui Mullins had already left, ruining their shoes in the ankle-high water running along the sidewalk. Mitch had been walking a little unsteadily; he'd been propping himself up against Jacqui as they went.

"Wow, what a weird night," Tommy Ellsworth told his wife after they'd seen everyone off. He picked the book off the coffee table and stared hard at it. "See now why I didn't want to keep this thing in the shop?"

Nicole nodded. "Yes, darling. I can just imagine what would . . . did you see the way Leona flew back across the room . . . ? And that thing—the smoke ghost—that was hanging in midair? I almost fainted from fright then . . ."

"Come on, honey, let's go to bed," Tommy said, setting off for the hallway and pulling Nicole along with him. He planted a loving kiss on her forehead. "I'll put the book away again, and we'll just forget all that spooky stuff ever happened."

They flicked off the living room lights and climbed the stairs.

But . . .

***

Over in the corner of the Ellsworth's living room, something was forming. An evil presence spawned by that night's ritual. It was tall and nasty and brooding, almost more impression that substance. It was summoned by the rhyme that had been chanted. Just as a question requires an answer, so the rhyme also required a response. And whoever had the correct response would live. The rest would die.

The forming creature was neither patient nor impatient; it just was. Once a man, once flesh and blood and capable of much love and tenderness, now it was merely a raging appetite of destruction; something that desired to wound and hurt, to tear soft flesh and break hard bones and spill blood. An evil thing that couldn't be killed because it wasn't alive; something that would only return to where it had come from when it knew what it needed to know. They had chanted the rhyme; they must provide the response.

And so the thing swirled amidst the shadows and became as substantial as it could; which wasn't very much. Still, in the end it 'existed' in the empty living room. It strode forward then back again, getting used to itself, sensing overhead the book that had freed it. Preparing itself for the bloody deeds to be done.

The most solid and obvious thing about it was the long glittering blade that hung by its side.

The Cleaverman didn't have much of a face, but what existed smiled wickedly.

CHAPTER 4

Nicole

Thunk!

The noise was a dull one. During the day it would have been swallowed up by any other of life's thousand noises. But this was 2 a.m. in the morning. Middle of the night. The only competition the sound had now was with the insects outside the house.

Thunk!

The sound finally woke Nicole Ellsworth. Nicole opened her eyes and stared up at the dark bedroom ceiling.

Thunk! The sound was coming from downstairs. She thought it had been louder this time—but maybe that was because she was fully awake now.

"What's that noise!? Tommy, wake up!"

She reached over a hand to shake her husband awake and realized that he wasn't in bed. She patted the vacant space on her right where he usually slept, then lifted her head and stared across at the bedroom door. The door was open. So as not to waken her, Tommy always left the door open whenever he left the bedroom at night.

Oh, he's just gone downstairs for a drink of water. He'll be right back.

The thought relaxed Nicole. Whatever the sound from downstairs was, Tommy would deal with it. Its source might be that kitchen cabinet door which always refused to shut properly. *Maybe he needed a glass from in there and afterwards . . .*

She smiled and tried to go back to sleep. But just as her eyes were shutting and she was about drifting sweetly away again . . .

Thunk!

The noise jerked her awake again. This time there was no mistaking that it had gotten louder. And there was something unpleasant about it too.

Nicole sat up and clicked on the bedside light. No way was she getting back to sleep now. In addition to the noise from downstairs keeping her awake, she was also curious now.

What's Tommy doing that can't wait till morning?

They'd both been inexplicably tired after the party. After a long goodnight kiss that had threatened to become full-blown sex but finally hadn't, they'd both fallen soundly asleep.

The noise came again. Thunk! And this time, even though she'd been expecting it, Nicole jerked when she heard it. Now that dull inexplicable sound worried her. Because . . . well, now that she was properly awake, Nicole's mind was feeding her alarming memories of the previous evening. What they'd all done downstairs in the living room after dinner.

But, no, that's just impossible—we didn't! We couldn't have! But Leona said . . . and we all saw . . .

There was a pause in the noises and Nicole tried to think. No, they hadn't really summoned anything, had they? *But I felt . . . I felt . . . ! Look now, the noise has stopped. Everything's fine. It was just the cabinet door again. See, I'll simply wait in bed for Tommy to return. He'll be back upstairs soon and we'll kiss again and fall asleep again. I'm just being silly here.*

So she sat in bed and waited. She couldn't relax though. She managed to keep calm for all of three minutes, her eyes tracking the progress of the second hand of the clock on the wall for lack of anything else to do. Occasionally, she'd glance from the clock towards the farther of the two bedroom windows. The storm had left a chill in the air and both windows were shut, but the drapes of that farther window were open, and she stared out at the night sky, which seemed as dark and brooding as a judge's eyebrows just before he pronounced a death sentence. Then she'd look back at the clock and see that only ten seconds had passed in the interim.

The longer Nicole waited, the more worried she grew. Tommy should have been back by now. What else could he possibly be doing downstairs?

Any moment now, Tommy'll step through the door. Everything's fine. Everything's fine, girl. You'll see.

But Tommy didn't step through the bedroom door. Instead the horrible 'thunking' noises resumed, faster now.

"Shit! Stop it," Nicole growled. Slightly angry now, she flung away the blanket and got out of bed. She was wearing pajamas and just remembered to slip her feet into her slippers. She hurried over to the bedroom door, walked out onto the stairway landing and yelled down the stairs, "Honey, keep the noise down, I'm trying to sleep!"

From where she stood she couldn't see down into the living room and still had no idea what Tommy was doing down there. The living room lights were on though, glowing through the hallway entrance and illuminating the foot of the stairs.

Then the smell hit her and she almost threw up. Last night's dinner knocked violently at the door of her throat and demanded exit. She staggered back against the hallway wall and swallowed and stood there gagging. What the hell?

The noise did stop though, and in that silent pause, Nicole tried to work out what it was that she'd smelt that was making her feel sick. The odor was a familiar one, for sure, and its nauseating quality came not from the fact that it was something naturally repulsive, but because there was so much of it. It was thick in the air, as if someone had shattered a bottle of perfume and the overflow of pleasant scent was overpowering the senses and thus becoming repugnant.

Thick and wet and yet very familiar. But an uncommon odor nonetheless.

Blood! Nicole realized at the exact moment that the thudding noises began again. *I'm smelling blood! Lots of blood! And raw meat!* It was the smell of an animal being slaughtered, after its throat had first been slit to let the blood out; now its belly was cut open and its guts and other viscera were exposed to daylight for the first and last time in its short life.

"Tommy, Tommy! Are you alright, baby!" she called and gagged again.

They had two guns in the bedroom and Nicole was a good shot, having spent time practicing at the Taunton Rifle and Pistol Club. But she was so worried now that her husband might have hurt himself that she didn't go back for the guns. Instead she hurried down the stairs.

As she descended to the ground floor, Nicole became aware for the first time of an alien presence in her home. Yes, the smell of blood and fresh meat both increased with her proximity to their unseen source, but now also she sensed something really nasty; something others might even say was unholy. Yes, she was used to such feelings—in the antiques trade one was eternally buying and storing objects and relics of dubious origin and intent; things better left buried with their dead owners or incinerated by those owner's heirs—but this was different. This evil was intense. It was 'active,' quite different from the 'passive' feeling one got on encountering say, an African fetish statuette. It was also very nearby.

"Tommy, are you okay?"

Nicole ran into her living room and saw what the evil presence was. There was an intruder in her living room.

Unable to believe her eyes, she skidded to a halt and gaped. She stood there staring, unable to scream simply because of the impossibility of what she was witnessing.

Her husband was being butchered by a ghost. But no, this wasn't a random ghost, this was the thing they'd summoned up after dinner. It had more substance now and looked like a man wearing . . . Nicole couldn't make out the ghostly man's clothes or if he was naked even, he seemed more dark imagination than actuality. Just like earlier, one saw him, could make out his head and torso and arms and legs, but all were black smoke and the spaces the smoke coiled around.

The one thing however about which there was no doubt, was the huge cleaver he wielded in his right hand. This wasn't shadowy at all— it was solid metal and horribly sharp, as evidenced by the pieces of Tommy Ellsworth that now lay neatly piled beside the coffee table. The rest of Tommy lay on the coffee table. There wasn't much of him there, just his head and chest. Nicole watched the shadow lift its giant cleaver and smack it into the bottom of Tommy's ribcage—Thunk! A slice of ribcage detached—two ribs, half of a vertebrae and a bloody shred of diaphragm. The Cleaverman pulled the slice off the bloody coffee table and repeated the action higher up Tommy's chest.

Thunk!

This time he seemed to split Tommy's dead heart in two, along with both of his lungs. There was a bright but brief spurt of blood. The blood passed through the Cleaverman as if he wasn't really there.

GOD, NOOOOO! TOMMY!

Nicole just stared and shuddered. Somewhere deep inside of her, a scream was welling up. It would be a scream to end all screams—the mother of all screams, as it were. But Nicole's scream wasn't ready to emerge yet, it was still growing inside her, being assembled from her terrors and her disbelief. Her teeth were chattering and her knees knocking and her eyes gaping, her breath escaping her in short gasps. Her throat felt tight. She wanted to run, but couldn't. Her mind screamed at her to turn around and dash upstairs and get out her gun, but she knew bullets would be useless against this thing in front of her.

Then call someone! Call the cops! No, not the damn cops! Call Leona! Call Leona—she'll know what to do! Call Leona!

But still, it seemed like she couldn't move. The reek of blood filled her head like surgical anesthetic and glued her to the air around her, glued her in place where she was. She just stared like a doll.

Despite the fact that she was certain he sensed her presence, the 'Cleaverman' hadn't once looked Nicole's way. He'd been intent on his grim task of dicing up her husband's corpse. But now, he rounded up that task. His ghastly ghostly arm moving in a blur, he chopped Tommy's head in two, then crosswise into four, swept the resulting mess of bone and brains off the coffee table to join the other human parts on the floor, and then, his giant cleaver streaked with blood, turned and stared at Nicole.

Nicole stared back at this creature of gas and shadows, this murderous phantasm.

His face was much like the rest of him, shades and twists of black smoke. It was a human face, however, and she had the impression that she was looking at a man in his late thirties or early forties. Dark angles amidst the shadows gave features to his face. He wasn't a handsome man and his face was twisted into a scowl as if he was angry about something.

The gas that formed the Cleaverman had a slight glow to it, as if he'd still be visible with all the lights turned off. Nicole looked through him and saw her husband's horrifying remains, a horrible glossy red as his blood dried on them and seeped into the living room carpet.

The Cleaverman took a step towards her, then another. There were maybe five yards separating them; any second now he'd be touching her.

Oh no—he's coming to kill me!

The mother of all screams that Nicole had been nursing like a baby now burst forth from her lips—a long and hard and endless note of anguish that contained both her fear for her own fate and her sadness over Tommy's death. Her voice rose louder than a wolf's howl; she felt like she was literally screaming her guts out.

The Cleaverman stepped closer still. He gave no impression of being in a hurry. About a yard from Nicole, he paused and opened his mouth as if to speak.

Letting that scream out, however, had released Nicole from her paralysis. She spun around and ran away from the Cleaverman. One step, two steps, three steps . . . Then she was outside in the short downstairs hallway and had reached the foot of the stairs. Her heart thudding 'bang! bang!' in her chest, she leapt up these two at a time, intent on reaching the safety of her bedroom. She imagined she could hear the Cleaverman coming after her.

But then, halfway up the stairs, she slipped and found herself sliding down them again.

"Oh, God, no!" she shrieked, grasping uselessly at the bannister rails as her body thudded down towards her death, her head bumping on each successive step.

But then, mercifully, Nicole's head struck the large bannister at the foot of the stairs and she knocked herself out cold.

CHAPTER 5

Carl . . . mostly

Carl Whitfield thought Susan Riley had great breasts. Her face was a little angular and her lips a little thin, but her breasts were fantastic. They weren't large, but were just perfect for her body.

Now as Carl sucked on Susan's breasts, slipping each of their nipples into his mouth, he remembered the other pair of magnificent breasts he'd seen that night. Yes, Angela Rossi also had a great pair. She wasn't pretty though, that was the thing. And she was too serious to boot. A man might date an unattractive woman if she was fun, but the way Carl had Angela figured out, she was clearly no fun at all. He knew she liked him, but he didn't see anything ever happening between them.

"You like what you're eating, don't you, baby?" Susan asked, running her fingers through his hair. She lay on her back in the large bed; he was kneeling beside her. Her enquiry was somewhat petulant, as if she sensed he was thinking of someone else.

He responded by pushing both of her breasts together and flicking his tongue left and right across her hard nipples. Then he licked up and down between their cleft. She moaned and slipped her right hand between her legs and began stroking her clitoris. Her other hand grabbed Carl's penis and began expertly stroking that too.

They remained like this for a while, teasing each other, and then Carl slipped on a condom and entered her. Susan gasped and shut her eyes. After a short pause, they began moving together.

The sex was slow and languid. They made love like fish drifting with the current.

It was 3 a.m. After leaving Nicole and Tommy's house, and dropping Leona Patten at home, Carl and Susan had driven down to the Clip nightclub in Taunton for drinks. They'd left Clip at 2:30, and returned here, Carl's apartment building on Carver Street. Carl lived up on the 3rd floor.

Their intercourse now was merely them burning off whatever spare excitement each retained.

Carl pushed his penis deep into Susan's vagina. She moaned loudly, tightened her legs around his buttocks and came. Her trembling and sounds of ecstasy pushed him over the edge too. His testicles tightened and the semen jetted out of them. When it was over, he lay like a stone on her.

After they separated, he lit cigarettes for both of them. They lay on their backs for a while, blowing twin streams of smoke at the bedroom's gray ceiling, then Susan draped a hand across Carl's chest and asked, "Hey, you wanna talk about the Ellsworths' now?"

He gave her a disgusted look. "C'mon, baby, I've already told you I don't need that nonsense in my head tonight." He gestured out of the window, at the black sky. "Maybe in the morning, when the bogeyman's gone back to bed. Right now, we don't wanna be putting ideas in the guy's head, do we?"

She looked upset. She felt like talking about it. But Carl ignored her. He didn't need any bad vibes tonight. It had taken him half the time they'd spent at the Clip nightclub to banish his misgivings over the outcome of that crazy ritual they'd performed at Nicole and Tommy's. He'd both seen and felt what had happened, and hadn't like what he'd seen and felt. That thing that had appeared, that had looked like a man made of smoke—at one point he'd had the unnerving feeling that the thing had been staring directly at him. That had been too much already.

Despite Susan's show of unconcern at the Ellsworths', once they'd left there she'd practically been trembling in Carl's car. She'd been itching to discuss it all night, but he'd kept shushing her. Talking about that supernatural stuff would have spoiled his night. It still would. Now he just wanted to relax and ejaculate another load in Susan, fill her rectum with his semen this time.

Almost as if she'd subconsciously latched onto his thoughts of sodomy, Susan now changed the topic: "So, baby, when did you first realize that Jeffrey was gay?"

Carl hid his annoyance. This was exactly what he didn't need. What the hell was her problem tonight? Now here she was again, raising another sore point. Not the fact that his brother was gay—he didn't give a shit who Jeffrey fucked—but the fact that Jeffrey was about *marrying* his damn boyfriend.

She repeated her question: "At what age did you discover that Jeffrey was gay?"

Dammit; she'd successfully disrupted his pleasant mood. He'd been trying not to think about his brother. At the moment Carl was very angry with Jeffrey.

"Carl . . ."

He sighed. "It was the day I caught him sucking off the boy next door. He was thirteen, I was fifteen and I came home early and found Jeffrey on his knees with Josh's cock in his mouth . . ."

***

It hadn't been a one-off either. More than once during their teenage years, Carl had caught his brother in bed with Josh Kramer, the kid who lived next door. The boys—both of them the same age—would either be fellating each other or Josh would have his penis in Jeffrey's ass; there'd always be a slight smell of excrement and a heavy stink of sweat in the air; two consenting young adults who seemed to be wrestling in bed or on the rug, their grunts of pleasure however betraying the real nature of their physical contest. Then—with semen dripping from both their lips or one of their behinds—the boys would fall apart like two halves of a hot dog bun.

Carl had kept quiet about Jeffrey being gay. The brothers had very little sibling rivalry.

Then came the root of the current problem tree.

After twenty years of lecturing college chemistry, their father Michael Whitfield had quit the teaching profession and set up his own company, Whit-Chem. He'd become rich practically overnight, and the family's standard of living had correspondingly risen.

Once the money started rolling in however, Carl lost all interest in studying. Both Whitfield sons were brilliant, and went to university. But while Jeffrey at least tried to read his schoolbooks, Carl discovered he enjoyed doing nothing. So he did nothing except indulge in sex, drugs and rock and roll. His grades dropped until he dropped out of university.

Their mother died around then and their father was too consumed by grief to worry about his older son's sudden waywardness. The company took his mind off his loss and so he devoted himself to it and left the boys to sort themselves out however best they could. He paid Jeffrey's university fees, gave both sons generous allowances and buried himself in work.

Six years later, when Carl was twenty-five and Jeffrey was twenty-three, their father stuck a gun in his mouth and blew his brains out. When they found him, his cold fingers were clutching a large portrait of his dead wife.

First came the burial. Then came the reading of the will. Carl now got a huge surprise. Though as expected, he and Jeffrey now became the majority shareholders of Whit-Chem, the company dividends wouldn't come directly to either of them. Their father had set up a lifelong trust fund for both of them. The money all went into this and they each got ten thousand dollars a month. They could withdraw more if they chose, up to a limit of twenty thousand dollars each, but only on Jeffrey's signature. Their father had cannily understood that Carl, who acted as if money grew on trees, might burn through their inheritance at the speed of light if given a chance. This proviso forestalled that.

Jeffrey Whitfield had a degree in chemical engineering, but like Carl, preferred an idle life. In that then, both brothers were similar; neither saw any point in working when they had no need to.

The difference between them was that Jeffrey had respect for money. He'd almost never drawn additional funds from their shared account. This was in marked contrast to Carl, who regularly asked Jeffrey to authorize transfers into his account well over their monthly limit.

And now Jeffrey had met Mike Rossi aka bodybuilder Mike 'Beefcake' and had fallen in love with him and the pair of them were planning to get married in a fortnight. This wedding presented Carl with two worries: First, that Jeffrey's own expenses were bound to increase, which might affect his own monthly withdrawals; and secondly, that Mike might exert a negative influence on his finances by convincing Jeffrey not to approve Carl's requests for additional money.

Which would be a disaster. Carl had expensive tastes. At the moment, he was barely making do on the fifteen to twenty grand a month that he got.

From whatever angle Carl regarded his financial future, he just saw dark days looming ahead.

"Some pussy for your thoughts?"

Carl turned to look at Susan.

"You've been looking all serious for like ten minutes now," she said drowsily, tracing manicured fingernails around his bellybutton, "staring at the wall instead of at my boobs. Do you wanna make it again, or do you wanna sleep?"

"I'm thinking of my brother's wedding," he said glumly. "He's asked me to be his best man."

"I just love weddings," Susan said, her eyes brightening, and completely missing his dour mood. "Especially gay ones. Two hot men tying the knot is just so hot! I always think of them both nailing me at once and instantly cream my panties."

Carl nodded. She'd said exactly what he expected her to. Sex was her business and she was perfectly suited to it.

Carl loved Susan's predictability. She was largely a surface person. Perfect T&A, but not much going on between her ears at any given time.

He loved the fact that she made very few demands on his intelligence. She didn't think much beyond the present. She existed in a perpetual 'now' and nicely anchored him there also. Susan's father Joe Riley was a respected Taunton judge. She seemed to have become an escort just to piss the old man off.

Carl, who was too lazy to put his own brains to good use, appreciated Susan's social outlook. Carl avoided dating intelligent women. Women like Jeffrey's soon-to-be sister-in-law, for instance—big-breasted-but-mousy attorney Angela Rossi. Women like that challenged him to think and Carl disliked thinking too hard on anything. It was best to just enjoy life—to view the flow of days and years as a continual big party. Drink and drugs and fast cars and a harem's worth of sexy women. He could afford it, so why not? Susan shared his viewpoint. She charged him $1000 a night for her company and of course, he didn't have to see her if he didn't feel like it.

Susan finally noticed that he was scowling and asked: "So what's the problem? You don't approve of your brother and his boyfriend getting married? You dislike gay weddings?"

He shook his head emphatically. "Sweets, I don't give two rat's farts about gay marriage; gay divorce is gonna be the problem. At least it's gonna be *my* problem."

She smiled, very amused by his statement. "I don't follow you."

Carl smirked. "Okay, view it like this: at the moment, my brother and I own controlling shares in our late father's company. Now if he marries Mike and then they get acrimoniously divorced, Mike just might end up owning some of those shares too. At the moment Jeff's too love-struck to ask Mike to sign a pre-nup. I've asked him to but he retorted that their love is true and will last forever."

Susan pouted and smoothed back her blonde hair. "But even if that eventually happens, Mike'll get half of *Jeffrey's* shares, not half of yours."

"The way our dad drew up his will, I'll be sharing the loss. Same as Jeff would if I was giving half away to a departing wife. And trust me, it's a lot of money to give away to an outsider."

She pouted. "I understand. I'm only trying to be helpful."

"Yeah, I know." Then he grinned at her. "But, hon, I'm hiring your pussy, not your brains."

For a moment she looked as if she'd get angry at what he'd said, but then she smiled greedily. "You're right, boss. Light me up another cigarette."

He did so and passed it across to her. She took a long pull, exhaled the smoke, then reached down and tapped his penis. She began to stroke it and nodded when it hardened. She masturbated him until he couldn't stand it anymore. Then he rolled on top of her and slid himself between her parted legs. This time he went into her anus instead. At first she grunted a little while he penetrated her, then she relaxed her sphincter to comfortably accommodate his manhood.

They made love like that, with him sliding slowly in and out of her rear passage and seeking the pleasure of a fresh release, as the night ground slowly on towards dawn.

CHAPTER 6

Jacqui, Big Dick & Steve-O

Wednesday evening in Taunton:

"Now, listen here, Dick," Steve-O was saying when Jacqui Mullins walked into his office at the Clip nightclub, "the reason I got you to handle shit like this is because I don't wanna dirty my hands cleaning the fan, dig?"

Richard 'Big Dick' Abbott, a hulking ex-heavyweight boxer, nodded meekly. "Yeah, boss." Six feet and five inches tall, Big Dick was dressed in a blue suit that seemed about to burst at the seams from all the muscle it contained. He had a shaven head, wore dark glasses over his pale eyes, and had a slight nervous tic at the right corner of his mouth, a souvenir from his boxing days.

Big Dick had been a good fighter, but he'd gotten into drinking and fast women and they'd ruined him. Now he worked as Steve-O's bodyguard. He also took care of other, unpleasant business that Steve-O might need him to tackle.

Steve-O was a short skinny man with a face that seemed a cross between a rat's and a weasel's. His brown hair was thinning and his suit bulged at the belly because of his paunch. Sitting there behind that desk Steve-O looked weak, but he had a killer's eyes and a murderer's black heart. It was a very bad idea to mess with him.

Jacqui nodded to both men, then sat on the edge of Steve-O's desk and crossed her legs.

"Not there, sweets," Steve-O said. "You know the drill now."

Jacqui smirked. She'd been expecting him to say just that. Sure she knew the drill; the whole point of her sitting on the edge of his desk was to fill him with lust from staring at her buttocks; lust was how she kept him in line. She slid off the desk and onto Steve-O's lap. She kissed him, then got on her knees on the Persian office rug and began undoing his pants.

She got his penis out. His crotch was sweaty, but just like she was ignoring the fact that Big Dick was also in the room with them, she ignored the sweat smell too, and took the penis into her mouth. She began playing with it, running her tongue up and down its length just like she knew Steve-O liked.

Steve-O nodded down at Jacqui, then rested a hand in her honey-toned hair and stroked it. "Oh, that feels real good, baby. I'm sure my dick tastes better than that of the loser you're married to, huh?" When she seemed about to take her mouth off his erection and reply him, he laughed and pressed her head back down on it. "No, no, don't reply, honey-pie, just keep doing what you're doing. You know I love your blowjobs."

Still laughing, Steve-O returned his attention to Big Dick, who stood there watching, his dark glasses hiding the cold amusement in his eyes. Big Dick crossed his hands in front of his crotch to hide his own erection.

Big Dick Abbott was fiercely loyal to Steve-O. Steve-O paid Big Dick a lot of money, which enabled Big Dick to maintain the expensive lifestyle he grown used to during his boxing career. So Big Dick did whatever Steve-O told him to. Which sometimes included hurting people who'd offended Steve; even Jacqui's husband if Steve-O demanded it. Like in this case, for instance:

"Now look," Steve-O went on in a cold voice, "this punk Dibbs needs teaching a lesson. So go over to his house tonight and teach him one. Rough—"

Then Steve-O stopped looking tough for a moment, grabbed Jacqui's head and gasped "Oh, shit, girl!" as he ejaculated into her mouth. He sat there quivering and breathing heavily for a few moments, while Jacqui, never one to swallow, spat his come out into a wad of Kleenex and wiped her lips clean.

While Big Dick stood looking on like a statue in a suit, Steve-O tucked away his manhood. The boss's blowjob taken care off, Jacqui had already gotten out her compact and was repairing her smudged red lipstick. She prided herself on giving good blowjobs, but they didn't do her makeup any favors.

Steve-O finally got control of himself again. "What I mean, Dick, is that you break one of Dibbs's arms or legs so he gets the point not to fuck with me and my finances."

"But, Mr. Steve—"

"But what, man?" Jacqui asked, walking over and seating herself sideways on Steve-O's lap, so that Steve-O had to look past her breasts to see Big Dick. "You can't take care of a little punk who owes Stevie ten grand?"

"It's actually twenty grand, hon," Steve-O corrected her. "He still ain't paid up for that coke he got from Sin Corbin back in March."

"Whatever, baby." She rolled her ass on his lap. "Big Dick's still just making excuses. Maybe he wants to fuck Dibbs."

Jacqui's makeup was perfect again, lacking any evidence that she'd just gotten through performing fellatio. Of course, Steve-O would have to wash the lipstick off his penis later.

"C'mon, Jacqui, you know I ain't gay." Big Dick marveled at how things worked out, but he was used to it now. Jacqui Mullins had been just a secretary; but now that she'd been promoted to Steve-O's bedroom lady, she was ordering him around too. The giant smiled coldly. He loved the way sunshades hid your eyes. Sure, they made you look cool, but wearing them also meant that girls didn't know when you were ogling them. Like now, for instance: Jacqui had no idea that he was studying her breasts and thighs. She was a really hot number—petite and shapely, and with that extra-tight ass in those skintight pants. Oh, he wouldn't mind slipping his rod into her love tunnel too, preferably from behind, where he could have a great view of that ass, and first he had to have those red lips of hers soft and cushy on his penis and sucking extra-hard.

But Big Dick loved rolling in that good green American currency, and being Steve-O's bodyguard was a nice cushy job with great benefits. Jacqui Mullins was Steve-O's woman and Big Dick wasn't about jeopardizing his fat paycheck by hitting on her. But there was still hope he'd get to fuck Jacqui anyway and quite soon at that. Steve-O had hinted to them both that he wanted to start recording pornos.

Big Dick was up for anything that would increase his paycheck.

He'd been in the room when Steve-O had asked Jacqui if she'd like to be a porno star. She'd been game enough. "But I'd have to divorce that deadbeat Mitch first," had been her one reservation.

Six-foot-five Big Dick was in a bad mood over the Dibbs issue too. And later, he'd likely take out his anger at Dibbs on some poor loser who'd have no idea what he'd done to deserve such an ass-whipping. And Big Dick, who really wasn't too smart after all those punches to the head he'd taken during his in-ring career, would greatly enjoy delivering that ass-whipping too.

But that was later. Now Big Dick said, "Well, boss, sure I can break one of Dibbs's legs if ya want. Thing is though, Dibbs works for Marko Velli. We don't wanna get Marko in a bad mood, that's for sure."

Steve-O snarled. "Marko's just some two-bit punk. He's just a hot-air balloon full of expired reputation. One big prick up his ass and he'll burst." But Steve-O didn't really believe that. Outside of their little trio here in his office, he'd never say what he'd just had. Marko Velli was the most feared and most ruthless of Boston's mobsters.

The thing was that until Big Dick's statement just now Steve-O hadn't known that Dibbs worked for Marko Velli.

Now, so that Jacqui didn't think he was frightened, he looked as tough as he could and growled at Big Dick: "Yeah, yeah . . . but we don't wanna start a gang war now, do we? It's enough trouble as it is making good money without worrying about some crazy Croat immigrant trying to slit our throats."

"So what we gonna do 'bout Dibbs then?" Big Dick asked. Big Dick wasn't fooled in the least. He knew that just his mention of Marko's name was making Steve-O shit hot bricks. And he knew Steve-O knew he knew how scared he was. But sexy and bitchy Jacqui Mullins didn't know. To her, Steve-O was the knight in shining armor who'd saved her from the bread line, even if his shining armor didn't zip up down the front due to his paunch.

"Send him away," Jacqui whispered in Steve-O's ear. "I gotta problem I need to talk about."

Steve-O nodded, huffed and puffed for a while, then told Big Dick. "Hey, get lost, man—my lady here wants to talk to me 'bout something important. Go kill someone or something. We'll discuss this Dibbs situation properly tomorrow and come up with a lasting solution to the jerk's bad attitude to financial settlements."

Big Dick shrugged. "Your call, boss. I'm just the errand boy," and he left them.

Once he was gone, Steve-O kissed Jacqui lightly on the lips. "Big Dick's getting slow," he said. "I may have to replace him soon." Then he forgot about his bodyguard. "So what's this problem of yours? Hey, first, girl, what happened to you last night? You were supposed to meet me here at eight. Yeah, I know it was raining an ocean, but I sent Dick over to pick you up anyway. He was parked at your street corner for half an hour. And I was calling your phone and it kept goin' to voicemail."

Jacqui squirmed on the small man's lap. "Wasn't my fault, honey. I tried to get away, but that deadbeat Mitch . . ."

Steve-O listened to Jacqui explain how her husband had dragged her over to their neighbor's house for dinner and what had transpired afterwards during the thunderstorm. While she spoke he stroked her hair and felt pleased with himself. She was a very nice acquisition to have.

Steve-O was single. His wife Sheila had divorced him five years ago for 'emotional cruelty', afterwards running off to Colorado with half of his money and both of their kids.

Steve-O had been dating Jacqui Mullins for six months now. They had a simple understanding: her loser husband had lost his job, had quit looking for another job and had begun drinking heavily; and while she needed help with their mortgage and bills and grocery purchases, the fortyish Steve-O needed a lot of help taming his libido. They'd agreed on financial terms and sealed the deal. Steve-O liked his new mistress a lot. She was compact and cute.

Jacqui had asked him to give her husband Mitch a job at the Clip nightclub, but he'd refused. Having the guy around was bound to become a nuisance. And a drunk like that could easily bring a gun to work and shoot the place up once he discovered the boss was balling his wife.

"I've never been so confused in my life," Jacqui said. "That thing in the air . . . it was . . . it was just . . . and the worst of it is, I just learnt that Nicole's in hospital now. Someone attacked and murdered Tommy last night."

Remembering how she'd felt when Mitch had called and told her, Jacqui began shivering. Mitch had of course been drunk again. He'd sounded amused while recounting the gory details he'd heard. "At least my blood's working, if I ain't," he'd told her over the phone.

She wondered how he could be so callous. At the moment she really hated him. She wondered why he couldn't just pull himself together and find another job. He'd slipped down and now was intent on pulling her down too. And she didn't intend sleeping in the trash with him.

Steve-O held Jacqui tight. "Nicole's in hospital? But how?"

Jacqui shook her head at him. "I dunno. Apparently someone broke into their house last night and hacked Tommy to bits. The neighbors at their end of our street heard her screaming and called the cops." Then her expression turned furious. "Goddamn Mitch—this is his fault. He's the one who provided the blood for that damn ritual . . ."

Steve-O nodded. He'd met Mitch a few times. The guy was a total douchebag. No way did he deserve a classy filly like Jacqui. Supplying blood for satanic rituals sounded right up the guy's street. Another reason why not hiring him had been the correct decision to make.

". . . If Mitch hadn't provided the blood for that stupid ritual, Tommy would still be alive," Jacqui insisted.

At this, Steve-O burst out laughing. "Come on, baby, you don't seriously think you people actually raised up something supernatural last night, do you?"

"Stevie, I saw the fucking thing with my own two eyes. It looked like . . . it was horrible." Jacqui tried her best to put her worries into words, but found the task impossible.

Steve-O couldn't stop laughing. "A group hallucination, that's all. It happens all the time. You said you'd all been drinking."

"Not that much. Mitch had a lot of wine but I mostly had coffee."

"Listen, honey, I'll tell you what happened to Mr. Ellsworth. You say they're antiques dealers?"

"Yeah, they own the 'Memories and Curios' place on Broadway."

Steve-O calmed himself. "So that explains it then. Someone broke into their house to steal their valuables and Tommy Ellsworth heard the noise and came downstairs to investigate and the intruder killed him."

Jacqui felt very unconvinced by Steve-O's explanation. What he was saying was exactly what she'd been trying to tell herself had happened to Tommy Ellsworth, but in truth, it struck her as too pat, like they were both making up an excuse for something inexplicable. Crazy shit didn't stop being crazy just because you didn't know how to deal with it. And anyway, Steve-O hadn't been there and hadn't seen it happen.

"Yeah?" she asked her lover. "So . . . so why hack him up like that?"

Steve-O grinned a smug grin. "They're antique dealers—they're sure to have lots of weird knives at home. In any case, stabbing someone's a whole lot quieter than shooting them with a gun."

"And that thing we all saw after Leona performed that ritual with Mitch's blood? What was that? Nothing too?"

"Yeah, nothing. That's exactly what it was. Nothing but the product of your drunken minds." He licked his lips and gently shoved her off his lap. "Now slip off those trousers and bend over my desk. You sitting on my dick's gotten it all hard again."

Jacqui got to her feet and complied. Being penetrated by a stiff penis and having orgasms seemed a nice antidote to her worries.

CHAPTER 7

Nicole

Nicole Ellsworth woke up at 9 p.m. Still groggy from the sedatives she'd been given, it took her a while to remember where she was. Looking left and right, she saw that she was surrounded by four cream-colored walls, in a small room with a single window. She was dressed in a thin blue gown and had a drip attached to her left arm.

Yes, I'm in hospital.

She felt so damn weak. She could barely move her body. And she remembered too why this was so:

The doctors sedated me when I began screaming that a monster had killed Tommy. They didn't believe me.

She felt as if her hysterics were about to return, but she was too doped up to really work up any emotion. All she could do was lie in bed and stare.

Nicole didn't remember arriving in the hospital. The last thing she recalled was sliding down the stairs. Then darkness. Then she was screaming at the doctors and being held down in bed and a nurse was slipping a needle into her arm. Then more darkness.

Someone must've heard me screaming in fright and called the cops.

Thankfully, someone else had left the lights on in her hospital room. She couldn't have stood it if she'd woken up in darkness.

Nicole began crying. Her husband's death filled her with intense misery. *Oh, my God, no—Tommy! Tommy!* Tommy had been a wonderful husband, a loving and caring man. She didn't know how she'd ever cope without him. Ten years of marital paradise and now he was dead. Butchered by . . .

Once she remembered how Tommy had died, Nicole's sadness became terror. That thing. That thing they'd made Leona summon. The Cleaverman. It had seemed a harmless joke, with half-drunk

39

Mitch baring his arm and offering them his blood . . . *But we succeeded. We actually brought the Cleaverman to life. God help us!*

Nicole was suddenly filled with a deep sense of urgency. With an immense effort she sat up in the bed. Once upright, she felt as if she'd just wrenched her soul out of her body. That was how tired she felt. But panic overwhelmed her exhaustion. She looked at the clock on the left wall: fifteen minutes after nine. She could hear footsteps passing outside her room, but no one was coming in to see her. And she didn't think it wise to wait.

I need to call Leona. I need to get to a phone and call Leona right now. I need to tell her what we've done. She may not even know that Tommy is dead yet. Maybe Leona can reverse the spell. Maybe if—

There was a closet on her left, beside the door that should lead to the bathroom. Her clothes should be inside the closet and her cellphone would be in there too. Then she remembered that everything had happened at night and that she'd been wearing pajamas at the time. Her cellphone was at home.

She tried to turn herself so she could put her legs down on the floor, but instead her strength gave out and she collapsed back down onto the bed.

She lay there, breathing hard. There was a red buzzer up on the wall beside the bed. She suspected it was to summon the nurses if she needed them. *But if I summon the nurses, what do I tell them? That I need to call a friend and warn her about the monster that killed my husband? That'll just get me sedated again, and once that happens I'll be helpless and . . .*

The light in Nicole's private room dimmed slightly then. She blinked and then suddenly, there he was again.

Oh no! It's the Cleaverman!

Just like the first (second?) time she'd seen him, Nicole wanted to scream but no words came. The Cleaverman stood at the foot of her bed, a floating mass of dark gray smoke that refused to solidify. She could see through him, could see the door behind him. His evil aura filled her hospital room. It intensified as he walked toward her, his insubstantial body passing through the bed and her legs, his immense cleaver scraping noisily over the bed's metal frame. Then he was right beside her, staring down at her, his smoky black eyes questioning.

"Wh-wha-what d-d-do you-you-you want wi-wi-with me?" Nicole sputtered up at the Cleaverman. Her heart felt like it was going to stop; that was how terrified she was. She glanced down at the immense cleaver by the creature's side. Large as a serving tray, the blade was clean of blood now and as reflective as a mirror. She saw her face in it; her terror echoed back at her.

"The riddle is the rhyme; the rhyme is the riddle," the Cleaverman said. His voice was strange, neither high-pitched nor low-pitched. It reminded Nicole of wind whistling through a tunnel. And there was misery in his voice; her creepy nocturnal visitor sounded unhappy.

"The riddle is the rhyme, the rhyme is the riddle," the Cleaverman repeated while staring intently at her.

"What are you talking about?"

Then she remembered. This was the statement he always told his victims. *But what the hell does that mean—the riddle is the rhyme? I don't know.* Then she understood why he'd not killed her last night: he'd not interrogated her yet.

But what's the correct response to this? Nicole racked her brain. *What is the . . . the riddle . . . that damn riddle . . . the rhyme . . . the goddamn rhyme, how did it go again?"*

Her terror prevented her from thinking straight. She couldn't even remember any of the words from the old spellbook. Oh, what had they been?

And then the Cleaverman raised his giant cleaver up over his head.

"No!" Nicole pleaded. "No! Don't!"

She tried to squirm away from the descending weapon, to roll her legs out of the bed, but she was too weak from the medication.

Thunk!

The cleaver chopped neatly through her right knee, completely separating it from her body. First came disbelief at what she was seeing—the shock temporarily anesthetized her as her knee rolled off the bed—next came pain.

As the Cleaverman raised his instrument again, Nicole began screaming. Her agonized flailing tore the drip out of her arm, jerking drops of blood across the floor.

Thunk!

Nicole's left leg got the same treatment as her right one, the gleaming blade slicing through both flesh and bone with ease. The pain forced her to sit upright in bed, mouth open wide and screaming, while blood jetted from the wounds where her lower legs had been. She managed a look at the Cleaverman. His insubstantial body wavered as if caught in a breeze. His huge cleaver was already bloody again. He had a look of intense concentration on his face, his lips curled down in displeasure.

Thunk! This time the angle of the blade's descent was different. Now it was Nicole's entire right arm, which had been stretched towards the Cleaverman in an imploring gesture, that separated from her shoulders and fell to the floor. With that arm gone, Nicole lost her sitting position and fell back onto the bed, squirting blood from all her wounds.

Now too, there was loud pounding on the door, and yelling voices: "Hey, let us in! Open this door right away! Hey, Mrs. Ellsworth, are you okay in there!?"

In response, Nicole screamed again, as, with his gaseous hand repeating its previous actions, the Cleaverman now hacked off her entire right leg at the crotch.

More banging on the door. "Hey, what's going on inside there! Hey, open this door right away, whoever you are in there! We've already called the cops!"

But Nicole already knew that calling the police was a waste of time. Her latter screams hadn't been to summon help, but simply to register her agony. Now she was just a limbless torso, and was amazed at how with no limbs, she'd not yet bled to death. But she knew that her death wasn't far off. Nicole was willing her end to come quickly.

All she did now was stare at the Cleaverman's smoke-face and jerk and shriek as he hacked away more and more of her. Her agony was such that she almost felt like thanking him for being so diligent in reducing her to her component parts.

Nicole's ghostly killer might finally have cut something vital, or maybe she'd just bled out enough, but it suddenly ended for Nicole Ellsworth. And she found death to be a blessed release.

***

The Raynham Outlook Clinic's staff tried for fifteen minutes to open the door to Nicole's room. They couldn't get it to budge. All through that quarter-hour, they could hear the sound of metal hitting meat—or so it sounded to many of them.

And then, when they'd tried everything and were waiting for the police to bring up a battering ram, the door clicked open by itself.

And what they found inside there on Nicole's hospital bed . . . was just a pile of bloody meat . . . a sight that left even the toughest of them vomiting. Those who couldn't get into the room's adjoining toilet puked on the floor.

CHAPTER 8

Angela . . . That Same Wednesday Night

Twenty-eight-year-old Angela Rossi lived with her brother Mike in a delightful little cottage on Elizabeth Drive, a quiet street near the center of town. Mike and Jeffrey (who was just visiting from his Boston base while he and Mike finalized their nuptial preparations) had the big bedroom, Angela had the small one. But once the men were married they planned to move up to Boston for good and then the house would be entirely Angela's.

Being a simple woman with simple tastes, this suited Angela perfectly.

Mike and Jeffrey were out tonight, visiting friends over in the neighboring city of Bridgewater.

Angela was home alone. Which was just great as it meant she could relax in peace and quiet. She'd had an incredibly stressful day down at the Taunton District Courthouse. They were trying Teddy Hobart for killing his wife Maddy. The trial had been on for a week now.

On the surface the case appeared simple enough: the couple had had a loud fight one evening, and afterwards when Maddy had fallen asleep, Teddy had slit her throat. The cops had the knife he'd done it with, with Teddy's fingerprints on it, and they also had Teddy's signed confession. Teddy, full of remorse, claimed he'd been sleepwalking when he'd killed his wife. He remembered doing it, and trying to wake up and stop himself, but he'd been unable to stop himself slitting Maddy's throat.

So far so good, the law would say. Spouses made up all sorts of excuses after anger got the better of them.

The problem in this case was that 49-year-old Teddy Hobart only had one hand—the left one; he'd lost the other one five years ago while trying to rescue a cat stuck in the middle of the road from an oncoming car whose driver hadn't noticed it. The cat survived the collision, Teddy's right hand didn't.

While reviewing the story in her mind, Angela made her way through to the kitchen and got herself a soda from the fridge, which she then carried into her bedroom.

The problem now was, that though the fingerprints on the knife that had killed Teddy's wife were definitely his, they were from his missing right hand. The knife was a new one, purchased online from Walmart by Maddy the previous week, so there was no chance of it having been forgotten somewhere in the house for the past five years.

And Teddy too, insisted that in the dream in which he'd killed his wife, he'd seen himself stabbing her with his missing right hand. To further complicate matters, the medical examiner had confirmed that from the position Madeline Hobart was found lying in bed and the angle of the knife's insertion, the wound that killed her had definitely been inflicted by a right-handed person. And Teddy had no identical twin.

Total spook city, Angela thought while getting undressed. *We've got to have a trial because he's confessed to killing her . . . but the case is going to get thrown out of court because, except he used black magic or telekinesis, there's no way he could have done it. How do you stab someone with a hand that doesn't exist? I'm definitely gonna ask Leona about this.*

That though, was a matter for tomorrow, when the trial continued.

With nothing else to do tonight, Angela Rossi stripped off and masturbated. Tonight she didn't use a vibrator, preferring instead the more intimate touch of her own hands on her aroused body. While satisfying herself in this way, she filled her mind with pictures of Carl Whitfield. *Oh, wow, is that guy handsome or what?*

But of course, she knew she had no actual chance with Carl. She was too ordinary, too plain (some would say 'homely'); all angles and awkwardness, where she intensely desired curves and confidence. It was the unfortunate cross of Angela's existence that God had given her brains but no looks.

But still, if she couldn't have the gorgeous Mr. Whitfield in real life, she could at least have him in fantasy.

Tonight she really enjoyed touching herself.

Such wasn't always the case. Some nights she'd be too tired to come, or too drunk, or too depressed even; she'd find that just when she'd be about to reach her climax, she'd remember some disturbing detail about whatever criminal case she was working on then and that would detract from her sexual pleasure.

But not tonight. Tonight, as she got increasingly intimate with herself, stroking her breasts, biting her lips and caressing her sex in those expert ways she'd trained herself to do over the lonely years—stroking her clitoris like it was a puppy, dipping her fingers deep inside herself as if prospecting for gold in her belly—nothing interfered with her enjoyment of herself. Her clitoris swelled and throbbed beneath her fingers; her nipples tingled, her thighs trembled. Finally the dam of sensation burst and sexual release flooded her and bore her off to its dizzy shores of onanistic ecstasy.

She came three times, each time visualizing Carl Whitfield simultaneously filling her with his semen and starting off a baby in her womb, and afterwards fell asleep with a tender smile on her face.

***

Angela was woken up by the ringing of her cellphone. She picked it up and saw that the caller was Jack Bishop, a friend and fellow Bristol County DA's assistant.

"Hi, Jack, why're you calling so late?" It was now a few minutes to ten.

He told her why.

"What? Dead!?" she gasped. "No, I hadn't heard a thing—I spent the entire day at the courthouse . . . and . . . I was over at their house just yesterday night."

"It gets worse," Jack said. Angela listened as he explained the impossible details of Nicole Ellsworth's death.

"Yeah, yeah, see you tomorrow." She hung up and stared at the bedroom wall. NO! What she'd just heard couldn't be true. It simply couldn't be true. Both Nicole and Tommy murdered? And in such gruesome fashion? Hacked to death, with Nicole murdered in her hospital room?

Angela sat there shivering, trying to wrap her mind around the impossibility of everything she'd just heard.

CHAPTER 9

Mitch

Mitch Mullins was sitting in Rudy's Truck Stop waiting for Joe Dibbs to show up. Rudy's was situated right by the Broadway overpass over the Blue Star Memorial Highway.

Mitch sipped his beer and checked his wristwatch. Then to confirm the time, he looked at the clock hung up on the wall to the left of the bar. 10:16 p.m.

Where the hell has Dibbs gotten to? Their appointment was for 9 o'clock, and Joe was hardly ever late when there was drinking involved.

Mitch drank some more beer and looked around Rudy's. The place was as rowdy as ever—drunken truckers and bikers and their women; two hassled-looking waitresses carrying trays of burgers and fries and weaving their way to and fro between the couples dancing to the twangy guitar noises spilling from the jukebox; cigarette haze floating through the air like rainclouds, and the smell of sweat and alcohol. The three overhead fans worked hard to cool the joint, but with little success. The proprietor himself, Rudy, a fat and hairy man in overalls and plaid shirt, poured whiskey for the men and women sitting at the bar and joked with them.

Mitch wanted to get roaring drunk, but was reining in his throat's desires until Dibbs showed and told what he had to say.

But where the hell was Dibbs? Dibbs had told Mitch he had a high-paying job for him if he was interested.

Sure, Mitch was interested. He was tired of Jacqui calling him all sorts of names—slacker, loafer, couch-potato, and those were the nicer ones—just because she was now the one paying the mortgage instead of him. She kept refusing him sex too.

47

Thing was, since losing his managerial job at Ellis Drake Inc., Mitch had been unable to get another that paid even half as good. That wouldn't have been too much of an issue, but then Jacqui had gotten that promotion at the nightclub where she worked and had begun earning thrice her previous salary. And that's when she'd begun giving him all that bad attitude. And that's when Mitch had begun drinking so much. And after a while the drinking had made him unemployable and the vicious circle had been complete.

Damn that woman—she's made an alcoholic out of me!

A sudden twinge of pain made Mitch glance down at his left forearm. He had on a long-sleeved shirt, so he didn't have to explain to his friends how the bandage had gotten on his arm.

He scowled, angry at himself. *What the hell got into me last night? Was it just the wine? Or was it that I just wanted to make some kinda idiot point? Whatever the reason, the fact remains that I handed over my blood for that crazy ritual and then Tommy got killed . . .*

Tommy's inexplicable death was one reason Mitch wanted to resume drinking. He didn't want to think about what he might have set in motion. The timing of their attempt to summon the Cleaverman and Tommy Ellsworth's horrible death seemed too much of a coincidence to Mitch. It was like flicking a switch and the lights coming on—impossible to separate cause from effect. As a result, he'd begun drinking early today—once he'd heard the news—quickly polishing off the half-pint of Wild Turkey in the kitchen. After that was empty, Mitch had intended to start on one of the bottles of Jack Daniels which he'd hidden in the closet in their guest bedroom so Jacqui couldn't throw them away.

But then Dibbs had called him with his offer of a job and Mitch had felt enough of a sense of responsibility to sober himself up a bit— after first calling Jacqui at work to pass on the grisly news. Then he'd drank a lot of black coffee.

So now here the fuck I am, almost stone-cold-sober and the sonofabitch ain't shown up. And his damn phone is switched off. It was now 10:30 p.m. *Where the hell . . . ? Sure, Dibbs ain't completely legit. I know he's got mob connections and this job of his might stink. But, by now I'm desperate enough to . . .*

"Hi, can I join you?"

Mitch looked up and quickly nodded. The speaker was a blonde woman in her late twenties. Slim, with dark eyes and a generous chest.

Dressed in a blue dress and boots. She slipped into the booth and sat opposite him.

"I'm Bev," she said once seated, extending her hand. Mitch shook her hand, then raised his own hand and tried to catch the eye of one of the waitresses.

"Here, lemme order you a drink. What'll you have?"

"No, don't bother," the blonde said. "I was just about leavin' and I wondered if you'd like to leave with me." She grinned at him. "I've been watching you for the past half-hour and thinkin', now there's a man I'd like to know."

Mitch digested her words. "Lady, I'd *love* to leave here in your company. But, hey, lovely as you are, honey, a guy's gotta know his limits. What's your company gonna cost me?"

She leaned across the table and whispered loudly so as to be heard over the jukebox. "Cost of a condom. Or a pack of 'em if you've got the stamina."

Mitch grinned back. "Well, sure thing then." His eyes, however, scanned her arms. Sure, she wasn't a prostitute, but she might be a junkie hiding a knife and ready to cut him up for her fix money.

She noticed him staring at her arms and ran her right index finger up her left forearm. "No tracks, baby. No, I ain't a junkie either."

Mitch sighed. "Sorry, but a guy can't be too cautious these days. Friend of mine got cut up really bad last night."

"So, which is it?" Bev asked coyly. "You coming, darling, or should I go home and jill-off to fantasies of what we'll both be missing?"

Mitch figured he'd awaited Dibbs arrival long enough. "Well, I'm supposed to be waiting for a friend, but then, he was supposed to be here an hour ago. Gimme a moment to settle up my tab and I'll join you outside."

She nodded. Mitch got up and walked over to the bar. After paying for the three beers he'd had, he asked Rudy to tell Dibbs—that was assuming the asshole finally showed up—that he'd left to handle some business and not to wait for him. He'd call Dibbs tomorrow.

He thanked Rudy and walked through the establishment's pleasant confusion out into the warm night where Bev was waiting.

"Your place or mine?" he asked her as they walked over to where his battered gray 2014 Ford Mustang was parked.

"Let's go to mine. It's nice and secluded. No chance of us being disturbed."

***

Mitch didn't feel any sense of guilt as he drove along the Blue Star Highway with sexy Bev riding shotgun beside him. In addition to Jacqui trashing his personality, she had also kicked him out of their bedroom. For three months Mitch had been reduced to masturbating and sleeping in the guest room. The last time he'd seen Jacqui naked was four months ago.

No wonder I drink so goddamn much. It helps kill my sex-drive.

So, no sex for three months. Mitch liked sex and he knew Jacqui liked sex too. So if she hadn't been sleeping with him all this while, that could only mean she was sleeping with someone else.

Mitch just wasn't certain who her lover was. Dibbs had hinted that Steve-O might be Jacqui's lover, or even that neanderthal Big Dick Abbott, who was reputedly nicknamed 'Big Dick' because he had a huge penis.

The upshot of all this was that if Jacqui was screwing around, Mitch felt that he was no longer required to be faithful to her.

Mitch studied the road ahead. Though still on the Blue Star Highway, they were now leaving the town limits and heading for Norton, at the moment cruising past Bunk Pond, which lay on their right. The land out here was mostly raw countryside with lots of trees and few houses.

He glanced over at his attractive companion. Bev sat with her hands in her lap and a rather grim smile on her lips, gazing intently through the windshield as if there were angels crossing the highway ahead. Other than to give directions to her home, she'd said little since they'd gotten in the car. Once, she'd reached over and squeezed Mitch's thigh. She'd felt his crotch, squeezed his hard-on a few times and then returned to her quiet highway vigil.

Watching her now as she watched the road ahead, Mitch interpreted Bev's facial expression as half lust and half disgust.

Maybe she's one of those religious girls who wanna fuck, but believe it's wrong to do so except you've a wedding ring on your finger. But no, it can't be that. She mentioned condoms . . . Hey, whatever the case, she sure is hot though.

"Turn off on the right here," Bev said abruptly, breaking up his chain of thoughts just before they reached Snake River. "Then drive slowly 'cos of bumps in the road. It's the third house on the right. You'll have to drive in quite a bit to reach even the first one though."

"I don't recall ever driving up this road before," Mitch said after making the turnoff.

She nodded. "Yeah, hardly anyone does nowadays. Most of the houses are empty 'cos the road's so bad. I ain't got a car and living here like I do, it's a pain to hitch rides to get to town."

They pulled up in front of the third house, a neat white cottage. The cottage lights were on.

"Hey, you ain't hiding a boyfriend in there, are you?" Mitch joked as he turned off the Mustang's engine.

She laughed and shook her head. "Nah, I just moved into the house. I'm single and live alone, so I leave the lights on when I'm out at night to discourage intruders."

Hearing that was a relief to Mitch, whose penis was now painfully hard. They got out and walked to the house. Bev unlocked the door and they entered.

The living room was small and cozy. Bev laughed. "Welcome to my house."

Something about her laugh—a weird undertone—put Mitch on alert that something was wrong with Bev. He stared at her for a moment, getting a strange vibe from her, a sense of expectancy that she was trying her best to hide. But then she kissed him and he realized that he was too sexually charged now to care if she was crazy or not. The testicular frustration that had built up in the interval since he'd last been with a woman now overrode his reason.

We're gonna make it now and that's that!

The television was on and was reporting about a weird court case—a one-handed guy who may or may not have offed his wife. Bev turned off the TV, then pushed Mitch down on the couch.

"You got anything to drink?" Mitch asked. "I just remembered I should've gotten us a pint of something back at Rudy's."

Bev smirked. "Oh, I've a lot for you to drink, honey, a whole sweet lot. But first how 'bout a nice blowjob to calm you down a bit? Your pants look like they'll explode if you don't get some satisfaction soon. And *then* we'll attend to your *other* thirst."

Mitch couldn't say no to that. He leaned back and let her undo his pants and slide them down his legs. She knelt between his legs and grabbed his penis and squeezed it.

Mitch groaned, but managed to control himself so he didn't instantly ejaculate in her hands. He pushed her back. "Take your dress off. I wanna see your hot body while you suck on me."

She straightened up on her knees and slipped her blue dress up over her head. Then she unhooked her bra at the front and flung it away. Staring into his eyes, she shook herself, making her breasts jiggle and her hair sway. Then she took hold of his penis again and began stroking it firmly.

Mitch watched her. Once more she had that look of expectation on her face. Only now, he understood what it was. *Ah, the girl just wants some lovin' . . . she's as sex-starved as I am.*

Bev slipped her mouth over Mitch's penis and sucked on him. Almost immediately, he felt himself about to come.

"Hey, slow down a little," he gasped, leaning forward to grab her breasts, which felt firm yet soft as pillows as he kneaded them. His palms seemed to tingle as they rubbed against her nipples. Everything felt electric—the night, each additional moment, her mouth sucking on him, the feel of her blonde hair as it swept over his bare thighs as her head bobbed up and down, her soft fingers tugging on his testicles and gently squeezing them . . .

She slipped her mouth off him and began licking down the underside of his erection, teasing the thick veins. She licked down to his balls, all the while continuing to stroke him firmly with her hand.

"Oh, shit!" Mitch groaned suddenly when life and death seemed to have focused in his testicles. "I'm gonna . . . !"

Bev immediately returned her mouth to his penis. Keeping her lips tight around his glans and sucking hard on it, she also kept stroking the penis's stiff shaft. She kept this up while Mitch ejaculated into her mouth.

"How was that?" she asked afterwards, while semen dribbled from the left corner of her mouth and down over her chin.

"Shit, shit, shit!" Mitch gasped. He'd forgotten blow jobs could be this great. Damn Jacqui and her vaginal economy. For the moment, words failed him. He lay draped back over the couch with his mind blown by her expertise.

She smiled down at him and Mitch missed the strange look in her eyes. "Alright, and now for that brew to revive you. Hold on, I'll be right back."

Yeah, this is the damn life! Mitch thought, surveying Bev's bobbing backside as she sashayed off across the living room. *A little nip of booze to revive me and I'm sure as hell gonna return the favor, honey! You'll be on your back and seeing stars in no time.*

Mitch relaxed. He could hear Bev fumbling about in her kitchen. She was making quite a lot of noise in there. It sounded like she couldn't find the booze and was rooting through her cupboards for it.

After a while Bev returned from the kitchen without any whiskey or wine bottles. Instead she was carrying a large white bowl. The look on her face was very serious.

"It's alright," Mitch told her, "I got plenty to drink at my place." He patted the couch. "Just come gimme some more." Just looking at her unclothed white body was getting him aroused again. His erection was back and he was looking forward to sticking it in her.

She shook her head. "I wanna show you something first." She looked tense and agitated, as if she was under immense internal pressure. Mitch felt mildly troubled again. She looked screwy.

"Hey, are you okay?"

But she forced a smile and said, "Watch me. I wanna show you something strange."

He nodded warily. He wasn't worried. Yes, his pants were still down around his ankles, but she wasn't holding a gun or anything, just that white ceramic bowl she was now putting down on the floor and squatting over.

He winced when he realized what Bev was about doing. "Oh no, girl, don't tell me you're gonna take a crap right here in your living room!"

She was already positioned over the bowl. "Don't worry, it won't take long."

Mitch saw the first brown chunk of excrement fall from between her buttocks and then he shut his eyes. *Hell no, this ain't something I wanna watch.* He could hear and smell her taking her shit, however. The smell wasn't in the least bit erotic. Mitch had already lost his erection. He hoped she'd get it over with quick.

"You're supposed to be watching me," her voice accused him.

Mitch kept his eyes closed. "Sorry, lady, but I ain't into that pervy shit."

She laughed. Mitch realized what he'd said. "I don't mean it like that."

"I'm finished. You can look now."

The excrement smell was thick in the air. He smelt it come nearer to him and felt Bev sit down beside him. "Hey, you ain't smearing it on yourself, are you? 'Cos if you are, I'm leaving here right now."

"No, I'm not gonna smear it on myself. I just want you to see it." Her hand reached under his penis and began playing with his balls. Mitch grunted. He was getting hard again, his penis throbbing against her deft fingers.

But that horrible smell! If only she'd get rid of that bowl.

"Hey, look at it, or else I'll pour it over your head." Her hand was still massaging his balls, getting him hard as a rock.

Panicked at the thought that she was serious about emptying her crap over his head, Mitch opened his eyes. She was grinning at him, the bowl of excrement in her free hand. Mitch couldn't look at it. He felt disgusted.

"Look at it," she said nicely. "I did it all for you."

"Take it away, for heaven's sake."

"Look, or else I'll drench you with it."

So Mitch looked. She held the bowl out over his belly so he could see its contents clearly. Bev's shit was brown and watery and full of . .

.

"What the hell are those white things?" he whimpered, pointing at the white oval balls in the bowl of excrement. The fecal smell made him want to throw up.

"They're *eggs*—boiled eggs, honey," she replied. "Cooked and unshelled. I've been keeping 'em nice and warm up my ass all day. Just waiting for you, darling. I've prepared these eggs just for you, and now you're gonna eat 'em."

"Hell no!" Mitch growled, sitting up. He shoved the bowl away. He did so carefully though, so the feces didn't spill on his body. "You're one sick woman, Bev. You give great blowjobs, but I'm not into that scat . . ." he corrected himself before saying 'shit,' "I'm totally not into that scat nonsense."

"It's not nonsense," she said angrily. "Life is shit. Shit is life."

Mitch was reaching down to pull up his pants when the knife flashed before his eyes. He froze. He had no idea where Bev had pulled it from. And now she had hold of his testicles again. The bowl of eggs and shit sat between their bodies.

"Here's the deal," she said sweetly as he gaped at her, placing the gleaming blade at the point where his scrotum met his crotch "You either eat my eggs or you lose yours."

Mitch stared at the bowl's revolting contents. There looked to be about ten shell-less boiled eggs in there, swimming in Bev's excreta.

"Shit!" Mitch groaned.

"Eggs," Bev corrected sweetly. "Delicious boiled eggs. Just a little smelly—my personal recipe." She stared crazily at him, her breasts sheened with sweat. "Now start eating, or do you want me to . . . ?" She nicked his balls, so he yelped in fright.

"Why are you doing this?" Mitch asked. While addressing Bev, he took great care not to move, conscious that one wrong move could leave him without his testicles. He could feel blood on his thighs from the little nick she'd just given him. "Why, why?" he repeated.

She mused on his question. "Psychology, I guess. It's just my nature to feed shitty eggs to people. Now pick up that bowl and start shoveling those delicious eggs into your mouth, or else your balls will be swimming in that shit too."

Mitch stared at her pleadingly, but her eyes showed that she was too far gone. She was somewhere distant from him, lost in her personal zone of crazy. Her face once more bore that expression of intense expectation, as if seeing him eating her poop would be the highlight of her existence.

Dreading what he was about to do, but dreading even more what she'd do to him if he refused to do it, Mitch picked up the white bowl and picked a brown-smeared egg out of it. He grimaced at it, then shut his eyes and opened his mouth.

***

He got home an hour later, parked the car outside his house and sat there staring at the front windows. The lights were on, meaning Jacqui was back home. He wasn't interested in seeing her. She'd most likely have gone to bed anyway.

He replayed his ordeal in his mind. That crazy bitch had made him eat up that entire bowl of eggs and excrement. And he hadn't dared throw up. Survival instinct had made him keep down everything he'd swallowed. Bev hadn't let go of his testicles until the bowl was completely empty.

Then afterwards, she'd kicked him out of her house at knifepoint and warned him never to come back except he wanted more of the same. Buck naked, she'd walked him to his car and seen him off. Mitch had left meekly, too traumatized to utter a single word. The thought of attacking Bev hadn't crossed his mind. He'd been relieved to escape from her insanity.

Go back there? To go back there, I'd need to be crazier than she is.

Mitch had no idea what his mouth smelled like. He imagined it smelt like an unflushed toilet.

What I need now is a whole tube of Colgate and like six or seven toothbrushes!

(Down the road the police vans had left Tommy and Nicole's place. They'd be back investigating the murder in the morning.)

Mitch got out of the battered gray Ford, locked it and let himself into the house.

Jacqui was in the living room watching a soap opera with a glass of milk in her hand.

"Oh, look who's back from the cathouse," she said on seeing Mitch. "Hey, you meet any nice syphilitic whores tonight?"

Mitch turned to look at her, then turned away again. At the moment, he had neither the energy nor the willpower for a contest of words. Jacqui had a nice glow to her, as if she'd been fucked, but tonight Mitch just didn't care.

"I'm trying to be social here," Jacqui called after him. "You could at least say hello. And thanks for that silly drunk call to my office informing me of Tommy's death. I guess you couldn't wait for me to get home to tell me the bad news, huh? Thanks for almost getting me fired."

He paused his trudge towards the bathroom, with its salvation of toothpastes and toothbrushes, to stare at her.

Jacqui misinterpreted his stare. "Shit, you're drunk again. Yeah, sure you are, that's why you called me at the club." She laughed. "I know your plan, Mitch but it's not gonna work."

"My plan?" This was the first thing he'd said since his ordeal.

She warmed to her taunt. "Yes, your plan, Mitch. You're trying to get Steve-O to fire me so I'll be out of work like you. Oh, man, you make me sick." When he didn't respond, she added, "Well, aren't you gonna say something, or are you just gonna stand there like a chunk of shit?"

He pondered on that for a few seconds, then walked over to her chair, leaned close to her face, opened his mouth and breathed on her.

Jacqui's reaction was immediate: "Oh, my God, what's that fucking smell? Shit!" She gagged and then, when Mitch breathed on her some more, she threw up all over herself.

He turned and headed for the bathroom again. He looked back once to see Jacqui, with puke all over her, now staring at him as if she'd get her gun from the bedroom and shoot him with it.

Mitch realized he didn't care if she did shoot him. Being shot tonight might ease his existential misery. He walked into the bathroom and locked the door so Jacqui couldn't get in to disturb him. Then he picked up both his and Jacqui's toothbrushes at once, held them together like one big toothbrush and squirted a massive hill of toothpaste over them.

He began brushing. He didn't think there was sufficient toothpaste in the world to clean the mess off his teeth and his soul, but he tried.

As expected, Jacqui shortly arrived and began pounding on the bathroom door. "Let me in, you slacker sonofabitch! Let me in! I need to clean up!"

Mitch ignored her and concentrated on brushing his teeth.

CHAPTER 10

Carl . . . Thursday Morning . . .

"Hi, bro," Jeffrey's voice came over the phone. He yawned loudly, then went on, "Sorry, but Mike and I were out real late last night. A friend just got in from Texas and we . . ."

"Hold on a moment," Carl told his brother. It was bright summer morning now; but he didn't yet feel right for the day. Clad in just his briefs, he peeked back through the bedroom door, where Susan lay wrapped in the bedcovers and dreaming, then quietly shut the door.

"Alright, I'm listening," he said, while crossing the large 3rd floor apartment to his kitchen to make himself coffee.

"Yeah," Jeffrey went on. "So you called me last night, but I didn't notice till just now."

"I need some money," Carl said flatly, feeling it was better to just come out with it at once. "I'm all out. Flat broke again."

"Again?" Jeffrey's incredulity was audible over the line. "You've washed out twenty grand in fifteen days *again*?"

"It ain't that much, kid. Rent and gas and . . ."

"And paying Susan a grand a night, which she then wastes on designer perfume and handbags. . . . Bro, when are you ever gonna see the light? She's leeching you."

Carl sat in the dining room and scowled over his coffee. "Don't preach to me, kid. I need five grand already."

"I'm not preaching, and stop calling me 'Kid'—there's only two years between us. As for the money, I don't have it."

Carl felt a chill go through him. No money? "What do you mean, you don't have it? We aren't bankrupt, are we? We can't be. Hey, listen, Jeff—I'll take the money as an advance on next month's allowance, like we've done before."

"When each time I had to pay back your debt? Oh no, not this time." Then his voice softened. "Carl, it's not that I don't wanna give you the money, but I've overdrawn the account 'cos of my wedding. The wedding's costing Mike and me fifty grand apiece. I took my half out of our trust fund and also another fifty to meet some other expenses."

Carl winced at the sums. "That's a hundred thousand you just withdrew." Then he felt confused. "But . . . but . . . Jeff, you've got money . . . all that cash you'd been saving up?"

"Oh, brother. Houses in Boston are so damn expensive, and we had to furnish it too . . . Anyhow, here's the thing: to get the hundred grand from the bank, I had to sign an agreement limiting our future withdrawals for a specified length of time."

Carl caught his breath. "How long?"

"Six months. For the next six months each of us has to get along on just ten thousand bucks a month. It ain't exactly the bread line, but . . . well . . ."

Hearing this, Carl felt another intense chill run through him. He gripped his coffee hard, as if trying to warm his soul with its heat. "What!? You should have asked me first."

"I don't need to, remember, bro? Dad made me sole signatory to the account. I don't need your approval to withdraw the money."

"It's my money too!"

"I know, and in the past you spent it as if the whole trust fund was yours. So don't flare up if just this once, I take advantage of our inheritance too."

Carl was stumped. Jeffrey had a point: Carl really couldn't complain. Yes, he had made similar withdrawals in the past—once when he'd wanted to buy his BMW X6, and then again, the time he'd taken that hot redhead supermodel on a cruise to India; after which she'd announced she was pregnant and would only have an abortion if he paid her $30,000 to do so.

"Alright, it's done," he said grimly. "Let's not fight about it. But, Jeff, I do need money now. I'm flat broke, bro."

"Look, bro, best I can do now is three grand. And that's out of my own pocket, not from the bank."

"Dude, how the hell am I supposed to survive for two entire weeks on just $3,000?"

"Simple . . . don't spend so much on that coke-nose in your bed."

"Hey, hey—she ain't a coke-nose. She's just high maintenance; needs a rich guy to take good care of her. Some women do, you know; like the Kardashians: those ladies have nervous breakdowns and develop yeast infections if they can't wear thousand dollar Gucci pantyhose. And . . ." he lowered his voice in case Susan unexpectedly walked out of the bedroom, "she's good business too. She gives me discounts."

"Discounts on her pussy? How low can you go, bro?"

"I think she's in love with me, is expecting me to propose to her."

Jeffrey laughed over the phone. "Or, hey, bro, there's another solution to your financial woes—go get a fucking job like everyone else in America. I hear Walmart's hiring greeters."

Jeffrey's laughter was so mocking that Carl almost flung his cellphone across the room. But the damn iPhone was damn expensive and from what Jeffrey had just told him, he was facing six months of privation. Just $10,000 a month to live on?

"You didn't have to say that," he told his younger brother. "That's not funny at all. You don't work either."

"No I don't, but I also don't spend all my allowance on hookers and drugs either, and then bitch about it afterwards. You started it."

"You're the one bitching now. Hey, Jeffrey, did you just wake up on the wrong side of the bed this morning . . . or did Mr. Beefcake shred your ass with his cock again last night?"

There was silence on the other end of the line, then his brother replied in an effeminate voice, "That's none of your business, honey. But if you'd really like to know . . . well, we had a threesome with our friend from Texas overnight, and by God, Rod's some stud. He can fuck for hours. And yes, my asshole does still ache, but in a nice and very satisfied way. Rod probed every inch of my rectum and then some. He discovered corners of my ass that I didn't even know existed. I haven't felt—"

"Spare me the gory details," Carl interrupted quickly, now wishing he'd not steered the conversation in that direction.

"Hmmph. Well, honey, do you want the three grand or not? I'm sorry, but it's the best I can do right now."

"Come on, bro, ask Mike if he can spare me some. Maybe make it five grand?"

"No, honey, this is entirely between us siblings."

Carl cringed. "Please, bro, don't call me 'honey'; we're brothers, not lovers. Yeah, alright, I'll take the money."

Jeffrey sighed and his voice reverted to normal. "Alright, bro, you'll have the money in two minutes."

"Thanks."

"Hey, Carl, you haven't forgotten Saturday, have you? The suit fittings for you and Danny?"

"No, I still remember." The fittings were being done up in Boston, so they'd agreed to drive up there as a quartet. Jeffrey and Carl and Mike Beefcake and Danny Foster, who was second best man, and who also used to be Mike's boyfriend. Danny apparently intended to perform his best man role wearing drag makeup. Mike was even suggesting that Danny (who moonlighted as drag queen Deidre Fabulous) wear a dress on that day.

Carl rolled his eyes at the thought. *Any more fagginess and I'm gonna scream myself silly.* Thankfully, Jeffrey was against Danny dressing like a bridesmaid. His thoughts were that if they wanted a bridesmaid, they should ask Mike's younger sister Angela to do it. Carl had strongly seconded that suggestion. He dreaded seeing the photo album of his brother's marriage up on Facebook and having all his ex-girlfriends ask him if he was in the closet himself.

"Okay," Jeffrey said. "Have to go now, Mike's calling me from the bedroom; see you on Saturday. The money will hit your account shortly."

He hung up. Carl sat there sipping his now cool coffee, then he walked out into the living room and turned on the TV.

Carl's mind was almost a blank.

He felt a slight panic start down in his gut and twist upwards around his spine, then reach forward to clutch at his heart with freezing fingers. No money? And for the next half-year? His mouth twisted up nastily.

This is exactly what I knew was gonna happen once this marriage stupidity of Jeff's got under way. This month it's the wedding preparations, but next month it's gonna be something else . . . and after that it'll be something else again for sure.

Carl could only see his younger brother's need for money getting worse.

A headline came up on the news and he turned up the TV volume.

***

Inside the bedroom, Susan Riley finally woke up. She rolled over onto her back, brushed her blonde hair out of her face and stared up at the ceiling. TV noise filtered in through the bedroom door.

She'd had the nightmare again. This had been happening every night for the past week and always at the same time. She'd have a night of sweet dreams or no dreams at all, and then just before waking in the morning, she'd slip into the nightmare.

What bothered Susan the most was that her nightmare was always the same one. In it she'd find herself talking to a tall creature in a moth-eaten gray cloak that hid its face, and who informed her that she was going to commit suicide. This hideous person—in her dream she knew instinctively that this was Death addressing her—never attacked her, he merely delivered his message and faded into smoke.

And then Susan would wake up feeling terrified.

Now, as Susan waited for her fright to pass, she tried to understand why she kept dreaming this. She'd never been a suicidal person, not even during her teenage years when her father had made her life hell. Back then, she'd instead run away from home. Fleeing hadn't worked out too well though. Each time, all Judge Riley had to do was make a few phone calls and she was quickly apprehended and returned back to him. As Susan remembered what happened to her afterwards each time, her buttocks twitched in sympathy.

But even then I didn't think of suicide. I thought of killing dad, I just never had the decisiveness to carry the plan out. But why am I now dreaming I'll kill myself?

By the time her terror had subsided she'd still not figured out the answer to this question. This too had been the pattern for the past week.

She got out of bed, wrapped herself in a blue bathrobe, and walked over to stare out of Carl's bedroom window.

The world outside was nice and green and summery. The pleasant sight soon put Susan in a good mood. She didn't forget her dream, but Susan was going to see the psychic Leona Patten later in the day and she figured she'd mention the dream to Leona and see what she made of it.

She went into the bathroom to wash her face and brush her teeth. She felt hungry. Time for some breakfast.

When Susan walked out into the living room she found Carl staring at the TV with a look of shock on his face.

"What's wrong?"

He turned to her in horror, then pointed at the television. "Tommy and Nicole both got murdered yesterday."

"What?"

Susan quickly sat beside Carl on the couch and they both stared at the television. The headline story was just replaying then:

"Well, viewers," the lady reporter said, looking quite depressed while talking, "Once again it's summer here in Raynham and in keeping with what is turning into a depressing yearly tradition, we've another murderer on the loose. At the moment I'm standing outside the Raynham Outlook Clinic, where last night, thirty-six-year-old Nicole Ellsworth was murdered in her hospital bed . . . In the predawn hours of yesterday, Nicole's husband Thomas Ellsworth was killed in almost similar circumstances and . . ."

As Susan listened to the horrible news bulletin, she felt the vague stirrings of terror again. She couldn't help but feel that the Ellsworths' deaths connected to her dream in some way, but she still had no idea how.

***

By the time Susan had made them both breakfast, Carl had gotten over his shock at the deaths. Breakfast was 'hooker basic': oversweet coffee, burnt toast and runny eggs; Susan Riley wouldn't ever win any culinary awards.

But this morning Carl was too engrossed in his thoughts to care about her lack of kitchen skills. As he smiled at his attractive companion across the breakfast table, his mind was working fiercely.

In the living room, the TV kept replaying the gory news, showing the exterior of the hospital intercut with footage of Nicole's hospital room, which was now occupied by State Police forensic officers. Then the picture cut back to the Raynham Channel's TV studios for expert analysis. These were the first murders in Raynham this summer and the local station was having a field day with the story.

After getting the gist of the story, Carl had lowered the TV's volume. The news now buzzed in the background like a subliminal drone.

Susan saw Carl looking at her and gave another of the shudders she'd developed on hearing the grisly news. She'd hardly touched her own breakfast.

"Carl, who could do such a nasty thing to the Ellsworths?" she asked him. "Whoever in the world would want to butcher Nicole and Tommy like that?"

He shook his head in silence, letting his face mirror her confusion. *Someone just like me,* he was thinking coldly. *Someone exactly like me.*

Carl had just realized that these murders, tragic though they were, had presented him with the opportunity to solve his financial problems.

If Jeff was to die in a similar fashion to Nicole and Tommy, the cops would think the same killer was responsible. It has to be done quickly though; tonight if possible . . . wait too long and they'll know it was a copycat killer.

It had just struck him also that his brother didn't yet know what had happened to the Ellsworths—Jeffrey had not mentioned it at all during their phone conversation.

Smiling now, he reached across the table and placed his hand over Susan's. Her fingers trembled under his.

"It's alright," he told her.

She looked at him with the start of tears in her eyes. He carefully concealed his amusement.

Yes, that's exactly what I'll do. Once I've gotten rid of Jeff, all the money's mine—the entire inheritance. No more pleading for Jeff's signature simply to buy a pack of cigarettes!

"Carl . . . Carl, you don't think that spell we cast at the Ellsworths' actually worked, do you?"

He patted her hand. "C'mon, don't be superstitious, baby. Spooks don't kill people. Not nowadays anyway, what with CCTV everywhere."

"Carl, we all saw something that night, and now . . ."

Carl refrained from rolling his eyes. He swallowed a mouthful of toast, sipped some coffee and told her, "Yes, we did. . . . Listen, just finish your breakfast like the bad girl you are and don't worry about the bogeyman." He pointed to the TV. "See, the cops don't seem to think a ghost killed them."

She scowled at him. "The report says the police are baffled."

"Baby, the police are always baffled at first. That's just cop talk. In a day or so, you'll hear them say they're making definite progress towards apprehending the killer."

"Here in Raynham? How many killers have the police here caught over the years?"

Carl nodded. "True, killers do seem to vanish into thin air in this town."

Just like me, he thought. *I'm gonna vanish too. Oh, this is just perfect . . . but I'll need a big knife to kill them with—no, a meat cleaver. Can't purchase it here. I'll need to drive out to Attleboro to buy it. Damn—I totally forgot: Mike's sister Angela lives with him! That's three people I need to kill. Heck—this is gonna take some planning!*

"Carl . . . Carl, are you okay?"

He snapped out of his bloody daydream to stare at her. "What, baby?"

"You look scary, like you're killing someone!"

He smiled. "I'm just horrified by the deaths." She'd eaten a little more of her breakfast and had the butter knife poised over a slice of unscraped black toast. He nodded his approval of her appetite while all the while planning:

I know Angela Rossi has the hots for me. How can I turn that to my advantage? I know—a date! I'll call and ask her out for dinner tonight. We'll have a nice time together with the money Jeff's just sent me and that way I'll be able to learn her schedules. But I gotta be careful now—Angela's a lawyer, she's a smart cookie. She earns her living with her brains, not with her ass (while thinking this he grinned across at Susan who was chewing toast while darting frightened glances at the television) *. . . she just might suspect me of something and that'll be the end of my plans. A shame to kill her too, she's got great boobs . . . if only she had the face to match them* (this caused another look over at Susan, who did have a great face to match her body.) *Angela is certain not to have a boyfriend or be getting laid much . . . she'll jump at the prospect of going out with me. Now, how do I ditch Susan tonight?*

That part was easy. Carl squeezed his face into a frown like he imagined he'd done the previous time she'd noticed. It worked.

"What's wrong, baby?" Susan shortly asked. "You've got the same look on your face as before."

"Oh, it's just financial woes," he said blandly. "I'm broke again and Jeff is being difficult. And I was thinking that we'd go down to Clip again tonight and party it up, but Jeff is just being such a jerk . . ."

He sensed an immediate change in her attitude. She didn't exactly freeze him out, but her concern for him vanished. Her gaze became cold and calculating, her eyes regarding him as if he was a piece of raw meat.

Oh, wonderful, predictable Susan, Carl thought with delight. *She only loves my bank account.*

"Are you okay, dear?" it was his turn to ask. "You seem a little cold all of a sudden. Maybe I should turn on the heating."

She shook her head at him. "No, it's just that I just remembered—wow, how could I have forgotten—I've some business to attend to for a couple of days. Hey, what's the time?" She reached across the table and pulled his cellphone across to her and tapped on the display. "8 a.m. already. I'm running late."

Despite knowing what to expect, Carl was amazed at the transformation that had come over Susan since he'd informed her he couldn't afford her services today. It was hilarious: she seemed almost allergic to him now; as if he was milk and she was lactose intolerant. Carl hid his amusement behind a façade of despair while Susan abruptly pushed back her chair and rose to her feet, walked around the table to his side and whispered, "Sorry, baby, but I'm in too much of a rush to do the dishes. You don't mind, do you?" and then hurried into his bedroom and shut the door behind her.

Once she was out of sight, he heaved a sigh of relief. True, Susan might be cold as ice, but this was one of the benefits of having a rental girlfriend. If he'd been dating a woman like Angela Rossi for instance, getting rid of her in a hurry would have proved much more difficult. Susan's attitude didn't offend him in the least. Carl knew that once he'd secured the family fortune for himself, Susan would come running back to him.

And speaking of the uncomely Miss Rossi . . .

Carl got up from the dinner table and quietly walked over to the shut bedroom door. He pressed his ear against it and waited till he heard the shower running.

Once he was certain that Susan Riley was busy trying to remove herself from his impoverished life as quickly as possible, Carl picked up his iPhone and called Angela Rossi, whose phone number he had due to the ongoing wedding preparations.

"Hello, Angela here." He had to admit that she had a nice voice. It sounded like she was in an office somewhere.

"Hi, Angela, it's Carl on the line."

"Hey, I'm surprised that you're calling me. Is it something to do with the wedding?"

He laughed. "No, not at all. I was just thinking about the other night at Nicole and Tommy's—"

"Oh, my God. It's just horrible what's happened to them!"

She sounded distraught at the news, so he pretended to be too. "Oh, it's really horrible. How could anyone . . . ?"

"Sorry, Carl, but I need to hang up now. The DA is looking at me funny. We're due in court in five minutes—it's the Hobart trial. Listen, thanks for call—"

"I actually called to ask if you'd have dinner with me tonight," he said quickly before she could hang up.

Her sharp intake of breath was audible over the line. "Would you like to?" he asked gently. "If tonight isn't convenient, we can do it tomorrow."

"No, tonight's perfect," she said in a rush. "I'd be delighted to have dinner with you." She laughed happily. "Listen, if I stay on the line a moment longer I'm gonna lose my job. Send me the dinner details via WhatsApp and I'll call you back during lunch break."

"Sure. That's great."

She hung up and Carl smiled with cold satisfaction. The fish had swallowed the hook. His plan was in effect.

He walked over and sat opposite the TV and turned the volume up again. To ensure that no one suspected him of the murders, it was important to get the details right. Fox News was covering another story at the moment, but Carl wasn't in a hurry. He had all day to plan.

Susan opened the bedroom door. He glanced up at her. In her lemon-toned pantsuit and blue shoes, red lipstick, blusher and green eyeshadow, she looked just perfect; polished up like an article for sale. But of course she was for sale.

She walked over to him and kissed his cheek. "Call me, baby, okay? Don't forget now. Maybe when Jeffrey feels up to being generous again?"

Carl nodded. He doubted she'd realized what she'd just said. But it didn't matter. Hardly anything she said ever mattered.

She left and he settled down to watch the news, which had just gotten back to the murder of the Ellsworths.

The Fox News anchorman was saying, ". . . Yet more grisly details are emerging of last night's brutal attack at the Raynham Outlook Clinic where . . . In other developments, Raynham Chief of Police Tina Kravitz is quoted as saying she hopes these deaths are an isolated incident and not the start of a new rash of summer killings . . ."

Carl smirked. *Keep on hoping, fat lady. You've at least another three stiffs coming up.*

CHAPTER 11

Susan

Susan Riley felt relieved once she was driving away from Carl's place.

I got out just in time, before he asked me for a freebie. Hell, I like the guy but business is business. No money equals no honey, querido.

In business one had to have principles.

Oh, she definitely liked Carl—for one thing, he was good-looking; for another, he wasn't kinky—but freebies were the death knell for a call girl; once she started handing out freebies on compassionate grounds, all her clients would want one. Discounts were okay, if the guy was low on funds, but no free sex ever.

What did Carl imagine she was anyway? The crotch-relief section of the Red Cross?

She turned her red Tesla Model S onto Broadway. The roads were all wet. It had rained in the night and the air smelt clean and fresh. She still felt slightly drowsy from last night's clubbing, but knew that would pass. This seemed an 'up' day for Susan. She had money in the bank and planned on going shopping later in the day to spend it. Susan could never see money in her bank account without remembering the latest trending fashions she'd seen in shops or online or in a magazine and feeling that compulsive feminine need to own them.

It ain't like I'm poor, but I'm still a whore. The reason for which doesn't require much psychoanalysis. I've got daddy issues . . . big-time daddy issues. I don't even particularly like sex that much but . . .

She reached under herself with her left hand and tenderly felt her butt crack as if it hurt. This wasn't something conscious; she did it without thinking. It stemmed from long ago. She was thirty years old now, but some trauma never left you.

***

13-year-old Susan had been called into the guest bedroom. This room was upstairs, at the end of a corridor at the rear of the large two-story house they'd just moved into.

Daddy had recently been promoted to judge and now his job consisted of sending people to jail. Susan loved Daddy—he was nice and really handsome, with that streak of white in his black hair, but sometimes he lost his temper with her. And when this happened Mommy never ever took Susan's side.

Today, Mommy led Susan into the guest room. Daddy was waiting there for them, staring out of the window. He turned around on hearing them enter. He had a stern look on his face, a lit cigarette between his lips, and her 8th grade high school report card in his hand.

Once Susan was inside, Mommy shut the bedroom door behind her. Mommy was small and blonde and quite pretty.

Daddy called Susan forward and shoved her report card at her.

"Your grades suck, darling daughter," he said in that juicy baritone of his.

She took the card from him. Yes, it was true, her grades were really bad, particularly in Math and Spanish. However, Susan wasn't really to blame for this. It was actually Mommy's fault. Mommy—Martha Riley—was obsessed with parties and keeping up with the neighbors; so much so that her only child was often left on her own at home to do whatever she liked. And anyone leaving a 13-year-old home alone must necessarily expect the worst . . . So, left to her own devices, young Susan Riley had played away all the hours when she should have been studying and now, well her grades were understandably atrocious.

But of course, her parents didn't see it that way. She could read it in her father's eyes that she was wholly to blame for her mother's parental negligence.

Her father's face never once lost its sternness. "Alright, daughter. If you won't read your books, your mother and I will have to punish you."

She tensed. "But, dad . . . !"

"Take your pants off, Susan."

"What?"

"You heard your father, little girl," Mommy said behind her. "Undress yourself. Take off your pants and panties."

Susan gaped at her father. "Dad, I can't get undressed in front of you!"

The well-respected Judge Joseph Riley blew smoke from his lips, then smiled calmly back at her. "I meant exactly what I said: take your clothes off, girl! You're supposed to go to university and become a lawyer, but instead you're wasting your time watching television and phoning boys. You need to be shown the error of your ways before it's too late for you to change them. Now get those panties off!"

"No, I won't do it. You can't whip me! You can't make me—!"

But then her father grabbed her and pushed her down on the bed. She tried to scream but he pushed her face into the pillow and she began struggling to breathe.

"Fighting will only make it worse," Mommy said.

Susan was already finding this to be true. So she relaxed and let her mother roll her jeans and panties off her legs. She couldn't see what was going on behind her, but she knew it would be very bad. "What are you gonna do to me!?" she squealed in fright.

"A little purging," her father replied. He flicked the ash from his cigarette off in front of her face, then waved its glowing tip at her. "One cigarette burn for each bad grade you got."

Susan shrieked, but there was no escaping her fate. And if she'd thought she'd be getting burned on her buttocks or thighs, she was mistaken. While Mommy held her firmly down, Daddy parted her legs and her buttocks and planted his lit cigarette against her tightly puckered anus.

"This burn is for Algebra," he said as she screamed into the pillow. "And this one for US History," he added after she'd calmed down, moving the cigarette a little higher and planting it against her anal sphincter again. "And this one . . ."

Susan stopped screaming and began crying. On the third burn, she pissed herself, flooding the bed with urine, some of which must have splashed upwards because she heard Daddy say: "Oh, heck, the little hellcat has put it out. Hold her down, honey, while I light up another. I've still got Yearbook to chastise her for. How anyone can flunk that is beyond me!"

13-year-old Susan Riley got five burns on her anus. Afterwards, Daddy left to meet some friends at the country club. Mommy cleaned up Susan's blistering, tormented anus and applied antiseptic cream to it. Then she held the traumatized girl close and rocked her like a baby. "It's all for your own good, dear," she said. "Now promise us that you'll get good grades from now on."

"Yes, yes," Susan readily agreed with tears running down her cheeks.

"Alright, darling," Mommy said. "Now just rest up and in a day or two, when you feel up to walking again, we'll go shopping. Your father says you need a wardrobe change. See, he loves you, dear. We both just want you to grow up to be a successful lawyer, not some dropout or hooker."

Susan was unable to walk for three days. And each day, after Daddy got back from his job of sentencing murderers to life imprisonment, he would cuddle her too and tell her that burning her had been for her own benefit. And warn her to read her schoolbooks, or next time she'd get the same again.

Susan's anus got burned eight times during her teenage years. The reason was always the same—bad grades. She never told anyone what was happening; she doubted anyone would believe her. And besides, she always got a fresh wardrobe afterwards and became the envy of all her friends.

Finally, however, Daddy realized that Susan simply wasn't as smart as he wanted her to be and would never become a lawyer and make him proud with her legal prowess. On the night before her sixteenth birthday, she got her final anal burning, eight cigarette scars for destroying his legal hopes in her. By now, she knew better than to protest and yell. She'd lain there and endured the agony. Of course, darling Mommy was once again on hand with the antiseptic cream.

The problem was, how did you complain about such treatment, convince anyone you were an abused teen, when the very next day after getting your ass burned for this last time, you received a brand new BMW convertible for your sixteenth birthday? And Daddy and Mommy threw a huge birthday party for you and your friends (complete with a five-tiered cake and your favorite local rock band) and were there smiling at you and telling everyone how much they loved you and how proud of you they were?

So Susan and her anus had finally been left alone. She'd gone to college for two years, then dropped out and gone to work at the Kohl's department store in Taunton. The work was boring, but she was bored anyway. She just didn't know what to do with herself yet. She'd been twenty years old and with no plans for her future.

Round about then her mother had died of lung cancer. After a year of mourning, Daddy had found himself a young blonde girlfriend of Susan's age. Susan had moved out of the house. She'd endured three more years as a cashier at Kohl's, and then quit to exchange sex for money instead. Which had been infinitely more profitable and, with all the drugs and partying and traveling involved, much more entertaining.

Prostitution had been her life for the past seven years.

All that teenage burning however had one ironic effect. Nowadays as an escort, Susan found anal sex very easy, even with huge penises. Her anus had almost no sensation left now.

***

So, yes, I do have daddy issues, Susan thought, as she steered her red Tesla onto Baker Road where the Pattens lived. *All in all, I may just have postponed my teenage rebellion.*

Or, why else did a woman who didn't enjoy sex that much become a prostitute? Susan didn't know for sure.

She was on good terms with her father and visited him regularly. Daddy—Judge Joseph Riley—had just broken up with his latest young blonde. Liz must have been blonde girlfriend number seventeen or eighteen; Susan had honestly lost count of them. Daddy never referred to the sordid past. Nor, since his wife's death, did he smoke anymore. Though disappointed that his daughter was an escort, Daddy was relieved that she was discreet about her indiscretions. Susan hadn't ever been arrested or gotten into any sex scandals.

Maybe I should get myself arrested, Susan thought as she parked in front of the Patten's house. *Shake Daddy up a little, throw a little turmoil into his well-ordered, respectable life. He really did hurt me back then . . .*

She parked the car and got out.

CHAPTER 12

Susan & Leona

The Pattens lived in a white cottage. The building had a screened-off porch on its right side, and a separate entrance on the left which led to the studio where Leona held her psychic consultations. This left-hand entrance was a black door over which hung a wide white sign decorated with a galaxy of stars, moons and planets arranged around the red words 'Psychic Readings.'

"Come in," Leona called out when Susan knocked.

Susan stepped inside. As she'd expected to be the case, Leona sat waiting on a couch. She would have heard Susan's car arriving and parking.

Leona's psychic studio had two rooms, with the front and well-lighted one serving as her reception area. After brief smiles and words of greeting, Susan followed Leona through into the larger rear room where she did her psychic thing.

This back room was shrouded in darkness, with its windows and both access doors obscured by dark blue drapes that one pushed aside to enter; and its walls and ceiling painted an extremely dark brown. Its floor was blood-red carpeting. The room's only furniture were the circular table in its middle and the three high-backed chairs arranged around that; and its only source of light were the three red candles arranged at the points of the white equilateral triangle drawn around the crystal ball set in the table's center. To one side of the crystal ball sat a pack of tarot cards.

"Sit," Leona told Susan. She was dressed in a blue robe that was studded with gems, a long and glittering silver necklace, and emerald earrings designed like insect eyes. Her eyelids were painted green, her lips blue. Her brown hair was clipped back.

Susan sat. "How're Paul and the kids?" she asked, both to make conversation and to help herself regain her composure. In this candlelit room, Leona looked incredibly spooky. Susan felt as though she needed to convince herself that she was still in the real world.

In addition, Leona looked miserable behind her makeup. She looked like she'd been crying. When they'd spoken on the phone before Susan had driven over, Leona *had* been crying. Susan understood Leona's grief: Leona and Nicole had been friends since childhood. They'd attended the same schools and same summer camps and later even dated in the same circles. As a matter of fact, Tommy Ellsworth had introduced Leona to her husband Paul. So the couple's death would be an especially heavy blow for her.

Leona grimaced. "Paul's off delivering tractors to Walnut Creek in Ohio. He'll be back tonight. Sandy and Junior are okay; in the car on the way to school this morning they were already planning how they were going to run riot over me this weekend."

Susan nodded. Leona's husband was a trucker—a big, brawny down-to-earth man who fit well with his seemingly ethereal wife. Their kids were ten-and-eight-years-old and were more than a handful.

Leona had meanwhile seated herself opposite Susan. She placed her hands on the table, stared moodily into her crystal ball, then said, "Alright, you're not here to consult me about your work life like you previously intended to, but concerning your nightmares."

Susan nodded. She wasn't surprised. Leona really did have the gift of foreseeing. Leona herself admitted that it wasn't perfect, but she was more often right than wrong. "Why do I keep having them?" she asked.

"Tell me what you see; the ball doesn't say."

Susan gulped. "Well, in each dream I meet Death, who nicely informs me that I'm going to commit suicide. The damn dream never alters and I only have it in the mornings, right before I wake up."

"Hmm." Leona stared into the crystal ball some more. "Let's do a tarot reading."

"Hold on a moment," Susan said, raising a hand to make her point. "Screw this, Leona. Everyone is in total denial about what happened to Nicole and Tommy. We both know—we *all* know—that that damn Cleaverman thing you summoned was what killed them, not whichever nonexistent psychopath the cops are currently busy chasing after." She realized her voice had gotten a little loud and paused to catch her breath. "Can I smoke?"

"Go ahead." Leona put down the pack of cards she'd picked up and then clasped her hands in her lap. "Well, you can't say I didn't warn everyone that night—it was a stupid thing to do."

Susan got her cigarette lit and dragged on it. She held the smoke in her lungs for a moment, exhaled, then nodded. "Yes, but that's medicine after death. I was as interested in seeing what happened as anyone else that night. I just—"

"I wasn't."

Susan went on as if she'd not been interrupted: "—didn't expect it to work. None of us did."

"I did."

Susan blew out more smoke. The gray tobacco haze fluttered between them like a ghost. She tapped her cigarette ash onto the round base of the nearest candlestick, then said, "Leona, for fuck's sake, stop it. Stop blaming us all."

"But *you are* all to blame." Then Leona sighed and nodded. "Oh, alright, I'll let it go."

Susan went on: "And now the thing we raised has killed two of us. And Carl doesn't want to talk about it because it's"—she made quotation marks with her slim fingers—" 'bad vibes' that'll ruin his pot and coke high, and you who brought the thing to life, you're also—"

"I'm more upset that *you* are."

Susan crossed her legs, then waved her cigarette at Leona, its trail of gray smoke making a creepy 'S' shape over the crystal ball. "Girlfriend, you seem remarkably composed for someone who's terrified. Me, I'm already looking over my shoulder, scared I'll be next for the chop."

Leona shrugged, her blue robe shimmering like sea waves over her body. "I don't think there'll be any more deaths, that's why."

"Are you sure . . . what makes you so sure?"

Leona shook her head. "I'm not one hundred percent sure, but I've been thinking; and from the look of things, we got off lightly." She shook her head and looked like she'd start crying. "No, I'm not trivializing Tommy and Nicole's deaths . . . but . . . look, Mitch provided the blood for the ritual and I performed it, and we're both still alive."

"You think Tommy and Nicole were sacrifices for the rest of us?" Susan asked.

"Yes, most likely because we invoked the Cleaverman in *their* house."

"Leona, I really hope that's true . . . 'cos, from the details of the deaths . . ." She felt unable to express what she felt—oh, what horror and agony their friends must have endured before dying! Instead, she pointed at Leona's crystal ball. "What do you see in there?"

"Nothing."

"And the cards? What do they say?"

"Death and life . . . betrayal and confusion." She tapped the deck of cards. "Life and death."

Susan leaned over the table. "What's that mean? That could easily be us all getting killed."

"I can't get a clear reading, each card I pick neutralizes the next one."

The conversation went on in similar vein, with Susan seeking an assurance of safety that Leona couldn't give her, and Leona visibly growing more and more irritated, until finally Susan growled, "Alright, alright, so assuming you're wrong and we're all gonna get killed no matter what—who was this Cleaverman creature anyway?"

Her question filled Leona with relief. Here now was something she could answer. She abruptly got to her feet and said, "Hey, you wait here for me. I'll be right back."

Susan stubbed out her cigarette on the base of the candlestick and lit another. With Leona gone for the moment she felt very nervous. She hated being alone in dark places, and in this particular dark room with its occult associations, she found it easy to imagine that the shadows the candles flung on the walls and ceiling were all dancing and had heads and hands and long deformed fingers that were reaching out for her. A child's nightmare translated into adulthood. Instead of staring at the shadows, Susan stared at Leona's crystal ball, trying to read her own future in the orb's dull interior. This was of course, impossible, and so Susan tried to pass the rest of the time she spent waiting for Leona's return picking cards off the psychic's tarot pack at random and peeking at them.

She quit doing this when she picked out the 'Death' card twice in a row, which she found scary because she'd thought a tarot deck only had one 'Death' card in it and she'd picked the second card from a different section of the stack—right near the bottom—after replacing the first 'Death' card at the top of it.

After that shock Susan simply sat in her chair with her legs crossed and blew smoke rings.

***

Leona returned with a tablet PC. She placed the device in front of Susan. "This is what the Cleaverman looks like—an artist's rendition, of course, though it's unknown who survived the Cleaverman to describe him." She felt a morbid satisfaction on seeing how scared Susan became on viewing the object of her fears.

"Ugh," Susan gasped. "And I thought the sneak preview we had of it that night looked horrible. This is way, way worse."

The artist's depiction was of a creature made of swirling smoke. It looked like a bigfoot with a wooly body instead of a furry one. The face was old and repellent and sunken, with tiny eyes, a long nose and uneven rotten teeth. The hands and feet possessed long pointed claws. Most obvious, and dominating the drawing was the huge cleaver that the Cleaverman carried over his shoulder.

Susan shuddered. This was the thing that had killed her friends?

"Now, listen up," Leona said, once more seating herself opposite Susan. "I've had a look around the internet for information on the Cleaverman, and there's very little of it."

"Was there anything in the spellbook Tommy and Nicole had at home? The one we used?"

"I think . . . yeah, there was some—on the pages right before the spell."

"What did it say?"

"I didn't read it?"

"Why not?"

Leona scowled. "You forget I was being hurried to cast the damn spell."

Susan let it go. She was interested in hearing what Leona had to say.

"Alright, legend has it that John Cleaverman was a butcher. A wacky, unpredictable fellow who lived in Springfield, Massachusetts in the 30's. Despite his eccentricities, John was happily married until the day a truck hit his car. His wife was killed outright, but John lost his memory and shortly afterwards ran amuck with a giant butcher knife . . . killed almost twenty people . . . then he mysteriously vanished."

Susan made a face. "That's just . . ."

"That's just *one* version of the story," Leona said, relieved that now Susan was listening rather than interrogating her.

"What's the other one?"

"That John Cleaverman was a philanderer who had an affair with a witch, a lady named Erin DeMornay. The legend says John got Erin pregnant, then left her to go back to his wife, so Erin cursed him, and now he's searching everywhere for his wife, only Erin made it so he can't remember her name. Then his lack of memory drove him mad, so he picked up a cleaver and began chopping townsfolk up like they were dead sheep."

"What was the wife's name?"

Leona shook her head. "No one seems to know. The Cleaverman riddle I read out that night; you remember the words?"

Susan tried and then shook her head. "All I recall is the first line— that one stuck in my head: 'Tell me the name of John Cleaverman's wife,' wasn't it?"

Leona nodded. "Yeah, that's all of it that I remember too. But there it is . . . see? It's a nasty curse, making a man look for someone whose name he can't recall."

Susan shrugged. "It's even nastier leaving a pregnant woman to fend for herself. Even if she was a witch. He knew what he was getting into when he took her to bed."

Leona shrugged right back. "Well, that's the second legend anyway. Then there's the third one."

Susan, who was now on her third cigarette, rolled her eyes. "A *third* version of events? Doesn't anyone know anything about this guy for sure?"

"Well, no . . . I mean, yeah. In this third version of the tale, John Cleaverman made a deal with the witch Erin DeMornay for eternal life—he wanted to be undead like vampires are—only something went wrong with the spell and afterwards he couldn't remember who he was. He loved his wife dearly, but could no longer remember her name either and the pain of trying to remember it drove him crazy. Also, while the spell did grant John immortality, it backfired so he couldn't enjoy living forever, but was instead consumed by a raging bloodlust . . ."

Leona fell silent. Telling the tale had drained her. Being sensitive to spiritual things had almost as many disadvantages as advantages.

Suddenly Leona was overcome with dread. This was a vague, anomalous dread; one impossible to pinpoint. She felt as though the shadows at the edges of her studio were alive and staring at her.

Yes, for certain they'd conjured up something nasty two nights ago. Leona had felt the astral turbulence of its arrival. The Cleaverman's coming had felt to her as if the universe had just defecated. This was Leona's exact mental image of the weird happening—in her mind's eye she visualized the old spellbook behaving like a magical anus. It had seemed to her like something putrid and undesired—ectoplasmic excrement—had entered the human world through the Ellsworths' living room . . . yes! The spellbook had shat out something that the afterlife no longer had a need for. And (viewed through the spyglass of metaphor) it had maliciously (or mischievously) deposited that horrible turd on Nicole's doorstep, for she and her hapless dinner guests to deal with . . .

Thankfully, the two hosts that night had borne the fallout of the summoning. They'd been the sacrifices that kept the others safe.

Leona said nothing more, but Susan had no further questions. Susan was already questioning the wisdom of having requested the information. She scared easily, and here, alone with a creepily-made-up medium in a candlelit room, surely hadn't been the best location to have heard this morbid trio of stories.

She watched Leona, expecting her to say something. But Leona was too drained to talk.

Susan got tired of waiting. She finished smoking her cigarette and didn't feel like immediately lighting another one, so instead she said, "So, I guess I'll just take your word for it that it's over then."

Leona nodded. "Yeah, I think so. I sure hope so anyway. But if not, look on the positive side."

"There's a *positive* side to these killings?"

"Yes. If there'll be any more victims, Mitch and I are the most likely choices. His blood, my tongue—he's a drunk, I'm a psychic."

"How can you be so damn calm about this?"

Leona laughed. "Because I'm joking, that's why. It's over, Sue."

"Well, I sure fucking hope so." Susan glanced at her watch, then stood up. "Hey, I must be going. Got a hot lunch date with a client."

Leona extended her hand. "Hey, you whore, don't forget to pay me first. Hundred and fifty bucks."

Susan scowled. "But you didn't . . . oh, whatever. What did you say about my nightmare again?"

"Sit down and I'll remind you."

While grumbling about inflation infecting the spirits and ether too, Susan got three fifty dollar notes out of her purse, placed the money in front of Leona, then sat facing her again.

Leona calmed her mind and soul and stared into the crystal ball. "Really frigging weird this is, girl. Apparently, in future you've a date with Death, but you're not gonna die . . ."

CHAPTER 13

Angela, mostly . . .

All through dinner that night, Angela thought of nothing else but what Carl Whitfield's lips would feel like pressed against hers, how his body would feel merged with hers. She imagined his manhood filling her to the brim (she was certain Carl's penis was massive, so much so that it was sure to hurt her a little at first when he put in in). She visualized how wonderful it would feel to fall asleep afterwards wrapped up in his muscular arms.

Angela did try to feel depressed over the deaths of her two friends, but it was an almost impossible task. She was too happy to finally have Carl to herself for a few hours. She didn't remember when last she'd been out with a guy this handsome—possibly never—so she intended to make the very most of this opportunity to impress him. Who knew when he'd ask her out again; or if he ever would. She'd fallen hard for Carl at first sight—not love, but a deep infatuation that given sufficient time and sufficient one-sided emotional nourishment might easily tip over into obsession.

They were dining at the R.O. Seafood Restaurant on upper Broadway. The dining room was about half filled and low background music created a nice ambience. He was having chargrilled oysters; she was having the garlic-and-butter lobster. The food was delicious, the accompanying white wine a delight to the tongue.

Carl wasn't drinking much though. "I had a couple of beers in the afternoon," he'd explained with a smile, "need to keep a clear head while I'm with you so I don't make an ass of myself."

"Oh, I'll forgive you almost anything tonight," Angela had replied dreamily.

If tonight's Eden of pleasure had a serpent, it was Angela's knowledge that there would be no sexual culmination to the evening—she had to work.

***

"I have to be in the office tonight," she'd explained when Carl had picked her up at home. "This Teddy Hobart case is driving everyone crazy."

On arriving at the cottage he'd asked after his brother and Mike, but neither had been home, so off they'd driven for dinner.

Carl had nodded as he'd driven past the Mr. & Mrs. Book Emporium, then turned the blue BMW X6 round a corner. "The Teddy Hobart trial? Oh, you mean the guy who couldn't have killed his wife because even though his fingerprints are on the murder weapon, they're from his amputated right hand?"

"The very same," Angela agreed wearily. She'd traded her drab work pantsuit for a low-cut white dress that showed off her breasts and thighs. Carl was clearly interested in her body; lots of men were. It was just her unpretty face that gave men reservations about her . . . "So," she'd finished, "with that case on and using up all my day-time, I'm backed up with other work I must clear up. Once you and I are through having fun, I head down to Taunton for the night shift." She sighed and faked a yawn. "I'll be lucky to get a couple of hours sleep before court resumes in the morning."

"I'll drop you off at the office," Carl had offered nicely. "Too bad we don't have longer."

Had Angela been less besotted with her handsome male companion, she'd have noticed the sly and 'very pleased' look that entered his eyes on her mentioning she'd be absent from home tonight. "Thanks," she'd said, "but please just bring me back home. It's best I take my own car to the office, so I can get back home in the morning."

***

"So what's the latest on the Hobart murder trial?" Carl asked her. They'd already discussed the Ellsworths' murders, both agreeing it was a terrible tragedy. And then, by mutual unvoiced consent to not ruin this pleasant evening with unpleasant conversation, they'd switched to

83

discussing lighter topics. Well, a little bit lighter. Though both gruesome and mindboggling, the Hobart case was at least an amusing one.

"You haven't been following the news?"

"Not too closely. Not today anyway. I was out of town making a few essential purchases." He grinned at her and she felt her heart melt with desire for him.

"Well," she said after a bite of juicy lobster, "today the defense had a replica of the bedroom where Maddy Hobart was killed installed in the courtroom. Not the whole thing, mind you, just the corner where the bed was. Then they got a female dummy and placed it on the bed in the exact position that Maddy was found. Then someone tried stabbing the dummy in the throat with his left hand."

Carl leaned forward over their table. "Yeah, I've seen something like that on TV before. Go on, please. So what was the outcome?"

Angela shook her head mournfully. "It merely confirmed what everyone already knew—Teddy couldn't have done it."

"So why try him then?"

"We have to. We have Teddy's confession to committing the murder. Yeah, I know it sounds really silly, but there it is: we're actually having to figure out a way in which he *could* have killed Maddy." She laughed. "We're doomed to failure though; already, the jury aren't buying any of what we're selling. And, Judge Riley is mad that we're wasting his time—"

"Sue Riley's dad?"

Angela nodded, hoping he wasn't about introducing Susan into their conversation. "Yeah, her daddy's overseeing things. And he's not pleased at all. "We—both the DA's team and the defense—were in his chambers at lunchtime and know what he said?"

Carl shook his head.

"He told us that if we bothered him with this nonsense for more than a week longer he'd have us all for contempt of court." She laughed. "He seemed dead serious about it too."

Carl also laughed. "I can't blame him. You all must be driving him nuts. And his daughter says he's a very straight-laced old fellow."

"Except for his hang-up about young blondes. Rumor has it that Judge Riley changes girlfriends about every six months."

"The question is: do they wear him out or does he wear them out?"

They both laughed some more. And then dinner was over.

Afterwards, as they crossed the parking lot to Carl's car, Angela felt great. Carl had been wonderful company—delightful, charming—everything she'd dreamed he'd be and more besides. That they wouldn't sleep together tonight was unavoidable and neither of their faults.

But, that's all for the best, she mused as Carl swung the X6 out of the restaurant's parking lot and onto the highway. *It's good to keep a guy dangling; give him something to look forward to.*

She'd noticed how he'd been eying her breasts all night. And so, when he dropped her off at home again and after walking her to the front door, gave her a nice gentle kiss on the lips, she pressed her chest hard against him, letting him feel how large and cushiony soft her breasts were; giving him something to lust after, something physical to remember about her, while whispering huskily in his ear, "Oh, Carl, I *really* enjoyed tonight."

She was utterly delighted to hear him reply: "Oh, so did I, Angel. Let's do this again sometime very soon." Then he was gone. In a daze she waved back at him and watched his car zoom off.

Then she flung her hands upward, then hugged herself tight with delight. It was a lovely night and she felt lovely.

He called me 'Angel' and he wants to date me again! Angela Rossi was practically floating on a cloud of romantic bliss while changing her clothes and heading off to the office again.

CHAPTER 14

Mitch

Early Friday morning, a few minutes before 2.a.m.

Dressed all in black, Mitch Mullins made his silent way through the trees flanking Elizabeth Drive.

To get here, he'd left his car parked two streets away, then proceeded amidst the woods that divided the streets. This way there had been no chance of his being detected by the homeowners, not there were many of those anyway. One good thing about a small town, particularly one like Raynham which was set amidst thick woodland, was the low house density; you couldn't see the neighbors for the forest.

Mitch parted the branches and leaves behind Steve-O's house. Then he set down his toolbox and spent some time finalizing his plans.

Mitch was here tonight for serious business. He was here to kill Steve-O, and possibly his wife Jacqui as well. He hadn't really made up his mind about Jacqui yet, but Steve-O was better than dead already.

Mitch's encounter with Bev (or the 'boiled-egg bitch' as he'd come to think of her) was partly responsible for his actions tonight. After that horrible experience—even now he felt like vomiting when he recalled what she'd made him eat—he'd wanted nothing more than to crawl into a hole for a few days to hide and rebuild his shattered ego.

Shit, I already know I'm a loser; but the bitch made me eat her shit!

Yes, all Mitch had wanted to do was hide and lick his wounds.

But see, Jacqui simply wouldn't let well enough alone. She'd kept badgering him, till he'd barely managed to restrain himself from beating her to a pulp—he'd been mad enough to kill her.

And then yesterday—Thursday—morning, he'd found the condoms in her handbag. Either because she didn't care anymore if he knew what she was up to or not, or because she wanted to humiliate him, Jacqui had left the handbag in the living room. All Mitch had had to do was walk past the armchair and peek down, and well, the damn purse was unzipped and the condom pack was right in plain view, on top of her lipstick and compact.

He'd opened the pack and noted that two condoms were missing. He'd almost expected to find the used condoms right there in the purse also, along with their load of Steve-O's semen (or was it Big Dick's? or both of theirs?).

Thing is, the condoms merely confirmed Mitch's suspicions. His friend Dibbs had hinted as much. (Joe Dibbs, by the way, was still missing—Mitch had called Dibbs's girlfriend, but she too hadn't seen him since Wednesday afternoon.)

Back then Mitch had laughed off Dibbs's suggestion of his wife's infidelity, but now . . .

Well, I'm a damn fool; Dibbs was right, Mitch thought as he stood there by the trees behind Steve-O's palatial two-story home. *But, no problem, I'm gonna fix everything tonight. I'm gonna fix Stevie's wagon real good.*

At first, Mitch had considered simply doing the right thing—getting a divorce. *Hell, by the time your wife wants you to know that she's cheating on you, you two are through. Face the damn facts, Mitch, you've been through for the past four months, ever since she kicked your ass out of the bedroom, claiming she got more sleep that way.*

But if they did it the legal way, Jacqui was sure to get the house. Mitch was dead broke, down on his luck and now a certified drunk to boot. There was no way he could afford a lawyer—so there went everything, including his run-down Ford Mustang. He'd be homeless in the blink of an eye. And with the run of bad luck he'd been having, Mitch figured it wouldn't be long now—maybe two years on the outside—before he'd be bumming coins on street corners; another anonymous stat for Uncle Sam to collate.

Two things had switched Mitch's outlook from passive to active.

Yes, the first was his revolting eggs-and-poop 'dinner date' with Bev. Filtered through that brown and stinky lens, Jacqui's admittedly sordid but nonetheless routine betrayal had assumed the colors of an unprecedented and thus unforgiveable offence, something that demanded violent punishment.

The second thing was the deaths of his two friends. Those deaths had given Mitch Mullins the idea to kill Steve-O and Jacqui and let whoever killed Tommy and Nicole take the blame for their deaths also.

Mitch hadn't ever killed anyone before. But . . . well, there was always a first time for every experience. And he realized he'd never have a better chance than tonight to commit murder and get away with it.

Staring up at the inky sky, Mitch agreed with himself that tonight, with its hidden moon and missing stars, seemed perfect for killing.

But first . . . Mitch suddenly felt his courage desert him. To bolster himself, he dug into his toolbox for his flask of whiskey. A nip of this and he was feeling much better. He put the flask away again, wedging it between the electric knife and axe. (He wasn't giving too much thought to how he'd chop the bodies up afterwards. He figured that once he had a corpse on his hands, the fear of jail would motivate him to deal with it.)

Feeling better now, Mitch leapt over Steve-O's fence and ran forward through the backyard. The house loomed large, lower lights off, upper lights on, its opulence becoming an additional reason why the man who'd stolen his wife had to die. The right edge of Steve-O's huge brown SUV showed by the building's edge.

The greedy sonofabitch. Has more than enough already and still has to take what's mine.

Just as he reached the rear wall, Mitch chanced to glance across the road, where he imagined he saw another man, also dressed in black, sneaking through the trees on that side towards the house opposite this one.

He ducked into hiding and scratched his head for a moment. *Hey, does the air reflect things, or am I seeing things? Or am I just frigging drunk? But no, I ain't had that much to drink. Just two beers for Dutch courage before leaving home . . .*

He peeked back out. His 'reflection' (if that was what it was) had disappeared. Sighing his relief, Mitch concentrated on entering Steve-O's house.

After deciding to kill Steve-O, Mitch had spent about an hour researching housebreaking online. Seeing as how he'd been drinking to steady his nerves at the same time, he now didn't recall too much of what he'd read, except that he needed to find a window, preferably the kitchen one, quietly knock it in, then reach inside the hole he'd made, feel about for the latch or key and turn that. So this is what he did.

While making his silent way along the left side of the house to the kitchen door however, Mitch did remember to keep watch for CCTV cameras. Not seeing any, he got the crowbar from his toolbox and gave the window in the kitchen door a sharp tap with the curved edge of the bar.

He gave a start at the loudness of the shattering glass.

Dammit, if someone heard that inside the house . . . !

But apparently no one had. For five minutes Mitch crouched by the kitchen door, waiting for someone to come and investigate. But no one did. So, feeling emboldened, he stuck his hand through the hole and turned the key. After another slight pause, he opened the door and stepped inside Steve-O's house.

A faint smell of food—fried meat—tickled his nose. Mitch quickly passed through the kitchen and crossed the rear corridor to the stairs. Leaving his toolbox at the foot of the stairs, he climbed the staircase with a knife in hand. Stab first, then chop into pieces, that was his plan. He'd considered bringing along Jacqui's gun also, but guns made noise and noise was something he needed to avoid tonight.

To his astonishment, there was no one in any of the three upstairs bedrooms.

Mitch stood by the front window of the last bedroom, staring down at Steve-O's front lawn and driveway. Steve-O had a stone flute-boy water fountain in the middle of his parking lot and there were three vehicles parked down there including Steve's brown SUV, so the wife-stealing sonofabitch had to be home. But if so, where the hell was he then?

Mitch began feeling scared. *What if they're waiting to jump me? But if that's the case, then why the hell haven't they jumped me yet? I've been in the house for ten minutes now and I ain't seen anyone!*

He was torn between the desire to flee and the urge to complete the bloody mission he'd come here for. His need for revenge won. *So Steve-O ain't upstairs? That doesn't matter. I'm gonna find him wherever he was, and when I do . . .*

While thinking, he'd been making his way back downstairs. Now he stood in the living room for a while, pondering what to do. *Should*

I check the downstairs bedrooms, or should I . . . ? Hey, hey does this damn house have a basement?

Now, listening along the corridor, he heard voices and laughter.

He grinned to himself. "Yeah, it's got a basement alright."

Mitch retrieved his toolbox from the foot of the stairs and walked back down the corridor, letting the voices guide him on. The door to the basement was right opposite the door to the kitchen. Shut when he'd entered the house, it was now wide open. Steps led down from it to a rectangle of light in which he saw a padded high-backed chair and Jacqui's bare left leg, the latter instantly identifiable by the hot-pink pedicure she'd just gotten done.

The thought that Steve-O was right at this moment having sex with his wife down there—less than ten feet away from him—filled Mitch with rage. He dropped the toolbox, pulled his knife out of his belt and prepared to dash down the stairs and stab the pair of them to death.

But then a warning flash went through Mitch's mind: *When I came in earlier, this door was shut, so who opened it? Who's come upstairs and where are they now?*

With this question in mind and the knife held ready, Mitch spun around to look inside the kitchen.

Oh, shit!

He had a moment's recognition that the naked giant facing him was Big Dick Abbott, and then the next moment, Big Dick's big fist collided with Mitch's jaw and knocked him out.

***

Something wet splashed on his face.

"Hey, wake up, asshole. We haven't got all night!"

More wet splashed on his face, then someone slapped him. Once, twice, thrice; each blow flinging his head from side to side.

Mitch opened his eyes and slowly focused them.

Oh, shit.

He was down in Steve-O's basement and bound to the high-backed chair he'd noticed from the top of the stairs. The chair had no arms, and lots of duct tape had been used to secure his wrists and ankles to its legs. He was also naked, now wearing just his socks. To further restrain him in position in the chair, a wide band of duct tape had been wound around his waist. Yet more duct tape formed a gag across his lips.

Jacqui was standing on his right, holding the half-full bottle of water she'd been splashing in his face. She was completely naked.

"Alright, he's with us again," she called out. "Dick, use your brains sometimes. The man's my husband; you didn't have to hit him so damn hard."

Big Dick shambled into view. "Sorry, girl. He was holding a knife and with my rod on display I wasn't about taking any chances."

Jacqui grabbed Big Dick's penis and began fondling it. "Yeah, they don't sell these in Walmart." Naked, Big Dick Abbott rippled with muscle. The man was as muscular as Jeffrey Whitfield's boyfriend Mike Beefcake, but was about six inches taller. His penis was proportionate to his bulk. Whoever had first nicknamed him 'Big Dick' had gotten it exactly right. Even half-hard, the organ was about nine inches long, and it was still growing as Jacqui's fingers teased it.

Mitch struggled against his bonds. He also tried without success to dislodge the strip of duct tape sealing his lips. His jaw ached where Big Dick had socked him. He wondered where Steve-O was, and why, if Jacqui was having an affair with Steve-O, she was naked with Big Dick. *Or are they having threesomes? But if that's the case, why the hell are they having their threesomes downstairs in the house basement?*

With her eyes fixed on his, Jacqui fondled Big Dick's penis to full erection. She giggled at Mitch's discomfort.

To avoid staring at her, Mitch now shifted his attention to the rest of the basement. To do so he had to turn his head. For the first time, he noticed the two video cameras on tripods.

He was craning his head to see better when he heard footsteps descending the stairs. He looked back just as Steve-O arrived in the basement carrying his toolbox. In his other hand, Steve-O (who thankfully had shorts and a tee shirt on), was brandishing Mitch's axe.

The little man was livid. He flung the toolbox down, then hurried straight at Mitch and slapped him twice across the face. Then waving the axe wildly, he shrieked, "You asshole! How dare you break into my house! I'll kill you for this! I should cut off your head."

Mitch squirmed and tried to get out of the chair. Steve-O looked like he really meant it.

"Careful with that axe, baby!" Jacqui yelped, ducking out of Steve-O's way. "You almost scalped me just now!"

Steve-O spun around to face her. "Can you believe this asshole you married? Honey, I think he came here to kill me . . . to kill us both."

Jacqui shook her head sadly. "Yeah, he's both a drunk *and* stupid to boot." She leaned in closer to Mitch. "Now, why the hell would you want to kill us both, lazy man?"

"Hmmph!" The way she'd been mincing around Steve-O, leaning on him and rubbing her naked breasts against him, made Mitch want to kill her even more.

Steve-O pulled Jacqui back and bent over Mitch himself. His frown had been replaced by a cold smile. "But, Mitch," he said in a voice that dripped oily delight, "now that you're here, I need to make you welcome. You're gonna star in my new movie."

Mitch had already figured out that Steve-O was making a porno, what with both Jacqui and Big Dick naked and the video cameras.

"I've already got one star, but two's even better," Steve-O enthused. "The fans will be screaming—no, they'll be *ejaculating* with delight at your performances."

What's he talking about?

"Turn him around, Dick!"

Mitch's chair was turned around. Now he had a clear view of Steve-O's recording setup.

The basement wall opposite him was draped with a US flag that covered it from top to bottom. In the middle of the flag the words 'USA' were boldly printed in large black letters.

In the foreground was a long red couch, almost a divan, with half of its back missing. This was normal enough for porn, Mitch guessed. What wasn't normal though, was the naked and bloodied man tied up in a chair exactly like the one Mitch was himself bound in. The man's mouth was gag-balled; a long stream of spit dribbled from its left corner. His body was covered with bleeding cuts, as if he'd been tortured, and his long dark hair was streaked with blood. The man seemed unconscious; either that or he'd been doped.

Mitch realized he knew the other captive. It was . . .

"You recognize Dibbs, don't you?" Steve-O said. "He's been here since yesterday—got tied-up in a business discussion." He gestured to Big Dick. "Wake the shithead up."

Big Dick nodded. He crossed to Dibbs's side, lifted the man's chin and urinated up Dibbs's nose.

Mitch watched in disgust as Big Dick directed the stream of piss inside Dibbs's face, the head of his penis pressed firmly against the man's nostrils. In a few seconds, Dibbs jerked awake. Big Dick didn't immediately stop pissing. While Dibbs tried to get away from him, Big Dick held his head firmly and finished urinating up his nose.

"I've been needin' to go to the toilet for a while now, boss," he said on letting go of Dibbs's head. Dibbs meanwhile was sputtering and dribbling urine out of his mouth and nostrils.

Laughing, Steve-O shook his head. "Fuck, Dick, you should've warned me, so I could catch it on camera."

Big Dick shrugged and pointed at Mitch. "Maybe, next time, we can do it with him, before . . . I'll just drink a few beers to fill up again."

Steve-O nodded. Jacqui laughed, but shook her head. "No, guys, he's *my* husband. If anyone gets to piss on him, it'll be me."

Mitch couldn't avoid the irony of this: *Night before last, a one-night-stand fed me her shit; now my cheating wife wants me to drink her piss.*

"Alright, alright, we'll decide on that later," Steve-O said. "For the moment, it's time to get our show on the road." He stepped back from his naked companions and gestured at Dibbs and Mitch, who were both staring at him in dread. "Welcome, gentlemen, to the official launch of USA Film Productions!" Then he lowered his voice and leered. " 'USA,' of course, stands for 'Uncensored Snuff Artists.' "

"Yeah, yeah!" Jacqui and Big Dick howled. "USA! USA!" Then, Steve-O included, they all began clapping.

Mitch half-expected them to get out glasses and begin popping champagne, they seemed that delighted. On hearing the word 'snuff,' he'd begun sweating bullets. *Snuff? They plan on killing Dibbs and I and filming it!*

He flexed his muscles against his restraints, but there was no chance of him freeing himself. So he stared helplessly across at Dibbs. Dibbs looked equally horrified, as if he too was learning of their intended fate for the first time.

Steve-O pranced over to Mitch. "Look alive, boy," he said, like he'd be doing them a favor by killing them. "You two are gonna be movie stars!" then he turned to face Dibbs. "This sonofabitch here owes me big money and refuses to pay up, so I figured I'd turn him into money. Ha ha, Dibbs, I'd like to see your Croat mafia godfather save you now."

"Fat chance of that happenin'," Big Dick said.

"Fat as Dick's dick," Jacqui agreed, grabbing the giant's penis again and squeezing it. Mitch wondered if she was high on drugs. It wasn't like her to act this uninhibited, particularly with no clothes on.

"You know, guys," Steve-O went on, strutting into the middle of the basement and turning around, his paunch sticking out mightily, "this truly is a great day for us! I'm gonna make me lots of money from snuff movies."

"And I'll finally be able to afford that new convertible I've been itchin' to buy," Big Dick said.

"And I'll finally be rid of that jerk," Jacqui said, pointing at Mitch.

Mitch stared at Dibbs, who stared back at him in equal horrified disbelief. It really looked like both of them were about dying down here tonight.

I always knew coming here tonight was a bad idea! I should've just divorced the bitch and let Steve-O have her! Shit!

"Alright, simmer down, everyone," Steve-O said, raising his hand for quiet. "Now let's get started on recording USA's first snuff feature production. The title of this little flick is *The Fucking Dead*."

"Hey, I thought it was *Fucking the Dead*," Jacqui instantly objected. "That's what you told me yesterday."

"And *I* thought it was *The Dead Fuckers*," Big Dick said, scratching his shaven head. "Or was that *Deadfuck*?"

The little gang boss shrugged. "Guys, this ain't high art we're making here. It's a snuff film—murder and tits and ass, in no particular order. No one gives a shit what it's called, so long as the title has both 'Dead' and 'Fuck' in it."

Big Dick and Jacqui nodded.

"Alright, so let's roll! Lights, cameras, action! Look busy, everyone!"

Oh fuck! Mitch thought when Big Dick got out a chainsaw. Now he really began struggling against his bonds.

CHAPTER 15

Carl

Nasty minds think alike. It was pure coincidence that Mike Rossi a.k.a. Mike Beefcake lived directly opposite Steve-O. It was also pure coincidence that tonight both men had dates with men who intended to murder them. It was also coincidence that both of those men were dressed almost exactly alike in black clothes, so that they looked like shadows (or each other's reflections) as they stalked though the trees to get to their destination.

They also arrived at their destinations at the same time.

One difference between both men, however, was that while Mitch had come as he was, Carl Whitfield, being both the more intelligent of the two men, and also the better prepared, had brought along a spare set of clothes to change into after the dastardly deed was done.

Getting into Mike Rossi's house presented Carl with no difficulty. On one of Jeffrey's previous trips to Raynham, he'd forgotten his keys to Mike's house in Carl's apartment. By the time Carl had found the keys, Mike had already given Jeffrey a replacement set; and Jeffrey had thereafter forgotten to collect the original set from Carl.

So now, Carl quietly let himself into the house. (Using the house keys automatically disabled the alarm system in the kitchen.) He entered through the back door and padded silently into the living room. There he dropped his bag of murder tools on the living room rug and sat for a moment reviewing his plans.

Simple enough. Now that Angela's out of the way for the night, I've only got Jeff and Mike to deal with. I'll take Mike out first, he's big and . . . no . . . no . . . Jeff dies first. A single blow to his throat . . . or stab him and then deal with Mike, then take care of Jeff for good . . . only thing is, if I leave Jeff alive, he might call the cops and . . .

The cottage was silent and all the lights were off. Not enough light seeped in through the drapes to see by and Carl didn't wish to part them anyway, so he worked by the light of his cellphone screen.

First, he got his two knives out of his bag and lay them on the rug. Both knives gleamed wickedly—each had a ten-inch blade that he'd spent a good part of the afternoon honing to razor sharpness.

Next, Carl got out the pair of axes. Both had short handles and were easy to wield; Both also had horrendously sharp blades. He'd purchased the axes in two separate hardware shops in the nearby city of Attleboro.

He checked his wristwatch. The time was five minutes past two. Time to get to work, as he expected he'd need at least an hour to chop up the two bodies afterwards.

After slipping on a pair of latex gloves, Carl picked up the pair of razor-sharp knives and headed down the side corridor. He paused for a moment outside Mike and Jeffrey's bedroom, the first door on the right. He felt no twinge of conscience, had no moment of doubt. His thoughts were cold and calculating. All Carl considered were the bright party lights at the end of the tunnel, the pot of cash at the rainbow's end. *Once they're both dead I'll be a rich man. I'll be set for life . . . and best thing of all is that no one'll ever even suspect I'm responsible. All I need to do afterwards is make a real mess of both of them.*

Before opening the bedroom door, Carl first of all placed his ear to the keyhole and listened. *If the pair of them are screwing . . . that might present a complication.*

But he heard no sounds of passion. So, finally he clicked the bedroom door open. He stepped inside the room, then, leaving the door open, stood awhile and let his eyes adjust to the faint illumination in the room.

He studied the figures in the bed. Mike was on the left, was lying on his back. Jeffrey was lying on the right, was turned on his right side with his left arm thrown over Mike's chest. Both men were naked, with the bedcovers down below their waists.

Watching them both sleeping, Carl almost felt like flipping a coin to chose who to kill first. An unfamiliar thrill filled him.

Okay, Jeff goes first. Oh, this is gonna be so damn easy, easier than taking the nipple from a baby's mouth.

He moved quickly to the right side of the bed. *Sorry, little bro, but I can't have you selfishly ruining my financial future.*

Carl did pause for a moment then. *Is this really necessary?* he asked himself. *No harm's yet done—I can still leave.* Then his lips twisted up in a greedy sneer. *No, screw that! I'm not going anywhere with all that money at stake. The money's mine!*

Picking his spot carefully, Carl stabbed the knife down, deep into his brother's neck.

After a second of anticlimax, when it seemed as if nothing had changed, Carl felt a spurt of warm wetness over his hand. At that same moment Jeffrey began thrashing and flailing. He sat up in bed, and Carl saw that just as he'd intended, the blade had gone all the way through Jeffrey's neck. Jeffrey was jerking like a spastic and blood was squirting left and right out of his throat.

Goodbye to Jeffrey then; time to deal with Mr. Beefcake.

Only problem was, Jeffrey's thrashing had woken his intended husband up.

Mike was drowsily asking, "What's wrong, darling?" when Carl leapt over the bed at him.

But Mike had exceptional reflexes. Seeing—or rather sensing—someone attacking him, he instantly flung up his left hand. The knife aimed for his throat gashed his forearm instead.

"Fuck!" Mike yelled and rolled sideways off the bed. Then, ignoring the blood streaming down his arm, he leapt at Carl in turn.

Meanwhile, Carl had fallen over onto Jeffrey, who—the knife handle still protruding from his neck—was now back down on his back and gasping out his last pathetic breaths. Carl, retaining sufficient presence of mind as the giant Mike came at him, reached over and tore the knife out of his brother's neck. The knife came free just as Mike landed on him.

"Who the hell are you, asshole?" Mike growled, grabbing Carl by the throat and squeezing. "What the hell are you doing in my house? What have you done to Jeffrey? Jeff, Jeff, answer me, baby, are you okay?"

Carl could feel the blood flowing down Mike's arm. He felt a moment's amusement that Mike couldn't see who was going to kill him, then thrust both knives deep into Mike's belly.

Mike howled in pain and let go of Carl's neck, which was a relief as Carl's oxygen supply was being shut off. He leapt away from Carl, which in turn jerked the knives out of his belly, then fell backwards off the other side of the bed.

A moment later he was up again and trying to open the top drawer in the left nightstand. "Shit, I'm gonna kill you now, asshole. I'm gonna blow your damn nuts off!"

Carl, deducing that Mike was going after a gun, didn't waste any time. Flinging away one of his knives, he ran across the bed, leapt off it onto Mike's back and stabbed the other knife deep into the big man's neck. Then he began sawing away at Mike's throat, feeling blood cover his hands as Mike's corded neck muscles separated like butter before a hot knife under the assault of the razored metal. Mike let go of the dresser and went down first on one knee, then the other. Carl didn't let go though, he kept sawing away at Mike Rossi's neck until both of them were down on the floor and Mike's head was almost completely separated from his shoulders. Only then did he stop slicing.

He lay there on top of Mike, breathing hard and with his entire body wet with blood, for about five minutes. Then, deciding he'd rested enough, he got up, pulled the window drapes tightly shut and turned on the bedroom lights.

***

Before he began the second stage of his gory task, Carl Whitfield had a snort of cocaine. The drug cleared his head and filled him with a manic intent to work.

Then, after cleaning Mike's blood off himself with a towel, he went to the living room to get the axes. He'd also brought along a hammer to shatter the bones with.

Carl stood studying the corpses for a while. He found it impossible not to gloat.

I've done it—ha ha! The inheritance is all mine now! No more sharing with Jeff and—he shot a glance at Mike—*big boyfriend over there! Ha ha!*

But now it was time to get down to work. Carl decided to start with Mike. Mike was larger and was thus certain to require more time and energy to cut up. Jeffrey was certain to be easier.

He dragged/lifted/rolled Mike's body up onto the bed again. *Dammit, this guy weighs a ton! It's like moving an elephant!*

He got it done though, and laid Mike out on his back. Mike's eyes were open and staring; Jeffrey's eyes were shut. Mike looked stuck in surprise; Jeffrey seemed to have had sufficient time to come to terms with his miserable and violent death—his expression was peaceful. Both men were equally covered in blood.

Carl raised one of the axes and brought it down in Mike's muscular chest. He felt a satisfying 'Thunk!' of contact and the impact jarred his arm. The corpse shifted slightly and blood dribbled from the wound.

This might take a while, Carl thought.

After that he lost himself in the task of rendering Mike Rossi to unrecognizable chunks. It was both sweaty and messy work. Blood leaked from the corpse and splattered him and he soon looked as if he'd been the one killed. But he persevered and after a hour was rewarded with the sight of an unidentifiable heap of meat and a skeleton.

By now though, he was already getting winded and realized he'd need the rest of his energy to convert Jeffrey into a similar meat pile. His arms and shoulders ached and if he'd not been covered with blood he'd have been bathed in sweat. So instead of attempting to pulverize Mike's bones with his hammer, Carl decided on a compromise. He used the hammer to shatter Mike's skull to pieces—wincing at the gunshot-like noise each strike produced—and then also shattered both of the skeleton's arms. He stuck Mike's forearm bones into the pile of meat, so that both hands stuck out like they were waving hello, then stepped back to examine the result.

"Yeah, looks like something a psycho would do," he said aloud. "Dammit, I need a frigging drink!"

To visit the living room now, Carl needed to first undress himself, otherwise he'd leave bloody footprints. He also had to remove his latex gloves. Once this was done, he walked outside in his underpants and poured himself a stiff brandy from Mike's drinks cabinet.

He sat in the chair by which he'd dropped his bag and sipped his drink and sighed. The living room was full of the odor of blood. Carl felt no twinges of conscience. He felt nothing except a deep sense of wellbeing at having almost completed his task.

His cellphone beeped then. He picked it up. Angela Rossi had just sent him a WhatsApp message. After noting that the time was now 3:16, he opened the message.

Just wanted to say thanks for the lovely evening, she'd written. *I'm up to my neck in files here. Speak to you soon. Angel.*

Carl laughed quietly to himself. If only she knew! But then he got to thinking: Mike's sister would make a perfect alibi to his murder. So Carl dialed her number.

She picked up almost immediately. "Oh gosh—I woke you up? I'm so, so sorry! Oh, I shouldn't've—"

Carl faked a loud yawn, then tried to sound very tired. "No, I got up to have a pee. The phone flashed while I was walking back to bed and I stopped to check it. How are things down at the office?"

"Crazy, just crazy. Once we get done with the Hobart case, we've another one coming up . . ."

While she spoke and he listened, he couldn't help thinking on how she might just be perfect for him. Yes, he'd always avoided smart women, but there was just something about this one . . . *Yeah, there is—her massive tits!* He laughed to himself, then said, "Hey, Angel, remember to be careful down there 'cos of the killer. At least until the bastard's been caught."

"You think he'll dare come to the DA's office? Oh, Carl, and I'm all alone in the building tonight . . ."

Now worried that she might decide to pack up work and hurry home before he was done here, Carl's voice took on a soothing tone. "No, no, I don't really think there's anything to worry about. At least nothing superstitious or silly like that."

"Are you sure there's no supernatural monster stalking us all?"

"I'm positive there isn't. I'm just concerned about you, that's all. I mean, we had such a wonderful evening together and I'm so looking forward to seeing you again and . . ."

As he rambled on, he had the firm assurance that he was telling her exactly what she wanted to hear. But it was time for him to get back to work. So he yawned and said, "Alright, Angel, I'd better get back to bed, and you'd better get back to work, except you wanna have to work overnight again tomorrow."

"Yes, Carl, I guess you're right," she said, her voice so gently erotic that it made his penis stiffen. "Sorry, I woke you, and thanks again for a wonderful dinner."

"Thanks, Angel. The pleasure was all mine."

She hung up and Carl stared at the phone in amusement. "Poor love-struck cow."

Carl had another snort of cocaine to pep himself up. Then he got up and reentered the bedroom to start butchering her brother's lover. He didn't bother to get dressed again.

***

An hour later he was through. The time was 4:09 a.m. Carl sat in the bedroom's single armchair, which stood beside an antique chest of drawers, and surveyed the damage he'd inflicted.

His attention was distracted for a moment by a pair of sunshades sitting on top of the chest of drawers. The sunglasses looked quite expensive and he also liked their design. He decided he'd take them along when he was leaving. The dead couple definitely wouldn't be wearing them anymore.

Finally he returned his attention to the mess on the bed.

"Yeah, now no one'll ever suspect *I* killed them," he said aloud, as if to convince himself of this fact.

The two piles of meat he'd created lay side by side on the bed. Maybe due to a latent case of sibling rivalry, Carl had gotten 'creative' with Jeffrey's remains. While staring at his brother's stripped skeleton, he had felt a rush of energy which he'd not felt when faced with Mike's bones. He'd put the energy to good use, breaking as many of Jeffrey's bones as he could, then dotting them into the meat pile until the result looked like a gory pincushion, with ribs and hands and feet sticking out of it. As if the meat-piles were hills, lakes of clotted blood lay between them.

Not bad, he thought. *And now I'd better go.*

This time, Carl took a hot shower before leaving the gore-splattered bedroom. After washing the blood off of himself, he toweled himself dry and then went to the living room to fetch the plastic bags he'd brought along. He put his bloody clothes and shoes and gloves in one of them, then rolled up his axes, knives, and the hammer in another. He didn't clean the tools off; doing so might leave evidence.

After this, Carl put both packages into another plastic bag—actually two bags doubled up to prevent any blood leakage—then carried this bag outside the house and left it in the grass near the back door.

Then he returned into the house and got dressed in the spare clothes he'd brought along. He also slipped on a fresh set of gloves. Afterwards he got a napkin from the kitchen and wiped down everything in the house he imagined he'd touched after taking his gloves off, including the bottle of brandy he'd drunk from and the glass he'd drunk the brandy with. Then he was ready to leave. It was 4.42 now, more than sufficient time for him to drive back home and get some sleep before all hell broke loose when the bodies were discovered in the morning.

He picked up his bag of tools and got ready to leave.

As he had throughout all the while he'd been committing the murders and chopping up the corpses, Carl felt totally calm at this point of departure. Never having killed anyone before, he wondered if this was how murder felt for everyone—just something you did to remove human obstacles in your path.

Then Carl remembered the pair of sunglasses he'd noticed on the bureau in the bedroom. He walked back there to get them.

After a final look over the bloody room to ensure he'd not forgotten anything incriminating, he stepped towards the chest of drawers.

Suddenly he changed his mind. He now remembered seeing Mike wearing these same sunshades when he and Jeffrey had dropped by two weeks ago. Mike had said then that Angela had gotten them for him as a birthday present.

Carl heaved a quiet sigh. *I almost convicted myself right there. If I'd taken those glasses and Angela noticed them on me, I'd be in jail for life before they got through reading me my rights.*

Relieved that he'd not been so foolish as to steal the dead man's glasses, Carl Whitfield left the cottage and its corpses and stole away into the night.

CHAPTER 16

Mitch & Dibbs & Jacqui & Steve-O & Big Dick

"What the hell is wrong with you!?" Steve-O yelled at Big Dick Abbott from behind the camera, his brain powered by cocaine. "Man, when I say, 'fuck the bitch,' I mean, fuck the bitch! Give it to Jacqui hard as a pneumatic drill!"

Jacqui scowled at Steve-O, then patiently explained: "The problem—which Dick and I have both discussed and agreed on—is that if he fucks me as hard as you're telling him to, I'm gonna lose my grip on the chainsaw. Not to mention that I'm gonna break both my ankles on these stilts you've got me wearing."

Jacqui was precariously balanced while stating this, with one elbow on the arm of the couch and both hands gripping the chainsaw. It was a small red chainsaw, one that a woman could easily manipulate. To enable her vagina reach the height of Big Dick's penis, she was wearing ten-inch high heels. Big Dick was behind her with his erection slotted deep inside her body.

To prevent recognition, Big Dick and Jacqui were both wearing wolf masks.

Dibbs, the target of the 'erotic wolves' (as Steve-O kept referring to them both), had on a pair of bunny ears and a bunny nose. He was still tied in his chair, but now his gag had been removed, so the camera could record his dying screams.

"Please!" Dibbs pleaded. "You can't do this to me!"

"Shut up, asshole," Big Dick growled at him. "If you dare make my wood go soft, I'll make you suck it hard again."

"So what's it gonna be, honey?" Jacqui asked Steve-O. "He fucks me too hard and I'm gonna topple over."

Steve-O quickly walked out between the cameras. He did some checking, said, "Yeah, we'll film it like you say," and hurried back into position. "Alright, action, erotic wolves!"

Jacqui started up the chainsaw again. She laughed as it hummed to noisy sputtering life.

"Nooooo!" Dibbs screamed pitifully. "Somebody help me, please!"

"Wooooo! Wooooo!" Big Dick howled in the best lupine imitation he could manage. Across from them, Mitch, who still had his mouth taped shut, sat and watched in horror.

"Now, get him, erotic wolves!" Steve-O yelled with glee. "Get that bunny-fucker!"

Jacqui eased forward slowly while Big Dick pumped her from behind. Walking on those ten-inchers while carrying the bright red chainsaw wasn't easy, particularly when each thrust of Big Dick's manhood into her body left her feeling increasingly sexually excited. But she was earning thirty grand for this, so she gave it her best.

Steve-O meanwhile, now switched cameras. Leaving the one on the tripod still recording, he grabbed another and hurried forward to get hand-held close-ups of the action.

"Alright, baby—start with his legs, but slowly," Steve-O directed. "We don't want him to die too quickly. And, Dick, remember: you don't stop fucking her no matter what."

"Yeah, yeah, boss, I gotcha. I'm in this pussy all the way to the finish line."

"NOOOOOO!" Dibbs screamed as Jacqui stuck the chainsaw into his right thigh. The insertion produced a backward eruption of blood and dislodged meat. The mess covered her belly and shoulders.

The noise of the chainsaw filled Jacqui's brain. Dibbs's blood and flesh kept splattering her. She ripped the chainsaw up through Dibbs's crotch, turning his penis and balls to shredded meat. She pushed the chainsaw into the hole she'd made between his legs. Dibbs's screams filled her brain now—his noises of agony being impossibly louder than the chainsaw. Big Dick fucked her harder and harder. More blood spewed back on her, splattering her face and breasts. Her nipples felt as hot as if they were melting.

"Yeah, fantastic!" Steve-O yelled, beside himself with delight at what he was filming. "Go, go, go, Jacqui!"

Jacqui began coming, the climax bursting up from her vagina to her brain in overlapping waves. Despite the firm hold Big Dick had on her hips as he pounded her relentlessly, she began toppling sideways, her trembling legs too weak to keep her balanced on the high heels. To steady herself, she pulled the chainsaw out of Dibbs belly and instantly stuck it into him again, this time aiming for his face. Dibbs's nose and mouth exploded and his teeth shattered and sprayed everywhere, but his skull presented resistance. Jacqui felt another orgasm racing in on the heels of the first one. She burst out laughing as the fresh waves of ecstasy hit her. To her surprise, her arms and legs found strength from somewhere and thus strengthened, she forced the chainsaw deep inside Dibbs's head. She came violently as the whirling, spitting blade punched through the back of Dibbs's head.

"Fuck!" she howled. "This is great!"

All this while Big Dick was still pounding her sex. She left the chainsaw spinning in Dibbs's mutilated remains and braced herself with her hands on her knees, waiting for Big Dick to come.

"Alright, time for the money shot!" Steve-O yelled with glee. "Big Dick, do it!"

Big Dick pulled out of Jacqui and stepped up to Dibbs. Jacqui pulled the chainsaw out of Dibbs's body. Big Dick started masturbating. Finally he ejaculated into the mess of brains and bone that remained of Dibbs's head. Then he stepped away and let Jacqui through again. As they'd rehearsed it earlier, she now began randomly slicing up Dibbs's corpse.

"Alright . . . cut!" Steve-O yelled finally. "Yeah, that's a fucking wrap!"

Jacqui turned off the chainsaw. She and Big Dick both removed their masks.

"How was it?" Jacqui asked, sitting on the couch to rest her trembling legs, and slipping off her ten-inch heels. "Did I do alright?"

***

"Oh, baby, you were fantastic! Fucking fantastic!" Steve-O enthused loudly. Cocaine always got him hyperactive like this.

At the moment, Steve-O, middle-aged, pot-bellied owner of Taunton's Clip nightclub, was floating on clouds of imagined future revenue.

He'd been surprised as hell when a friend had informed him of the 'R.O.C. Dark Elite,' a secret group of worldwide private collectors who paid top dollar—often as much as two hundred thousand dollars per movie—for snuff flicks. And then . . . right on cue, this two-bit punk Dibbs had made a nuisance of himself.

With Steve-O's new connections, Dibbs was money in the bank, income just begging to be made.

Jacqui had needed so little convincing to take part in tonight's video shoot that Steve-O suspected she was actually a closet psychopath. Damn, the pro way she'd handled that chainsaw, chopping Dibbs up like he was so much lumber. It looked fantastic on camera.

Big Dick, of course, was doing this purely for the money; that was Dick's style. Steve-O had no problems with that.

"Alright, time for a coke break, everyone." Steve-O put down the handheld camera and waited for Big Dick to bring the mirror. Once the cocaine arrived, they each did a few lines, then Big Dick pointed to Mitch and asked, "So, how we gonna do him?"

***

Mitch began fidgeting in his chair. His head was rife with crazy ideas of what they'd do to him too.

Steve-O was rushing everywhere in jerky motions like a spastic ape. The little man looked demented. Big Dick and Jacqui weren't even bothering to wipe the gore off their bodies. Jacqui was red all over; Big Dick less so, but with the cocaine they were snorting, both of them looked as manic as their boss.

Steve-O finally calmed down a bit. Standing between Jacqui and Big Dick, he nodded at Mitch. "Yeah, we gotta come up with something creative here. I wasn't expecting him, only had a script for Dibbs's death written. But hold on and lemme think a bit . . ."

Steve-O scrunched up his face till he looked like a confused raccoon, paced back and forth for a few seconds and then returned to his previous place. His eyes gleamed as he announced: "I got it! *Balls of Meat!* Or maybe . . . *Balls and Chunks of Meat* . . . I'll decide later."

"*Balls of Meat?* What's that about?" Big Dick asked.

"Yeah?" Jacqui shook her head. "Sounds ordinary to me, honey."

Steve-O retreated across the basement to behind his mounted video cameras, then gestured at the other two to join him. "Group huddle, folks—we don't want Mitch to know what we've planned for him. His fear and surprise on camera have to be genuine. The audience must feel his shock and horror in their crotches—the true essence of cinéma vérité. Ha ha!"

Mitch stared at the pair as they joined Steve-O and began whispering. Knowing they were planning something nasty, he began struggling against his bonds again. The sight of Dibbs's mutilated remains provided him with great motivation to break free. However, his struggle was as futile as before; his plight remained the same; his arms and legs remained tightly taped to the chair. His eyes strayed over to where his toolbox lay. What was worst was that Mitch no longer felt even the slightest hint of intoxication; now he desperately wished for a drink to dull his terror a little. But what he really needed at the moment was to be well away from this crazy basement and these crazy people.

Steve-O got back behind the camera.

"Alright, everyone, ACTION!"

Jacqui and Big Dick put on masks again. This time though, Jacqui wore a half-face cat mask that left her lips free. Mitch was soon to discover why this was. She also didn't bother with putting her high heels back on, instead leaving her feet bare and flexing her big toes so her hot-pink pedicure flashed in the basement lights. Having been in her shoes, her feet were about the only part of her body not coated with blood.

Then Big Dick picked up a pair of pruners and Mitch's eyes bugged out in fright.

The masked pair approached Mitch. Once they were right in front of him, Jacqui got down on her knees and grabbed her companion's penis and began jerking on it with both hands.

"Hey, Dick . . . a little more to the right . . . yeah, that's fine. Let me get this focused before you start on him. Okay, Jacqui, now get working on that dick with your lips, get it swelling, honey. Dick, rip the tape off his mouth now!"

"Yeow!" Mitch howled as the tape came off his lips. He breathed in deeply, then yelled, "STOP!"

He'd screamed so loud that his intended killers paused and stared at him.

"Hey, man, listen!" Mitch gasped. "I'm sorry I came down here tonight. I didn't intend to kill you . . . I was just gonna scare you into leaving Jacqui alone." He made doe's eyes at his wife. "I love this woman, man. I just couldn't stand the thought of anyone else having her."

Jacqui took her mouth off Big Dick's penis and burst out laughing.

"Man, that's such a sad story that it's making me lose my wood," Big Dick said mournfully. The muscular giant looked down at his giant love muscle, which was indeed drooping.

Steve-O frowned at Mitch. "See, kid, I wouldn't have killed ya if you'd not come downstairs here. But now you know my business."

Mitch began sniveling. "I won't tell a soul! I wasn't even here tonight. Hey, Mr. Stevie, look, I'll even help you dispose of the body. I'll team up with you guys. I need a job right?"

Steve-O seemed to mull this over. "Jacqui, what do you say?"

"And you can have my wife too!" Mitch yelled. "You can fuck Jacqui day and night! I'll even buy your rubbers for you! I'll move her things over to your house so you two can have your privacy! I'll even pay for the divorce! She can have the house, the car, my bank account—everything!"

Steve-O was still staring at Jacqui.

Jacqui pushed up her cat mask to reveal her pretty face. She wiped her lips with the back of her hand, plucked a piece of meat off her left nipple, then shook her head emphatically, her face taut, her eyes bright with a narcotic glow. "Stevie honey, my husband's a lazy, unmotivated bum who drinks like a fish. He'll fuck your business up like he's fucked up his life and our marriage. First chance he gets, he's gonna get drunk at Rudy's and spill the beans about this basement to everyone who walks in there for a drink."

"Hell no, I won't do that!" Mitch screamed, then he glared furiously at Jacqui. "What the hell's wrong with you, you spiteful bitch! Why would you tell lies like that about me!?"

"I'm not lying, Mitch. You're a worthless drunk!"

"I'm gonna quit drinking! I will! I will! I'll join Alcoholics Anonymous!"

Jackie spat on the floor. "Even then you still won't be worth dogshit!"

"He ain't completely worthless," Big Dick said with a cold smile. "Dead, he's worth a lot of money to us. Alive"—he threw a meaningful look at Steve-O—"boss, you'll be paying him a salary."

Steve-O grinned. "Sorry, Mitch, but money talks. I like making it more than I like spending it. You're worth at least your weight in dollars. You're a loser and no one's gonna miss you, not even your wife."

Jacqui smirked. "Hell no, I won't miss the sonofabitch. All he does nowadays is get drunk on my money and make a fool of himself." Leaping to her feet, she jabbed a manicured fingernail into Mitch's left arm. "Guys, I told you how he got this bandage, didn't I? Using his blood for some dumb demon-summoning ritual?"

"Hey," Big Dick said worriedly, flipping his wolf mask up so it sat on his head like a baseball cap. "I heard on the news yesterday, how some woman was chopped to pieces in hospital. Is *he* responsible for that?"

"What woman?" Mitch and Jacqui both asked at once.

"Some woman named Nicole or something. I can't remember her surname."

Jacqui gaped at Mitch. "Nicole's dead too?"

"How can she be dead?" Mitch asked. "How the hell can Nicole be dead?"

"Dunno know if it's the same lady you two know," Big Dick said, "but she was locked in her hospital room and the nurses and interns all heard the sound of chopping and they couldn't get the door open to save her, and when they did get the door open she was just a pile of meat left." He looked worriedly at Mitch. "So, Jacqui, you're saying your husband here is responsible for doing that?"

"NO!" Mitch yelped. "Don't blame me for that too! I don't know anything about that. I just wanna get home alive—!"

"Shut the fuck up, all of you!" Steve-O shouted. "You're trying to ruin my fucking movie!" The little man with the big paunch picked up the coke mirror and held it out to his assistants along with a straw. "Listen, powder your noses again, both of you, and then we resume shooting."

Jacqui turned away from Mitch with a snort of disgust. "So, you've decided, Stevie?"

"Yeah, we'll do him too. It means an additional thirty grand for each of you."

Jacqui took the straw from Steve-O and connected its end to one of the white lines on the mirror. She sniffed that one up, did another line up the other nostril, then straightened up, wiping her nose. "Sixty grand really ain't bad for a night's work. That's twice my last-year's salary."

"And there's a whole lot more where that came from, for both of you," Steve-O explained. "Just—I don't wanna hear any more hogwash about the bogeyman! Kapish?"

Big Dick took the coke straw from Jacqui. "Sure, we dig you, boss." He sniffed up three lines of cocaine, then grinned at Mitch, his eyes bright as headlamps. He clasped his hands together and flexed his fingers. "Alright, Jacqui honey, suck me hard again and let's fix your husband real good."

"No!" Mitch pleaded as Big Dick approached him again, pruners once more held in hand.

"Now, don't get upset 'bout your wife and me," the giant told Mitch, leaning forward till Mitch could smell his breath. "She's got a huge ass and I got a huge cock and we both want 'em to be good friends."

"On film, that is," Steve-O quickly corrected. "Away from the movie set, Jacqui's all mine. Ha ha ha." He pointed between the cameras. "Your wife's mine—all mine now, Mitch the li'l bitch! ha ha ha!"

"Mitch the li'l bitch? Ha ha ha! Boss, you're too funny. How the hell am I ever gonna keep a hard-on if you keep cracking me up like this?"

"Jacqui, please, help me. I'm sorry 'bout everything I ever did to hurt you, honey. Please!"

She blew him a kiss. "Sorry, li'l bitch, goodbye."

"Action!" Steve-O yelled from behind the camera.

Jacqui and Big Dick both slipped their masks back down over their faces. Big Dick took up his former position. Jacqui once more got down on her knees and began fellating him.

Mitch stared at the giant's giant penis getting larger and harder. "No . . . no . . . no . . . no!" he gasped, unable to think of anything else to say. He'd seen torture scenes like this before in movies. The pruners were clearly intended for cutting off his fingers and toes, and after that, who knew what else?

"Wait a minute," Steve-O said, then hurried out from behind the camera.

"Dammit, my cock's gonna go soft again, boss!"

"Jacqui, keep sucking him. This won't even take a minute!"

Jacqui hadn't even removed her mouth from her partner's manhood yet. Steve-O picked up Mitch's axe from where he'd dropped it on entering the basement. "Alright," he said, placing the axe on the floor near Jacqui's feet. "That story about the woman getting butchered in hospital just gave me a great idea. Yeah, so when we're done with the chainsaw, Jacqui, this time you *hack* Mitch to bits, alright?"

"Hmmph, hmmph," she agreed around her mouthful of erect penis.

Steve-O hurried back behind the camera. "Alright, let's get on with it!"

"No more delays?" Big Dick asked.

"No, but just remember, man—this time the money shot ain't on his face. Remember how we planned it: you wait until he's almost dead, then you chainsaw open his belly. Then you jerk off and come on his spilling guts while Jacqui's licking your asshole . . . then you both step back so I can catch the creampie on the handheld . . . and *after* that she hacks his remains to bits. You got that?"

Big Dick nodded. "Yeah, it's a little tricky to remember, but I got it."

"NO!" Mitch howled in horror. "You can't do this to me! You can't!"

Jacqui took her mouth off Big Dick's erection for a few seconds. "Shut up and die like a man, you worm!"

She resumed her fellatio. Big Dick meanwhile, groaning in pleasure, now leaned forward with the pruners. He didn't go for Mitch's fingers though. Instead he reached down between Mitch's legs—

"No no no no no . . ."

—Flicked Mitch's fear-shriveled penis up—

". . . No no no . . . please, dear God, no . . ."

—then grabbed Mitch's scrotum—

"NOOOOOOOOOOOOOOOO!" Mitch shrieked as Big Dick neatly snipped off his testicles.

"Great! Fantastic!" Steve-O yelled from behind the camera. "Wave them around, then shove them in Mitch's mouth. Try to make him eat them!"

Mitch was twitching in his chair like he was being electrocuted. He was in so much agony that he couldn't even stare down at his mutilated crotch, but instead looked straight ahead. He didn't even react when Big Dick grabbed his jaw and shoved the testicles into his gaping mouth.

"Have some nuts, dude," Big Dick said. "Sorry, but we're all out of beer at the moment."

Mitch's mouth went slack around the horrible thing inside it. His mind seemed to have emptied itself at the moment of his castration. He couldn't even feel the blood streaming from the wound.

"Great, great!" Steve-O yelped. "Now rub the blood on Jacqui's boobs!"

This was quickly done, with Jacqui not stopping her relentless fellatio. Her head moved like a piston over Big Dick's manhood; back and forth, back and forth.

And then, suddenly, the atmosphere in the basement began to subtly alter. No one at first noticed the chill that was settling over the place.

"Alright, Dick, get the chainsaw!"

Jacqui let go of the big man's penis and as previously scripted by Steve-O, began giving her castrated husband a lap dance. She sat on him face-to-face, and as she ground her buttocks on him, she also stirred the bloody testicles in his open mouth with a finger.

"Good," Steve-O cooed at her, moving in close with the handheld camera. "You're a real star, baby."

"I never knew I had it in me," Jacqui said, working her hips as Mitch's blood smeared her buttocks. "Though maybe it's just 'cos I hate him so damn much." Blood was all over the seat of the chair and was spilling down to the floor. Mitch was still alive, but something seemed to have died in him, the way he sat there twitching with his head cocked back and his balls on his tongue.

"Shit, I think I'm gonna come again," Jacqui said.

"Go for it, baby! Frigging go for it!"

She grabbed Mitch's shoulders. "Oh shit shit shit! Meat balls! Meat balls! I gotta have my meat balls!"

Then she dug the two testicles out of Mitch's mouth with her fingers and while undulating in orgasmic ecstasy, proceeded to crush both balls to pulp in her little fists, letting their pinkish mush seep out between her clenched fingers. Then she turned her cat-masked face towards the camera and groaned, "Well, I sure hope he's got some kids stored in the sperm bank." Then she began laughing maniacally.

"Alright, perfect, Jacqui honey. Now get off him—he's bleeding more than I expected. We don't want him dead before the chainsaw . . . hey, what in the mother-frigging hell is that?"

"What?" Jacqui looked up and saw what both Steve-O and Big Dick were staring at. Something black and smoky was forming in the air near the closer of the two tripod-mounted cameras. It was a man, a man made of smoke. They three could make out hollow facial features amidst the haze of his head, with eyes like shallow infant graves and thin unsmiling cadaverous lips. Down by the creature's right hip, gripped in fingers that were wormlike tendrils of black gas, swung the hugest meat cleaver any of them had ever seen.

"What in the mother-frigging hell is that?" Steve-O repeated, swinging up his camera to cover the smoky apparition.

"It's the thing I told you we conjured up at the party," Jacqui moaned in terror. "The Cleaverman. Oh shit, it's come for me!"

The Cleaverman's ethereal face took on a questioning expression. "The riddle is the rhyme; the rhyme is the riddle," he said.

"What the fuck is it saying?" Steve-O asked.

"I don't know what that means!" Jacqui yelped. "I don't fucking know!" She grabbed and shook his arm. "Put that goddamn camera down, baby. We're all about to die here!"

"Calm down," Steve-O whispered. "It isn't blocking the way out. We can get past it and up the steps."

But Big Dick, chainsaw in hand and cocaine in brain, was striding boldly up to the smoky figure.

"Dick!" Jacqui yelped. "Don't do that, Dick!"

Big Dick Abbott either didn't hear her or didn't care for her warning. He yanked the chainsaw's starter cord and the power tool sputtered back to life.

"The riddle is the rhyme; the rhyme is the riddle," the Cleaverman repeated.

"Huh? What the hell you talking about, gas-head?"

Big Dick lunged at the smoke-figure, sweeping the chainsaw right to left through its body. The black smoke parted, then reformed itself behind the whirling blade.

"Huh?" Big Dick said, then stared at the ethereal creature he'd tried to kill.

"Dick, get away from that thing!"

But it was too late. As Big Dick Abbott backed off, the Cleaverman raised his giant cleaver and brought it down again. Big Dick raised his chainsaw to block the cleaver, but it was useless. The giant cleaver sliced through the steel chainsaw as if it was paper, then went on down, down through Big Dick's wolf-masked head, down through his torso and crotch.

The cleaver popped out between Big Dick's legs. Big Dick fell apart in two equal halves, though his right half got more of his penis.

The Cleaverman stepped between the corpse's halves and stared at Jacqui and Steve-O.

"The riddle is the rhyme—"

Jacqui ran for the door.

Without seeming to turn at all, the Cleaverman flung his cleaver at her. The giant blade flashed through the air and thunked into the farther wooden jamb of the basement door. Jacqui, who'd been about exiting through that door, shrieked in pain and froze. For a split second, the Cleaverman's blade could be seen lying horizontally inside her body, bisecting it into two, and then Jacqui's shapely hips and legs collapsed to the floor. Her upper body—from her waist up— remained atop the cleaver, with blood pouring from her truncated torso like red wine from a punctured or shattered cask.

Jacqui looked down at herself and screamed, blood spurting out over her tongue and lips. With her cat-mask on, she looked like a lioness chewing raw meat.

The Cleaverman gestured with his fingers. Like Thor's hammer, his cleaver jerked out from the door frame and returned to his hand. Jacqui's top half fell on top of her bottom half. Her guts slithered out of her like red snakes. She was already dead, her eyes wide open and staring.

The Cleaverman stared at Steve-O. A cold glow surrounded the Cleaverman, icy light like flickering fluorescent, purple dying neon. These dancing electric tendrils, which seemed to possess malevolent intent of their own, were constrained from self-expression by the greater darkness that they acted as a chute for. Their light penetrated the Cleaverman's sparse black form like blades of ultraviolet starlight, wrapping him as though the spectral being were a package of darkness.

Steve-O almost couldn't handle the horror of viewing the Cleaverman's face. That face, like a billowing gray bag caught and blown by winds from forever; scarecrow hair like burnt straw, as ethereal and non-existent as little transparent tubes ferrying frothy black gas from the interior of the Cleaverman's head to the middle of nowhere; a nose like a misshapen and charred potato; lips that were really nothing but gateways to the chaos beyond human existence; and the mouth itself was Hell's deepest and blackest pit, a chasm so vast and bottomless that all the flames of hellfire couldn't light it. The two flaps on the sides of the phantom's head might have been ears, but might just as easily be shards of fragmented darkness, or the sails of two ships sailing on the seas of fate.

If John Cleaverman wore clothes, they were rags woven from nothing, garments assembled from the fabric of the void and stitched together with the thread of timeless wicked intentions.

"The riddle is the rhyme; the rhyme is the riddle."

Steve-O flung the video camera at the Cleaverman and ran. The camera passed harmlessly through the Cleaverman's spectral form. Steve-O, however, slipped on a smear of Mitch's blood. He stumbled, but righted himself before he went sprawling.

Steve-O didn't dare look back. He made it safely to the basement stairs and vaulted up them.

I got away, he thought as he reached the landing. *I got away!*

Then, as he raced along the corridor towards the living room, he felt a horrible pain in his legs. As he lost his balance and toppled to the floor, he saw the Cleaverman's blade, floating ahead of him like a suspended metal surfboard.

Steve-O stared down at his legs. Both had been severed at the knees and were spraying blood all over his expensive rug.

In shock, he turned to look for his lower legs. Both lay behind him, and he also saw the deadly smoke creature approaching. The Cleaverman was either walking or floating down the corridor.

The Cleaverman made a gesture with his hand. Sensing fresh danger, Steve-O looked forward again. The giant bloody cleaver, which had paused in midair, was now reversing itself, coming towards him at speed. It began spinning fast, flipping end over end.

Steve-O was in too much agony to duck. As it passed him, the cleaver sliced his right arm off at the shoulder. Screaming in agony, Steve-O collapsed onto his back and began jerking left and right, much like Mitch had done a short while before.

And then the Cleaverman was bending over Steve-O, with that huge demonic blade raised high and his smoky, ethereal face as merciless as Death itself.

Steve-O was in so much agony now, he couldn't even plead for his life. He stared at his truncated shoulder, at the blood flowing out of him, and prayed he'd die quickly.

And then the glittering blade came down and chopped off Steve-O's other arm at the elbow, and then it came down again and severed his right leg halfway up the thigh.

As his blood splashed the walls left and right of him, Steve-O began screaming blue murder.

And, staring at the Cleaverman's hazy face, with its eyes like pits of tar, Steve-O realized that his prayer wouldn't be answered—despite the ghastly severity of his wounds, he wasn't going to die quickly at all.

Some things were worse than death itself, Steve-O realized, and dying like this, being slowly hacked into little bits by a thing from his worst nightmares, was one such thing.

He kept on screaming. And his head was the last thing his killer chopped up.

CHAPTER 17

Cleaverman

After he was through chopping Steve-O into little pieces, the Cleaverman returned to the basement. He pulled the two pieces of the female corpse over on top of the halved male corpse and got to work hacking them both up. As the ghastly specter performed his grisly task, his mind received flashes of memory, vivid impressions of the time before this no-time he now existed in, that time when he had been human. The ghostly apparition saw himself behind the counter in a neat shop, with skinned dead animals hanging from hooks. People told him what they wanted and he chopped the animals up.

Thunk! The blade landed; the corpses split into more pieces.

A woman—she wasn't like this one whose head he'd just cut off; she was tall and willowy, with long black hair and pale blue eyes—a woman stepped out from the rear of the shop and kissed him tenderly on his cheek . . . but who was she?

Thunk! His immense cleaver rose and fell and the wet flesh and bone beneath it parted like the Red Sea before Moses.

Rage and sadness filled the Cleaverman's heart. The dark ghost felt that if he could just remember this beautiful woman . . . or at least recall her name . . . all would be well with him.

The riddle is the rhyme; the rhyme is the riddle.

What did that mean? The Cleaverman mentioned this, but he neither knew the rhyme nor riddle. If he'd had any idea what they were, he might have been able to remember *her* name.

Her name! What was it? Until he knew the answer, he would remain in a hell of torment, a deep anguish that, impossible as it seemed, was even greater than the agony of those he killed, those unable to help him.

117

Once, maybe twenty human years ago, the Cleaverman had known the answer. A woman had told him his woman's name. He'd been happy for a while. But then he'd forgotten her name again—oh, she!—his beauty with the flowing and glossy black hair. His memory of her had faded a little more with each passing day, until there remained not even its echo of itself, and his misery had resumed.

Thunk!

He was done with these two. They had been useless to him—had given him no help—and now they were useless to themselves too. Their deaths should serve as a lesson to others who didn't know . . .

The Cleaverman turned away from the pile of bloody meat that was his latest creation, and walked towards the man tied to the chair, his dark gaseous legs splitting around the metal of a collapsed tripod as he stepped forward.

He paused beside this man, the man whose blood had revived him.

The words were once more in his mind and on his lips: "The riddle is the rhyme; the rhyme is the riddle."

The man in the chair didn't answer. He couldn't answer. His penis was still intact but his scrotum was gone. There was a huge pool of blood under the man's penis, but it was congealing now. The man would live, though his testicles were now a useless mush that his dead wife had smeared across his hairy chest after pulping them.

The castrated man was unconscious. He'd been unconscious on the Cleaverman's arrival in the basement, and so hadn't heard the question.

The ghostly Cleaverman pondered whether to revive him, but finally decided against it. In his current condition he was unlikely to understand what was expected of him. He would return to speak to this man.

Sooner or later, he too would have his chance to live or die.

Satisfied with his bloodshed, but with his longing and quest still unsatisfied, the Cleaverman faded from view.

CHAPTER 18

Angela . . . Friday Evening . . .

. . . Coming home tired out . . . the smell of murder—blood and body fluids . . . investigating . . . screaming! . . . getting her phone out . . . dialing 9-1-1 . . . dialing Carl . . . collapsing in a chair while her eyes filled with tears . . . detectives and forensics . . . Carl arriving . . . she and Carl's joint confusion . . . sedatives . . . bed . . . the sweet relief of sinking into darkness, of knowing nothing . . .

Oh, my God, Carl! It's so horrible!

Angela Rossi jerked awake with those words ringing in her mind. For the first few seconds after awakening she felt completely dissociated from her surroundings. She stared at her bedroom walls and yet had no idea where she was. Her bosom was full of the sort of terror that she suspected drove people insane.

More memories and images assailed her:

. . . Entering Mike and Jeffrey's bedroom . . . bloody insanity . . . skeletons and meat, chopped intestines like sausage links; human flesh piled high on the bed as if the Devil was making sandwiches . . . the shock of recognition of what she was staring at . . . collapsing into the bedroom chair . . . puking and screaming . . . running out into the living room and screaming some more . . . looking around for her cellphone, screaming at the 911 operator . . . a delay, then the screech of Ford Crown Victorias out in the driveway and an endless flood of perplexed men streaming into the house . . .

Angela finally got a hold of herself. She was still trembling when she got up though. She sat on the edge of her bed trying not to panic. She succeeded in keeping her fear under control; but this was more due to the sedatives the paramedics had made her take than to any mental fortitude. Similarly, she didn't weep now. She felt empty though, all hollowed out; an emotional husk.

Someone—Carl hopefully—had undressed her after she'd dropped off to sleep. She had on just her bra and panties now.

Carl was here with me! Where is he now?

Then she spotted Carl's note propped up on the nightstand. *Had to head out of town, Angel,* he'd written. *Damn thing can't be put off, even in a family crisis ☹ I'll call you later, or come over.*

Had Carl called her yet? She didn't want to be alone now! She placed the note down and picked up her cellphone. No, he hadn't called her yet. She however had eight missed calls from Leona Patten.

Leona's last call had been at 3:46 p.m. Angela's cellphone showed the time now as 4:15. *Damn—I slept the whole day away.*

The terrifying images of her brother's and Jeffrey's deaths returned to scare her. Oh yes, she was scared. And . . . it sounded as if she was alone in the house. Had the cops all left?

Her heartbeat quickened in panic. How could they leave her alone at a time like this? With murder and insanity in the air? Evil thoughts fluttered like birds at the windows of Angela's mind; they knocked like infernal mailmen intent on delivering envelopes of doom. Angela refused to let these thoughts in. It wasn't yet time to consider them. Those were thoughts of damnation; thoughts that housed you in a padded cell.

She stood up. After first pulling on an oversized black tee shirt that hung below her hips, she crossed to the bedroom door and opened it. She stepped out into the corridor, and realized that she seemed to be alone in the house.

Angela's bedroom was on the right side of the cottage, the master bedroom and guest bedroom were both on the left side of the building. Mike and Jeffrey had sometimes entertained visitors in intimate ways; this sleeping arrangement had meant Angela got a good night's sleep notwithstanding the bumping and grinding going on elsewhere in the house.

So, to get to their bedroom, she had to cross the living room.

On stepping into the living room, Angela discovered that she wasn't alone in the house. Marie Beck, a young policewoman who was also a friend of hers, sat in a chair reading a paperback romance.

Marie smiled sadly on seeing Angela. "I was asked to keep an eye on you to make sure you were okay," she said. "Mr. Whitfield had to leave for a while, but he promised he'd be back. How do you feel now?"

"Sad and very messed up," Angela replied, making an effort not to break down in tears. "I feel like I'm going crazy. I don't understand how this could have happened."

Marie nodded sympathetically. "And at your neighbor's house too."

"What?" It slowly filtered through Angela's mind what Marie meant. She recalled hearing, during her morning freakout, someone saying similar murders had occurred in the opposite house also. That house belonged to Steve-O, who owned the Clip nightclub. "Marie, who got killed over there?" While speaking, she walked to the front windows and parted the drapes. Steve-O's luxurious house was done up in yellow 'Crime Scene' barricade tape. "Who got killed, Marie?"

She felt Marie approaching behind her. "There were four corpses. From the I.D we found in their clothes, Steve-O was one victim. Another was a local hoodlum named Joe Dibbs. The other two corpses belonged to Steve-O's bodyguard Richard Abbott, and his PA, Jacqui Mullins."

Angela felt chilled by the information. "Jacqui's dead too?"

The policewoman shuddered. "All four bodies were as fucked-up as your brother's and his boyfriend's—hacked completely to pieces. Just wall-to-wall gore. There was a survivor though, but he was unconscious."

"Who?"

"Mitch Mullins, Mrs. Mullins' husband. He was badly injured. He's in the ICU, though the doctors expect him to make a full recovery."

Angela stared across the street and thought deeply. *Okay, this isn't happening. That party we all attended at the Ellsworths' house . . . and now five of us are dead? And Mitch is in the ICU? Even though no one's going to believe me, I'd better accept the truth that we're all jinxed—everyone who attended that dinner party that night is jinxed. The only reason I'm alive now is because I wasn't home last night!*

Once again the panic surged up in her, seeking to take her over. Now she choked it down with determination. *The one thing I can't afford to do now is lose it. If I lose control of myself, I'm dead meat—and I mean that in a literal sense. That thing, whatever it is—isn't taking prisoners. Only God knows how Mitch survived. And he's not in any condition to tell.*

She turned to Marie. "Could you please make me a coffee?"

The policewoman smiled back reassuringly. "No problem. Would you like a bite to eat too?"

"No, I don't think I'll be able to prevent myself from throwing up. Just coffee, please. Thanks."

While Marie made coffee, Angela quickly stepped through the north hallway entrance that led to her brother's bedroom, immediately coming face-to-face with the yellow 'Crime Scene, Do Not Cross,' tape sealing it off. The bedroom door was shut. Leaving the tape in place, she opened the door and stared into the room.

As she'd expected, the entire mess was now gone. The bed sheets had been stripped off, and the mattress also carted off for analysis. There were wide patches of blood on the walls and on the light brown carpeting, but it had all dried.

What Angela found most bothering as she stood outside the doorway with its barrier of yellow tape, was the smell. The bedroom windows were shut and the smell of death was thick in the room: blood and urine and excrement from shredded intestines and also several chemical smells from the forensics guys.

Her eyes fell on Mike's sunglasses which sat on the antique chest of drawers he'd bought from the late Ellsworths. The sunshades looked like demon eyes surveying ruins. The sunglasses were her birthday gift to Mike; she'd wanted to give him something special and had found these online. Remembering how much Mike had loved those glasses brought tears to her eyes again.

"Here's your coffee."

Angela turned and accepted the steaming drink from Marie. "You should just about be getting off work now," she told the woman after checking the time on her phone. "Give me a minute to have a bath and get dressed and I'll drop you off at home."

"Oh, no need to do that," Marie said quickly. "You should stay home and rest. Everyone was in favor of moving you to a hospital bed, but Mr. Whitfield nicely said he'd look after you."

"It's no trouble. I'm fine now—well, about as fine as I can possibly be after seeing my brother and Jeff butchered, but I'll survive. Besides, I really need to see someone over your way, so dropping you off isn't any bother at all."

Marie nodded.

That settled, Angela hurried back through the house to clean herself up. Once she'd shut her bedroom door, she quickly dialed Leona Patten's number. Then she stepped into the shower and turned on the water, so the sound would prevent Marie from overhearing their conversation. She didn't want the cop thinking she was losing her mind after losing her brother.

Leona answered the phone. "Oh my God, Angela, this is just horrible!"

"Leona, tell me flat out: are all these deaths the Cleaverman's work, or not?"

Leona's voice was panicked. "They are, they are! I thought the deaths would stop with Nicole's and Tommy's but I was dead wrong!"

"Even though you were wrong, I don't want to be dead. What can we do?"

"How soon can you get over to my house?"

"I'm on my way over already. I just wanted to make sure you'd be home before setting out."

"Oh, I'm home alright. Paul's back home too now. We're about to have a conference on this. See you soon then."

While showering, Angela realized that her conversation with Leona had done very little to calm her nerves. *Leona sounded panicked on the phone. If my psychic friend is that panicked, what hope do the rest of us have?*

CHAPTER 19

Angela, Susan, Leona & Paul

"Yes, Aladdin, so we've let the damn killer genie out of the magic lamp. How do we shove it back in again?"

After saying this, Susan Riley crossed her legs and flipped a cigarette up into her mouth and lit it. She sat smoking in silence, her gaze asking someone to suggest something.

They were gathered in Leona's living room, which, mostly so the Pattens' kids didn't make a nuisance of themselves and destroy something valuable, had very little in the way of occult paraphernalia on display. There was just the single crystal ball above the electric fireplace and two tarot almanacs on the wall.

Leona looked spooky again, in a long white dress and ancient-Egypt makeup. She sat on the couch beside her husband Paul, who was a large man with short black hair and a beard, wearing denim pants and a dirty white shirt with rolled up sleeves.

Susan was in the armchair on the couple's left. She was dressed like she was on her way to someone's bedroom—spandex-tight red leather pants and peep-toed high heels, an almost see-through pink silk blouse that showed she wasn't wearing a bra, and enough makeup for all three women present; plus sunglasses in her yellow hair.

Angela Rossi was seated on the right of the Pattens. Her gray clothes gave the impression that she'd just come from the office. This was accidental but routine enough for Angela, who didn't really buy clothes except for work.

The Patten's two kids were playing out in the backyard.

The topic was how to return the Cleaverman back to where he came from.

"I'm not exactly saying that we're sitting ducks," Angela said, "but . . . well, except we do something, that's certainly the way it looks to me. And I don't like the feeling at all."

All three woman looked equally frightened.

"I still feel like I'm being pranked," Paul Patten said. "But the death toll says otherwise. Nicole and Tommy, Jeffrey and Mike, Jacqui, Steve-O and Big Dick . . . and Mitch in the ICU with his balls cut off. Shit!"

The TV had been on, with its endless loops of news about the deaths—gory details about each killing plus how the FBI were already on the scene, with their top profilers hard at work—but the Pattens didn't want their children accidentally seeing that. Viewing it also made the adults nervous, so they'd turned the TV off.

***

"I'm sorry to hear about your brother's death," Paul had told Angela on her arrival.

She'd shrugged it off. "Yeah, but at the moment I've no time to grieve. That comes later, if we survive this crazy thing we've set in motion. I haven't even called my mom yet to tell her—I've no idea what to say to her. She was supposed to come down for the wedding next weekend and now . . ."

The big man had frowned then. "So, it really did happen that night like Leona and Susan claim it did?"

Angela had nodded. "I saw the Cleaverman materialize with my own eyes. The nasty thing was as real as Mike's corpse." She spoke without weeping, looked about the room at them all. "I got home from work this morning and . . ." her voice was about breaking but she kept its tone hard and cold, "and I found two piles of chopped-up meat in my brother's bed. Later on, a cop told me how Jacqui and her boss were given the same treatment across the street. So yes, the Cleaverman means business. He's made us three—four, if you count Carl, who was also there—"

"We tried calling Carl," Paul had said. "His phone's switched off."

Angela had nodded. "He said he had to rush off somewhere."

***

"The Cleaverman means business and he's made us four his business," Leona said quietly now, echoing Angela's earlier comment. "We're the only four left and unless we solve his damn riddle, we're all as good as dead."

"Mitch is still alive," Paul reminded her. "That makes *five* of you."

"When Mitch wakes up in hospital without his testicles, I'm sure he'll wish he were dead too," Susan said after spilling a long plume of smoke from her nostrils. "He'll also wish he'd not been so willing to donate his blood to summon the Cleaverman. That lush is really to blame for all of this."

"We're *all* to blame for it," Angela corrected her. "I don't recall you or I or anyone else objecting while Mike was taking the blood from Mitch's arm. Leona did warn us that we were playing with fire, but we wouldn't listen."

"Yeah, yeah, so diarrhea happened and now the air conditioner's covered with it," Susan said, sucking on her cigarette again. "People, how the fuck do we dispatch it back to where it came from? That's what I wanna know."

"We need to solve his damn riddle," Leona repeated.

"What riddle?" Angela asked. "Is there a riddle associated with the Cleaverman?"

Leona got up, her flowing white dress making her seem ethereal, like she was about to fade away into nothingness. She stepped away from the couch and stood beside the coffee table, this position meaning her husband and friends were now arranged in a rough semicircle about her. "The riddle is the rhyme; the rhyme is the riddle," she explained to Angela. "That's what the Cleaverman supposedly asks his victims before chopping them up."

"But that's a statement, not a question," Angela reasonably pointed out.

"I think that's just to confuse us," Leona replied. She gestured to her husband. "Paul and I have been trying to figure it out. The conjuring rhyme in the spellbook is a riddle—"

"Tell me the name of John Cleaverman's wife, right? I sort of remember that much."

"Yeah, that's it." Leona plumped her butt down on the coffee table and began wringing her hands. "The riddle seems to be that we need to work out the name of John Cleaverman's wife from the summoning rhyme and tell it to him. That's the only way he won't chop us all up."

"That's all? I thought we'd need to sacrifice a virgin"—Angela scowled at Susan—"or a slut. Alright, so let's do it." Angela looked questioningly at Leona. "So where's the riddle? And why, if that's all we need to do, do you still look so worried?"

"We don't have the spellbook," Paul explained. "It's over at Tommy and Nicole's place."

"And," Susan quickly added before Angela could phrase her next question, "although Leona's been able to find the rhyme online, it's incomplete."

"Incomplete? How do you mean?"

"Show her, Leona."

Leona picked up her tablet from the coffee table, tapped its screen on, and handed it over to Angela, who shuddered visibly on seeing the artist's rendition of the Cleaverman. "Yeah, that's him alright," she said, "but like he's been working out in the undead gym or something."

"Bottom of the webpage," Leona instructed.

Angela scrolled down to where the writing was. " 'Tell me the name of John Cleaverman's wife . . . loved all of his life . . . one day in strife . . . you, my friends . . . give up your lives.' " She nodded at Leona, her face pale. "I see what you mean. The first line is the only complete one, the other four are filled in with dashes."

Paul Patten nodded too. "Whoever posted that damn thing online clearly didn't want anyone trying it out like you guys did." He got to his feet. "Hey, do any of you ladies want a cold beer?"

Angela shook her head. "Coffee for me, if you've got it—black, no sugars. I'm still recovering from the sedatives the paramedics gave me."

"Beer for me, man," Susan said.

Paul nodded and looked at his wife. "You want something too, honey?"

She shook her head. "At the moment I'm too worried to think straight. Alcohol and caffeine are both certain to make that worse."

Paul left them and headed for the kitchen.

"What do the cards say?" Susan asked when he was gone. "Have you consulted the tarot again about our dilemma?"

Leona made a vague gesture towards the far side of the living room, flipping her fingers at the wall the living room shared with her psychic studio. "Same as last time, girl—murder, death . . . betrayal."

"Betrayal?" Angela asked. "What does that have to do with this?"

Leona shrugged. "I don't know and the cards refuse to be any clearer. Just about everything to do with the Cleaverman is vague and shadowy. I clearly sense our dead friends' distress over their violent deaths—they're sad and very angry at being torn from this life and tossed into the rolling void. But concerning us the living, I can discern very little about our fates." She gave a dramatic wave. "The benevolent spirits are silent. The malevolent spirits appear very amused at our plight. I spread the tarot and the cards keep neutralizing themselves, as if . . ." She gazed helplessly at her two friends. "As if the Cleaverman is himself blocking off the cards from warning us, or is shuffling the pack to deceive us."

CHAPTER 20

Paul

While the coffeemaker worked, Paul Patten stared out through the kitchen windows and listened to the racket his kids were making.

The kids were up in their treehouse, doing whatever eight-and-ten-year-olds found to do up in treehouses. Neither Paul nor his friends in the neighborhood had had one as kids and so he didn't know. Paul figured the kids were most likely just listening to music or watching cartoons—he'd rigged the treehouse up with electricity for them, even though before he'd run the wires, Leona had warned that the electricity might set both tree and treehouse on fire. Paul had almost changed his mind then, but the kids had already got it in their heads that they'd be able to watch TV in their treehouse and they kept insisting. Wife said no; kids said yes. Paul was in the middle with both sides equally loud and insistent.

In the end Paul had asked Leona to consult the spirits and find out whether or not the kids' treehouse was going to burn down. The spirits replied that there was more chance of President Trump being struck by lightning than of the treehouse burning down. Though a democrat, Paul had figured those were no odds at all. So the kids got their electricity.

Now, he listened a bit, heard some juvenile laughter, and relaxed a little. At least *they* were okay.

Because Paul himself didn't feel okay at all.

Dammit, I feel like someone pulled the plug of reality while I was off trucking tractors to Walnut Creek, Ohio. Sure, Raynham's a weird town anyways, but since I got in from Ohio, it's like being in a parallel universe. Damn!

Being a trucker, Paul was used to strange happenings, but not like this. And the craziness had actually begun last night, when he'd been driving home.

That . . . Shit.

Paul cringed on remembering what had happened . . .

***

It had been 3 a.m. He'd been rolling along the Blue Star Memorial Highway, heading home. At the time, Paul didn't have any flatbed trailer connected, he was driving just the truck's cab.

Somewhere on his way out of Norton—he'd just passed the Red Mill Village condo complex, down the road from Mansfield Municipal Airport—Paul Patten had stopped to pee. Too canny a traveler to walk into the roadside woods in the dead of night, he'd exited the cab and pissed by its front tires.

Later he'd wondered why in the heck he'd not simply completed the drive—he'd been less than ten minutes away from arriving at Rudy's Truck Stop, near the Broadway overpass. Rudy's would be closed to patrons at this hour, but the place had an outdoors restroom where he could relieve himself.

But when the need to pee comes over a man, when he feels like his bladder's gonna burst if he don't whip out his manhood already and water the grass, there's just no helpin' it.

So, no, Paul really didn't think that what happened was in any way his fault. After all, he'd peed along the highway lots of times.

This time though . . .

"Hey, mister, can I get me a ride?"

Paul was about zipping up when he heard the voice behind him. Despite his shock at someone addressing him out here in this lonely place, he managed to zip up without catching his penis in his fly.

Then he turned around to see who'd addressed him.

It was a woman. She was of average height and had pale hair. She wore flip-flops, jeans cutoffs, and a short-sleeved shirt knotted at the navel.

First off, Paul checked that she wasn't carrying a gun. Even though he didn't see how such could be the case at this time of the night, this woman could have been waiting here for someone to ambush; there were lots of crazies out on the highways.

There wasn't much moonlight, but he finally decided the woman was unarmed. She was standing with her hip cocked to the left, with one hand resting on that hip while the other dangled by her right thigh.

"What . . . what the hell are you doing out here this late, woman?" Paul asked. He'd now gotten his confidence back. He towered over her by at least a foot, in addition to which her hundred and twenty pounds would be no match at all for his three hundred. Even if she did have a gun, he had a shotgun up in the cab. Trucking interstate, one didn't take chances.

"I was hitchin' home from Foxborough and the randy bastard ditched me here 'cos I wouldn't suck him off."

That made sense to Paul. Lots of guys got ornery if you gave them a boner, and then refused to chew on it a little. It bothered him a little though that he couldn't see the woman's face clearly. She wasn't hiding it from him, but the moonlight just wasn't hitting it right.

"I might be able to give you a ride. Where you headed?"

She cocked her hip the other way. "Right your way, I'm guessin'. I'm headed for Raynham. I live right on the outskirts of town."

Paul made up his mind. "Alright, you can ride with me."

She stepped up close and he smelt her. She smelt sweaty, delicately perfumed and yet in some way unpleasant. He boosted her up into the cab and she scooted across into the passenger seat. He climbed up himself, shut the cab door and then flicked on the overhead light to see her better.

She looked ordinary enough. Country girl in her late twenties. Dirty-blonde hair, dark eyes, long oval face. Very pretty in a farmer's daughter kind of way. She made him wish he wasn't married, so he could chat her up. And yes, there *was* something disagreeable about her, but he didn't know what it was. He looked down at her body, then looked away. The sight of her bare thighs was giving him an erection.

"My name's Bev," she told him as he turned the starter key. "Thanks for picking me up."

"I'm Paul," he'd responded as the cab resumed rolling down the highway.

He'd driven for three minutes, just rolled across Snake River, when she'd said, "Here's my turnoff right ahead here on the left."

Paul nodded and pulled up to the roadside. He leaned over to let her out. "Alright, miss, home you go now. Been a pleasure ridin' with ya."

She made no move to get out of the cab though.

"What ya waitin' for?" Paul had asked. "C'mon, honey, we're at your stop now. I'm in a hurry to get home to the wife and kids."

Instead of getting down though, Bev had begun undoing the buttons of her top. She wasn't wearing a bra. Her breasts were large and plump and left Paul almost speechless.

"Ah, Bev, what're you doing?"

She'd wrapped a coil of her blonde hair around a finger and smiled at him. "I'm just thinkin' that seein' as you've been so nice to me where that other guy was such a jerk, I'd like to give you what he wanted but didn't get." To make her point, she pulled her shirt fully open. "What do you say, Paul?"

Paul almost bit his tongue. "Well, see, like I was sayin', I'm married, and Leona won't like it—"

She giggled. "But Leona ain't getting' it, Paul, except she's a dyke maybe. Is Leona a dyke, baby?"

"Hmm, well, no . . . I mean, I don't think she is, but . . ." Try hard as he might, Paul couldn't clear her offer of herself from his mind. The sight of her breasts had finished the job of inflating his penis that glimpsing her bare thighs had begun. The cab interior now felt uncomfortably hot on this cool summer night.

"I'm flattered, Bev, but you really don't have to do this," he finally stammered.

She leaned across, grabbed his erection through his pants and squeezed it while flashing her teeth at him. "Oh, but I insist, Paul. So, why don't you just lock up this truck and walk me to my front door and then we'll have a ball and I promise not to tell Leona what we did." She giggled. "And the best thing of all? I ain't a hooker. There's no charge involved."

Pretty as Bev was, there was no way that Paul could refuse such an offer. Sure, he *was* worried that his psychic wife might afterwards paranormally perceive what he'd done, but even that valid concern didn't successfully dissuade him. Quickly convincing himself that what Leona didn't know couldn't hurt her, Paul Patten had locked the truck's cab and followed Bev home to the white house halfway down the unnamed lane.

It was a bit of a long walk to the house, but once they'd arrived there, Bev had been as good as her word. They'd done it twice on her living room floor—first she'd given him a blow job and ridden him to a climax, and then he'd penetrated her doggy-style, squeezing those juicy breasts and sliding his manhood in and out energetically, while she moaned and gritted her teeth and came so loudly that he was glad she didn't have any nearby neighbors.

Then, while he'd been lying panting on the floor and trying to get his breath back, she'd gotten up to use the bathroom. She'd taken the used rubbers along, and he'd heard her flush them down the toilet. Then he'd smelt her using the toilet, and then . . .

And then . . .

She'd reappeared carrying a white bowl and crouched beside him. "Something to revive you," she'd told him, with a manic smile on her face.

He'd leaned up to see what she'd set beside him on the carpet. "Holy mother of God!"

"Just some boiled eggs with the shells all removed," Bev said, while at the same time pressing a revolver between his legs. "Start eating, baby."

Boiled eggs Paul could cope with. But this wasn't just boiled eggs—the white ceramic bowl was filled with a mixture of boiled eggs and excrement, and she'd included a plastic spoon to stir it all up.

He'd glanced at her thighs. She hadn't wiped; there was shit dribbling down her left thigh. He glanced back at the bowl and noticed there was something else mixed in with the eggs and poop. It looked like patches of roadkill: raw meat and hair—a squashed paw and flattened head—and what might have been blood and sand.

He stared up at Bev again. "Are you frigging crazy, woman? Who the frigging hell is gonna eat this mess?"

Her manic smile didn't falter. "You are, Paul. I make a point of feeding my lovers after we've done the nasty, and here's the meal." She jabbed the revolver harder into Paul's crotch. "Now, honey, you either start feeding or start bleeding. You don't start scooping those eggs up and eating them right away, and I'm gonna start shooting. And trust me, honey, no one's gonna come to your rescue before I blow your balls off."

"Please . . ."

"Don't try my patience, darling." She lifted a spoonful of poop to his lips. "Open wide . . ."

"Please," Paul squeaked through firmly shut lips. "Please!"

Bev grinned and put the spoon back down. "Oh, so you think I'm playing a game with you, do you, Paulie?" He felt the gun painfully jab his scrotum. "Okay, so *let's* play a game. Here's the rules, honey. Now, I'm gonna count to three. On 'three,' you lose your left ball. Then on the next 'three' you lose the right one. . . . then . . . Alright, you got that? . . . Great, let's go then. . . . One . . . two . . ."

Paul grabbed the spoon and lifted a mouthful of eggs and feces to his mouth and ate it.

"Wow, you win, honey!" Bev yelped in unfeigned delight. "Now, we start again. One . . . two . . . Wow! You win again, Paulie—you're a world champion shit-eater! Alright, here we go for round three. Keep that poop down, honey, keep that shit down! One . . . two . . . YEAH!"

This went on until the horrible mess of eggs and excrement and hairy flesh was all gone. It didn't matter that Paul vomited half of it back out, Bev made sure that he ate everything in the bowl.

Then: "Get out," she'd ordered him at gunpoint, pushing him naked out of her front door and flinging his clothes after him. "And if you ever come around here again, I'll call the cops."

Paul arrived home an hour later. He'd been relieved to find Leona soundly asleep; on those nights when she felt sexy she'd wait up impatiently for him to get in and make love to her.

Last night though, he'd felt too ashamed to face her. He'd gazed in on Leona's peacefully slumbering form, then silently padded to the bathroom and got the bottle of Listerine. Then he'd hurried to the kitchen and spent fifteen minutes gargling to get the taste of shit out of his mouth.

***

I oughta just be glad I survived it, Paul thought now as he poured Angela's coffee. *I was real lucky last night. That Bev girl was so nutty she could've been chipmunk food. She could've blown my damn head off. I'm gonna be real careful who I pick up from now on.*

The memory of last night's humiliation brought a bitter taste to his mouth, then he shrugged it off and managed a grin. *She wasn't bad in bed though. Not bad at all—sucked good dick—gave me a fantastic blowjob—just what came after made the whole thing so distasteful. Yeah, serving a man eggs like that is real disgusting. But, on the bright side of things, Leona's so worked up about this Cleaverman business that there's no chance in hell of her paranormally picking up on what happened.*

Paul laughed, got two beers out of the fridge, and exited the kitchen.

CHAPTER 21

Angela, Susan, Leona & Paul

Paul returned to the living room. He handed Angela her coffee and Susan her beer, then sat back down on the couch facing his wife.

"The webpage doesn't list the poster . . ." Leona was saying, swiveling on the coffee table to face them in turn, "so there's no way to contact him or her and find out if they actually know the full version of the rhyme."

"So, the only thing we can do," Paul said, sipping on his Bud Light, "is break into the Ellsworths' house and find the book and try to work it out. It's obvious that we need to work out the name of the Cleaverman's wife, that's all."

Susan pointed her latest cigarette at Angela. "She's law enforcement; maybe you shouldn't say that with her here."

Angela rolled her eyes. "So's your dad, Sue. And he'll likely be the one to sentence us all for breaking and entering anyway." She nodded to Paul, "I'm with you on this. I'd rather have her dad sentence me than die looking like burger patty and have him attend my funeral. When shall we do it? When do we visit Nicole and Tommy's place?"

Paul looked thoughtful. "Are the cops through investigating the place now?"

Angela nodded. "Yeah, sure. Besides, with these new deaths, no one'll even give a thought to Nicole and Tommy's house."

"Tonight then," Paul said, lifting his beer to his lips. "Tonight at around midnight, once the kids are sound asleep. We'll park near Mitch and Jacqui's place and make our way through the trees. Shouldn't take us long to get there and back."

"That's cool," Angela said. "I'm going with you." Then she frowned. "Damn! I really wish Carl would call. I'll feel so much better knowing the Cleaverman hasn't gotten him too."

Susan raised an appraising eyebrow. "Why? Are you two dating now?"

Mug of coffee clasped in both hands, Angela shook her head. "I wouldn't call it dating. We just had dinner last night." She shrugged. "I thought *you* were his girlfriend."

"Don't play dumb, like you don't know how I earn my living," Susan said dismissively. "I'm a good-time girlfriend. And at the moment Carl's finances aren't in Olympic shape and he can't afford my company." She ignored Paul and Leona's disapproving faces, stubbed out her latest lipstick-smeared cigarette and then rolled her eyes and half got up from her armchair in shock. "Hell no—I don't believe it!"

"What's wrong now?"

Laughing, Susan settled back down into the armchair. "Hey, bad news can be good news too."

Angela frowned. "Sue, I've no idea what the hell you're talking about. And I don't think either Paul or Leona have either. Have you suddenly remembered something important about the Cleaverman, or else what is it?"

"The Whitfield inheritance," Susan explained. "Now that Jeffrey is dead, all the money is Carl's."

"If he survives the Cleaverman too," Paul said with a scowl. "And unless we get that damn book soon and unscramble the riddle it contains, there's a high chance of that not happenin'."

"I just realized," Leona said worriedly, "that it's actually very foolish, us three gathering here like this; as dumb as asking a cat to babysit a mouse. If the Cleaverman materializes now, we're all dead meat."

On that statement, Susan got to her feet. "Well, guys, I have to leave now anyway."

Angela scowled at her. "You're not coming with us to . . . ?"

Susan shook her head emphatically. "You don't need me anyway. You've got the muscle"—she pointed at Paul—"the brains"—she pointed at Angela—"and the mystic woman"—her wagging index finger finally froze on Leona. "So, honestly I don't see what you need a slut for too; it ain't like the Cleaverman needs a blowjob."

Angela rolled her eyes. "Duh? Safety in numbers?"

Susan began checking her makeup in her pink compact and touching up her blusher. "According to Leona, it's more like temptation in numbers. The more of us there are there, the greater the likelihood of Mr. Cleaver-mad turning up to chop us up."

"Cleaver-mad? Ha ha ha. Yeah, that sounds about right," Paul said, though his expression wasn't the least bit humorous. He took a sip of his beer, scratched his chin reflectively for a moment, then tugged on his beard. "Hmmm, can you at least babysit for us? Otherwise, we'll need to leave the kids alone while we're gone."

Susan shook her head sadly. "Oh, I'd honestly love to make myself useful, but I honestly can't. Unfortunately, I've a date at midnight, and it's one I can't get out of." She frowned. "I would if I could—don't think I'm making light of our current situation—but this was booked ages ago, and if I don't go tonight, my reputation might be ruined for good."

Her comment made Angela laugh. "Sue, you no longer have a reputation. You and Crystal Parr are in contention for 'most overused vagina in Massachusetts.' What's there left to ruin?"

"My bank account, I guess." Susan either missed the insult implicit in the remark, thought Angela was making a joke, or simply didn't care either way. She bent over and hugged Leona. "Sorry, I can't watch your kids tonight, but I honestly gotta run—this is so frigging important."

And then she hurried off out the front door. There was silence in the living room until they heard her car start up.

"That's one very airhead woman," Paul said reflectively as Susan's car pulled out of the driveway.

Angela laughed. "I've the feeling she's trying to distance herself from what we're planning to do. She thinks we're gonna get busted for sure tonight . . . and daddy—Judge Riley—will be incensed if she involves herself in any scandal."

"I've never understood that," Paul said with a perplexed look on his face. "How does a respectable judge end up with a prostitute—alright, an escort—for a daughter? And she's his *only* kid? Is that the result of bad parenting, daddy issues, or what?"

Leona shook her head slowly. "Yeah, Susan's an airhead, but maybe she's smarter than the three of us. I'm already getting a bad vibe about us breaking into the Ellsworths' house. And it ain't the cops I'm scared off."

Her husband nodded and finished his beer. He stood up and pulled her up off the coffee table top and held her close. "Yeah, me too, hon.

But what else can we do? I definitely don't wanna watch you—either of you girls—get chopped up by this Cleaverman." He checked the time on his watch, then turned to Angela. "We've still got quite a while before midnight. What you gonna do? Stay here with us or go home and drive back later?"

When Angela didn't immediately respond, Leona said, "She might as well stay here with us till midnight. I'm just about starting dinner, so she'll eat with us and the kids." She peered into Angela's eyes. "I really don't think you should go home right now anyway. Your house must be full of ghosts."

Angela gave a start at the comment and looked worried. "Ghosts? Do you really think so?"

Leona gave her a comforting smile. "Merely a figure of speech. But considering the deaths in your house, the atmosphere there can't be good for you right now. Being alone there will surely set you to thinking morose thoughts. The spirits are sad."

Angela nodded. "Yeah, you're right. I'll stay here with you guys." She drank the last of her coffee, then got out her phone. "But dammit, I'd really feel a lot better if Carl would just call us."

"I'm sure he's okay," Leona said. "I don't sense that anything bad or weird has happened to him."

"So why doesn't he call me?"

Leona shrugged. "That, I can't sense. The answer to that question seems tangled up in the greater scheme of things." She looked inquiringly at her husband.

Paul headed for the kitchen. "Considerin' that question requires another beer, I think."

"Come and help me make dinner," Leona told Angela, taking her by the hand and leading her after Paul. "Working at something will take your mind off of Carl and the other things."

Angela followed her meekly. All three adults tried to keep their minds off what was still to come that night, off what they had to do.

CHAPTER 22

Carl

At about the same time as Angela and the Pattens were having dinner, Carl Whitfield sat in his living room pondering his options.

He'd lied to Marie, the policewoman who'd been left at Angela's house to keep watch over her while she slept. There had been no urgent business to attend to. He'd just needed an excuse to leave the place.

Carl was frightened. No, he wasn't scared of the police finding out what he'd done. With the way he'd carried out the murders and cleaned up afterwards, there was no chance of them suspecting he was responsible. In that sense, last night's operation had been a fantastic success.

I'm rich now—the inheritance is all mine!

But apparently, the Cleaverman was a real supernatural entity, one as murderous and malevolent as Leona had claimed it was.

Shit!

So now, Carl, laptop on his lap, sat staring at his TV as the latest details of the murders scrolled across the bottom of the screen:

'SIX KILLED IN ELIZABETH DRIVE MASSACRE. GAY COUPLE MURDERED BY SERIAL KILLER. TORTURE DUNGEON DISCOVERED. FBI SAY NO LINKS BETWEEN THESE AND LAST SUMMER'S KILLINGS' . . . and so on and so forth. The news anchorpersons looked like they were trying hard to conceal their intense delight at having this latest juicy news item tossed in their laps.

Carl liked the 'Gay Couple' angle. It set the cops off on an additional wild goose hunt.

Maybe I should've painted something homophobic on the bedroom walls. But that might've been too leading. But back to the real problem . . .

140

The 'real problem' as Carl saw it, was discovering how to deal with the Cleaverman. It hadn't escaped his notice—Carl was after all very intelligent even if he was also extremely lazy—that it was mere good luck on his part that the Cleaverman had selected Steve-O's house rather than Mike's for his massacre.

So, last night my life hung on a flip of a coin, and I had no frigging idea. It could just as well have been me, Mike and Jeff that the Cleaverman targeted.

Since leaving the Rossi's house Carl had spent four hours online, researching the Cleaverman. Maybe he just didn't know the right keywords to input into Google, but he'd found out very little of use. This Cleaverman fellow didn't seem to be any kind of a regular urban nightmare.

All the while he was searching, Carl was aware that his life's stopwatch was ticking, his God-given allotment of personal time running out, each passing second dragging him nearer to a rendezvous with a gory death.

Finally Carl had found a page with a version of the spell, but the spell had been incomplete. Damn!

But . . . there was still a ray of hope. On another of those few pages about the Cleaverman, he'd found a passing mention of how to revoke the spell:

The rhyme is the riddle; the riddle is the rhyme.
Extract the riddle from the rhyme and unriddle it in time,
Then unriddle to the Cleaverman the riddle of the rhyme,
Or else your life truly ain't worth half of a dime.

So, Carl at least knew how to fix the problem. He just needed the complete spell they'd cast three nights ago. Unriddling it should prove easy—Carl was great with puzzles, riddles, and ciphers. He figured he could easily crack this one too. And then all he had to do was wait for the Cleaverman to show up, and tell him the answer.

The fact that he might actually have to stand face-to-face with the monster that had mercilessly butchered four of his friends filled Carl with dread. But even that was a lesser evil to consider.

Do I even have sufficient time to do it?

This was another problem now. The complete spell was in the spellbook Leona had cast it from. That spellbook, in turn, was in the Ellsworths' house.

The only solution Carl could see, was him breaking into the Ellsworths' house and finding/stealing the spellbook.

Yeah, that's what I'll do. What time? . . . 2 a.m. should be fine. There's more houses on that street than on Mike's . . . I'd best give everyone time to start snoring.

A massive surge of dread suddenly swept over him. He looked around, expecting to see someone there with him in his living room. But there wasn't anyone; he was alone. Looking down, he saw that his hands were shaking. (Both of his arms still ached anyway from last night's effort of chopping up the two corpses.)

He thought of getting up and raiding his stash of hash, but then had second thoughts. In addition to making one sloppy on the job, marijuana sometimes also made him feel paranoid. *And if there's one thing I can do without right now, it's additional paranoia. Some coke might've helped, but I'm fresh out of summer snow.*

Carl studied the TV for a while. At the moment the Raynham Chief of Police was being interviewed. Tina Kravitz was a massively obese woman, a mountain of flesh in a police uniform; despite which she still managed to be disarmingly pretty. At the moment though, that pretty, fat face was creased up in a disgusted scowl.

"I'm here now with Tina Kravitz, the Raynham Chief of Police," the young female interviewer told the camera before turning to address her subject. "So, Chief Kravitz, why do you imagine serial murderers constantly pick your little town of Raynham to do their dirty business in? By now you must agree that it's more than a coincidence."

"I dunno, Sherri," Tina Kravitz replied, "I guess the FBI's team of profilers are better equipped to answer that one. But in my li'l opinion, it's all most likely to do with the 'copycat syndrome'—I mean, once a place gets some kinda reputation, all the crazies wanna help it live up to that reputation." Tina Kravitz raised a fat finger and looked menacingly at the camera. "And, speaking on behalf of all the good and law-abiding citizens of this fine town, I must add that some of our locals might try to capitalize on this bad reputation as well; or maybe you're damn commie sympathizers or whatnot and wanna cause waves of violence in support of ISIS or North Korea. But don't try it, folks—we'll catch ya, just like we're gonna get the sicko responsible for all these killings that're goin' on now."

The young woman with the microphone nodded. "So, ma'am, you clearly don't agree with the suggestion that Raynham is built on one of the Earth's six hundred and sixty-six gateways to Hell?"

The police chief laughed without mirth, the action making her massive bulk shake in an intimidating fashion. "Aw, c'mon now, Sherri. A gateway to Hell, in this enlightened time and age? That's of course pure superstition. And malicious slander and calumny to boot. Who the hell suggested such a silly thing anyway?"

"Well, Chief, we spoke to a woman named Sin Corbin and she claims—"

"Oh, sorry to interrupt ya, Sherri," Tina Kravitz said, "but you really should choose your interview subjects better. See, I know Sin Corbin real well—we're first cousins—and let me tell you somethin' 'bout her . . ."

The next news item concerned the Hobart trial. Apparently both sides were locked in a stalemate. Teddy Hobart had taken the stand today, and during his testimony had told the court that he'd deeply loved his dead wife Maddy, and had no idea why he'd murdered her. Teddy had also insisted that he'd been sleepwalking at the time.

"Crazy-ass old fart," Carl said in disgust, then his eyes widened. "Oh no! I forgot to call Angela!"

Seeing Hobart and remembering that Angela was part of the prosecution at his trial had reminded him of this oversight. Angela must be wondering where he'd gotten to. *And I mustn't do anything to harm our fledgling romance.*

Carl had silenced his cellphone so no one could disturb his research. Checking it now revealed that Angela Rossi had called him eight times already, her most recent call being thirty minutes ago. In addition to Angela's calls, he had one from Leona Patten and three from her husband Paul.

Dammit, the shit's already hitting the fan. The only person who hasn't called me is Susan, but then she's likely coked-up and busy getting butt-fucked somewhere and has no time for worry at the moment.

He grabbed the remote and turned off the TV. Then he shut his laptop, moved it off his lap and onto the couch, and stood up.

After stretching a few times, Carl picked up his cellphone again and called Angela. She didn't pick up. He tried calling two more times, but now received an intercept message. For some reason, she'd switched off her phone.

Shrugging, Carl walked into the kitchen to make himself a sandwich. *She'll see that I called her that first time anyway. And at the moment, I really can't worry about her—I gotta worry about keeping myself alive; which of course, should keep her alive too, so long as the Cleaverman doesn't call early to collect his answer. Then we're both screwed.*

He drank some wine along with his sandwich, with the result that he shortly began feeling sleepy. Which was good, he felt. *It's just 9 p.m., if I doze now, later on I'll be fresh for the night's work.*

And besides, being a little tipsy helped keep his mind off the task ahead. He found it absurd that he felt more worried by the thought of a simple break-in into Tommy and Nicole's empty house than he had when he'd been planning to murder his brother.

Yeah, 'cos now, my own damn life is on the line!

After setting an alarm for 1 a.m., Carl turned off his phone and went to bed. In a few minutes he was asleep.

CHAPTER 23

Angela, Leona & Paul

"And so here we are," Paul said as they stepped up to the back door of the Ellsworths' house at a few minutes after midnight.

The house lights were all off. The gray-and-brown two-story looked as dead as its owners. The night was dark and because it had rained earlier, the grass was all wet. There were still lots of clouds overhead and the light wind blowing meant the rain might return. The night itself didn't seem eerie, but they each had their own fears to contend with, particularly the looming specter of death.

"I hope the kids'll be fine," Leona said worriedly as Paul jimmied his crowbar between the lock and the door jamb. On this dark night she was dressed in black: a long-sleeved black blouse hand-painted with gray moons and a long black skirt. Black boots with pointed toes. Her makeup was also entirely black. She sighed. "I hate us leaving them alone in the house like that."

"We had no choice," her husband reminded her. "If we get in any trouble here, a babysitter would be a witness that we weren't home."

"Junior and Sandy will be fine," Angela told Leona with a comforting smile. "They were both sleeping like babes when we peeked in on them. We'll be back at your house before they even realize we're gone. And besides, you left your phone on your bed for them with that written instruction to call Paul if there's any trouble. They'll be fine, you'll see."

"It was completely selfish of Susan to desert us like that," Leona said. "Her ass is on the line here too."

Paul laughed. "At the moment, honey, Susan Riley is most likely peddling her ass for money. Well, now you know she ain't no hooker with a heart of gold."

"And we still can't get Carl on the phone either," Leona said.

145

"At least we know he's alive," Angela pointed out. "He did call me right before my phone died."

"So, Carl was alive three hours ago, and he hopefully still is now," Paul said.

"Don't be so pessimistic," Angela said. "I'm worried enough as it is."

"Okay, I'll be optimistic then. Maybe Carl was Susan's trick for tonight and they're both balling right now while we're tryin' to save y'all."

"Ugh, that's even worse," Angela said.

"Just tryin' ta look on the bright side of things."

Leona shivered. "Honey, it's really cold out here. Open the damn door and let's get in where it's nice and warm?"

Paul gave the crowbar a hefty yank and the lock broke outwards—only a glittering metal tongue held the door in place now. He wedged the crowbar back into the gap and this time forced it forward. With a loud splintering of wood, the door flew open.

"And . . . we're in," he said with quiet satisfaction.

However, Angela winced at the noise. "Damn, man, that was so *loud*. Someone may have heard it."

"Yeah, honey," Leona agreed. "And, with two dead couples on this street, everyone else must be sleeping with one eye open now."

Paul nodded. "Alright, girls, back behind the trees. If no one shows up to investigate in five minutes, we're in. If the cops do come, we'll run back over to where we parked the car and try again later after they've left."

The three of them quickly retreated behind the wall of maples just outside the Ellsworths' rear fence and waited. Five minutes, then another five, just to make sure.

While they waited Paul checked the revolver he'd brought along. He'd also brought along his shotgun, but the women had insisted he leave it back in Angela's car, which they were using tonight because its somber gray color was less likely to attract notice than was Leona's red jalopy.

No one showed up to investigate the noise. It began drizzling; they heard peals of distant thunder and saw far-off flashes of lightning. Water began dripping down on them through the tree leaves.

"Hey, let's get into the house before we get soaked," Leona said finally, nervously clicking her flashlight on and off.

So she, her husband and Angela crossed the backyard again and let themselves into the Ellsworth house.

***

Once they were all inside, Paul shut the door and clicked his flashlight on. Its beam filled the rear hallway with shadows.

"It's been just two days since their deaths and the place already smells abandoned," Leona said as she followed Paul along the hallway.

"It's the lack of ventilation," Angela explained. "All the windows are shut now so there's no longer any airflow."

They reached the foot of the stairs.

"Which way?" Paul asked, adjusting his gun in his waistband.

"Upstairs," Leona said. "Tommy most likely returned the spellbook back upstairs after the summoning."

"Yes, that's logical," Angela agreed, pulling her gray jacket tight around her as if she was cold. "Let's go, already. Just being in here is giving me the creeps."

Paul led the way upstairs. The stairs creaked beneath his weight. Viewed from behind in the semi-darkness, he looked much like a bear hunting honey.

"The book should be in their bedroom," Leona said when they reached the upper landing. "This way."

They followed her right, into a large but cluttered bedroom containing lots of antique furniture.

"Has to be in here," Leona said, clicking on her flashlight and hurrying over to the small bookshelf by the right wall, where she quickly checked the spines of the few volumes it contained. "It's not here though."

"Here it is," Angela said, walking over and picking the spellbook up from the left nightstand.

The others joined her at the foot of the bed.

"The Book of Summonings; yes, this is it," Leona confirmed with relief in her voice. "Now let's go downstairs to the living room."

"What do we want there?" Angela asked. "We should leave here before someone comes. We forgot to shut the bedroom drapes. Anyone looking from next door will think a burglary's going on in here."

"Oops," Paul said and switched off his flashlight. Then he walked over to pull the drapes shut.

"Listen, we don't have time to argue," Leona insisted. "You and Paul come down to the living room with me."

Carrying the book, she turned and briskly exited the bedroom.

They followed her back downstairs.

"Someone definitely got killed in here," Paul said as his flashlight illuminated the dark living room. "That goddamn smell . . . like roadkill or worse." He crossed to the windows. "I really wish we could open the damn drapes instead of keeping 'em closed. It stinks worse than a slaughterhouse in here."

Angela sat on the couch by the hallway entrance. "So, yes, well we're here. Leona, what's this about?"

"Hold on and I'll explain." Leona strode over to the coffee table, which was both covered with dried blood and now stood inside a wide dark patch that disfigured the green rug. She knelt down in the dark patch and sniffed the table, running her fingers along the deep grooves in its congealed red coating that indicated where the Cleaverman's blade had gashed the underlying wood. Then she whispered a prayer over the table and returned to sit beside Angela.

"So what are we doing down here?" Angela asked impatiently. "We really should just leave."

Paul, who was standing by the TV, nodded down at Leona. "She's right, honey. Hanging around now that we've gotten what we came for is just plain stupid."

"There's a good reason," Leona explained. "I can sense good spirits nearby—I'm hoping they'll help us solve the riddle."

Angela looked unconvinced but said, "Alright, let's give it a go."

Paul nodded too. "Worth a try."

Leona opened the book to the relevant page. Paul sat on her left and illuminated the book with his flashlight. Angela sat on her right and stared grimly at the page.

Leona read out:

"Tell me the name of John Cleaverman's wife,
An Angel Maria he loved all of his life.
Never a nag like Jenny, never one day in strife.
You, my friends, have just one chance to survive:
Answer this riddle or give up your lives."

After that they each read it through silently three or four times.

"Can't make head or tail of it," Paul admitted, scratching his brow. "So what's her name?"

"Must be either Jenny or Maria," Leona said, a frown on her blackened lips. "Those are the only two names in the rhyme."

"No, there's three names there," Angela corrected her with a smile. "Angel's also a name; a form of Angela."

"Okay," Paul agreed, stroking his beard, "so, we've three options, or—considering that it's a riddle—maybe six, if we adjust 'Jenny' to 'Jennifer,' 'Angel' to 'Angela,' and 'Maria' to 'Mary,' or 'Rosemary' even."

"Wow, that's quite a lot of options," Angela said. "And 'Angel' could also be 'Angelina' or 'Angelica.' " She made a face. "I think Leona's right and *we are* going to need supernatural help in unravelling this puzzle." She nudged Leona with her elbow. "Go on, do your thing."

Leona left the couch and sat cross-legged on the rug with the spellbook open by her feet. Then she placed her palms on her knees and shut her eyes. Her face settled into a placid expression.

"Yes," she said after a few moments, "I can sense the spirits nearby. Tommy and Nicole both sense our distress and wish to assist us . . ."

CHAPTER 24

Angela

Angela watched Leona with misgivings.

I'll be so relieved once we've left this house. If I knew this was what Leona had in mind, I'd have suggested she do it upstairs in the bedroom.

But it was too late for that now and Angela knew it. Now, Leona was totally into her trance, her eerily-made-up face bearing a look of concentration as if she was listening to someone or something.

In addition to the garishly made-up psychic meditating opposite her, the house itself wasn't helping Angela's mood. Having belonged to a pair of antique dealers, this place was too full of outlandish junk to not conjure up weird feelings in the semi-dark created by the beam from Paul's flashlight, the batteries of which now appeared to be dying. In this regard the stuffed animals on the shelves by the television were particularly bad offenders. Already frozen in lifelike poses, the dim illumination gave the stationary raccoon, bat and cat corpses an additional illusion of life. The stuffed brown bear standing upright sentinel on the opposite side of the room, in the far corner past the windows, was menacing enough already, but whenever the light caught its glass eyes, they seemed to Angela to gleam with realistic fury.

Oh, how I wish Carl were here right now holding me in his arms.

Angela felt that if Carl Whitfield was here with them, things would be fine. At the very least they'd have one more brain to help solve the Cleaverman's riddle. During their dinner date Carl had really impressed her with his intelligence.

But he wasn't here, so Angela Rossi, Bristol County DA's assistant, was alone with her peculiar bogeymen. It was still drizzling outside, and that, reminding her of the fateful night in this same room when they'd summoned the Cleaverman, filled Angela with dread.

Also dreadful in a personal sense to Angela, were the six grandfather clocks arranged against the far wall of the Ellsworths' living room. In this case, the problem was of the clock faces seeming like human faces. To a lawyer like Angela Rossi, that array of tall and narrow horologes looked like an unsympathetic jury. And Angela Rossi was very aware that they were committing a crime by being here and that the longer they remained here, the greater the chance became of their being discovered. And of course, once that happened, her name was going to be in the newspapers and her career was going to be in the gutter.

But being shamed out of court is way better than being dead.

"Hear and help me, you benevolent spirits," Leona whispered. "I need your assistance!"

She fell silent again and Angela turned to Paul. "This is taking too long," she whispered.

He yawned and shrugged. "Can't rush her when she's like this."

They waited while Leona sat in her trance. Now, Leona almost seemed to be glowing in the darkness, her black clothes shining as if emitting a faint radiation. Suddenly she opened her eyes. Her gaze was frantic and staring, fixed on nothing. Her face twisted up as if she was in pain.

"Leona . . ." Angela began, but Paul shushed her.

"At the moment she can't see or even hear us," he whispered. "She's over in that other world."

Angela nodded and calmed herself. *This had better work,* she thought. *Leona looks possessed.*

Still staring sightlessly ahead, Leona picked up the open spellbook. She held the book at chest height but didn't look at it. Speaking to those 'others' she was communicating with, she said, "Now help me answer this riddle," and then intoned:

> *"Tell me the name of John Cleaverman's wife,*
> *An Angel Maria he loved all of his life.*
> *Never a nag like Jenny, never one day in strife.*
> *You, my friends, have just one chance to survive:*
> *Answer this riddle or give up your lives."*

As Leona spoke, Angela became aware of a strange undercurrent rising in the living room; a chilling, spooky feeling that sent shivers down her spine.

Something's wrong, she thought. *Something's very wrong in here!*

But Angela couldn't place a finger on the problem. She stared at Leona. Her psychic friend still seemed possessed. Leona was still holding the Book of Summonings up in front of her but staring vacant-eyed over the book's top. Her pale skin and black clothes still gave off that barely discernable glow. She was still speaking too, muttering either words or an incantation under her breath.

Then Angela realized that Leona was actually quietly reciting the Cleaverman spell again.

Oh my fucking God, that makes three times! she thought in alarm. *She already read it out once when we were trying to decipher the riddle ourselves, and now she's read it out twice to the spirits who she's trying to get to help us!*

Panicking now, Angela turned to Paul. "Man, we've got to stop her! And we've got to get out of here right away!" She wasn't whispering now; she didn't care if folks in the nearby homes heard her. This was life and death, too precious to worry about reputation trifles over.

Paul looked at her in confusion. "What do you mean? She's trying to solve—"

Angela shook her head. "You don't get it, man! All you need to do to summon the Cleaverman is read out the spell three times and shed some blood."

Paul nodded. "Yeah, I know that. But there's no blood here, so there's no danger."

"No blood?" Angela pointed past him. "Look at the coffee table."

Sudden worry dawned on Paul and he turned to stare at the coffee table. The dried blood that had coated the top of the coffee table was glowing. It burst into flame as they watched.

Oh my God, no! Angela thought.

"Oh hell," Paul said. "We gotta get outa here right now!"

They both turned back to Leona. "Leona . . . !"

Leona was still staring sightlessly into the room, only now the expression on her face was one of absolute terror. Still holding the book out, she gasped: "The riddle is the rhyme? Her name? I don't know! I don't know!" Her eyes and mouth gaped even wider. And then she screamed: "No! Stay away from me! STAY BACK! STAY BACK!"

There was no one in the living room except the three of them, but suddenly the air above Leona Patten flashed a bright silver. It was the briefest of flashes, but the next second, both of Leona's outstretched forearms detached from her elbows and fell into her lap. Blood spurting from her elbows, Leona toppled over backward. She lay there twitching in shock, her mind still locked in the paranormal realm she only could sense.

"No!" she gasped. "No, don't kill me!"

Paul dashed to her side and grabbed her by her shoulders. "Leona! Leona! Honey, say something!" The fire on the coffee table had now gone out, but a smell of burnt flesh lingered.

And then armless Leona, her eyes seeing something only she could see, sat up and smiled at Paul. "The Cleaverman says to ask you a question, honey, and if you don't know the answer, you're gonna die like me." She laughed insanely for a moment. "The question is this . . ."

Angela plugged her ears with her fingers. She didn't know if this counted or not—the question after all wasn't intended for her, but she wasn't taking any chances. She lip-read what Leona was telling/asking her husband: *The riddle is the rhyme; the rhyme is the riddle.*

But Angela didn't believe Leona was in control of herself any longer; it seemed like something evil now had a grip on her. For one thing, only something unholy could have made an experienced medium/psychic like Leona recite the deadly Cleaverman rhyme three times with blood nearby. For another thing, with both of her forearms chopped off and ejecting jets of blood the way they were doing, Leona should have bled to death by now, but she wasn't dead yet. Her evil message delivered, she'd fallen back to the ground where she kept smiling like she was crazy.

But Death was coming for Leona for sure. Angela could see the black gaseous swirl forming by her head. In five seconds the black smoke had the form of a man holding a monster cleaver in his right hand. Just like Leona before she'd had her arms cut off, the smoky man also seemed to glow slightly.

Oh my God, he's here! Angela realized. *We're all going to die!*

Paul, shocked by his wife's injuries, hadn't yet noticed the evil black apparition that had materialized beside him.

Angela, her fingers still stuck in her ears, wanted to flee, but she knew she couldn't leave just yet. *I need to get the spellbook before I go anywhere, or else I'm as good as dead myself.* The sight of the Cleaverman filled Angela with an intense urge to wet herself from fear; she barely managed to contain her terror. Somehow, her dread of her fate if she panicked overrode her fright.

The spellbook was wedged between Paul's foot and Leona's legs. Angela took her hands from her ears and stepped tentatively towards it. But it was then that Paul realized that they had company in the living room.

"Shit!" he growled.

Angela didn't know if Paul Patten sensed the gleaming blade's descent, but the huge trucker stepped back from his wife at the exact moment that the Cleaverman chopped her head off. Leona's head rolled towards Paul. He leapt out of its way and drew his revolver from his waistband.

Paul began firing at the smoky apparition. "I'm gonna kill you, asshole!"

"Fuck!" Angela gasped as the bullets passed harmlessly through the Cleaverman and smashed out the living room windows. The noise galvanized her into action. Taking advantage of the distraction, Angela ducked down and grabbed the spellbook. Once she'd gotten it, she looked at Paul.

"Paul, let's get out of here! The cops will be here any second now!"

But Paul wasn't listening. His eyes were still focused on the Cleaverman. It made for a crazy standoff. On one side of the living room, the Cleaverman stood over Leona's decapitated body. On the other side, Paul was pointing his gun at the apparition.

"FUCK YOU, ASSHOLE!" Paul screamed at the Cleaverman— loud enough to rouse the entire neighborhood if the gunshots hadn't already—and began firing again.

From a safe vantage point by the living room entrance, Angela watched the Cleaverman fling his giant cleaver at Paul. She watched the giant blade travel through the air like a javelin, watched it punch all the way through Paul's chest, lifting Paul off his feet and pinning him to the wall like a trophy head. She watched the Cleaverman advance on the shrieking trucker, walking like a ghost; rolling across Leona's corpse and across the carpet as if he had castors in his smoky feet.

Then, keeping her own shrieks in so the Cleaverman didn't notice her too, Angela turned and ran along the rear hallway and out of the house.

Despite the rain, she didn't stop running until she was safe in her car, and even there and then she didn't feel in the least bit safe.

I got the book! I got the spellbook! I've bought myself some time. I've bought some time.

These were the sole thoughts in Angela's head as she drove herself home.

CHAPTER 25

Susan . . . Thea's House

The night rustled past Susan Riley like black silk.

She sat, as comfortable as a princess, in the back of a white stretch limousine. No hurry and no worries. Shoes off, legs crossed, she enjoyed the ride as the vehicle seemed to float along.

The limo had picked her up from home at midnight, ten minutes ago.

Tonight's client was Thea Dee Marlowe, a retired rock goddess who lived out on the outskirts of Attleboro. Like Susan had told Angela and the Pattens, this appointment was a month old. Thea Dee Marlowe had hired Susan on a friend's recommendation, via susanrileyservices.com.

The rain was heading east and they soon drove out of it.

Susan leaned forward and poured herself a brandy from the limo's minibar. She had additional options of either listening to music or watching a movie on the vehicle's entertainment system, but felt in the mood for neither.

She smiled coldly to herself as the limo rolled through the city of Attleboro.

Yeah, this is the way to travel. Riding in luxury like this one can forget about life, both its good and bad aspects.

At the moment, Susan was on an 'up.' She'd done a few lines of coke before leaving home, just to get herself in the mood for anything. Thea Dee hadn't yet told Susan what her specific sexual interests were. For all Susan knew, the old girl might want to be whipped. Susan had no objections to doing pervy stuff; it just cost more.

Susan sipped her brandy and they left Attleboro behind. The ride was so smooth that she felt she wasn't even moving. The limo driver was an uncommunicative Chinese man named Chang. He addressed her "Yes, ma'am, no, ma'am," and such like, but said little else. It didn't matter, Susan didn't feel like talking much either.

They turned off the main highway. She poured herself another drink. The alcohol and coke were working. She felt luxurious: pampered, cared for and slightly wired with expectation. She felt the way she expected she'd feel if she were Carl Whitfield's wife. It was an amusing thought. She got out her cellphone from her purse and called Carl. But Carl's phone seemed switched off.

"Where are we now?" she asked the chauffeur via the intercom.

"Outskirts of Attleboro, ma'am," came back the respectful reply. He had a slight accent that reminded her of old Jet Li movies.

Susan put her cellphone away again. Then, after a long sip of her brandy, she permitted herself a moment's seriousness. Her friends should be at the Ellsworths' house right about now.

She frowned at the thought of how she'd evaded accompanying them on their quest for the spellbook. *Maybe I should have gone there with them. Yeah, right, who'm I kidding? I'm worried enough already without dropping that in the mix too. I don't need an additional fright-fest with the Cleaver-maniac. Not after I already had that goddamn recurrent dream of meeting Death again this morning. And he told me exactly the same thing as always—that I'm soon gonna commit suicide.*

Yes, Susan had had the dreaded dream again. Herself, wearing a skimpy red party dress and standing on an empty black plain in the middle of nowhere; and Death, as tall as a hill and with the blade of his scythe hanging in the sky like the new moon. Death had been dressed in a tattered gray robe and hood that obscured all of him except his gleaming eyes. He'd loomed over Susan, staring down at her in a way that made her feel completely insignificant.

The red glow from Death's eyes had framed her like twin spotlights. She'd felt cold, freezing.

"You'll commit suicide tomorrow," Death had said, in an echoey voice that sounded like ten rotten corpses all talking at once.

"But why?" she'd asked in confusion. "Why?"

"Because you'll want to."

"But I don't want to," she'd protested.

Laughing, Death had turned and walked off. Susan had remained there staring after him, and then, as usual, she'd woken up and it was morning. This time the fear had remained with her for a good while afterwards.

The dream still made no sense to Susan. *Why the hell would I wanna kill myself, right when things are looking so good for me? I mean, Carl's back on top again—with Jeffrey suddenly dying like that—that means lots of money for me . . . hmm, except if he's suddenly gotten sweet on that dog Angela. She looks like a cow—not pretty and massive dugs out to here. If Carl gets serious about her . . . I'll have to do something about that, get the bovine bitch out of the way before she ruins my business over there. I'll need to publicly embarrass her so badly that she'll steer clear of Carl forevermore.*

While making a mental note to crash Angela Rossi's romantic wagon, Susan unconsciously tapped her purse. The action reminded her of the pistol in the purse. The gun was a Ruger LC9. Compact and lightweight and reputed to pack quite a punch. She'd owned the gun for ages, but in the upper circles of prostitution that she moved in, it hadn't proved necessary and she'd taken to leaving it at home. But now, with this worry about the Cleaverman and her supposedly impending suicide at hand—she suspected some drug dealer planned to murder her and frame her as having killed herself—she'd decided to start carrying the LC9 again. So now, whoever assaulted her would be in for a deadly surprise. Male or female, she'd just point the weapon at the attacker's crotch and pull the trigger.

She reconsidered the dream. During the day she'd realized its positive aspect: *If I'm gonna kill myself, then the Cleaverman won't be killing me. That's one bother less.*

This knowledge and reasoning was why, although Susan Riley was as upset by her friends' deaths as her other friends were, she could still go about her business with a semblance of normalcy.

"We've arrived, ma'am," Chang announced over the intercom.

***

Thea Dee Marlowe's house was very old. Susan had been locked in her thoughts for most of the approach up its long driveway and now, when the chauffeur opened the limo door for her, she was very impressed. Constructed mostly of dark stone, it was a very large house, and a big house always meant big money. The mansion sprawled extensively on either side of the columned central pavilion that framed its main entrance.

Susan knew a little bit about Thea Dee Marlowe's life. She'd had a very successful music career, recording three number one albums as lead vocalist with the rock band Slain Jane. Then something went wrong and she left the band. There were two versions of what had happened to Thea Dee. One version said the shock of her husband's death had devastated her. The other, more malicious version (and probably the more accurate one) said Thea's hard partying and extreme behavior had done her in. Anyway, in the end, she'd quit the music business.

Thea had never come out as a lesbian—she'd been married after all. But one of Susan's clients was Bruce Baxter, lead guitarist for the Urban Fairies, and he'd told Susan that the real reason why Thea Dee had been kicked out of Slain Jane and replaced by the arguably less talented Janet Orgasm, was that she'd made a practice of seducing the other members' girlfriends.

Touched by a familiar stroke of vanity, and the need to prove her own desirability to a rock legend, before exiting the limousine Susan got out her compact from her purse and double-checked her makeup. Oh, she knew she had a very elegant face. In contrast to her voluptuous figure, her face was very thin, almost skeletal, with its skin stretched tight over the long skull like a mask her soul was wearing. If not exactly classically beautiful, she was very alluring. Men (and lots of women too) went for her in a big way; that was the important thing.

The Chinese chauffeur waited with polite deference to her beauty, until she'd finally satisfied herself that she looked her best and stepped out of the long car.

"Please climb the steps, Mrs. Marlowe is expecting you," the man said with a deep bow, shutting the vehicle's door after her.

She turned to nod her thanks and something weird seemed to happen. Chang's Asian features suddenly seemed to alter, so that he no longer looked human. His face appeared to narrow; while his slanted eyes twisted into empty vertical slits. His mouth too twisted till it ran from his nose to his chin instead of from side-to-side, with teeth like dirty shards of glass filling the slit-like black maw. In addition, two spiky downward-curving horns jutted from each side of his forehead.

Shocked by the terrifying change, Susan took an involuntary step backwards.

"Are you alright, Miss Riley?" Chang asked.

"I . . . I-I . . ." she gasped in horror. But the man was just himself again; an everyday Chinese person.

She took another step back and blinked. *Was that just an illusion?*

After another respectful bow, the chauffeur reentered his stretch limo and drove off to somewhere on the right side of the building.

Once he'd left her, Susan hurriedly ascended the steps to the pavilion's marble floor and strode between the high stone columns to the front door. Illusion or not, she still felt spooked.

She rang the doorbell.

Thea Dee answered the door in person. Susan was relieved to see her. Thea Dee was tall and shapely, and had short, reddish-toned hair. Now in her mid-forties, Thea's face showed clear signs of her years and of her wild-girl rock past, but she was still attractive. Her eyes were black, her lips a deep pink. She was barefoot, and dressed only in a blue silk negligee that did more to reveal her body than to conceal it. A slightly nauseating perfume that Susan was unfamiliar with wafted from her.

"Hi, I've been expecting you," Thea said warmly, then instantly stepped aside to let Susan walk in past her. "I hope your ride with Chang was smooth."

"It was fine," Susan replied, strolling into a marble foyer filled with gothic busts, a few of which were rather macabre in design. "You've got quite a collection of these."

Thea Dee laughed. Although she possessed a warm voice in the middle female register, her laugh was strangely unpleasant; not as bad as fingernails on chalkboard, but not far off either. After being spooked by the chauffeur's imagined transformation, Susan was glad both when they left the rather creepy vestibule and when Thea's mirth ceased.

"Come upstairs with me," Thea said and led the way across a wide and luxurious living room towards a spiral marble stairway.

Thea's living room had a tasteful mingling of old and new furniture, and side by side on its walls, fighting for place with Thea's collection of gold and silver records, hung an extensive collection of paintings. Most of the paintings, however, depicted ghastly scenes and happenings: morbid sights such as men and women being crucified upside-down or gutted and decapitated, skewered babies being barbequed or fried in oil, and cities burning with horrible monsters flying in the flames that consumed them. And all these paintings were distressingly lifelike.

The gruesome art put a definite damper on one's enthusiasm for the fantastic house. Still Susan felt herself compelled to stop and stare at the paintings. "These are some creepy artworks you've got here," she said, shuddering.

"They weren't originally mine," Thea replied. "My late husband Edgar was a painter of the macabre."

"Your husband painted all these? Wow, he was really talented—even though I don't care at all for his subjects." Susan vaguely recalled that Thea Dee had married some steel-inheritance multimillionaire, who'd then died during a fishing trip—the story was that a shark had ripped Edgar Marlowe's guts out and that he'd died screaming his love for Thea.

"He painted *all* of them," Thea said with pride. "Every single one's an original and I've collectors offering me ludicrous sums to purchase them." She pointed across the room. "Edgar's favorite was that one there."

Susan looked at the painting she'd indicated. "Ugh!" she couldn't help exclaiming.

The painting Thea Dee had pointed out was of a woman. *Well, maybe it's not supposed to be a woman, but it's certainly got a woman's boobs and a pussy and . . . shit, how can anyone be that damn ugly? This lady makes Angela Rossi look like Miss Universe!*

She wasn't exaggerating the portrayed woman's lack of comeliness. The woman had the kind of body a porn star would kill for, curves that men would fight wars to bed . . . but her face . . . Susan felt sick just looking at it. How Thea's husband could have painted something this ugly was beyond her imagining.

"That's supposed to be Death," Thea Dee said.

"She's ugly as sin," Susan said.

"Well, you know they do supposedly live together."

"What are you talking about?"

"The wages of sin is death—so the Good Book says. Death is Sin's daughter. Edgar painted Sin too—but that's in one of the bedrooms."

Susan scowled and looked back at the weird image. It was a really nutty painting. Instead of Death wearing 'his' traditional cape and hood and carrying a scythe (like Susan had seen in her recurring nightmare), 'she' was wearing just a wet *Fat Alice* tee shirt against which her nipples protruded, and red high heeled boots (no panties), and carrying a shotgun. And her nose was the size and shape of an erect penis.

And then, just as Susan was about to look away from the painting, her mind seemed to play tricks on her again. The painted Death first smiled at her and then in a rather melodramatic move, she stuck her shotgun under her ugly head and blew it off.

For a moment, Susan felt relief at Death's suicide; her having no head at all was a definite improvement over the one she'd had. But then the swirl of haze that had enveloped her unbeknownst to her blew away and her mind was abruptly clear again. And the painting of Death looked exactly the same as before.

What's going on here? Susan asked herself. Then she turned to Thea Dee. "Did you see what just happened?"

"*What* happened?"

"To the painting . . . it just . . ." Susan shut up. Telling Thea Dee what she'd seen would make her seem silly (which she wasn't), or drunk (which she might be—how many brandies had she had on the ride over?).

"Don't worry 'bout it," Thea Dee said reassuringly. "Lots of people see strange things in this living room. Edgar was always telling guests that this house had an occult charge."

"Oh, they do? It's not just me then?"

"Oh, screw that and come screw me instead," Thea Dee said then, lust brimming over in her voice. "Come on, honeypot, I ain't paying ya to be an art critic." Tugging on Susan's arm, she steered her back towards the spiral marble stairway. "I can't wait to fuck you, girl. I've been dying to do so all month."

This was language that Susan understood: intense fuck, exciting sex, magnificent cock, glorious cunt and superlative orgasm. Education working overtime in bed. The creepy feelings evaporated. She forgot about Death's imagined suicide and climbed the stairs behind her famous client.

CHAPTER 26

Susan . . . Sex

Thea Dee led Susan along a pink corridor arrayed with more busts and grim paintings and gold records, to a white door.

She pushed the door open. "Welcome to my bedchamber."

Susan stepped inside. The bedroom was huge, with blue walls and lots of windows. With unvoiced lustful intent they moved quietly towards the large bed and lay down on it. This wasn't the time for words, but for the communion of flesh and desire.

"Fuck me silly, bitch," Thea Dee moaned throatily as she discarded her negligee and settled on her back. "Make this really worth my money."

Susan needed no further urging. She stripped off in a flash, flinging her clothes to the floor, and got on top of Thea.

Thea Dee spread her legs. Susan went between them, seeking out her soft center, dipping her tongue into its juicy depths, both tasting and teasing it. The hole was already dripping when she arrived at it, and as she tended to its needs, it gushed even more sexual juice. Thea Dee moaned and shuddered. Susan dug her fingers into Thea Dee's vagina and thrust them in and out. Thea Dee gasped and groaned in surging ecstasy, her first climax lifting her like a bird. Susan kept her mouth glued to Thea's sexual orifice, licking and sucking until her climax was over.

"Was that good for a start?" she asked when Thea Dee stopped straining on the bed.

"Fuck me with this!" Thea Dee handed her a strap-on harness fitted with a blue dildo. "Fuck me real good."

Susan slipped into the harness. "Here we go, honey,"

Slowly, she slid the dildo into Thea Dee's dripping sex. Then she began thrusting in and out with firm, hard strokes. Thea Dee instantly wrapped her legs around her back and Susan leaned forward and kissed the other woman.

She was surprised at how bitter Thea's mouth tasted. As nasty as if she ate garbage for a living.

Thea Dee, groaning and squirming beneath Susan as the dildo filled and thrilled her, laughed at the look of disgust on her face. "My single failing as a lover—I've incredibly bad breath. The kiss of death, one might say. You'd be amazed at how many sexual relationships I've terminated just by kissing the person." Then she frowned. "But I'm paying you to satisfy me, not to be my dentist, so you've no excuse not to kiss my mouth."

"Do you like it up the back door too?" Susan asked, seeking an escape.

Thea Dee nodded eagerly. "I adore anal sex."

"Then roll over, bitch. I'm gonna ass-fuck you till you beg for mercy!"

Thea Dee quickly rolled over. Susan surveyed her buttocks for a moment, then slapped them hard with both hands. "Hey, up on your hands and knees!"

Thea Dee assumed the correct posture for doggy-style penetration. Susan first lubricated Thea's anus with spittle, then inserted the dildo. She began thrusting again. Her insistence on them being on their knees soon proved futile, as, after a violent thrust from her, Thea Dee simply collapsed down onto her belly again. Thereafter, they had sex like that, with Susan keeping up a barrage of hard penetrations on Thea Dee's ass hole, while the woman, with both of her arms hidden beneath her body and both hands penetrating and caressing her sex, seemed to dissolve into a series of endless orgasms.

The grinding of the dildo against Susan's crotch saw her becoming increasingly aroused, until finally, unable to control her lust any longer, she hastily slipped the dildo out of her companion's anus. She pulled the harness off and flung it away over the side of the bed, then rolled Thea Dee back onto her back and gasped at her fevered face in a fevered torment of her own, "Quick, make me come too!"

Thea Dee reached down between Susan's legs and began stroking her. Susan had imagined herself an expert at stroking clitorises, but this was something else altogether. She had no idea exactly how Thea Dee was touching her—after the first few seconds the rock legend seemed to have twenty or thirty fingers caressing her crotch in different ways—but the effect was fantastic. Before Susan knew it, she was floating on clouds of ecstasy—having orgasm after orgasm after orgasm in a landslide of seemingly endlessly increasing sensations that made her hope her client wouldn't in turn charge her afterwards for sexual services provided.

CHAPTER 27

Angela

More scared than ever before in her life, Angela Rossi paced back and forth across what was now her living room. Her thoughts were as dark as her hair. She mentally examined the Cleaverman riddle from every possible angle, sure that at any moment now, the monster would appear, ready to chop her into little pieces.

With her own life clearly on the line, her brother's grisly death had paled into total insignificance. Twice already during her pacing, her feet had randomly led her into the master bedroom where Mike and Jeffrey had been murdered. (The first time, she'd even been unaware of herself ripping the 'Crime Scene' tape off the door.) She'd walked in there almost in a trance, and on realizing where she was, had stared at the wall above the bed's headboard as if the bright red splashes it was now painted with were a sort of coded writing system, a secret language which, once itself interpreted would in turn shed perfect light on her deadly problem.

Tell me the name of John Cleaverman's wife,
An Angel Maria he loved all of his life.
Never a nag like Jenny, never one day in strife.
You, my friends, have just one chance to survive:
Answer this riddle or give up your lives.

However, the bloodstains held no answers for Angela. Staring at them only galvanized her horrified mind to further futile exertions to solve the Cleaverman's riddle.

She made her way back to her living room wondering: *What the hell is his wife's name? Nine or ten options to choose from and I'm no nearer an answer than I was an hour ago.*

166

She'd not called the police to report the Pattens' deaths either. *What can I tell them? Nothing they'll believe. Besides, those gunshots would have woken up the entire neighborhood anyway.*

She sat in an armchair facing the TV. The TV was off, but had it been on she'd have been unable to focus on the news anyway.

It was the middle of the night, but adrenalin had Angela more awake and alert than drinking an entire pot of coffee would have achieved. And she didn't dare shut her eyes anyway. If she closed her eyes for more than thirty seconds, terrible images formed in her head. She'd see Leona's hands falling off her body, then her head rolling off her shoulders, with blood jetting everywhere like water gushing from a fire hydrant. She'd see the Cleaverman—that inexplicable black swirl of gas and soot—flinging his cleaver at Paul, and Paul being pinned to the wall like a bug affixed to a corkboard. She'd feel a resurgence of the terror she'd felt when she fled the Ellsworths' house, the sort of terror she'd often seen gorgeous 'scream queens' portray in horror films—the sort of terror she'd assumed must be overacted, because of course no one could possibly be that frightened. But she had been *that* frightened. She'd escaped on autopilot—somehow understanding that she needed to get to her car no matter what else happened tonight.

She sat and pondered the riddle. By now, after reading it fifty or so times, she'd memorized the lines. The spellbook lay on the coffee table. The Book of Summonings. It seemed so ordinary. How in the world could something so little have created such a large and murderous problem?

This was crazy. Angela Rossi felt as though the universe had gone mad around her. There were things—horrible, nasty things like motor accidents, airplane crashes, rapes and serial killer abductions and terrorists attacks—that you knew happened, but didn't expect them to ever happen to yourself. And then there were other things—things that you knew wouldn't happen to you simply because they were impossible things, the products of fevered or fanatical or unstable imaginations; things one only saw in the movies; things the movies confirmed weren't real.

And when those impossible things happened to you . . .

Had it been just this morning—*No, this is past midnight, we're in Saturday now*—just yesterday morning that she'd come home from work and found the bodies? Oh, but it seemed so long ago, as if the duration of one's life was measured in experiences and not minutes, hours, and years. Time seemed to have slowed down completely and at the same time actually sped up. So much had happened in the past day that Angela felt as though in that short interval she'd lived twenty-four years instead of a similar number of hours.

And where the hell is Carl anyway? If he were only here with me now, holding me close and telling me we'd make it out of this mess alive, I'd feel a whole lot better about my chances of survival. Carl's phone was still turned off. None of the many texts that Angela had sent him had yet been delivered. But somehow, Angela sensed that Carl was still alive. *No, Carl Whitfield isn't dead. I'm certain he isn't!*

Why he wasn't answering his phone though, she had no idea.

CHAPTER 28

Susan Meets Death

At last, when Susan was certain her personal ecstasy couldn't get any greater in that bed, Thea Dee leaned over her and kissed her.

It was a deep, hot, completely uninhibited kiss. Ordinarily such a kiss would be termed 'passionate.' But this kiss which Susan Riley shared with Thea Dee Marlowe went beyond the boundaries of human intimacy. It was a dark and nasty kiss. And its nastiness extended much further than mere disgust created by Thea Dee's outrageously bad breath.

No, this kiss seemed to alter Susan's perceptions of the world. While their lips were in contact Susan felt like she was being sucked up into Thea Dee's aura. And when their lips separated . . .

Susan was in the same bedroom, but not with the same woman. If her companion *was* a woman. Leaning over Susan was the female nightmare depicted in that horrible painting downstairs. In person, Death looked even worse than Edgar Marlowe's portrayal of her. All her horror was in her face, however. Her body was still exquisitely Junoesque, sexually alluring in every aspect; but her face . . .

If Medusa's gaze turned men to stone, Death's horrifying visage would freeze the Pacific Ocean.

Just as Susan had earlier remarked to Thea Dee downstairs, she'd never seen anyone so ugly in her life. With that nose like an erection and eyes like festering sores and a mouth that a shark would be ashamed to exhibit to other fish, and ears like bleeding batwings, and the whole horrible mess being so disproportionate and mismatched . . . no hair at all, the bald scalp scaly and cracked open like rotting zombie flesh . . .

But all this, of course, ended at the top of her neck. The body carrying the head was perfect in all details and in addition had sexual lubrication and saliva smeared all over its thighs (though the vagina between them looked like a jagged cut in the back of a dead and rotting kitten). And those fantastic breasts had smears of lipstick on them . . . Susan's purple lipstick. Which meant . . .

I just had sex with . . . with her? Susan was horrified.

"Hello, I'm Death," Death said. "But I think you already know that."

In response, Susan quickly sat up against the headboard and began shivering. "What . . . What . . . ?" She was too shocked to flee. Too frightened to do more than voice her incomprehension. "Where's Thea?"

"*I* am Thea Dee when I feel like being," Death said. Then she gestured behind her. Thea Dee Marlowe lay there, sleeping. Only this version of Thea was as transparent as a ghost—Susan could see the bed through her—and her transparent body bobbed up and down on the bedcovers as if moved by a gentle breeze. She was faintly blue in color and there was nothing inside her body; nothing at all. She was a plastic bag, a human balloon.

"I am who I am," Death replied Susan's now even more puzzled gaze. "I have many guises—some prettier than others." Gesturing at the transparent woman, Death laughed, and yes, it was that same nauseating laugh that Thea Dee had had. "Yeah, she's a cute body, isn't she? Great to fuck in too."

Susan nodded while inching her way towards the edge of the bed, so she could leap down and run away.

"Stop!" Death said. "I'm not here to kill you."

Susan stopped. "You're not?"

That nasty laugh again. "Of course not. Why should *I* kill you? I don't need to. You'll soon do my job for me."

"You mean . . . ?"

"Yes, your wildest dreams will soon come true—you're gonna kill yourself, ha ha!"

Death or not Death, Susan had to respond to that: "That's just a bad joke, and in bad taste too."

Death looked mournful, which made her look even worse. "Sorry, I couldn't help myself; in my line of work I've few occasions for humor. But alright, your nightmares will come true then. You'll commit suicide and that'll be it. It'll be over for you."

"I won't die tonight, will I?" Susan asked tentatively.

"Actually you will. In . . . well, let's see . . ." She looked at the wall clock, "Okay, it's one-twenty-six now. You'll kill yourself in three hours."

"What?" Susan felt terror rising in her like a current of toxic black sludge. "What?" Then she calmed down a little. "But you . . . you're Death, aren't you? So why are you here?"

"I live here, remember?"

"Don't get fucking cute with me. You know that I frigging mean: you arranged this meeting for a reason . . . What is it?"

Death smiled. "I hadn't been laid in quite a while and since you're about to die anyway . . . well, I thought . . . well, you know how it is."

Susan shook her head. She felt bolder now. "And no, that's not it—sex isn't the reason you lured me here. If that was all you wanted, you could hire any hooker you like"—she gestured at the transparent female balloon that lay beside them—"Thea's rich, remember?"

Death sighed. "Susan, believe me—it *was* the sex. Eddie Rockstar pointed you out at a party and I loved the shape of your ass." She faked a gasp and moan of ecstasy, an action that made her lipless mouth split sideways almost to her ears, revealing a mass of teeth like broken bones and a tongue like a strip of lacerated and bleeding muscle. "Orgasm is truth," Death gasped in self-mockery. "As true as dying. That's why I love sex so much, and particularly having lots of juicy orgasms, what the French call *la petite mort*—little deaths."

Susan shrugged. "Have it your way, lady. I only like sex when I get paid afterwards. Times like that, I have no trouble climaxing. In fact, the more I'm paid, the better and longer I orgasm."

Death grinned. "So, you understand then; I knew a prostitute would. Just the same way as I kill both men and woman without prejudice, I love sex with both sexes." Susan saw that Death's nipples were still hard; and her magnificent breasts seemed almost to be straining towards her, trying to touch her for more loving caresses.

"Yes, I do understand that sexual enjoyment is universal. But no, I still think you're fooling with me. Hey, you, tell me the real reason you enticed me here."

Now Death shrugged. "Oh, alright. I want you to give a message to your father for me."

Susan now looked perplexed. "Dad? You want me to give a message to dad? But . . . why? What message?"

Death got up off the bed and stared down at Susan. "Tell him to lay off young blondes for a while. They're bad for his health."

Susan laughed at that. "Ha ha ha ha ha! You're sure you're not simply some joker in a mask and this isn't just some elaborate hoax?"

"Do you honestly believe that, Sue?"

"Maybe. Prove to me that you're Death."

The hideously ugly woman scowled at her. "What?"

Susan nodded. "You heard me, bitch. Give me a demonstration. Prove who you really are."

Death scratched her chin, a chin like a torn mess of chicken skin. Then she pointed at the transparent Thea Dee.

Susan shook her head. "Not good enough by half. She might really be a balloon." She leaned forward, sharp fingernail extended. "In fact, I think I'll just pop her bubble right now."

"Don't!" Death yelped.

Susan was surprised at the alarm in the gruesome woman's voice. "Why not?"

"Use your brains; the ones in your head, not those in your ass. If you kill her, where do I return to after this discussion?"

Susan extended her finger closer to the ghostly Thea. "That might be good proof. If I burst her and you're stuck—YEOW!"

A flaming pain had just started up between her buttocks, right on her anus. "Oh, shit!" The fire burnt her there for two seconds, then was removed, only for the pain to instantly repeat itself again. "No, nooooo, daddy! Noooo! Stop burning me!" she howled.

Then in shock, Susan realized what she was saying. She hadn't felt pain like this since she was fifteen, since those last times when her father had burnt her anus with his cigarettes because of her bad grades at school. "Yeoooow!" she howled again. "Daddy, please please, please stop it!"

It was a reflex cry, one which back then she'd quickly discovered was a waste of time. Judge Riley had never shown her mercy, sometimes her pained yelps had even angered him enough to give her additional 'bonus' burns. The flaming agony came again and Susan gripped her thighs and howled some more as her ass crack burnt. Tears began streaming down her cheeks.

The anal pain reduced to a hot itchy throbbing. Susan gaped speechlessly at Death.

"Do you believe in me now?" the hideous woman asked her, her ridiculously long nose bobbing. "Or would you rather take another hot trip down memory lane?"

"I believe. I believe!"

The heat between Susan's buttocks instantly vanished. Gasping, she flopped back against the headboard. She grabbed a pillow and clasped it tightly. "You really are Death. Shit!"

Death sat back down on the bed. She sat on Thea's legs. Susan noticed that Death was either sitting *inside* Thea's body, or sitting *through* it—there was no compression like you'd expect with a balloon. She shuddered some more.

"So," Death said, "just tell your father to lay off the hot young blondes for a while."

"Sure, sure," Susan quickly agreed, fearing a repeat display of the pain she'd just felt. "I'll tell him whatever you want."

Death nodded. "Nothing more. Just that, that young blondes are bad for his health. And as for you—"

"Hey, wait. We just had sex with each other, and it was good, wasn't it?"

"Fantastic. The best I've had in a long while."

"So why kill me then?"

"Everyone dies sometime. Death is the unchangeable rule of life— i.e. it ends."

A chill wind of terror blew over Susan, its cold seeming to penetrate deep into the marrow of her bones. "My father is twenty-eight years older than me. He's due to die soon, take him instead."

Death turned her back on Susan and strode over to the bedroom's walk-in closet. Her words floated back to Susan: "Sorry, honey, but you don't get to decide who goes and who stays. Actually, I don't either. I'm just the collector. Everyone alive has a predetermined lifespan and my job is to make the machinery of transition run smoothly."

Susan scowled at the closet's wide-open double doors. Her position on the bed meant that she couldn't directly see Death, though she caught glimpses of the hideously ugly demigoddess as she turned and bent while selecting what to wear. Once Susan was even treated to the absurd sight of Death posing in front of the closet mirror with a party gown held pressed to her body, her maw-like eyes filled with a question of how the garment would look on her knock-'em-dead figure.

"Hey, how 'bout giving me some info then?" Susan asked finally, controlling her frustration so she didn't get another burst of anal pain. Hearing herself uncontrollably begging 'Daddy' not to burn her anymore was just too pathetic.

"What sort of info do you want?"

"What about the afterlife? Is there one?"

Death, her face reflected in the closet mirror, smiled. "Oh, you'll find out soon enough."

Susan tried again. "Yeah, yeah, only it's too early in the a.m. to go looking for a preacher. . . . So, you're saying the Cleaverman won't kill me then?"

"No, you'll kill yourself. I've made that perfectly clear already, young woman. You're gonna die by your own hand . . . and in about three hours from now."

The 'young woman' comment stung a bit. "Will you at least tell me *how* I expire?"

Death reappeared in the doorway, dressed in black stretch pants and a dark leather jacket. She was barefoot. "No, I won't. Otherwise you'll create all sorts of complications by trying to escape your fate, which is futile anyway."

"Can you stop the Cleaverman?"

"I won't—at the moment he's working for me . . . makes my job easier. He's still got a few more souls to collect."

Susan's fear was mixing with anger. "You're not very helpful, you know."

"It's the nature of my job. Like they say, it's a dirty ass, but someone's gotta wipe it."

"So what *can* you do for me then?" Susan felt desperate now. *This all can't be true—I'm too young to die!* She felt she had to salvage something of her existence before . . . before it was all over. Because she was certain Death was telling her the truth.

But is she really telling me the truth? Maybe all this is just a con. Maybe this is just a trick after all. Susan looked more closely at Death's head, taking her time to seriously consider the woman's gruesome features. *They seem eerily realistic, too realistic to doubt, but Thea Dee*—she glanced briefly at the motionless and transparent rock legend—*Thea was once in showbiz and those guys are special effects and makeup wizards. So, it's very possible that that's a latex mask she's got on . . .*

Death laughed. Something about this particular laugh made Susan look at her sharply. "Huh?"

"You now doubt that I'm telling you the truth about your death. That's fine. What is truth anyway? What actually happened, what you want to believe happened, or what everyone else says, thinks, or feels happened even if you know they're all wrong?"

Susan understood what she meant. "*You're* messing with my thoughts? You're making me doubt you?"

Death nodded. "Yes, I don't want you too worried about your future. This way your death will still come as a massive shock to you. Consider it additional payment for our wonderful time of lovemaking." Then Death turned and walked towards the bedroom window nearest her, which was now open and letting in air and moonlight, the drapes blowing almost vertically in the sudden gusts of wind.

"I'm leaving," Death said, staring out of the window as two massive pairs of birdwings sprouted from her back. One set of wings rose from her shoulder blades, the other emerged halfway down her spine. All four wings were as black as night, with long and beautiful glossy feathers like brushstrokes of darkness. Extended out to her sides, each of Death's wings was six feet long at least. Seeing Death like that, with her wings spread, and a look of solemnity on her gruesome face, rendered Susan speechless. Some sights command silence.

"I'll see you soon," Death said, folding her wings back in and then leaping up onto the windowsill, where her unshod feet transformed into bird's feet with long black talons. "I've a collection to make over at the Bristol County Jail." And then she slipped away into the night.

"Hey, wait!" Susan called after her, leaping over Thea Dee and running to the window.

But Death had already vanished. Susan imagined that she saw a huge black bird winging away on the night winds, its glorious and giant dark pinions leaving white trails in the air.

Susan stood there with the cold wind blowing in her face. "She said I've just three hours to live . . . three measly hours." She turned to the wall clock. "Actually, now, that's more like just two hours and forty minutes. Da fuck?"

CHAPTER 29

Carl

No, no no!

Carl sat at the wheel of his car, parked down the road from the Ellsworths' house. He'd turned off his headlights before turning onto Hall Street and now was relieved that he'd had the foresight to do so. The far end of the street swarmed with police vehicles. Blue lights flashing. Crisscrossing yellow flashlight beams. The cops were out in full force.

It was raining.

Carl realized that his mission to retrieve the spellbook from the Ellsworths' house had just crashed and burned. *No damn way am I gonna be able to sneak in there unnoticed with this massive cop presence everywhere. Dammit! But what the hell could've happened again, to bring them all over here tonight, with the sky like this?*

Carl had to know. So, leaving its engine running, he got out of his car and made his way forward to see.

He got within thirty yards of the police undetected. Then he paused behind a tree and watched.

He saw a stretcher being carried out of the house to the medical examiner's hearse-like white van. The body on the stretcher was covered with a white cloth that was splotched with red patches—making Carl wonder why they hadn't simply used a body bag to move it—but then a gust of rainy wind blew the cover away and Carl gaped. There was no body on the stretcher, just a mass of shredded meat.

The Cleaverman was here!

Right then, one of the ambulance men stumbled and several pieces of corpse flesh fell off the stretcher, one of them being a severed arm.

The men moved on with their stretcher. Another man picked up the spilled body parts and followed them. Behind that man another stretcher was being carried out of the Ellsworths' house.

Carl had seen enough. He quickly retraced his steps back the way he'd come and got into his car again. The rain picked up then. Realizing his luck as the rain became a downpour, Carl put the BMW in reverse and leaving its headlights off, reversed all the way to the end of Hall Street and back out onto East Elm Street.

While driving home again, Carl's mind was filled with questions: *Who the hell just got killed back there?* The answer was instantly obvious to him: *That must've been Leona and maybe Angela. They went after the spellbook too and the Cleaverman showed up and killed them both. Oh my God! What am I gonna do now? Shit!*

Carl had no answer to this question. He was shivering as he drove home and this wasn't just because he was now soaked to the skin. He was now terrified. Carl sensed Death's net drawing in around him, leaving him with no escape.

Any second now, any second at all, the Cleaverman can come for me too! And I need that damn book, and the damn book is still in that damn house, which is now swarming with damn cops. What the damn hell am I gonna do?

The positive side of this—if there was one—was that with these fresh murders occurring, no one would ever suspect him now of murdering Jeffrey and Mike. *But that's not much help to me if I get killed before I can spend any of the money I've earned myself by killing both of them. I need that God-damned spellbook! I'm the only one left now and I don't intend dying like the others have!*

His cellphone was still turned off. He hadn't wanted anyone calling him tonight. He still didn't want any callers, at least not until he had some form of resolution to his dilemma. He didn't know for sure that Susan was dead too, but he assumed as much. *Even if she's alive she won't be much help anyway. All Susan has in her head is sex for money.*

While steering his car through the mid-night darkness, only one solution presented itself to Carl: *I'll have to try again, attempt another break-in later tonight, early in the morning when the cops must've gone for a break and none of the neighbors have woken up yet. Sure, it ain't much of a chance, but at the moment it's the only one I've got.*

On reaching home, Carl decided there was no point in sitting and waiting to die. He changed his clothes and then drove out again, looking for somewhere to get drunk instead. Not too drunk though, just enough to pass the two hours before he intended returning to the Ellsworths' house again.

He figured he'd be safer too amidst a group of people. Carl thought the Cleaverman would be less likely to attack him in front of a lot of witnesses.

The time was 1:52 a.m on Saturday morning.

CHAPTER 30

Susan

After watching the night sky for a while, Susan turned back towards the bed. She was just in time to see the transparent 'Thea Dee' apparently vanish. Thea Dee flickered out of existence like a bad movie effect. And then Susan realized that she'd been played for a fool and understood too exactly how it had been done.

That thing was a holographic projection! And the so-called Death bitch too. She was never here to begin with! Everything was a massive hoax!

Susan walked over to the bed. Staring down at and touching the spot where Thea Dee had supposedly lain only made concrete her refutal of those recent events. *It was a damn hologram!* She pondered long and hard on this, and the more she did so, the more convinced she became. And now that she thought about it, Susan realized that she'd not touched Death once in all the while they'd been conversing, nor had Death touched her.

So why then did I feel my ass burning?

She finally put that down to subconscious suggestion. She'd expected something nasty to happen while 'Death' had been threatening her, and Daddy's cigarette punishments to her teenaged behind were really the worst horror she could imagine then.

"Hey, Thea, I'm onto you! Ha ha ha! You can't fool me! Alright, the gag's over now, show yourself!"

Susan thought this would make Thea Dee Marlowe reveal herself. She expected the wealthy widow to reappear grinning from some concealed door near the closet or windows. But Thea Dee didn't show.

"Hey, Thea! Where are you? Frigging come out of hiding and pay me!" Thea Dee had paid Susan an advance of $2,500 via her website and owed her that much again as balance. Susan didn't think a woman as rich as Thea Dee Marlowe would balk paying, but . . .

"Hey, Thea, okay I'm leaving now! You can deposit the balance in my bank account!" Now a thread of doubt had slipped into Susan's mind. She doubted her own doubts. *What if I didn't imagine it all? What if Death really was here—if I actually did fuck Death and talk to her and . . . no, that's too silly to even imagine!*

But still, these fresh doubts had unsettled Susan Riley. Feeling rather nervous now, she began collecting her clothes from the floor and getting dressed. She dressed hurriedly. She felt a sudden need to get far away from Thea Dee Marlowe's house.

Thea Dee didn't appear all the while that Susan was dressing. Susan no longer expected her to. Finally, Susan pulled on her shoes and walked into the bathroom to reapply her makeup.

'DON'T FORGET TO WARN ASS-BURNING DADDY ABOUT THE BLONDES!'

The message was scrawled on the bathroom mirror in bright red lipstick. Susan gulped at the sight of it and decided 'to hell' with doing her makeup in there. She backed out of the bathroom, picked up her purse from the chair where she'd dropped it and dashed out of the bedroom. At the top of the spiral staircase, she pulled her gun from her purse.

Nobody's screwing with me again tonight!

She went slowly down the marble stairs, so as not to slip off her high-heels and fall the rest of the way. This house seemed just the right sort of place to break one's neck in.

From the bottom of the stairs, she walked straight out to the foyer, glancing neither left nor right. She didn't wish to look at any of the macabre wall-hung paintings, with their endless depictions of human agony, inhuman evil and infernal torture and brutality. She particularly didn't want to look at that painting of Death. What if when she looked at it, she found the painting blank now, as if Death had stepped out of it to go somewhere? She clearly recalled her hallucination (if it had actually been one) of Death's suicide. Ugh! That was just so creepy . . . another special effects joke for sure. Susan contemplated that maybe what she'd thought was a painting was really a large TV monitor cunningly recessed into the wall, and that she'd actually watched a CGI-animated scene from a movie. Despite which, she still didn't intend to turn and confirm her suspicions of such a massive hoax being played on her by this house's now seemingly vanished hostess.

She felt relieved once she was out of the extensive living room and crossing the foyer to the front entrance. The Ruger LC9 was still tightly clenched between her fingers, her knuckles almost bone-white from the pressure she was exerting on its grip. She was so on edge, she was guaranteed to shoot anyone who startled her.

Which was why she surprised herself by not firing when the front door of the house opened by itself as she reached for its handle. She was simply too startled to pull the gun's trigger, that was all.

She stood there staring at the Chinese chauffeur who now stood in the doorway, uncertain what would happen next, recalling the previous occasion when his unreadable face had altered shape to some kind of demonic visage, his slanted eyes switching to the appearance of keyhole slits.

The moment hung heavy with Susan's expectation of violence of some unspecified kind. Then Chang's inscrutable features altered into a smile.

He gestured to Susan's gun with obvious amusement. "Please put that away, Miss Riley. Mrs. Marlowe said both to take you back home, and to give you this."

He handed her a stuffed white envelope. "It is the remainder of your fee."

Susan put the gun back in her purse and accepted the envelope with trembling fingers. She sneaked a peek at its contents. A wad of crisp hundreds. Much too many to be just the balance half of her payment. She looked up enquiringly at Chang.

He smiled as a chill breeze blew in through the door and past him. "Madam says she enjoyed your services so much that she would like a repeat performance next Friday night. The additional money in the envelope isn't an advance payment for that, it is merely a bonus for tonight." While Susan digested this, Chang added: "And now, Miss Riley, if you'll please come on out to the car, so we can set off. It looks like it's about to rain again."

She followed him quickly, stashing her earnings into her purse as she crossed the marble patio. The payment she'd just received had served to confuse her the more. *If Thea Dee is Death—no, stop thinking like that, that's crazy—she wants to see me again, meaning I'm not gonna die .. . ? It's all just a joke?*

Before getting into the limo door that Chang was holding open for her, Susan looked back at the massive house, with its impressive atmosphere of wealth and decadence. *Thea pays well. She's definitely worth several repeat visits. But I'll insist on no more creepy jokes . . .*

She got into the limousine and Chang shut the door. The Chinese chauffeur then got into the front of the vehicle and they set off, with Susan throwing one last glance back at the building as they reached the foot of the driveway and turned onto the highway. She couldn't help herself: she felt as if Thea Dee Marlowe's house was itself a special effect—a movie set or rock video set—and might cease to exist—wink out of existence—once she was herself out of sight.

Once the limousine was again passing through the city of Attleboro, Susan relaxed. The lyrics to a Slain Jane song played through her mind:

You're the best friend nobody has,
And nobody wants,
Ain't that sad . . .

Susan wasn't sure, but she thought this was one of the band's earlier songs on which Thea Dee, and not Janet Orgasm, had sung the lead vocals.

Then her thoughts turned to her father. She hadn't seen him for a week, not since that crazy Hobart trial had commenced. The last time they'd had dinner together, he'd been complaining about how his most recent blonde girlfriend had left him, citing his jealousy as her reason for breaking up with him.

Susan suspected there might be something incestuous in her father's unrelenting genital assault on young blonde womanhood. *Is he imagining they're all me? That'll at least explain why Daddy keeps breaking up with all of them in disappointment.*

That thought both made her laugh and made her remember Death's instruction to warn her father, which made her frown.

Should I tell him or not? An imagined twinge of pain in her anus made her decide, *Yes, I'm gonna call dad right now and get it over with. I'll just joke that too much sex at his age is bad for his health.*

But just as she was reaching into her purse for her phone, it rang anyway.

At first Susan thought her father was the one calling, which would have been quite a coincidence. But the Caller ID showed it was Bobby West, one of her rich clients.

She instantly forgot about her father and became all business again.

"Hi, Bobby," she purred into her cellphone, "what's happenin' hon?"

"I got a friend in town tonight and we need a girl for some fun. Are you up for it?"

"Sure, if the money's right. What am I gonna get for this?"

"I got five grand here waiting for your pussy and ass to come collect it."

Susan grinned like a cat in the darkness. "Oh, I'll be right over. Get ready to ejaculate a lot, honey."

After disconnecting the call, she leaned forward and pressed the intercom.

"Yes, Miss Riley? We're almost at your home now."

"No, Chang, I've had a change of plans. Keep on going right past my place and turn left when you hit Center Street . . ."

After giving the chauffeur the directions to Bobby West's condominium, Susan poured herself a brandy and relaxed back sipping it. This Friday night—*Oh, it's Saturday morning now*—was turning out to be very lucrative indeed.

A brief worry about the Cleaverman flitted through her mind. She dispersed with it as effectively as one would swat a pesky fly. *Oh, Death already told me the Cleaverman won't get me, so there's nothing to worry about.*

Susan and the limo rolled on through the night. The time was fast approaching 2 a.m.

CHAPTER 31

Angela

The rain had just stopped.

Angela couldn't fight off her sense of impending doom. Each second that passed, she expected to see the Cleaverman materialize in her living room and kill her.

Almost two hours into her vigil with the spellbook, she'd still had no success in cracking the rhyme.

Angela, Maria, Mary, Marie, Rosemary, Jennifer, which is it? Okay, maybe it's a trick: his name's John, so maybe her name's Joanna?

It was useless and Angela realized it was.

Carl still hadn't contacted her, her last call had gone straight to his voicemail again, joining the queue of the previous six.

Carl Whitfield, where the fuck are you? I need you to be here with me on this! As a personal rule, Angela generally avoided profanity, but her current dire situation appeared to demand it.

To distract herself, she'd finally switched on the TV. Nothing really new, just the rehash of yesterday's events in court at the Hobart trial. She figured she might as well watch it since she'd not been in court.

She was almost amused to see how bored Judge Joe Riley appeared by what was going on. The accused, Teddy Hobart, sat with his defense team, looking resigned to his fate. Both Teddy and the DA seemed equally bemused by this crazy joke of justice they were forced to be a part of.

Angela's mind returned to her own worries. She muted the TV and got out of her armchair just as a 'Breaking News' headline began scrolling across the bottom of the screen. She figured the update would be about Paul and Leona's deaths. She had no intention of listening to that.

She got up and walked back into Mike's bedroom. There she sat in the chair by the chest of drawers and tried to think. This time she'd brought the spellbook along with her. She opened it to the Cleaverman riddle and focused her mind on the puzzle. After a while she shut the book again, nudged Mike's birthday glasses slightly to one side, then leaned her right arm on the antique chest of drawers and laid her head on her arm.

And then the room seemed to alter slightly, with the edges of things becoming just that little bit less defined, enough to make one feel uneasy without knowing why. Angela, who was already tense and nervous, never noticed this beginning of the changes.

By the time she'd realized something was amiss, a thin pillar of smoke was already swirling right in front of her, between her and the bedroom door.

Almost at the same chilling moment as she realized that her escape had been cut off, she heard the terrifying statement:

"The riddle is the rhyme; the rhyme is the riddle." Smoke spilled from somewhere, filling the bedroom and stinging her eyes.

The Cleaverman stood there staring at her, his gaze expectant. His eyes were so dark and scary that Angela almost passed out from fright. As the dizziness rode her brain, she sputtered out, "I don't know the answer! I don't know her name! Help me, someone! Somebody, please HELP!"

The Cleaverman's expectant gaze switched first to one of intense disappointment and then to one of rage. He raised his immense blade high above his ghostly black head.

"NOOOO!" Angela screamed as the blade came down and separated her left arm from her body at the shoulder. "NOOOOOO!" she screamed as the Cleaverman once more raised his cleaver . . .

Then she woke up.

Her heart was racing, thumping hard in her chest. She was still seated in the chair, with her head laid on her arm on the chest of drawers. It took her a few moments to realize that it had all been just a dream; there was no Cleaverman in the room with her. She was alive and safe, not being murdered at all.

Oh, thank God! A massive wave of relief rushed over her, like cool shower water on a hot summer day.

Angela sat up and as she did so, her hand knocked her dead brother's sunglasses off of the chest of drawers. The sunglasses flipped through the air and landed on the carpet. Her eyes focused on the floor at the time, Angela heard a slight 'click' as the glasses hit the carpet, and then watched a microSD card pop out of the left arm of the sunglasses, up near its hinge.

For a moment she stared at the glasses, then she picked them up and slid the SD card all the way out of its slot.

The sunglasses were 'spy-glasses'—they contained a miniaturized video camera. Angela had found them online and bought Mike a pair for his last birthday. She knew he and Jeffrey used the glasses to record gags—practical jokes and such like—when they were out with friends. She also suspected that they used them to make personal sex tapes (the video quality was extremely good and she remembered that before she'd shifted them, the sunglasses had been positioned facing the bed).

But had Mike's spy-glasses recorded anything last night? And if they had, what had they caught?

Angela checked the record setting on the sunglasses. She saw that it was both turned on and set to voice-activated. Then she got up from the chair and went to play the microSD card in her laptop.

***

Angela watched the video files in her bedroom, sitting cross-legged on her bed.

As she'd suspected, the positioning of the sunglasses on the antique bureau hadn't been incidental. The first recordings featured her brother, his fiancé, and their friend Rod, who'd stayed over at the house two nights ago. Lots of fellatio and masturbating one another and then both men had tag-teamed Rod, one in his mouth, one in his ass, and then they'd repeatedly switched positions. It was a fun-fuck free-for-all with lots of condom usage and ejaculations.

There were eight files of this gay (in both senses) threesome, lasting in total for about two hours—it was a 256 Gb card. Susan closed each file after determining it was more of the same.

The ninth file, however, was very different from the previous ones. This one, timestamped for 2 a.m. the next night, was recorded in the dark. The bedroom lights were off and most of what the spy-glasses captured was shadow and whatever interpretation the viewer's mind would cast on them. Then the racket began.

"What the hell is going on?" Angela asked herself aloud. She'd expected to once again see the dark, smoky ghost she'd encountered earlier tonight, but was sorely disappointed. What she could make out in the video seemed to be a man with a knife attacking her brother and his boyfriend. There were shrieks and yells and lots of limbs flailing, along with flashes of silver.

She heard Mike yelling: "What the hell are you doing in my house!? What have you done to Jeffrey!? Jeff, Jeff, answer me, baby, are you okay!?" Then there was a lot more scuffling and noise, and then: "Shit, I'm gonna kill you now, asshole. I'm gonna blow your damn nuts off!" And then commenced a lot more fighting and there seemed to be someone riding on Mike's back.

It was horrifying, witnessing what was clearly a home invasion with murderous intent. What Angela was seeing on her laptop screen was so shocking that for the moment she forgot all about her troubles with the Cleaverman.

Then, with the loud slumping of the fighting figures, the noise ended. The video cut out at that point due to the silence in the room.

With her heart seemingly in her mouth, Angela clicked on file number 10. File 10 was timestamped as being recorded five minutes after the previous one. This time the bedroom lights were on.

Carl? Carl? What the . . . ?

Angela had no words, not even in her mind. For a long stretched-out moment that seemed to last forever, her thoughts froze and her shock and horror traveled direct from the laptop's screen to her emotional response, totally bypassing her rationality. Dismay and incomprehension flooded her.

Carl? Carl?

Carl stood there, as bloody as a butcher, but lacking the apron. Jeffrey lay dead on the bed with his throat torn to shreds. Carl dragged Mike up onto the bed. Mike, his eyes open and staring, was as dead as Jeffrey and bleeding from a multitude of stab wounds. His head was almost completely detached from his shoulders.

Carl took a snort of white powder that Angela deduced must be cocaine. Then, as if he'd set the camera to record his murderous deeds, he turned towards it and grinned demonically. Then he walked out of range of the camera and the file ended.

Angela sat there in her bedroom feeling completely numb. She simply couldn't believe what she was seeing. *Carl killed Mike and Jeffrey? But . . . but . . .*

Now Angela had begun feeling really angry, which she definitely preferred to feeling scared of death. She'd really loved her brother. And to imagine that a man she'd thought she might be falling in love with had done this to him?

She clicked on the next video. This was much worse: Carl hacking up Mike's body beyond recognition, then arranging his flesh in a morbid heap on the bed . . . exactly how she'd found it yesterday morning . . . Carl sticking Mike's forearm bones into the pile of meat, arranging them so that both hands stuck out as if they were waving hello, then stepping back to admire the result.

"Yeah, looks like something a psycho would do," Carl said aloud with an evil and self-satisfied grin on his handsome face. "Dammit, I need a frigging drink!"

She watched Carl get undressed and walk out of view again. The video ended then. From the file's timestamp and its length, Angela knew what had happened next:

That would have been when he noticed he had a WhatsApp message from me—It was a quarter past three when he called me back! And all the while he was playing me for a fool, setting me up and seducing me! Carl, you goddamn shithead! Oh, how could you do this to me? Yeah, you're gonna explain it to the damn trial judge. And I know why you killed them too: it had to be for the money, that damn Whitfield inheritance. You greedy asshole!

Strands of hair got in Angela's eyes and she flicked them away with an angry gesture. She was so angry with Carl Whitfield now that the tears she felt these horrible video revelations should have brought to her eyes simply wouldn't come. Yesterday morning she'd wept her heart out, but now, the sheer extent and callousness of this brutal violence had shoved her far beyond the boundaries of mere grief. In a case like this, sadness seemed sadly insufficient.

You murdering sonofabitch, she silently raged while clicking on the next video file. *Oh, you're gonna rot in jail forever for this, you damn bastard!*

Angela watched Carl dismantle Jeffrey's corpse too. Then, really, really disgusted and angry, she got up and headed for the living room, where she'd left her cellphone. "The cops are gonna make short work of you, you lowdown murderer," she growled aloud. "In fact, if I get a hold of Jerry Townsend, I'll ask him to accidentally fill you with lead so you'll arrive DOA at the morgue!"

But when she reached the living room, her gaze flickered to the television, which was now broadcasting the news of Paul and Leona Patten's deaths. The sight of their bodies being carried out of the Ellsworths' house on rain-drenched stretchers reminded Angela of her own plight.

Oh dammit! I haven't solved the riddle either, and if the Cleaverman shows up now . . .

Angela felt enraged and sickened by Carl Whitfield. Though she hated letting him off the hook for even a little while, she'd just remembered she needed his input to solve the riddle. *He just might know the answer—Jeffrey was always insistent that Carl was a whiz at ciphers and such like. But what greedy lover boy doesn't know, is that once he's solved the Cleaverman riddle for me, he's taking a one-way trip to the stone motel.* She frowned grimly. *And I'm gonna plead with the DA to allow me prosecute Carl. I'll even fuck him for the privilege to be the one to send lover boy away for life.*

She felt satisfied with that. She'd use Carl Whitfield for the moment, and once he was no longer useful . . .

She no longer felt worried that Carl hadn't yet called her. *He has to sooner or later. Once he hears the news about the Pattens' deaths, he'll come running to me, enquiring if I know what they found out. He has to. He'll want to remain alive to spend all that money he's gained by killing Jeffrey.*

Angela smiled coldly. *But I've got the spellbook and Carl hasn't! Which means ten-to-one, he's certain to get butchered by the Cleaverman before he can even spend a dime of the money! Hahahahahaha! If that isn't ironic, I don't know what is.*

Slightly relieved and with her rage partly mollified by her plan for revenge, Angela returned her attention to the television. She at once found herself engrossed in the news. It seemed that something new had just now—at 3 a.m. on Saturday morning—developed in the Teddy Hobart case.

Angela picked up the remote and clicked up the volume.

CHAPTER 32

Teddy Hobart . . . Two Hours Ago

I did it, but hell no, I didn't do it.

Teddy Hobart lay in his cell at the Bristol County Jail and House of Correction in North Dartmouth. Late though it was, he couldn't sleep. And it wasn't just the noise of the rain keeping him awake either.

Teddy was tallish, with short black hair and a bald patch in front. The way he lay on the prison bed, with his right arm thrown over his belly, made it instantly obvious that he had no right hand.

The cell had bunks for three prisoners, but fearing a repeat performance—as in another inexplicable killing—Teddy was being housed alone in here. From what he could tell too, the other prisoners were relieved that they weren't sharing with him.

Teddy could hear the prisoners in the adjoining cells snoring. For him though, sleep just wouldn't come. He'd tried everything he could to relax his mind, but nothing was working. Now he stared through the bars of his cell at the drab corridor wall, listening to one of the guards walk the block.

"Lotsa damn rain tonight," he heard the man tell another, "though it seems to have blown itself out now."

Tonight was a bad night for Teddy. For one thing, his missing right hand was playing 'ghost tricks' on him again. He'd look down at the stump—his prosthetic hand had been taken away from him so he couldn't kill himself with it—and feel like the hand was still there. He'd feel it flexing, feel it hot and cold. Normal enough, for sure, but unnerving when you're on trial for murdering someone with it.

Worse still, each time Teddy felt that he just might fall asleep after all, just as his eyes were about closing, he'd see *her* and the shock would immediately jar him awake again.

He'd see a momentary flash of his dead wife Maddy.

Teddy Hobart had been living in dread of Maddy since the day he'd killed her. The thing was that he kept seeing her. And at the craziest of times too. He'd be eating breakfast in the jail dining hall and suddenly Maddy would be sitting beside him. Or he'd shut his eyes for a second in his cell and when he opened them again, she'd be sitting on the bed opposite his. She'd not say anything, just stare angrily at him, with that horrible stitched-up gash in her neck reproaching him as well.

Or he'd be taking a shit and suddenly Maddy would be right there in the toilet with him, standing half inside and half outside the cubicle, with her body bisected by either the wall or door. She wasn't a true ghost though—she was quite solid. Yesterday she'd even handed him the toilet paper to wipe his ass with.

And of course, Teddy was the only one who could see her.

Maddy always wore her wedding gown, which was what she'd been buried in, and she reeked of embalming fluid. Aside from her stitched-up neck, she really didn't look too bad though, but it was unnerving to see her.

Teddy had thought that by now—after she'd appeared to him almost forty times—he'd have gotten used to it, but such wasn't the case. Each of her appearances held fresh dread for him. The creepy way he felt just before she materialized was impossible to get used to. He'd just feel scared, and then he'd feel more and more scared until she left him alone again.

Most upsetting of Maddy's appearances were the times when she'd simply be sitting in midair; like yesterday in court. She'd appeared floating beside Judge Riley.

And I don't dare tell anyone 'bout that, 'cos if I do, I'll be branded 'crazy' and everyone—both prosecution and defense—are gonna be utterly delighted with that. They'll simply forget about the trial and label me as criminally insane and lock me away.

Teddy didn't intend to spend the rest of his life either in jail or in an asylum. He didn't intend to crack up and start screaming that he could see his dead wife, which might be exactly what she had in mind to accomplish by her continual appearances.

No, he hadn't meant to kill Maddy and that was that. *I loved her and I've no idea what in the hell really happened that crazy night. Yeah, I know I did it, but hell no, I didn't do it.*

Most nights since then, he had nightmares in which he relived himself committing the murder in vivid detail, tearing Maddy's throat open and gaping helplessly while her blood poured everywhere. Then he'd wake up sweating.

Hell yeah, I certainly do remember how this nonsense began. Yeah, I borrowed and read that book on black magic—The Book of Summonings. Poor, poor Maddy kept warning me to leave the damn book alone, but I was adamant about finishing reading it and I even played wizard, reading out spell after spell aloud. Then Maddy sneaked the spellbook away from me and returned it to her cousin Tommy Ellsworth and I got mad at her for doing so, and I figured that was that. But it clearly wasn't, 'cos it was the weekend afterwards that all this mess began.

Teddy desperately needed the hauntings to end.

Because if they didn't . . . The sight of him fleeing the witness box screaming would be more than sufficient evidence to have him committed.

Acting normal was tough enough as it was. Teddy felt so close to cracking up now, it was like his mind was doing its absolute best to fall to pieces on him . . . as if his brain . . . sometimes it felt to him as though each lobe of his brain had now fragmented into a hundred writhing worms of demented mental meat, and that each of those angry worms of disbelief and fear and confusion wanted to go its own way out of his head and was pounding on the insides of his skull and screaming to be set free. Since his arrest he'd constantly felt as though, if a neurosurgeon peeled back his scalp and sawed his head open, that person would find such a mess inside his skull that they'd give up their medical practice for good.

Hey, what's that?

Teddy's silent vigil of staring at the corridor outside his jail cell was interrupted by the sound of beating wings above and behind him. Startled by the loudness of the sound, he turned on the bed and stared up out of the cell window. It had just stopped raining and the clouds had cleared up. The moon was huge—unnaturally so—and framed inside it was the silhouette of . . .

Is that a winged woman? A winged . . . woman?

The figure that Teddy was seeing through the barred window was female enough, but it also had four large wings, two on either side of its slender body, one wing flapping above and below each of its spread arms.

The woman flew in place in the moonlight, not approaching nearer. Teddy, however, sensed an intense aura of evil surrounding her.

Dammit, I'm losing it! he thought desperately, looking away from the window and gripping his head between his left hand and the stump of his right forearm. *Maybe there is a conspiracy to drive me crazy after all. Then they can ditch the trial.*

Scared that Raynham and Taunton law enforcement were indeed trying to drive him out of his mind, Teddy Hobart slipped a peek out of his cell window again.

Jesus, she's still up there!

The winged woman still floated up there. And she seemed a little closer now. Teddy didn't understand what was going on, but he had the feeling that the winged specter was waiting for something. Was she waiting for him?

Then, suddenly, he felt *her* again. His dead wife. Teddy felt Maddy's creepy presence nearby, as unpleasant as if mud was being poured on him.

He didn't need to turn around to realize that just as he'd dreaded, she'd come to visit him tonight. Fright pulsed through him. *No matter what Maddy does in here tonight, I gotta control myself. I gotta keep my voice down; that way no one'll suspect anything weird's going on.*

With that resolve in mind, Teddy turned from looking at the flying woman to staring at his dead wife.

Heck! Teddy thought next in alarm, leaping up off the bed to confront her.

Yes, it *was* Maddy there in the cell with him. Wearing her dry-cleaned satin wedding dress and reeking her embalming fluid perfume as usual, with her thin face pale with death, her gray eyes like those of a grilled fish and her graying hair falling long and straight down to her waist.

But tonight, Madeline Jane Hobart wasn't visiting her husband's cell just to glare at him. This was instantly obvious, both from the cold smile on her face and from the two large knives she was now lifting as she advanced on Teddy.

"Maddy, don't!" Teddy screamed as she stabbed him. The knife in her left hand penetrated the space between his neck and right shoulder. She left the knife stuck there and, now holding her second knife with both hands, stabbed it hard and deep into Teddy's belly.

"No, Maddy, don't!"

"Hey, keep it down in there, Hobart!" a tough cop voice called from down the corridor. "You wanna dream 'bout murderin' your dead wife, do it quietly!"

The pain from the first knife stab had paralyzed Teddy, but not for long. As Maddy swiped the second knife across his belly, slitting him wide open from left to right, Teddy tried to fight her off. He hit her with his stump, but she turned her head and bit into it, stripping a massive chunk of skin and muscle off his right forearm with her teeth.

Teddy finally succeeded in pushing Maddy back with his good hand, but as she retreated, she dropped her knife and dipped both of her hands into his belly, coming up with two handfuls of his intestines. She pulled hard on these and his guts unreeled out of his belly, dripping blood all over the cell floor.

"Noooo! Hellllllllp!"

"I'm warning ya, Hobart! Better keep that goddam noise down!"

"NOOOO!" Now Maddy had begun shredding his intestines to pieces with her hands and tossing them around the enclosure.

The guards arrived and looked confused. Teddy understood what their problem was: they couldn't figure out how he'd gotten a knife stuck in his right shoulder, and even more confusing, why his guts were seemingly yanking themselves out of him in a straight horizontal line, and then separating into little pieces and flinging themselves across his cell.

Teddy looked out of the window at the flying woman again. She'd now descended and was peering into his cell through the window bars. He wanted to beg her for help, but she was smiling at him as if she was enjoying his pain. The winged woman also had the most horrible face he'd ever seen in his life, demonic in the extreme. In addition, Teddy was in so much agony anyway that he couldn't even form words anymore—each time he tried, his mouth gushed out blood instead.

He looked down from the demoness at the window to Maddy, who was laughing silently as she disemboweled him, then back up at the demoness. He realized now that her morbid gaze was also strangely welcoming.

Already confused by what they were witnessing, the two prison guards were even more perplexed when the tangled rope of Teddy's guts plopped to the cell floor as if someone had dropped it. And then—both guards saw the footmarks that appeared in the blood on the cell floor as if someone invisible was striding across the cell towards Teddy—they both gasped as the gash in Teddy's belly opened up wide and both of his kidneys flew out of him, seemingly of their own accord. After that came several other organs which neither man knew the name of.

Neither guard made any attempt to get into the cell. The man who had the ring of keys dropped it in shock. The other man puked through the bars of the cell door onto the cell floor.

And neither guard could understand why, while Teddy Hobart was being torn to shreds like this and dying, his gaze remained fixed on the window of his cell, almost as if he was staring up at the brilliant moon.

CHAPTER 33

Carl

" . . . In leaked information just reaching us, we've received news that the fingerprints on the knives used to murder Teddy Hobart belong to his dead wife Madeline Hobart. Official sources are yet to confirm this information, but if true, this will be the latest eerie twist in a case that has baffled state law enforcement from the get-go . . ."

Simply more Raynham summer craziness. Carl turned the car radio off. Head full of his own worries, he'd not been paying any attention to the bulletin anyway. Uncanny stuff happened in Raynham all the time. You either got used to it or you got the hell out of town.

Carl had just pulled up outside the Clip nightclub. But something was clearly wrong. Instead of the usual Saturday a.m. party atmosphere one expected to find here, with cars arriving and people entering and leaving, there was nothing. The parking lot was empty and all the club lights seemed turned off. The entire place looked deserted.

"What the hell is going on here?"

Then his eyes found the 'Closed Until Further Notice,' sign on the front entrance, and he winced and slapped his forehead in disgust at himself.

Carl, distracted and worried, had forgotten about Steve-O's death. The Clip nightclub wouldn't reopen for business until it had new management; that was if it ever reopened at all.

Carl sat there in his blue BMW X6, thinking that maybe he'd have to go get drunk at home after all. But then there was a sharp rapping on the front passenger side window.

He turned and saw a woman knocking on the glass. She seemed young, maybe in her mid-twenties. Blonde hair, dark eyes. Her halfway unbuttoned pink top gave him a good view of her cleavage.

196

She gestured at him to roll down the window, so he did. She looked more lost than dangerous.

"Hi," she said pleasantly, once he'd rolled down the glass, "Can you give me a ride home?"

"What're you doing here at this time of night anyway?" he asked cautiously.

"Same thing as you, I think—wanted to go clubbing, forgot the place was closed down." She grinned at him. "So how 'bout it? Can I get a ride back up to Raynham?"

He nodded and released the door locks. "Yeah sure, get in." She seemed harmless enough. Carl figured that driving her home would provide him with a distraction until he felt it was safe to attempt entering the Ellsworths' house again.

"Thanks a mil!" She opened the door and climbed into the car. Her pink skirt matched her top and she was wearing red shoes.

"Hi, my name's Bev," she said brightly, extending her hand. "Thanks so much for taking me back home. I hope you'll come in for a drink once we get to my place."

***

And so it was that thirty or forty minutes later—he'd lost track of time since she'd knocked him out with what had felt like a baseball bat—Carl awoke to find himself tied to a chair in a windowless room that he quickly surmised had to be the basement of Bev's house. His arms hung down by his sides, duct-taped to the chair's rear legs, his own legs taped to the chair's front ones.

He'd been stripped naked while unconscious. His clothes were draped over another chair on his right. Both chairs were pulled up to a rough wooden table. The table was bare except for a white ceramic bowl. The bowl contained a spoon, but was otherwise empty. Carl stared at the table and bowl, trying to figure out what was going on.

The basement door was on his right and was shut. The room was empty except for a set of shelves on the wall behind him. A single yellow bulb hung overhead.

Oh heck, what the hell have I gone and gotten myself into tonight? Doesn't this rain of poop ever end? First it's the Cleaverman trying to stop me enjoying my new wealth, and if he's not bad enough . . . now I've gone and picked up Psycho Bitch too!

He was doing his best to ignore the headache he'd awoken with.

"Hey, Bev!" he howled at the door. "Hey, Bev, come and untie me!" He doubted she'd let him go so easily, but it was worth a try. "Hey, Bev!"

She opened the door a few minutes later. She entered smiling. She was naked too and for the first time he noticed that her belly was quite swollen.

She was also carrying a gun, a silver revolver, the sight of which sent chills of fear down Carl's spine.

"Hi, honey," she said sweetly, "I've been waiting for you to wake up."

"Let me go right now!" Carl raged at her, the sight of the firearm threatening to unnerve him. "You've no right to tie me up like this!"

She giggled. "I *know* I've no right to tie you up, Carl. That's why you're downstairs in my basement." As if to emphasize her point, with a flick of her bare foot she kicked the basement door shut again.

When the door slammed shut, Carl lost hope of ever seeing daylight again, or of spending his ill-gotten gains.

"What do you want with me?" he asked. "Listen, you don't have to do this. I'm rich, I can make you rich too, Bev. Just don't do this to me."

She leaned on the table and turned, so her breasts were almost in his face. Despite his plight, he couldn't help but focus on them. They were lovely sexual cones, with juicy pink tips that, come to think of it, were swollen.

"Don't do *what* to you?" she asked him. "You don't even know what I want from you."

That was true; Carl didn't know. "Wha-wha-wha d-d-do y-y-you wa-want?"

"Nothing."

"Nothing?"

"Nothing dangerous. "First I'm gonna suck you off. Then I'm gonna feed you, and then I'm gonna set you free."

She's crazy! "Why tie me up just for a blowjob?"

"You'll find out soon enough." Then she got under the table, got on her hands and knees between his legs and began playing with his penis. Then she took his penis into her mouth and began sucking on it.

He stared down at her head bobbing in his crotch and began getting hard.

He had to admit that she was great at fellatio. And also, seeing as she'd said she'd set him free afterwards . . .

I might as well go along with it. Shit, when there's no escape, relax and enjoy the rape.

She removed her lips from his member. He spotted her eyes beneath the table's edge, staring up at him. Dark in color, they regarded him with vicious amusement. There was an unspoken hunger in her gaze. For a moment, he hoped she wasn't crazy enough to bite his penis off and try to feed it to him. *Is that why she put the bowl on the table?* At that thought, a shock of fear ran through him. But she'd resumed sucking his penis, and he managed to shrug off his worries about her and concentrate on the thrilling sensation of her mouth on his swollen manhood, and of her delightful fingers on his balls and thighs.

She rubbed a finger up the cleft of his ass and tickled his anus and he spurted fiercely in her mouth; his sexual discharge felt like a cannon going off in his crotch. She kept sucking on him, draining him of come and energy.

"Please, please, enough!" he moaned when the feel of her lips on his penis grew almost painful. He wished she'd not tied him down; he'd have pulled her head away from his crotch.

She had mercy on him, removing her mouth from his softening manhood and slipping out from beneath the table to face him again.

"That . . ." Carl gasped at her, "lady, that was one of the greatest blowjobs I've ever had in my life."

She grinned at him mischievously. "See, I told you you had nothing to worry 'bout." She leaned on his shoulder so her breasts were pressing against his right ear. "Now, you just eat up what I'm gonna serve you like a good boy and you'll be untied and out of here in no time."

Carl nodded weakly. "Yeah sure, Bev, whatever you say." Then he winked and nodded towards the white bowl on the table. "I bet it's just milk and cereal anyway."

She grinned back. "Well, you got the milk part right at least."

Carl had no idea what to think when Bev climbed up on the table and, facing away from him, squatted over the white bowl. Then he saw the black butt plug she'd blocked her ass with.

"You've gotta be shitting me!" he gasped when, after placing the gun down in front of her, she reached back and began pulling the butt plug free from her anus. Carl simultaneously began tugging against the duct tape she'd used to secure his arms to the chair's rear legs.

The plug popped free from her ass hole. Bev squealed as if it had hurt a little, then she discarded the sex toy over the side of the table and said, "No, Carl honey, I ain't shittin' you. I've been keeping this dinner nice and warm up my ass all night. Storing it just for you, and you're gonna eat it all. Baby, you're gonna love what I've got in store for you!"

Gripping both sides of the table to steady herself, she positioned her anus dead center over the white bowl. Then she grunted and her anal ring began opening again . . .

Oh, hell no, Carl thought in panic. *I gotta get out of here. I ain't eating her—!*

But then, both his thoughts and his attempts to free himself stalled when he saw what was coming out of her behind.

First was a thin dribble of milk into the bowl, then something white plopped out. Carl stared at it in confusion. Is than an egg? A boiled egg?

Another boiled and unshelled egg followed the first out of her anus, then two more and a gush of milk. Then there was a brown deluge of feces over the eggs and milk. Then more eggs and milk, then more excrement. Carl could only look on in dismay.

Bev, meanwhile was grunting really hard now—she sounded as if she was really hurting. "Just a li'l bit of protein left up my ass, honey— I must've stuffed it in extra deep, damn thing feels like it's jammed in my colon."

Her anus had shut up for a while. Now it spread again and something black emerged. The ass hole spread wider as the thing got larger and larger.

A rat! She stuck a dead rat up her ass! Oh, fuck!

Carl could only stare as the dead rat plopped on top of the mess of milk, feces and eggs in the bowl. The brownish mess was already slopping over the rim of the bowl onto the table top; this final extrusion splattered Bev's ankles and feet with shitty milk.

Bev climbed down from the table and grinned, first at the disgusting mess in the bowl, then at Carl.

"Oh, yum yum, honey. Looks delicious, don't it?"

"You've gotta be shit . . . kidding."

She looked a little upset at his lack of enthusiasm. "You don't like it, honey?"

He gaped at her in amazement. "It's a pile of shit and eggs and a dead rat. Why in the world would I like it?"

Now she looked as hurt as if she'd been his wife and he'd just criticized dinner. " 'Cos I spent ages preparing it just for you, honey." Her expression turned intense and mean. "And you're gonna eat it and love it, honey . . . or else . . ." Her gaze strayed to the gun.

"C'mon, Bev, you don't mean this," Carl pleaded. "This is all just a joke, right? What you really want is for me to eat your pussy, right?"

Bev shook her head and picked up the revolver. "Carl honey, what I desire more than anything else in the world right now, is for you to eat these soft-boiled eggs, with all of the natural seasoning I've spiced 'em up with. You can fuck me afterwards if you feel like—but eat these eggs first!"

Carl shut his eyes and refused to look at the shit-filled white bowl. "No, Bev. No matter what you do . . . YEOW!"

He instantly opened his eyes again. He had no idea where she'd gotten the knife from, but she'd just jabbed his left thigh with it. There was a little blood, but Carl couldn't dwell on his hurt, because Bev now shifted the knife to his penis.

"You either feed or you bleed," she said, sticking the knife's tip into his sandy-toned pubic hair; not cutting him, but making certain it hurt. "For inspiration, imagine your life without your dick."

"Please!"

"No. Eat up, honey."

"I can't. You've tied up my hands."

"What the hell do you think the knife is for?"

She freed his right hand and stepped back.

After a pleading glance at her, which resulted in her making a slashing gesture at him with her knife, Carl picked up the spoon and began to eat up the mess of eggs and milk and shit.

***

It was the rat that did it.

"Hey, let me chop that up for you," Bev offered nicely when Carl tried unsuccessfully to bite through its black fur with his teeth. "I'd have cut it up earlier, but it's easier to stick a rat up your butt when it's still in one piece." She looked questioningly at Carl, her eyes shining with a crazy woman's delight that she was getting what she wanted. "Should I? It's okay if you'd rather swallow it whole, but if I cut it up it'll be easier."

Carl nodded dully at her. His whole mouth was covered with excrement and it had painted his chest brown too; along with vomit from the two times he'd thrown up. He was holding the rat in his freed right hand, and both the rat and his fingers were covered with shit and egg fragments.

Carl was no longer thinking logically. His mind lacked a framework on which to hang and process his current experience. Somewhere in his distressed consciousness spun the knowledge that he was living on borrowed time—that there was a book he needed to find before the night ran out or else the Cleaverman would kill him. His shocked mind, however, no longer considered the Cleaverman as a serious threat. There seemed to be no point. Life was shit . . . and boiled eggs. His brain seemed to have relocated to his taste buds and all he could taste in his thoughts was feces.

Carl was taking solace—gaining strength to go on—from the fact that the bowl was now half empty. He'd persevered and would persevere. Emptying the bowl was a small price to pay for keeping his penis intact. *Three more eggs to go; two more turds to eat; maybe a cupful of ass-chocolate-flavored milk to drink up . . . and this damned rat.*

The shit-coated rat was about the size of his fist. There was no way he was going to be able to swallow it. If he dared try, the dead rodent would stick in his throat and choke him to death. *Maybe*—he stared dully at the white bowl—*maybe dying is actually better than finishing eating all this crap! Aw, man, even being butchered by the Cleaverman has to be preferable to this.*

Bev had meanwhile bent over the table. She collected the rat from him, laid it on the table and concentrated on slicing it up. To do this effectively, she placed her gun on the table, gripped the rat firmly in her left hand and sliced its head off with the knife in her right hand. She wasn't paying any attention to Carl.

Carl saw his chance and took it. He drew back his free right arm, then punched Bev in the head as hard as he could. The blow stunned her and she staggered back from the table. Before she could recover herself, Carl leaned forward and grabbed her revolver from where she'd left it.

"Hey, you've got my gun," Bev said when she straightened up again.

"Yeah, now frigging untie me!"

"No, I won't. You ain't finished your dinner yet." Knife raised, she took a step towards him.

Carl shot her. For a moment, as his finger tightened on the trigger of the revolver, he was scared that the weapon was empty and that he'd just dug himself into an even deeper pit, but then the gun discharged loudly, its noise in this small basement room almost deafening Carl.

More from luck than anything else, the bullet hit Bev in the neck. She collapsed to the floor and lay there twitching, with blood squirting from her throat. Her eyes focused on him and seemed to be pleading with him not to hurt her again.

Carl took careful aim and shot Bev again. This time the bullet blew her brains out. Her head jerked up on the impact, then settled down again, with the rear half of her skull missing.

Carl heaved a sigh of relief and placed the smoking revolver down on the table. Then in anger, he swept the bowl of eggs and excrement and the dead rat off the table with his hand so they splattered on Bev's corpse.

He spat and spat to clear the taste of feces from his mouth. *Crazy! . . . Psycho bitch! How in the . . . ? Shit! Just look at me!*

He took his time with getting free. Bev's knife had dropped under the table. Carl realized that the only way to reach the knife was to topple his chair over onto its side. The danger in toppling the chair over however was that he might knock himself out in the process.

Finally, he slid the chair over to Bev's body and let it fall on her, using her crotch as a pillow for his head. Then he levered himself forward and got hold of the knife.

After that he freed himself easily and two minutes later was back up on his feet.

Then he pulled the chair upright again and sat on it, staring at Bev's naked corpse. He needed to think.

Now I've another dead body to deal with.

The fact that he'd killed her didn't bother him. He was still too angry at her. *Anyone who feeds shit to people deserves to be shot dead. And what kind of a sick freak keeps boiled eggs, milk and a dead rat in their rectum all day long?* (If he twisted he could see the black butt plug where she'd discarded it.)

However, the prospect of another round of corpse cleanup depressed Carl immensely, mainly because it meant more delay in returning to the Ellsworths' house. And more arm and shoulder pain from wielding the damn axe.

Still, there was no escaping it. He'd have to cut up Bev's body like he'd done to Jeffrey's and Mike's, make her look like another victim of the Cleaverman. It was helpful that Bev lived so far out of town. Even more satisfactory to his plans was the fact that she lived alone.

By now Carl had calmed down sufficiently to plan with a clear head. The steps he needed to take were obvious, he just had to arrange his actions in the correct sequence so as to evade detection when the cops found Bev's remains.

His clothes were still draped over the back of the other chair at the table. There was no point in putting them on yet, not until the gory task of chopping Bev up was completed.

Then he reconsidered that: *Nah, I need to get dressed anyway—I gotta get the axe out of the trunk of my car. But I can't get dressed looking and smelling like this, so I gotta shower first, then get dressed and fetch the damn axe . . . then get undressed again to chop her up . . . then I'll wipe the basement down, then I'll be out of here; hopefully before anyone drives up this way and notices my ride parked out front. No, I think I'll move the bimmer closer to the house, maybe park it around the back . . .*

With that more or less resolved, Carl got up. To reach the chair that had his clothes draped on it, he had to step over Bev's corpse. While doing this, he ran his eyes over her nubile form, from her splayed feet to her shattered crown, where her brains decorated the floor around her scattered pale hair. Though very dead, she still looked strikingly attractive and obscenely sexual, this latter impression a product of how her spread thighs revealed her wet womanhood. He had the scary impression that her nipples were still hard—as though she'd climaxed while dying. For some reason that possibility scared him more than her corpse did, and he made the sign of the cross to protect himself from her ghost.

He retrieved his clothes and shoes from the chair and stepped back across Bev again. Next he picked up her gun off the table and then exited her basement and climbed the basement stairs to go find a bathroom.

Bev's bathroom was quite grimy and smelt as though it housed a dead rat somewhere. Carl turned on the shower and washed the feces, milk and vomit off of himself. Ever since Carl had imagined that dead Bev's nipples were hard, he'd been assailed by an eerie feeling like he was being watched. The feeling was here with him now in the shower. He found himself worrying that someone would enter the bathroom and hack him up with a knife. He wished he'd brought Bev's revolver into the bathroom with him.

He finished bathing without incident. Despite which he felt intense relief on leaving the bathroom alive.

Then he dressed quickly and afterwards checked the time on his cellphone. 3:38 a.m.

Time to get to work. I gotta get the hell outa here and fast at that.

While crossing Bev's living room to her front door, Carl really felt nervous.

Calm down, man. There's no danger here. No one's gonna find the crazy bitch for ages! A woman who keeps rats up her ass ain't gonna have too many friends outside of a loony bin. Maybe she's even an escapee from one and is living this far out of town so no one notices her. So no one's gonna find her either. And by the time they do, she'll have decomposed anyway. Stop worrying. Just get the axe from the trunk of the car . . . No, frigging NO!—move the damn bimmer out of sight first, then . . .

And that was when the door handle on the front door clicked down and the door opened.

Carl, who was six feet away from the door then, froze in shock. *Who the hell? I thought Bev said she lived alone. Oh, shit, I've a corpse downstairs in the basement and . . .*

Quickly, he slipped Bev's gun from his pocket and waited. He couldn't shoot this person up here—too much noise with the rain now over. He'd take he or she down to the basement and kill them down there. He shook his head. It was crazy: you killed one person, and then you had to kill another person to cover up for the one you'd killed and so on.

The door swung wide open.

"Hi, Carl honey! I'm home!"

It was Bev. The same Bev whom Carl had just left downstairs with a fatal bullet wound in her throat and her brains blown out of the back of her head. Now she was standing there on the threshold and grinning at him. She was as naked as he'd left her on the cold basement floor, but neither her neck nor head showed any signs of injury.

"That wasn't at all nice what you did to me down there," Bev said. "Shooting a woman like that, and when all I wanted to do was feed you. And after I gave you such a fantastic blowjob too." She wagged a chiding finger at him. "Call it pride if you want, hon, but I'm great at giving blowjobs. Lotsa men have told me so."

"Oh, sh-sh-sh—!" Carl stammered. His fingers opened and he dropped the gun, hearing its dull thud on the carpet. He realized he'd just disarmed himself, but it didn't matter. Fear of a kind he'd never experienced before now filled him. He gaped at Bev in terror. "Sh-sh-sh—!" Staring at her there, he seemed to lose the ability to breathe— his chest tightened up and seemed to have become a vacuum; the very act of respiration regressed to a memory of an action that he'd once performed.

The woman who should have been dead laughed and stepped inside the house. "Sh-sh-sh—? . . . You mean, 'shit?' Oh, you want some more dinner, honey?"

Carl breathed again. His throat and chest unconstricted. His body trembling, he pointed a finger at her. "You-you-you—!"

"What kinda psycho are you anyway?" Bev asked, her eyes gleaming in that insane way they did. "Killing women like that, and I was gonna keep my word and let you go too. Answer me, Carl, why'd you kill me just now?" Then she grinned brightly at him. "But that ain't a problem, honey. I ain't a girl to keep a grudge, particularly not with a guy as handsome as you are, 'specially not one with a sweet hard cock and nice tight buns and abs like you got. Tell you what we're gonna do, hon: you and me are gonna go back downstairs again and I'll make you some Saturday morning breakfast. How would you like that? I just found a rotting groundhog outside and it's keeping nice and warm up my backside now, just for you, baby, just for you . . . just a li'l groundhog, mind you, honey, there's only so much my li'l butt can handle . . . and afterwards I'll give you another world-class blowjob and then . . ."

Carl had stopped listening at her first 'groundhog.' Now he was focused on escaping from here. He was terrified, his body quaking with fear. *I killed Bev and she's not dead! She's not human! She's not human!* It was taking him all of his willpower not to shit himself. He felt like his bowels might let loose at any second. But Carl most definitely wasn't about shitting himself here and now. If he did, Bev might make him eat the excrement.

Bev was reaching out to swing the front door shut when Carl made his move. To grasp the handle she'd stepped sideways, leaving a gap between herself and the door frame. Carl darted into the empty space, not stopping when she yelped in pain as he knocked her out of his way.

Then he was running for his car. Running like the wind. There was a cold breeze blowing now and the sky was lightening as though dawn would break shortly. The leaves of the nearby trees were rustling as if they were laughing at him for being a coward and fleeing from a woman.

"Come visit me sometime, honey!" Bev called after him as reached his car and began fumbling in his pockets for the keys, hoping he'd not left them in her house. If he had . . . he'd be running all the way back home then.

But he got the keys out and got the car unlocked and leapt in.

As he twisted the key in the ignition, he gaped back at Bev. Nude and pretty, she was standing in her doorway and waving vigorously at him.

"Or better yet, I might come visit you at home," she shouted over the noise of the car engine. "Bring you some nice warm backside viddies—eggs and fresh meat! Only you can't fuckin' kill me again, hon! If you dare kill me again I'll be fuckin' pissed at you!"

Fuck this! Carl put the blue BMW in reverse and backed out of her driveway as fast as the vehicle would go. Then he put the car in forward gear and sped off, not caring if the bumpy road trashed the car's transmission.

All the time he was speeding home, he was scared shitless.

CHAPTER 34

Angela

"Hey, Ramsey, it's Angela. . . . "Thanks, man, I'm still in shock myself over Mike's death . . . Ram, I need you to track a call I received last night for me. . . . Time? At three-eighteen in the morning. . . . Yeah, 3:18 a.m. . . . You got that? . . . Ram, what I want to know is which Raynham cellphone towers did the caller's phone signal bounce off to reach my number . . . Nothing major, but I'm working on a case and I want to get my facts straight . . . comparing evidence so the defense attorneys can't pull a swerve on us again. . . . Only thing is, I need to keep this completely secret, man. The DA'll have my head if I screw this up . . . Thanks, Ram. . . . Huh? . . . Oh, Hobart? Yes, yes, it's been confirmed that his dead wife's fingerprints were on both of the knives he was murdered with. I'm so confused, no idea what I think about that anymore. Only thing I'm sure of, is that Judge Riley's going to be delighted to see the last of the case and of us all. . . ."

CHAPTER 35

Susan

Susan and her two clients were playing 'sandwich' in Bobby West's living room. They were propped up in a corner of the couch. She was lying on her back in the middle of the two men, with Bobby underneath her and Bobby's friend Jack kneeling facing her, with one of his legs on the couch, the other on the floor. Bobby was slim and handsome, Jack was large and ugly, dark and hairy. Jack had the larger penis of the two men and accommodating him was quite a stretch, but Susan was used to stretching that way.

"Oh, yeah, this ass is so tight!" Bobby gushed while fucking her with short energetic upward thrusts, which Jack matched with forward thrusts of his own while also squeezing her breasts. Bobby meanwhile kissed and licked Susan's back and shoulders.

She could feel the two men rubbing against each other inside her body, their stiff penises almost making contact through the thin wall of meat that separated her vagina and rectum. It was an enjoyably distracting feeling. It was particularly sweet when both men synchronized their thrusts so that one of them was entering her while the other was pulling out and vice versa.

Normally, Susan could reach orgasm like this, but tonight wasn't one of those times. Possibly she'd already exhausted tonight's quota of climaxes with Thea Dee Marlowe, but most likely she was just distracted. After an initial round of drinking to get everyone in the mood, she'd been having sex of one kind or the other with both men for the past hour and a half, with long pauses in-between so the guys could catch their breaths and re-inflate their erections. The living room floor was littered with ripped condom wrappers and used condoms. Both men seemed horny as hell tonight, even Bobby, who was normally shot out after two orgasms. She suspected they'd both used some hard-on pills.

She'd been paid—the five grand was safe in her purse, so now she concentrated on giving the men value for their money, and luxuriating in the feel of their hard sweaty masculinity crushing her soft feminine form between them.

While moaning sounds of pleasure, her mind wandered and wondered and she remembered and pondered tonight's adventures.

She no longer believed that Thea Dee was Death. Nor did she believe either that she'd die soon. She gasped while the men stuffed her intimately and dug her fingers into Jack's ass cheeks, then stared at the clock on the mantelpiece. The time was now four minutes to four.

"Oh wow, honey that's so deep! Oooh, I just love your rod! Yeah, baby, drill my ass like that!" *Death said I'd kill myself in three hours—that's like in thirty minutes time. Yeah, right, like that's gonna happen.* "Oh, Jack, pound my pussy harder, honey! I need your cock deep in me!" *But I'm still gonna call dad and warn him 'bout the blondes—I'll tell him a brunette psychic told me to caution him about dumb blondes. It's a great joke! Ha ha ha!*

"Yeah, baby, squeeze my tits hard. Oh-oh-oh God, oh shit, I'm goddamn cooooooming! I'm-I'm-I'm comiiiiing!"

Susan felt no guilt at faking orgasms. It was what hookers and porn stars were paid to do. That was what the client expected—a smoking hot performance for their money—not you lying there like a dead fish. If the guys who hired her hadn't wanted an active woman they could have instead masturbated to sad memories of their dead grandmothers. So Susan Riley made a point of delivering in bed.

"Oh, oh, oh, oh, oh! You guys are great," she moaned and pretended to slump back on Bobby, which seemed to set him off too, because he tensed then and spurted. Then he lay limp beneath her while Jack leaned over them both and pumped hard and furiously until he came as well.

They separated, panting as if they'd been lifting weights. Bobby fetched a CD case from his bedroom and using it as a tray, sliced up some lines of cocaine for the three of them.

Jack clicked the TV on. There was a CNN bulletin on about how Teddy Hobart had died in his cell in 'Shocking and Mysterious Circumstances.'

"Man, turn that crap off," Bobby said, staring up from snorting a line of coke. "We're here having a sex party tonight, not trying to be conscientious citizens. Though I know you damn attorneys can't help but wank over court cases."

"I've been following this one," Jack said. "It's quite intriguing."

"Man, wait till you're back in your law office on Monday. Don't'cha realize it's bad to bring work home with you?" Bobby shoved the CD case towards Jack. "Here, dude, do a few lines; they'll relax your social conscience."

After Jack had taken the CD case from him, Bobby grabbed the remote control and clicked the TV off again. Then he laughed. "Hey, Jack, I forgot to properly introduce you to our lady of the night."

Jack, rolled up hundred-dollar-bill connecting his nose to the CD case, tilted his head. "What're you on about, Bobby? She's hot as hell and a fantastic lay—what more do I need to know 'bout her?"

Susan knew what was coming, but couldn't help laughing anyway.

Bobby grinned broadly. "Since you're so interested in the Hobart case, let me introduce you to the presiding judge's daughter—Susan Riley."

Jack's eyes widened as he turned to her. "You're Joe Riley's daughter?"

She nodded, then gestured to the CD case. "Hey, man, don't hog the coke. I gotta relax my conscience too."

Jack reigned in his surprise, then bent over the lines of cocaine again. When he handed Susan the CD case and improvised straw, he asked, "Doesn't your dad have a problem with what you do for a living?"

She shrugged, noting in passing that the CD they were using as a coke tray was Kimchi Chocolate Stereo's *Optimal Heresy* EP. "Sure he does, but . . . hey, we all gotta make some money." Then, not wanting to get bogged down in questions of family and morality, she skillfully changed the subject: "I assure you tho', my dad's gonna be utterly delighted that this Hobart case is over. You guys have no idea how much it pissed him off. He'd be so angry on the phone when I called him that—"

"Hey, you two," Bobby said, "no talking shop—let's screw some more."

So that's what they did. Their eyes bright, their minds on fire, their nerves tingling from the white narcotic powder, they resumed their sexual activities.

"Let's go into your bedroom," Susan suggested to Bobby when he grabbed her breasts. "The bed will be much more comfortable."

"Our long dicks can't wait that long," Jack said, stroking his erection and then grabbing her buttocks and squeezing them hard.

"It's just five yards to the bedroom door," Susan protested with a giggle.

"But this five inches is in too much of a hurry," Bobby said, pointing down at his stiff and throbbing penis.

Susan burst out laughing. While Jack fondled her ass and ran his fingers up and down the cleft of her buttocks, Bobby moved the coffee table over to near the television so that they had almost the entire rug to themselves.

This time, Susan got on her hands and knees, then Bobby plugged her mouth with his penis while Jack filled her rectum with his larger one. They rocked back and forth like that, with Jack holding Susan's hips and pounding her really hard. With her mouth full of penis, Susan couldn't make any erotic noises even if she wanted to, so her mind could wander all it liked. She sucked Bobby's manhood automatically. Fellatio was something she didn't need to think about anymore. She'd performed it so many times that it was second nature now.

Spurred by Jack's question, her thoughts kept going to her father. If only the old guy could see her now. *He'd have a heart attack for sure. Maybe I should take a selfie—me, with my nose powdered with coke and with two dicks up my front and back holes—and email it to him. Ha ha ha!*

She'd done so once before, when he'd pissed her off. That time, he'd asked her uncle Peter Hathaway, a preacher here in Raynham, to caution her on the error of her evil ways.

Back then, she'd had Marie Beck—her roomie at the time—stick four cigarettes up her butt while she lay on her back naked with her legs folded up on her breasts. Marie had then lit the cigarettes, and while they burnt and smoked, had taken a series of increasingly lascivious photographs of Susan. (They'd had a real giggle while doing it. Marie was a cop now and they still laughed uproariously over what they'd done whenever they saw each other.)

Susan had emailed the photos to her father on his birthday, the email headed: "Happy Birthday From My Burning Asshole, Judge Daddy!"

Her father hadn't spoken to her for six months after that. She'd figured the photo that had really upset him had to be the best of them all: her legs folded up against her breasts again and her vagina packed with burning cigarettes—Marie must have wedged about fifteen of them in there—and the inscription: 'Judge Daddy's Little Whore Wishes Him Many Happy Returns' scrawled across the white cheeks of her ass (which she was spreading wide so that her anus gaped) with red Sharpie.

She tensed for a moment while Jack pounded her ass extra-hard. *This guy's like a frigging Jackhammer! Doesn't he get laid at home? He's wearing a wedding band. Maybe his wife hates anal.*

She thought of her father again and did her best to grin around the penis gagging her. *I really don't think I'm doing this just to piss dad off anymore. There must be something I get out of it too, and not just financially.*

She heard Bobby and Jack slap palms over her body, then shake hands. "Oh, this is some prime French asshole," Jack groaned as he fucked her, while Bobby grunted assent, his hips tensing by her head as he approached his climax. Finally the two men joined hands across her back and synchronized their thrusts into her entrance and exit holes. She rocked with them, slackening her throat so Bobby's penis was able to slide right into its depths. Both men quickly ejaculated and fell back on the bed again. Both of them lay panting, their erections dwindling in their condoms, their bodies wet with sweat. Susan felt cooler and less sweaty since she hadn't been doing any work.

"Yeah, that was great," Jack gasped with great enthusiasm. "I gotta have you around more often, baby."

She gave him a wide hooker grin. "I'll come whenever the price is right, honey. And rest assured you'll definitely come too. Lotsa times in fact."

She could tell they were both done for the night. Bobby was languidly smoking a cigarette, and with the way Jack was gasping for breath, she figured he'd used up all his own libido too for the time being. So she left both men lying there and went to have a shower. If either man wanted more sex later, a blowjob should suffice to settle them.

213

Walking through Bobby's bedroom, she smirked at the neatly made-up bed. *All that sex would have been much more enjoyable in bed—I might've even come myself—but of course, the customer is always right.*

She remembered the intense stares of coke-fueled lust in both men's eyes as they'd borne her down to the rug and penetrated her, and the frenzied sex that had followed. She laughed. "Yeah, those five inches couldn't wait to walk five yards alright. Neither could the other seven inches."

Laughing at that, she stepped into Bobby's bathroom.

While her chosen mix of hot/cold water spilled over her, she stared out of the bathroom window. The sky was quite light now, Saturday about to break dawn.

She deliberated on what to do today.

Well, first of all, once I get home I'm gonna sleep till noon. Then . . . I haven't got any clients this afternoon, so it's a perfect time to drive over to Attleboro and visit that shoe shop. I need some pink shoes to go with that new handbag I bought last week . . . and those really high heels with the thong straps . . . and the matching bikini . . .

The water felt nice and warm. The shower peppered her skin sensually with its little jets. She ran the soap across her breasts as if she were masturbating. *Oops, I forgot Carl. I need to call him and . . . now that he's wealthy again, I'll ask him to take me shopping. During the trip to Attleboro I'll have more than enough time to talk that big-dugged cow Angela out of his life. Some half-priced sex won't hurt either, or even a freebie—but of course I'll charge him extra next time.* She yawned. *Yeah, so that's my plan for the day. Sleep, call Carl . . . no it'll be better if I call Carl before I go to bed, so he doesn't make other plans, possibly even to see that bitch Angela.*

Susan suddenly felt weird. She realized that even though the shower water was a lovely warm temperature, she'd begun shivering as if she had a cold or a fever. And all of a sudden she sensed something eerie in the air. Something inexplicably unnerving.

She turned off the shower. Without its warmth wrapping her in a liquid blanket, the chill quickly intensified. Susan just as quickly realized that she wasn't shivering from a physical sensation of cold, but rather from fear. Yes, suddenly she was deathly frightened without knowing why.

She grabbed a towel from the towel rack and stepped up to the bathroom door.

"Bobby, honey? Jack?"

But of course the bedroom was as empty as she'd left it five minutes ago. And now the door from the bedroom to the living room was shut. *Did I shut the door when I came in here? Yeah, I might have.*

Still feeling her inexplicable fright, Susan stepped out into the bedroom. She toweled herself dry and listened. She could hear voices out in Bobby's living room. Soft, then louder. She leapt in place at a loud yell of pain.

Are they beating each other up? Wrapping the towel around her body, she hurried to the bedroom door to fling it open and see what was going on out there.

A loud noise made her jump. She leapt back from the door in fright and discovered that her teeth were chattering.

What the hell is happening? She couldn't explain it—the fright was just there, filling her like bad juju. Something was wrong out in the living room.

She could feel it, she could sense it. The wrongness—call it 'evil' if you liked—was seeping through the walls and drenching her, similar to how the shower water just had. But where that dousing had been warm and soothing, stirring erotic feelings in her loins and breasts, this dousing was chilling and abrasive—as if her nerve endings were being run over a cheese grater—and the only feelings it produced were those of sheer terror.

She heard a scream. It sounded like Bobby screaming. Or was that Jack screaming as if he'd just been castrated?

He's killing him! Yes, he is. I need to call the cops!

But just who was killing who? Susan didn't know and she needed to find out. And the only way to do that was to open the living room door. And she also needed to open the door because her purse was out there in Bobby's living room and both her gun and her cellphone were in her purse. Her protection and her connection to the outside world were out there.

While she decided what to do, a rain of staccato sounds like muted gunfire spilled in through the shut door. It sounded like Bobby and Jack were punching each other out.

She looked around. No, Bobby didn't have a phone here in his bedroom. His cordless was outside in the living room.

Unable to control herself and realizing that if she didn't do something right away she'd soon start shrieking like she was insane without knowing why, Susan quickly opened the bedroom door.

Then she stood staring. She couldn't believe her eyes. The most far-out scenario she could imagine wasn't half as insane as what she was looking at.

Bobby West lay in pieces on his blood-drenched couch. His body was neatly arranged too—his severed head up at one end, his severed feet down at the other, with the rest of him arranged in sequence, and with about four inches of space between contiguous parts of him, like for instance, his lower legs and thighs. And so it proceeded up the length of his entire body. The one exception was Bobby's belly, which was a shredded mess: a four-foot-square area in the middle of the couch was covered with exploded meat. The couch itself was chopped up, bloody foam spilling from the rents the killer's giant blade had made in it while butchering Bobby.

It's the Cleaverman!

A dark, brooding and ominous gaseous swirl hovered beside Bobby's corpse, an arm like woven tendrils of bonfire smoke raising then slamming down the biggest cleaver Susan had ever seen, down into the mess of Bobby's abdomen.

Thunk!

Susan shrieked as blood flew and gore spewed. Bobby's already destroyed torso was destroyed even more.

The evil present in the living room was discernable by the five senses. Susan *felt* the evil pressing on her, she *smelt* it, and she could *taste* its foulness on her tongue and filling her throat. Sound-wise, it hummed in her ears and the Cleaverman also seemed to be breathing. And then there were the other sounds to deal with too: the whistle of the cleaver through the air, its thudding impact in flesh and bone and the underlying wood, then the squishy noise of its removal, along with the splatter of blood on fresh surfaces and the splat of flesh on the same.

And of course she had the visual picture of it all—the Cleaverman himself—horrible, horrible, exceedingly horrible. Susan couldn't see his face yet because he was looking away from her. He was still mostly intangible, though much less so than on that scary night at Tommy and Nicole's house when they'd summoned him from the darkness.

Then she remembered Jack. *Where is he? Has he escaped?*

But no, Jack's naked body lay between the coffee table and the TV. From where she stood, he seemed to have a deep and wide gash in his back, as though someone had been trying to chop him in two from behind but hadn't quite succeeded. Not yet anyway. The limp way that Jack lay and the wide red stain on the carpet around his body assured Susan that Jack wasn't about going anywhere.

Oh, Jack's jackhammered his last asshole for sure!

She was surprised at her own joke, at how calm she now felt. Well, not exactly calm, but despite the horrors before her, she felt that she had an excellent chance of getting away alive. *Death said the Cleaverman won't kill me! I'll kill myself. And I'm not about doing that, so . . .*

She felt supremely confident about this. The question now was how to safely leave Bobby's condo. The Cleaverman was standing opposite the TV, and the living room door was over on his far side. Susan would have to walk past him to reach it. Hell no, she wasn't about attempting that.

Bobby lived up on the fifth floor, so she couldn't exit through any of his windows. But the condo's back door led out to a rear balcony which connected to a zigzag metal stairway designed to also function as a fire escape and she realized she could escape that way.

Susan turned to flee that way, but then she remembered her money. *Hey! There's nine thousand five hundred dollars of my hard-fucked cash in that purse and no way in hell am I running away and leaving it for the police to hold as evidence. And by the way, where are the damn cops? The police station's only half a mile away! And this is a goddamn condo, for God's sake! Didn't anyone hear Bobby's screams?*

The Cleaverman still wasn't looking her way—the demonic smoke-creature seemed completely unconcerned about her, which she figured bought her a few seconds. Now he was chopping Bobby's head into little pieces, the thudding sounds of which reinforced to Susan her need to hurry and get away from here as fast as she could.

Where's my purse? Where's my purse? Where'd I drop it again?

As she watched the ghostly figure chop Bobby West into smaller and smaller pieces, her confidence of a moment before crumbled like a trampled biscuit. Yes, Death had said the Cleaverman wouldn't kill her, but still, hanging around and watching him work seemed like a very bad idea.

Susan trembled like an oak leaf dreading its autumn fall. As one part of her mind quaked with horror and atavistic dread, another tried to understand how this was even possible in what was supposedly a modern and rational world. Cause and effect ruled in everyday life, or rather they should rule, except one knew drunken fools like Mitch Mullins, who leapt to donate blood to the paranormal blood bank.

So, Mitch wound up with both his balls cut off and pulped to mush? Well, it serves him right for getting us all into this supernatural mess.

That however, was neither here nor there. Now's problem was the Cleaverman, who wielded his glittering blade with the kind of fury one reserved for one's choicest enemies—Susan winced and her butt tightened sympathetically—or maybe teenaged daughters who consistently flunked their exams and in so doing extinguished their doting father's hopes of their overachieving in life.

The blade rose and fell and the heap of raw bloody meat that had recently been making love with her became progressively less like chopped-human and more like burger patty.

Desperate now, she scanned the living room for her purse. And now her primary consideration wasn't even the money. Susan considered forgetting the purse, but decided that doing so would be foolish. *My ID's in that purse too. Dad's gonna be fucking irate if the cops find any evidence of me being here tonight! Ballistic won't even start to describe it! Which reminds me—my gun's in there too!*

Then she spotted her purse. It was on an armchair, wedged under a throw pillow.

Thankfully, the armchair in question was on Susan's side of the ghostly murderer, not over by the entrance, although to retrieve it she would still have to get close to Jack's corpse.

She dashed forward and grabbed the purse, taking care not to spill its contents. She couldn't help looking at Jack though—she couldn't control the impulse. Hidden from view by the coffee table at her previous position, now she saw that the entire top of Jack's head—everything above his ears—was missing, sliced off in a clean bloody line. The angle at which his head was bent meant that she couldn't see inside his skull, but she'd seen enough.

Her heart racing like mad, Susan turned and dashed for Bobby's back door. She'd managed to keep the bath towel wrapped around her, but avoiding a display of public nakedness was hardly on her mind now. She just had to get away. Seeing Jack had reinforced to her mind the stupidity she'd exhibited in remaining to pick up her purse.

I must've been crazy to keep staring like that. What's the matter with me!?

She reached the rear door, unlocked it and slid back its heavy bolt, then yanked the door open and dashed outside.

And instantly halted. She'd almost run right into the Cleaverman. *Wha . . . ? How the . . . ?*

Somehow, the very creature she was fleeing from had gotten outside before her. The Cleaverman stood there on the balcony, as insubstantial as skywriting, his sooty form outlined against the night by the faintest of pale radiances, the smoky material forming his body tossed and shredded by the wind that blew over the balcony. The wind sliced through him, displacing parts of his body into dangling tentacles like shredded cloth that flapped free before fusing back to his ethereal substance. His feet seemed both to touch and not touch the floor.

Now too Susan saw the Cleaverman's dark face. A ghostly face that wasn't even really there. Eyes like abandoned coal mines, nostrils like tar pits and a mouth like a never-ending chasm. Hair like a cap of dirty rags was draped over his skull.

Those murky eyes. They bored through her like drills.

Susan gaped at the Cleaverman on the balcony. The blue metal stairs she'd sought to reach for safety were visible through the gaps in his body; at once so near and so far away. She gaped down at his right side, where his cleaver, the only substantial thing about him, hung in his ghostly fingers. The gigantic blade dripped with blood; the blood of the two men she'd just slept with. Along with the wind slicing through the Cleaverman blew gusts of intense evil also. These evil breezes swirled around Susan and caressed her in the doorway.

With a terrified shriek, Susan backed into the house again and slammed the door. She quickly relocked the door. She was about also sliding the bolt back into place when she saw that the Cleaverman's body was already passing through the door, tentacles of his paranormal substance seeping effortlessly through the hard wood and then wavering like fingers questing for her.

She turned and ran back to the living room. He was coming for her, she knew it.

In her terror she found some courage. Once she was in the living room again, she made no attempt to flee to the front door. She was certain the Cleaverman would be waiting for her outside that one too. Instead, she got her Ruger LC9 pistol out from her purse, then whirled to face her evil pursuer.

The Cleaverman was already approaching her, his ghostly feet seeming to float over the rug.

"The riddle is the rhyme; the rhyme is the riddle," he said, fixing her with a questioning look.

Susan thought: *Leona said this is a question about his wife's name! What's his wife's damn name?*

"Is her name Maria?" she asked the Cleaverman. "Or maybe Megan, or maybe Cassandra?" *Shit, Sue, try to remember some outlandish names!* "Or Lana . . . Brooke, Barbara . . . Sasha . . . ?"

The apparition's facial expression switched from questioning to angry. He began raising his cleaver.

"Joanna or Danni . . . Lizbeth . . . Ivanka?"

The blade was coming down. Susan flung herself away from it, landing on the coffee table. Lying there on her back and with Jack's arm digging into her side, she began firing.

Bang! Bang! Bang!

The bullets from the LC9 streaked through the Cleaverman's body and punched holes in the condo wall.

Bang! Bang! Bang!

The Cleaverman once more turned to face Susan. If his evil aura had terrified her before, now that it was focused on her it rendered her almost nerveless with terror.

The blade streaked down again. Susan twisted to get out of its way. She rolled left, but instantly realized she'd rolled on top of Jack, and rolled back again. As she fell off the coffee table onto the rug she felt a shattering pain in her left arm. She looked back at it and shrieked. Her left forearm—everything beneath the elbow—was missing. She looked up. Her forearm lay on top of the coffee table. She looked back at the fresh stump, which was gushing blood freely.

Terrified, Susan gaped up at the Cleaverman. "Genevieve! Magda! Carmella!" she screamed, desperate to save her life. "Rosa! Irene!"

But the Cleaverman's enraged look never altered. The giant blade came down again and bit into her left knee.

This time, when Susan got through screaming, she gasped in disbelief. The Cleaverman had split her entire left leg into two, all the way down from thigh to ankle, completely separating the halves, so that it now looked like she had two thin legs instead of one normal one. She could see her flesh and separated bones inside the ghastly wound; and blood, seemingly buckets of dripping blood.

Oh no! I can't die like this! she thought desperately as her gaze flicked over to the couch, at the mess that remained of Bobby West. *Better that I die by my own hands than this way! I'd rather kill myself than end up like Bobby!*

The Cleaverman's evil gaze brooded. His giant cleaver removed her right ankle.

Susan suddenly realized that despite her agony, she'd not dropped her gun. She hoped she still had at least one bullet left in the Ruger LC9 with which to end her own life.

Then she relaxed and grinned. She laughed up at the Cleaverman, who was just raising his giant cleaver again. The blade hovered in the air as if its owner wasn't sure where to hit her next.

"How dumb of me to ever doubt that," she said aloud, greatly amused by the pathetic absurdity of her situation. "Of course I do have bullets left in the damn gun. How the hell else am I gonna be able to commit suicide?"

Still laughing, Susan Riley shoved the barrel of her pistol into her mouth and pulled the trigger, feeling a split-second's satisfaction and relief when the gunshot noise assured her that she'd succeeded in ending her own life before her phantom attacker could.

Had Susan been facing the wall clock then and been able to see the time, she'd have realized that Death's grim prediction had come true: it was now precisely 4:26 a.m. She'd died exactly three hours after Death had told her she would.

CHAPTER 36

Cleaverman

Once the woman was dead, the Cleaverman got down to his grisly task of dismembering her and the other male corpse.

He worked expertly at this job and very quickly reduced both bodies to little more than meat and bone meal.

But he felt sad while wielding his mighty blade.

This woman had had the right idea—names. *Her* name—the name he needed to know. Once he knew *her* name, this cycle would end.

But she'd gotten the name wrong. And now she rested with Death.

But there were still three others. Would *they* know the answer to the riddle? He frowned down at his cleaver, which once more hung pristine clean, razor sharp and gleaming like a mirror, by his side. If they too didn't know the answer, Death would soon welcome them also in her grim clutches.

By now the Raynham police force, alerted by the gunshots, were busy destroying the front door of Bobby West's condo with a battering ram to let themselves in.

But by the time the policemen entered the living room and stared speechless at the gory remains of the three recent lovers, the ethereal and deadly John Cleaverman had already vanished.

CHAPTER 37

Carl

A rogue breeze rustled Carl's bedroom window drapes and made him shiver. He woke up and sat up.

It was bright Saturday morning. Carl though, didn't feel bright in the least.

After escaping from Bev's house, Carl had fallen asleep from sheer exhaustion.

He'd not slept well though. He'd had a horrible nightmare. A vivid and nauseating nightmare.

In Carl's nightmare he was lying on a wooden altar, bound and helpless, while a giant pink anus that was bordered by buttocks the size of mountains distended next to him. Then an equally giant wolf made of feces pushed its way out of the anal cave and began eating him.

"Worship Bev!" the shit-wolf howled as it feasted on Carl. "Worship great Bev!"

Even now that he'd woken, Carl kept seeing Bev's pale pink ass hole spreading and the dead rat's black head emerging as if from a cave; the ass spreading yet more and the rat plopping down onto that mess of shit and eggs . . . and then himself bound and helpless and being forced to eat it up.

And then I killed her and she came back to life! She goddamn came back to life again!

His mouth tasted funny. The horrible taste made Carl get out of bed and brush his teeth. While brushing them, he stared at the mirror over the washstand. His handsome face looked haggard and drawn, like he'd aged overnight.

I look scared. Hell yes, I'm scared. More scared than I've ever been before in my damn life! What am I gonna do now?

Carl realized that he now had *two* problems. Two ginormous problems.

The first problem was of course the Cleaverman. He needed to find a solution to that dilemma. *I was too damn scared last night to return to Tommy and Nicole's place and see if the police had left for awhile. And by now, their house is gonna be swarming with cops again.*

On getting in from his ordeal at Bev's, Carl had instantly tried calling both Leona and Paul Patten. His call to Paul's phone had gone unanswered. Leona's phone had been answered by the couple's young daughter Sandra, who sounded drowsy, like she'd just gotten out of bed. Sandra Patten had told Carl that her parents weren't home. Sounding puzzled, the girl had then explained that her parents had left a note on their bed saying they'd had to hurry out of the house and to call them in case of an emergency.

Carl had thanked the child and hung up. Then he'd sat shivering, realizing he'd *not* been wrong, that he *had* seen the cops bringing Leona's and Paul's remains out of the Ellsworths' house. Then his exhaustion had overcome his terror and he'd fallen asleep and had his nightmare.

Avoiding becoming a victim of the Cleaverman was Carl's number one problem.

Carl's number two problem—and paradoxically, the one he currently found the more terrifying—was Bev. *She said she might visit me at home!* Carl hadn't seen the Cleaverman, but he'd both met and had sex with Bev and then . . .

Help me, somebody! Each time he heard a movement in the corridor outside his apartment, Carl imagined it was dead (undead?) Bev coming to visit him with her white bowl and her ass full of eggs and shit and—*Did she actually say a rotting groundhog?* After his nightmare, Carl no longer doubted that Bev had been telling him the truth, that she *had* stuck a dead groundhog up her rectum . . . just for him.

So, it's either a ghostly executioner is gonna come and kill me 'cos I don't know his wife's name, or a psycho zombie chick's gonna come and feed me poop!

He didn't understand how a simple foolproof plan to enrich himself could have paddled so far up Shit Creek.

He went into the living room and powered up his laptop. The only way out he could figure now for himself was to research non-stop all day long, as if his life depended on his finding a complete version of the Cleaverman riddle—because it actually did.

His phone rang.

Carl scowled at the cellphone screen. *Dammit, it's Angela again. Is this the twentieth time she's called me or what?*

Carl was in two minds about Angela Rossi. On one hand he was relieved that she was still alive—mainly because it meant one more human shield between himself and death. On the other hand, the very thought of her irritated him. He hated how she kept calling him, as if there was more between them than just dinner and a fleeting kiss.

And a lot of corpses too, he corrected himself. *We're connected by six or seven corpses.*

After one more glance at the phone, Carl dropped it beside him and reached instead for the TV remote.

He clicked the television on and then almost instantly dropped the remote control as if it was a rattlesnake.

No! No! No!

". . . Two hours ago, a team of police officers and FBI agents forced their way into the Briarcliff Road condominium home of Mr. Robert West to discover a terrifying scene of massacre . . ."

His mouth hanging open in shock, Carl sat and trembled as the news bulletin filtered through him, each word filling him with its individual quota of dread. The newsreader was a young Mexican man in a cream-colored suit who himself looked both confused and terrified, as if he expected to be the psycho murderer's next victim.

". . . Initial investigations have revealed one of the victims to be Miss Susan Riley, daughter of Judge Joseph Riley, currently the trial judge in the Teddy Hobart murder case, which itself took a bloody and ghastly turn this same night when Mr. Hobart was murdered in his jail cell under extremely suspicious circumstances . . ."

Susan's dead! Carl felt as if he was trapped inside a massive garbage compactor and it was closing on him. At any moment now he expected himself to implode into a thousand bloody pieces.

". . . Raynham law enforcement officials are baffled as to how the murderer escaped the scene of his crime with the building surrounded and both house doors locked from within . . ."

Carl's phone beeped a message notification. He snatched it up and made a face at the screen. Angela Rossi again. What was the woman's problem? Couldn't she just leave him alone? Call after call after call . . . and now texts too?

Carl, if you're alive, answer the damn phone. It's frigging urgent! It's a matter of life and death!

Carl had no time for Angela's paranoia; he had more than sufficient paranoia of his own to deal with. He dropped the phone again. *I daresay it's urgent, you silly cow. I'm gonna be killed next, I can just feel it!*

His phone beeped again. Another message notification. After confirming that this message was also from Angela, Carl didn't bother reading it. He turned his phone off. Then he turned the television off also.

Then he made himself a cup of coffee. After which he began desperately surfing the internet, looking for a solution to his problem.

All of a sudden, his concerns had inverted themselves. Carl was no longer worried in the least about Bev showing up. He'd gladly eat Bev's shit if it would keep him alive. All that filled Carl's mind as the minutes ticked away into hours was finding a complete version of the Cleaverman riddle and ensuring his own survival.

***

Two hours later, Carl was no closer to ensuring his own survival. By now he was biting his nails with nervousness. His search of the internet had turned up nothing—just the same blanked-out version of the Cleaverman riddle.

And he'd accidentally compounded his nervousness. After searching for an hour and realizing he needed to take a break, Carl had turned on the TV again. By the time he'd realized he'd made a mistake he'd already dropped the remote and was already riveted to a gory description of exactly what the Cleaverman—who the non-superstitious cops were describing as the Raynham Butcher—had done to Leona and Paul Patten.

Carl had sat listening, staring hypnotized at the TV screen while blindly feeling about him for the remote control so he could turn the TV back off, which finally resulting in him knocking the remote off the couch and onto the floor, an action which broke the morbid spell that had entranced him. He'd grabbed the remote off the floor and turned off the television. And then for good measure, to ensure he didn't repeat his mistake and re-traumatize himself, he'd unplugged the TV from the wall.

Now Carl was busy pacing his living room carpet, walking rapidly as if trying to escape his fate.

That goddamn riddle must be available somewhere. I gotta get hold of the book! But the cops! Screw the cops! They don't live there, they'll have to go home soon and then I'll . . . but what if the Cleaverman shows up before the cops leave the Ellsworths' house. Dammit . . . I'm screwed . . . I'm screwed . . . I'm—!"

Carl jerked to a halt like he'd walked into an invisible net. He'd heard something. *What the hell was that?*

The sound came again and he almost relaxed. It was just someone buzzing his front door. Then he was instantly nervous again. *That has to be Bev. It has to be! The crazy biatch has come to visit me just like she threatened and I'm . . . !*

Imagining he already smelt feces in his living room, he hurried into his kitchen and grabbed a large cleaver. Sure, bullets hadn't killed Bev for good, but maybe chopping off her head would work.

The buzzer kept ringing. The sound filled Carl's brain as if whoever was at his front door was trying to drive him insane.

But if I kill her and she stays dead, I'm gonna go to jail. No one's gonna believe she resurrected that first time! They'll think I've committed a regular murder, not paranormal self-defense. Shit, I'm screwed. I'm totally screwed.

The buzzer kept ringing. It looked like Bev wasn't about going anywhere. Carl thought of calling 911, but didn't. He knew that by the time the police arrived, Bev would have made herself scarce, and then he'd be charged with making prank calls and wasting precious police time while the town was in the middle of a serial killer crisis.

If only they knew the frigging truth. Oh, God, what am I gonna do now?

Carl looked desperately around his living room. *I don't own either a Bible or a crucifix! If I did, I'd . . . Hey, dude, think—how 'bout if you just eat Bev's damn poop and eggs so she goes away and then you can forget about her and get back to working on your real problem?*

Carl finally rushed across to the door and peered out of the spyhole, which, having already made up his mind on who his visitor was, it hadn't previously occurred to him to do.

He was both surprised and relieved. It wasn't Bev out there, but instead Angela Rossi. Angela had a frightened yet determined look on her face, like she was prepared to stand there all day ringing his buzzer except he let her in.

So he let her in. She seemed to leap back when the door swung open, but then she sagged with visible relief.

"Hi," she told Carl, then pushed her way past him into the living room.

Carl locked the door, then followed her. "What . . . what . . . ? This isn't a good time for visits. Look, I'm right in the middle of something important."

Ignoring his protests, Angela walked over to an armchair and sat down. "You goddamn asshole. So you've been home all this while. You could at least have replied my phone calls."

He stared at her. She looked extremely pissed off. In passing, he also noted that she was wearing tight black pants and an even tighter white tee shirt that showed off her mountainous breasts and valley-deep cleavage to what would have been, under other circumstances, devastating effect. She didn't seem to be wearing a brassiere either. Carl found himself torn between Angela's breasts and her anger.

"I . . . I . . . I've been busy," he finally sputtered at her.

Angela smiled coldly. "So, when you didn't reply . . . Carl, you jerk, I've been calling you for four hours. You didn't reply, so I decided to come over and see if the Cleaverman had already paid you a visit."

"I've been trying to find a solution to the Cleaverman riddle," Carl said in his own defense, then he walked to the couch, sat down and picked up his laptop again. "It's hopeless though. I can't find a complete version of the rhyme anywhere."

Angela laughed. "You could have saved yourself the bother. I've got the book here with me. That's why I've been calling you all morning."

CHAPTER 38

Connection

Carl felt an intense surge of relief on hearing that, like what he imagined an about-to-be-boiled lobster might feel if it was suddenly saved from the chef's pot and returned to the sea again.

He looked at Angela expectantly, his gaze requesting her to produce the spellbook. But there was something else in those dark eyes of hers, something deeply forbidding, that made him draw back from her as if she was about to bite him. Even before Angela's next few sentences rocked him to his very core, Carl realized that she was extremely angry with him.

"Where is it?" he asked when she made no sign of pulling it out of her large brown handbag. "We need to—"

"Not so fast," she said, silencing him with a raised hand. "There's stuff we need to discuss first."

"Angel, the damn Cleaverman wants to kill us both. What could be more important than our damn lives?"

She laughed, and it was a cold laugh that chilled Carl through and through. It wasn't an amused laugh. The sound emerged from Angela's mouth without affecting her facial features. Her homely face remained set like a death mask. Her thin and pale lips were grimly parted, the fake mirth vibrating them in its passing like a winter wind fluttering the drapes of a suicidal widow's bedroom windows. Her eyes were as emotionless as frozen jelly. Finally she said: "My brother's life and *your* brother's life, which you took away by killing them."

Carl stared at her for a moment, feeling numbed as the words sank in. She knew? How the hell could she know?

"Oh, no," he said, making a show of shaking his palms at her to emphasize his plea of innocence. "Hell no—I didn't do that. Hey, baby—don't you dare accuse me of that. That was the Cleaverman's doing."

Angela smirked. Then, leaning forward in her chair, she handed her cellphone over to Carl.

Carl accepted the cellphone with shaky fingers. Once again, he had that feeling of being stuck in the jaws of a compactor that was about to pulverize him; as if he'd strode unawares into a minefield from which there was no possible escape without losing some part of his body.

The phone screen flashed damning images at him. His heart dropped into his stomach. He saw himself, covered in blood and with a shred of Jeffrey's intestine tangled in his hair, leaning on the short haft of his crimson-bladed axe, which in turn rested on top of Mike Rossi's severed head, which itself rested on the pile he'd made of Mike's flesh and innards. He was laughing like a maniac.

I look absolutely insane, Carl thought, seeing a one-way trip to the state penitentiary in his future. *They're gonna lock me away forever.*

He saw the cataclysmic crash of his grand enrichment scheme. The extent of his fall from grace terrified him. For the past two days, he'd floated daydreaming on a cloud composed of millions of dollars; only to now . . .

Carl looked up from the phone screen, on which he was brutally divesting his brother's left thigh of all its meat.

"What do you want?" he asked Angela Rossi, feeling like a man who stood on the verge of a precipice, with a yawning black chasm behind him and a giant hungry gator approaching him. "Money? I'm wealthy now. I'll share it with you. Just don't share this with anyone else."

He was shocked when she began laughing. "Share it with me? Oh, hell yes, you're gonna share everything with me, Carlie."

Carl waited meekly.

"We're getting married, Carl," Angela said. "That's what I want from you. Nothing more and nothing less. Just your hot body, your pretty face, and above all, your hard dick in me daily, for the next half-century at least."

CHAPTER 39

Angela . . . The Proposal

"Married?"

"Yes, married."

"You can't be serious."

"Baby, don't be more of an asshole than you've already shown you are. I *am* frigging serious—we're getting married." She pouted at him. "Honey, I love you. I want you. I'm having you. And at the moment, your balls are stuffed so deep in my pussy, it could be a handbag and your pubic hair the zip."

Angela got to her feet and strutted across Carl's living room floor. "One peep out of me and you're finished," she confidently informed him. "You're fucked, literally. You've a choice to make . . ." She leaned over the coffee table and stared at him. "It's a very simple choice, really, elementary school stuff: would you prefer to spend the next fifty years of your life in prison with no chance of parole, with muscular hunks with dicks the size of aerosol cans raping you day and night, with black men exchanging your sweet and tight white ass between themselves for cigarettes and favors . . . or . . ." here, she preened herself—it wasn't by accident that she'd both ditched her bra and chosen a tight tee shirt which showed off her physical assets to best advantage, "or, would you prefer to spend those fifty years of nights and days with me? With me loving you and pampering you and . . . I frigging assure you the sex will be second-to-none. And . . . with me there's also no chance of your catching any nasty diseases like Susan was gonna give you sooner or later."

"Susan's dead," Carl said quietly. "The Cleaverman got her."

"I know," Angela said sweetly. "And it's all for the best for us. I wouldn't want you spending your hard-murdered money—sorry, darling, *our* hard-murdered money—on prostitutes."

While making her speech, Angela been watching Carl closely. She still didn't know how he'd react to her marriage proposal. Really, he had no choice at all. It was either her way or the penitentiary; but men could be stubborn as mules sometimes.

She'd considered turning him in—right up till the moment when he'd opened his front door and she'd seen his gorgeous face again, she'd agonized over doing the right thing and calling the police to come arrest him for killing both of their brothers—but she'd managed to control herself, to rise above her sense of loss and her sense of outrage, both emotions which demanded recompense and justice. She'd also had to overcome her sense of ethics, that deep understanding of right and wrong drummed into her mind in law school.

Screw that. A girl's gotta catch a few breaks every now and then. And unpretty me snaring myself a rich and handsome husband's a hell of a good start!

She realized Carl was smiling coldly at her.

"I could kill you too," he said quietly. "We're alone in here now and there aren't any witnesses. The police would never realize it's not the same serial killer."

Still bent over the coffee table with her big breasts dangling in Carl's face, Angela laughed in Carl's face. She'd expected this.

"I already told you not to confirm yourself as an asshole, darling," she told him. Then straightening up again, she backed off to sit in her armchair again. "No, you can't kill me—not ever. Honey, I'm a *lawyer*, and a damn good one at that—I graduated top of my class. Before coming over here, I already backed up the evidence of your murders—this video and five others are backed up in six different cloud storage sites, along with instructions to my lawyers"—she burst out in honest laughter at the surprised look on his face—"Carl, honey, lawyers have lawyers too." Her face and voice both turned hard and cold again. "So, yes, playboy, in the event of my death, I've left instructions with my lawyers to open several cloud storage accounts, and just in case those have been somehow deleted by hackers, to also play several DVDs I left in their custody this morning. And I don't need to tell you what those cloud accounts and DVDs contain, do I?"

"But . . . but . . ." He was very amusing to watch, worse than a drowning man clutching at barbed wire. For a moment, Angela felt very offended. True, she wasn't a beauty, but she wasn't *that* bad-looking. She just wasn't . . . whatever it was that men kept chasing after like dogs in heat.

During those few moments, she almost sent Carl off to jail simply for wounding her vanity. But then she put things back in perspective: *But now I'm getting me some and that's that.* Oh, she intended to really put Carl through his paces in the bedroom. For the foreseeable future, he'd be humping like a camel . . .

I'm frigging passionate too. I just haven't had much chance to show it.

She was relieved when Carl's shoulders sagged. She'd defeated him. She permitted herself a grin of triumph, let him see her gloating over him.

It didn't matter. He was hers now. All hers now. "And you can't ever cheat on me," she added. "Not even once—not even when I'm pregnant and fat or old and ugly—or else I'll dump you in the slammer anyway, and I'll—"

And it was right then that the air between them began swirling into a helix of black and gray smoke beside the coffee table.

She sat and stared at the arriving Cleaverman. Her mouth gaped wide in horror at his terrifying form. She felt like screaming but stifled the emerging noise with both palms pressed to her mouth. This wasn't the time for mindless panic. This was the time for strength, though truth be told, Angela honestly didn't think strength was any use here: she'd *seen* what the Cleaverman had done to the Pattens.

"Carl!" she finally gibbered in fright, looking at Carl and realizing that her future husband hadn't yet noticed the phantom killer, that he was miles away from her, mentally lost in sad reflection of his fate. "Carl, frigging snap out of it! He's here! The Cleaverman's here!"

CHAPTER 40

Carl

Angela had deduced right: On hearing her demand and her terms and conditions, Carl had done more than just sag. He'd withdrawn deep inside himself.

Now he had three horrors: the Cleaverman wanted to kill him; Bev wanted to 'feed' him; and Angela wanted to marry him.

Carl figured that he just might escape the first two fates, but not the third. Angela Rossi—pleasant and homely and with that massive chest of hers—had him by the short hairs. There was no escaping her. He stared at her and felt physically sick. He didn't feel disgusted because of Angela—she wasn't ugly, merely plain and awkward—but because of all the pretty and sexy women he wasn't going to have any more. Just this one, morning, afternoon and night. And she was guaranteed to get fat too—women like her always got fat after a while. And if there was one thing Carl didn't like, it was fat women.

But . . . he thought quietly, *being rich and having a fat wife is definitely better than languishing in jail and suffering nightly colon inspections from guys with erections the size of my forearms. Who knows, sex-starved as she is, Angel might even do anal* . . .

On that amused if ironic note, accepting that his playboy days were now over for good, Carl Whitfield refocused his mind back out of his miserable reflections and once more became aware of his living room. And that's when he realized that he and Angela were no longer alone in the room.

The Cleaverman had come to them. Unbidden, unwanted and unwelcome, the monster was here nonetheless.

The evil animated swirl of black smoke that formed the Cleaverman was already speaking: "The riddle is the rhyme: the rhyme is the riddle." The dead demonic voice echoed through the living room. The figure's recessed gassy eyes were sunken pits that seemed to descend through his head to the depths of Hell, to where Satan held court in abysmal infernal caverns while watching damned souls roast over pits of burning sulfur and brimstone. The Cleaverman's mouth was a cave that begun nowhere and ended nowhere. If this horrible creature's eyes led to Hell, his mouth then must be the Devil's torture chamber. Tattered and wavering gaseous rags seemed to cover him. To Carl's mind the rags seemed a representation of John Cleaverman's one-time butcher outfit.

Carl felt as frozen as if his bones had been emptied of their marrow and liquid nitrogen had been poured in to fill them up again.

Carl sort-of imagined a swirl of concentrated biological fumes— the semi-toxic gaseous exudations of a murdered corpse hurriedly buried in a shallow mountainside grave, a body accidentally unearthed by a hungry wolf on a hot summer night after the winter frost and spring thaw had had nature's rotting way with it; he visualized that swirl of noxious fumes reacting in anger to the violence of its death, and in its rage becoming more than it was ever meant to be; created by violence, it had in turn assumed the horrendous nature of its makers and become one with the evil that had seeded it.

This, to Carl's horrified mind, summed up the Cleaverman. There are things so scary that one doesn't dare remember them; and other, even scarier things that one doesn't even dare think about or see. And then there are things that must not exist, because if they did exist, existence would become madness. Carl understood this now with a shattering clarity.

And the eyes . . .

The Cleaverman's eyes were like no eyes that Carl Whitfield had ever viewed before. Eyes were meant to be bright, to be communicative and reassuring. But John Cleaverman's eyes were wells of unending darkness. The expression in those twin smoky depths in the Cleaverman's face was impossible to put into words. Pain and death were both emotions expressible on a mask of human skin, but this was beyond that. The Cleaverman's gaze conveyed a spectrum of emotions of such intense revulsion that for several seconds Carl actually felt his sanity collapsing from sheer terror. He felt awe as if in the presence of God.

I have stared into Hell and it's staring right back at me, he thought.

Now Carl understood the meaning of absolute fear. Above everything else that was terrifying about the ghostly apparition that had just joined them in his living room, the most scary thing about the Cleaverman was the irrepressible aura of evil that radiated from him. The outflow of negation issuing from this abominable creature was like nothing that Carl had ever sensed before; and from the look on Angela's face, she felt the same way.

Carl's gaze now became riveted on the Cleaverman's huge cleaver. He'd never seen one so big in his entire life. It gleamed like a colossal razor blade, one potent enough to slice the sun to shreds. He visualized it hacking the life out of him like it had done to Tommy and Nicole Ellsworth, to Steve-O and Jacqui and Big Dick, and to Paul and Leona Patten and finally Susan Riley and whoever she'd been sleeping with at the time. The sequence of images that came to Carl's mind were utterly terrifying ones; flying clots of blood and ripped-apart shredded meat and mingling spilled body fluids.

And then, suddenly, his trance of awe faded and he was again there with his terror and the Cleaverman's riddle that he needed to resolve to stay alive.

The Cleaverman turned his dark gaze on Angela. Intense fright etched all over her face, she had the spellbook out now and was hastily flipping through its pages.

"The riddle is the rhyme; the rhyme is the riddle." The voice echoed everywhere like death seeking an escape into life. Now the black gas swirl sounded angry. Its edges flickered with a cold blue fire.

Angela had gotten the right page open. "I don't know!" she shrieked at both Carl and the Cleaverman.

"Throw me the book!" Carl shrieked back at her. (For a moment, he'd actually considered waiting for the Cleaverman to butcher her first. But that would mean his going to jail once her will was read out; so he'd realized he had no choice but to save her.) The Cleaverman was already lifting his giant blade.

Angela flung the book at Carl, its pages fluttering like wings in the air. The book crackled with static electricity as it passed through the edge of the Cleaverman's body.

The Cleaverman's blade was now held high. At any moment now it would fall, and that would be it for Angela Rossi, who was cringing in her chair, too frightened to make a jump to safety. Her breasts rose and fell, keeping time with her terror-fueled breathing.

"Hey, wait!" Carl told the Cleaverman. "I know the answer. I've written it down somewhere in the book. Just don't hurt her. Whatever you do, don't hurt her!"

He was relieved when the Cleaverman froze just as the blade began descending. Slowly, the phantom slaughterer turned to face Carl.

"The riddle is the rhyme," he said. "The rhyme is the riddle."

He stood waiting, his body writhing in the air that formed it.

"Just wait," Carl said. "Wait and I'll tell you what you want to know. Just be patient for a minute or two."

The Cleaverman said nothing. But he lowered the cleaver to his side again.

"Good, good," Carl said with a confidence he didn't feel. "Just calm down and let me find where I wrote it down and then I'll tell you."

Carl had no idea what the riddle's answer was. He flicked desperately through the book. Through gaps in the Cleaverman's gaseous body, he saw Angela staring at him with hope in her eyes. But where the hell was the damn riddle written? At a point he opened a page and his eyes locked on a strange title. "What the hell?" he said to himself, but then realized he had no time to further investigate his discovery. Death, personified in the eerie specter that stood before him, was waiting. He searched on, cursing the fact that the page Angela had opened had shut again when she'd flung the book to him.

"A few pages from the back," she mouthed at him.

But Carl had just found the riddle/rhyme:

Tell me the name of John Cleaverman's wife,
An Angel Maria he loved all of his life.
Never a nag like Jenny, never one day in strife.
You, my friends, have just one chance to survive:
Answer this riddle or give up your lives.

Carl stared at it, and roved his mind across the words on the page. There was an answer here, and it had to be a simple one. *I'm frigging good with puzzles and ciphers. I can crack this. I can do this.* He glanced at the Cleaverman, whose ghostly face was locked in an expectant expression. "Just one more minute, smoke guy, I got this."

Then it hit Carl and he began laughing.

"What's the matter?" Angela asked worriedly, as if scared he'd just lost his mind.

Carl laughed even louder. Then he pointed at the Cleaverman. "Dude, your wife's name is Tanya. Now, please leave us alone. My fiancée and I have a wedding to plan."

"Tanya?" the Cleaverman asked in some wonder, his facial expression of anger slowly changing to one of peace. "Tanya?"

"Carl, are you frigging sure?" Angela asked.

Carl nodded confidently. "Yes, her name's Tanya. Alright, Smokey, like I said, goodbye."

Carl was relieved when the Cleaverman began to fade. Though certain he'd cracked the puzzle, he'd had a moment of intense doubt right after he'd told the Cleaverman the answer. What if?

But it *was* over.

"Yes, Tanya. Yes . . . her name *is* Tanya," the fading ghost acknowledged, with a smile on his morbid face and pleasure in his echoing voice.

Soon all that remained of John Cleaverman was his immense silver cleaver and the dark ghostly fingers that gripped it.

And then those too winked out of existence. And then all that remained was for the lingering traces of implacable evil in the living room to fade away also.

CHAPTER 41

Carl & Angela

"How the hell did you figure that out?" Angela asked after the Cleaverman vanished, then she leapt up and hurried over to Carl's side on the couch. "I've been cracking my brain at it for at least ten hours and you figured it out in under a minute. . . . Oh, oh shit! And I was so scared and confused when he appeared that I completely forgot to plug my ears like I did the last time I saw him. I just didn't remember at all."

"Plug your ears? Angel, what are you talking about?"

"When I went with Paul and Leona . . . I put my fingers in my ears so that I didn't hear what the Cleaverman said. But this time, when he looked at me, I just couldn't . . . I just couldn't, like my hands and arms just wouldn't obey me." She calmed herself and remembered the question she'd been asking Carl: "But how did you figure out the riddle? I thought my brain was going to burst from how much thinking I did and I still couldn't work it out."

He shrugged. "It's easy."

"Easy?" She gaped at him. "Carlie, Tanya isn't any of the names in the riddle."

He nodded, now pleased with himself. "Yeah, but it's there in plain view." He pushed the spellbook at her. "Just read the first letters of each sentence downward."

"Lemme see." She snatched the book from him. "T . . . A . . . N . . . Y . . . A . . . You're right. Man, you're a genius."

"No, I'm not. I'm just lucky." He scowled. "Maybe *unlucky*—your soon-to-be husband, remember?"

She draped an arm over his shoulder and squeezed his muscles. "Would you prefer the alternative? I can still arrange it for you if you'd like."

He shook his head. "Not after all this crap I've been through. He scowled. "I'd rather eat your pussy three times daily than suck stinking convict dick day and night."

She leaned against him and kissed him on the cheek. "That's a smart man. I'll be good for you, you'll see. Oh, I'll be really good for you, Carl. Just don't ever cheat on me and we'll be fine."

Carl nodded glumly. "Yeah, yeah—all you women are the same anyway. No chance of letting me off the hook?"

She shook her head and her thin lips twisted up in anger. "None at all, darling. After all, you did kill my older brother and I loved him dearly and . . ." She suddenly looked shocked. "Oh no, I forgot about mom!"

Carl stared at her in alarm. "What happened to your mom?"

Angela explained: "My stepdad called me to tell me that my mom saw the news about Mike's death on CNN—they live in Columbus, Ohio—and that she instantly fainted. She's been sedated and each time she wakes up she groggily asks if I'm alright or if I got murdered also. And I promised him that I'd call her and then plumb forgot."

Carl relaxed again.

"Are you sure it's over?" Angela asked after a moment.

"Yeah, I think it is," Carl replied. Angela was still leaning on him and now that the Cleaverman had left them both alive, the feel of her soft breasts on his naked torso was creating a familiar feeling of sexual tension in his groin. He was surprised and relieved that she'd decided not to turn him in. True, it was going to be hard living with her . . . or maybe it wouldn't be—she seemed genuinely in love with him, and from the way the feel of her soft body pressed against his was already giving him an erection . . .

An erection that Angela had noticed, because its swollen tip had just pushed its way out beneath the left hem of his shorts.

She reached down and touched it. At first she touched it tentatively, as if she was scared of it, or unused to seeing erections, which Carl suspected was the case. Then, as if realizing that the swollen penis in her little hand belonged entirely to her now, Angela grasped it firmly, pulling back Carl's shorts with her other hand and exposing him fully, both phallus and balls.

She giggled with pleasure. "Oh, what a beauty."

Carl managed not to moan as she stroked him, with an expertise that almost matched Susan's.

Then she let go of his erection and got up off the couch.

"Alright, darling," she said, leering down at him with eyes that were now portals of lust. "I'm going to have a bath now, and once I'm all cleaned up I want you to come and make love to me. I like sex to be really nice and gentle, you know. I need you to treat me like a lady in bed, like my body is made of gold and my kitty-cat spun from silk and . . ."

Carl nodded and she left. His penis was still hard and showed no signs whatsoever of deflating. Having sex with her would be good therapy. Despite defeating the Cleaverman—had they actually defeated him?—he felt infinitely stressed out; the result of all the hours spent worrying and searching for the Cleaverman riddle online, while ironically, the riddle—in the person of Angela Rossi (he could hear her turning on the shower water)—was busy worrying and searching for him.

Carl got up and walked over to plug in the TV again. Then, with his penis sticking out in front of him like a lance, he returned to his spot on the couch and turned the TV on. Angela was singing in the shower. Carl winced; she had a *very* bad voice.

There was a new news headline now, one that instantly deflated Carl's erection:

'TRIAL JUDGE DIES IN SHOCKING CIRCUMSTANCES.'

Carl turned up the volume.

". . . Of twists and turns, there's been yet another shocking twist in the Teddy Hobart murder case. This morning Judge Joseph Riley was found dead at home in his bedroom. The judge—who'd been overseeing the Teddy Hobart trial, had apparently choked to death on a mixture of boiled eggs and excrement and what are believed to be the decaying remains of a small rodent. It will be recalled by viewers that Mr. Hobart was himself killed sometime during the night.

"At the moment, the primary suspect in Judge Riley's death is a young blonde woman who was reportedly seen walking away from his house.

"Mrs. Laura Wilson, Judge Riley's housekeeper, said that when she arrived at the old widower's residence this morning, she met an attractive blonde woman in her mid-twenties who was just leaving. The woman, who said her name was Bev, claimed the judge and she had spent the night together. She walked off while Mrs. Wilson entered the house . . . and was quickly alerted by the smell of excrement to investigate her employer's bedroom, where she discovered his corpse. The Raynham police are requesting anyone with leads to come forward.

"Earlier this morning, Judge Riley's only daughter, Susan Riley was found hacked to pieces in a Briarcliff Road condominium apartment belonging to Mr. Robert West. Also murdered in that attack were Mr. West and Mr. Jack Clarke, a successful attorney residing in . . ."

Carl gaped at the television. *Judge Riley is dead?*

Then he remembered something. Carl recalled that weird thing he'd noticed in the spellbook while searching for the Cleaverman rhyme, but which his desperation hadn't given him time to properly investigate. He reached for the spellbook, which Angela had left on the coffee table.

Angela was still singing in the shower. Her voice sounded better to him now, or maybe he'd begun getting used to it. The newscaster was still talking, but Carl's mind faded her out. Angela had left the spellbook open to the Cleaverman rhyme. After picking the book up, Carl quickly flipped backward through its leaves until he found what he was looking for:

THE BOILED-EGG WOMAN.

Occasionally summoned along with the Cleaverman is the creature known as the Boiled Egg Woman. A kind of mischievous minor demon, the Boiled Egg Woman usually appears to her victims as a young woman with blonde hair . . . She calls herself Bevv, an abbreviation of 'boiled egg woman' with the two vees in her name forming the 'W.'

The specific reason why the Boiled Egg Woman appears along with the Cleaverman are not known—some occult authorities claim she was John Cleaverman's sister or daughter, while others claim she was his mother or lover—but once summoned to the human realms, Bevv remains active for exactly as long as the Cleaverman does, vanishing back into the ether at the exact instant he does.

The Boiled Egg Woman—Bevv—is believed to be harmless enough . . .

Carl read this and tried to keep a straight face. He almost felt like shouting out his relief at having killed two birds with one stone. *Ha ha ha! Both the Cleaverman and Bev—or Bevv—are gone! No one's coming to feed me poop!*

Then he sobered. *I'm still getting married to plain-as-butt Angela and . . . dammit, whoever said marriage was an institution wasn't lying—being married to that woman's gonna be almost like being locked away!*

The shower noises had stopped. He turned off the television and grimly willing his penis to rise back to erection again, turned and walked into his bedroom.

To Carl's surprise and strange dismay, the moment he saw Angela sprawled naked on his bed, his penis leapt to full rigidity again.

CHAPTER 42

Angela

Angela moaned and gasped and tingled as Carl thrust and sweated and grunted on top of her. His penis filled her vagina the way a chocolate bar fills a hungry mouth. She was wet and juicy and her heels clenched tightly on Carl's buttocks and her breasts throbbed and tingled as they pressed against Carl's hairy chest.

No doubt about it; Angela Rossi (shortly to be Angela Whitfield) was enjoying herself to the fullest. And from the look in her fiancé's eyes, so was he.

Angela's primary regret as she approached her sexual climax was that it was evil and murder that had brought them together.

But all's fair in love and war, she thought giddily as her senses melted away in delicious orgasm. *I won! The good girl won! What's important is that I got the man I wanted. Yippee!*

The End

ABOUT THE AUTHOR

Wol-vriey is Nigerian, and quite tall.

He believes there actually are things that go bump in the night.

He writes horror fiction—for adults only, please. And also some surrealist stuff.

Wol-vriey blogs at: *http://oddityfarm.wordpress.com*

WOL-VRIEY
BIZARRO AND TRANSGRESSIVE FICTION

BOSTON POSH (BUD MALONE #1)

In 2028 AD, the USA is a nation ravaged by hungry dragons and dinosaurs. In Boston, Massachusetts, private eye Bud Malone is hired to rescue a kidnapped heiress. But nothing is as it seems.

Malone works to unravel a tangled web involving Boston Chinatown, a 200-year-old woman with a 9-year-old body, white robots, a human-liver-eating psychopath, a golem, a porcelain dragon, and a snake goddess with a crush on him. There's also a woman obsessed with chicken sex. Then Malone meets Posh Lane, a gorgeous call girl who's desperate to quit her pimp.

Romantic sparks ignite between Posh and Malone, but Posh's past suddenly catches up with her in a BIG way. To save Posh, Malone agrees to run a quest for Earth's new rulers, the Forks. But, Malone has no idea that agreeing to the Fork's odd request will send him on the weirdest trip he's ever been on in his life.

BOSTON CORPSE (BUD MALONE #2)

MAGIC CAN BE MURDER! - Drag queen Lucy Tang is back in Boston, and is hell-bent on settling her vindetta against casino owner Sookie Ling. And suddenly, Bud Malone, PI, has the case of his life to resolve.

When Boston's robot police force are baffled by a mind transfer case, they come to Malone for help. The one person who can likely help Malone out here is the witch Soledad Bathory. But Soledad seems to know a lot more than she's telling him. It's a case not made easier when Malone meets Soledad's beautiful cousin, Josephine 'Slave' Bailey. Slave has her own plans for Malone, most of which involve teaching him BDSM and making him her new Master.

Oh, and Rick Rogers owes Sookie Ling a whole lot of money, a gambling debt that's going to be literally Hell to pay!

BOSTON CORPSE - Not your average detective novel!

Burning Bulb
PUBLISHING

WOL-VRIEY
BIZARRO AND TRANSGRESSIVE FICTION

BOSTON LUST (BUD MALONE #3)

"Bless it, Father, for she has sinned."

Seven murdered gay women, all their bodies completely drained of blood. All also with large parts of their bodies dissolved away like acid has been pumped into their veins.

Bud Malone has to find the female vampire preying on Boston's lesbian population.

Then Malone meets the beautiful Trudi Carmen and the case gets even more tangled. Trudi needs Malone's help in recovering a ring that's gone missing. But how in the world is one little black ring related to either the dead women or their killer?

Resolving this case will lead Malone deep into Lucy Tang's legacy—The Abstracta. And then to the city of Genesis.

Boston Lust—Just when you thought Bean Town was safe to visit again.

HELL DANCER

Six people find themselves trapped in Detention, a nightmare realm where the demonic Schoolmaster is hell-bent on reforming them . . . until they die.

Porn superstar Venus Deluxe came to Springfield, MA to party, and next found her life hanging by a thread. One wrong answer will mean her death.

Suspended BPD detective Tanya Rockford was trying to stop one kind of violence, but found a terrifying another. With her and her companion's lives hanging in the balance, it's going to take all of her courage and resourcefulness to escape this hell she's stumbled into.

Porn stud Chad Cannon has made a career from his ten-inch penis. Here in Detention, however, it's his brains that matter. He'll soon be hoping all the pot he's smoked over the years hasn't completely messed up his memory.

The three students, Sherri, Jordan, and Mike? They were all just in the wrong place at the right time. Will anyone survive Detention? The evil Schoolmaster doesn't plan on letting that happen . . .

Burning Bulb
PUBLISHING

WOL-VRIEY
BIZARRO AND TRANSGRESSIVE FICTION

VAGINA MUNDI

Rachel Risk is a professional thief with super-strong hair that can stretch like tentacles to manipulate objects. Ashley Status has both a digitally augmented brain, and 'muscle-purses' in her arms and legs in which she stores inflatable objects—cars, guns, rocket launchers, etc.

When Raye is framed as the fall girl in a jewel robbery, the pair flee Chicago's vengeful robot gangsters and take refuge in the Hotel Bizarre, where the gorgeous 'vagina singer,' Femina, is performing for a week.

But the Hotel Bizarre is even stranger than its name suggests, and very soon Raye and Ash are involved in an deadly adventure, a struggle for survival the likes of which they'd never imagined possible—with loads of deviant sex, drugs, music, and violence at every turn. And just what is the old woman in the skin desert really doing with all those cats glued to her walls?

VAGINA MUNDI—a Bizarro Hymn in praise of WOMAN!

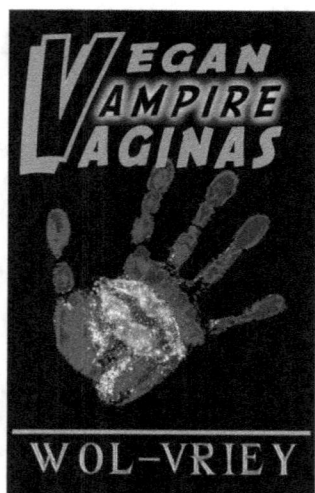

VEGAN VAMPIRE VAGINAS

The biggest bank heist in US history. And Tom Palmer can't remember pulling it off. And no, this isn't your standard case of amnesia. After a one-night-stand gone horribly wrong, Boston salesman Tom Palmer wakes up with a vagina implanted in his left hand. Then his day gets worse.

Tom is transported across space-time to a nightmare version of Boston, one where the Bizarro virus has transformed half the population into cannibals. Worst of all, Tom discovers that in this new Boston, he's the infamous gangster Pussypalm, wanted for robbing the Federal Reserve Bank of Boston a year ago. He also learns that the vagina in his hand is prophetic, i.e. it talks . . . after sex.

With 130 people left dead during his bank heist and six billion dollars missing, Tom knows he's living on borrowed time. It is in his best interests not to remember anything. Because once he does . . .

Burning Bulb
PUBLISHING

WOL-VRIEY
BIZARRO AND TRANSGRESSIVE FICTION

VEGAN ZOMBIE APOCALYPSE

In the post-apocalypse worlderness, zombies rule the earth. They're allergic to meat, and brains literally make them explode. Zombies now eat blood potatoes, parasitic tubers grown in the flesh of humancows corralled in maximum security farms. Two fugitives meet in the ancient ruins of Texas. The first is Soil 15-f, a womancow who's escaped her farm a week before she's due to be killed and her blood potato crop harvested. The second fugitive is Able Kane, former head necros food technician, now sentenced to death for heresy. But Soil is no ordinary humancow.

Unknown to herself, she's the vegan zombie agricultural revolution, and the zombies desperately want her back. And the necros equally desperately want Able Kane dead. He's fled with a forbidden discovery which will reshape the world for the worse if used. And Able is just hardheaded/misguided enough to use it.

MELANIE NEMESIS CATCHPOLE

In Springfield, Massachusetts, Melanie Catchpole is hired to fetch back a magic teddy bear worth millions of dollars from a warehouse across town. Problem is, the warehouse is down in Springfield's O-Zone—that totally weird sector of the city where Bizarro fell to Earth. The 'O' is a fairytale land, a place where dreams and nightmares literally live and breathe..

Worse still, the gingers—mutant cannibals—prowl the O. The gingers have already eaten everyone else Melanie's employers sent to get back the magic teddy bear.

Accompanied by the handsome but ruthless Doug Fisher (who she finds sexy but doesn't dare entrust her heart to), Melanie enters the O-Zone. Melanie and Doug are instantly caught up in an adventure they'd never have believed credible even if written as fiction . . . and Melanie's used to experiencing the very weird as the norm.

And now, additionally, there's a mystery to unravel: What does the dark, freezing-cold being called The Fixer want with Mary, the barkeep's daughter?

Burning Bulb
PUBLISHING

WOL-VRIEY
BIZARRO AND TRANSGRESSIVE FICTION

BIG TROUBLE IN LITTLE ASS

From Bizarro master storyteller Wol-vriey comes a truly weird western tale that will leave you awe-struck and on the edge of your seat...

In the town named Little Ass, tight-assed prostitute Rosa overhears a gunslinger's plans to assassinate rancher Edison Bennett. Once the badass Bennett learns of the plot, he ensures there'll be hell to pay for any attempt on his life!

Yes, it's going to take all of gunslinger Jude's shooting prowess, his eclectic collection of strange firearms, a trusty horse that requires an owners' manual, and the help of the lovely and invigorating Nell (who's EXTREMELY odd when the going gets weird), to survive the Bizarro hell that Edison Bennett unleashes in order to hold onto the land that he'd stolen from Madam Zizi.

BIZARRO 101 (A BASIC PRIMER)

Welcome to the strange place:

A collection of 37 flash fiction stories designed to introduce one to the Bizarro/New Weird Genre.

Weird, dreamy, nightmarish, absurd, sad, surreal, humorous . . . this collection of tales is all this and more.

***

"This primer is the very essence of any and all styles and types of Bizarro writing. Wol-vriey collects, distills, and bottles up these 37 tiny stories for your sensory enjoyment. This is an absolute must-read for anyone new to the genre, because it demonstrates the scope of what Bizarro is, and what it can be."
　　　　　　　　　　　　　－Teresa Pollack, Bizarro commentator and blogger

Burning Bulb
PUBLISHING

WOL-VRIEY
BIZARRO AND TRANSGRESSIVE FICTION

Dr. Orgasm

Courtney Taylor is young, intelligent, beautiful, and successful. She also has a boyfriend who loves her deeply. The problem is, no matter what Courtney does, she can't climax during sex.

When Florence Rigid's communist forces destroy the city of Metaphor, Courtney and her friends Teresa, Highball, Miki, and Heather are cast into the midst of a quest to find the only person able to save the land of Innuendo—Dr. Carol Orgasm, wanted by the communists for developing the O-Pill, a wonder drug that grants women sexual ecstasy on demand.

The communists will do anything to get their hands on the O-Pill and prevent its reaching the millions of Innuendo's women. But Courtney desperately wants that pill too. And so it's now a race between Courtney and the communists to find Dr. Orgasm first.

And Courtney has no choice but to win this race. She must win it: For her own orgasm . . . and for the freedom of female sexuality everywhere.

PUSSY TRANSMISSION

Pussy Transmission were the most decadent Pop Art ensemble of the 90's. Led by the beautiful painter Isis Lynch, the trio revolutionized the art world. Then suddenly, without explanation, Pussy Transmission vanished into historical obscurity. Now, twenty years later, three women come to Lynch Place. Lily and Nina are journalists desperate to interview Isis Lynch. Raven, on the other hand, wants to find her boyfriend, who's gone missing inside Isis's house. Raven's worried—she's heard that Pussy Transmission broke up because Isis began dabbling in black magic . . . with devastating results. All three women will shortly wish they'd never left home. Particularly once the rats in Lynch Place start warning them that they're going to die . . . and Raven meets Betty Butcher, the bouncy supernatural psycho who's intent on chopping her into bits. Pussy Transmission, Baby! Just because . . .

Burning Bulb
PUBLISHING

WOL-VRIEY
BIZARRO AND TRANSGRESSIVE FICTION

GIRLS ARE NOT SMILING

Welcome To The Road Trip From Hell

Pagan is demon-possessed.

Lori is suicidal.

Britt is just terminally pissed off.

Meet three young Boston women on the run from the law, each with problems that will fuse into more than the sum of their individual parts, becoming a holocaust of sex and violence and terror, a literal rain of blood and horror and gore and evil.

And if that wasn't already bad enough, Pagan's pet demon is slowly transforming her into something both unspeakable and unholy. Truly, these girls aren't smiling.

BLUE NIGHTMARES

Consummate EVIL is coming. It is relentless and unavoidable. It is Blue.

Jessica Schreiber is seeing things. Very horrible things. Since arriving in Raynham for what should have been a relaxing vacation, she's been seeing *The Big Blue*.

Jessica is smelling things too—dead and rotting things that she can't see. She is sure those dead and rotting things are dead people. Lots of dead people.

Jessica's worst nightmares will soon become her reality. Her reality will soon become a terrifying nightmare.

The tentacled residents of the House of Death have a lot that they wish to show Jessica Schreiber. They have a lot that they wish to tell her. But will she survive long enough to learn their lessons?

Burning Bulb
PUBLISHING

WOL-VRIEY
BIZARRO AND TRANSGRESSIVE FICTION

BRAINCHEW

It was supposed to be a simple jewel heist, but it went badly wrong. Chuck got shot and died.

Lance hid his friend's corpse in the Pleasant Street Cemetery. But that was a big mistake—there was something undead, something extremely hungry . . . something eXXXtremely horrible, buried in the Pleasant Street Cemetery.

And Lance had just woken it up.

They called the monster Brainchew because it ate brains. Human brains. And it preferred those brains fresh from the heads . . . of the living.

And now it was awake again, Brainchew planned on feeding big-time tonight. Oh hell yes, it did.

BRAINCHEW 2: OUT OF THEIR HEADS

After Tiff Hooper recognizes Josh Penham, the man who abducted her and kept her in his basement and abused her, she brings her three friends to Raynham for a night of well-deserved revenge on him.

Only things don't go according to plan.

It is never a good idea to leave a corpse in Raynham's Pleasant Street Cemetery. You run the very real risk of awakening what lies underground there. And that thing—Brainchew—is more horrible and more evil than anything the average mind conceives of even in its worst nightmares.

Brainchew is back! And this time the monster is extra-hungry. But there are plenty of delicious human brains about tonight, and Brainchew intends to eat them all before dawn.

Burning Bulb
PUBLISHING

WOL-VRIEY
BIZARRO AND TRANSGRESSIVE FICTION

DARIA: AN EROTIC NIGHTMARE

Even the best laid women can go wrong.

Daria Simpson is HUNGRY. She's HUNGRY for sex and bloodshed and death.

Shelly Parker just wanted to have a threesome with her boyfriend Craig and her best friend Erica. Everything was shaping up nicely for their weekend of sexual fun and games, until they stopped at the creepy Crossway Diner and met Daria.

From the moment they met Daria, EVERYTHING went wrong for them; and it went wrong in the most horrific and terrifying of ways!

Daria: Paranormal service has been resumed.

WET BONES

Greg is about learning the hard way that you don't mess with Aunt Grace.

Nine completely fleshless skeletons recovered in the Massachusetts woods. Two detectives on the trail of a horrible, hungry monster.

Broken-hearted Allie Jackson has a date with a creature from Hell.

Things are about to get well out of hand for everyone, and in horrifying, terrifying ways they don't expect.

Burning Bulb
PUBLISHING

WOL-VRIEY
BIZARRO AND TRANSGRESSIVE FICTION

MR. UGLY

When a rotting corpse appears and starts butchering Raynham's youths, there's really only one question that needs answering:

Is this faceless and rotting monster Peter Howard, or isn't it?

Problem is, Peter Howard died 15 years ago. So how can he possibly be back from the dead and murdering people with such relentless and incredible brutality?

Peter's mother Malicia, who's just been released from the lunatic asylum may have the answers to the crazy puzzle, but the two detectives investigating the deaths don't even know the right questions to ask her yet.

BRUTAL

Jane Winters is 28 years old.

She works as a checkout cashier in a department store. She's an attractive woman with a winning personality. She has both a photographic memory and an I.Q. of 189.

She's met the man of her dreams.

But she's also a cannibal with a unique and very scary mode of operation.

The group known as TULIP (The Urban Legend Investigation People) are out to either prove or disprove the legend of Insane Jane.

But have TULIP bitten off more than they can chew?

Burning Bulb
PUBLISHING

WOL-VRIEY
BIZARRO AND TRANSGRESSIVE FICTION

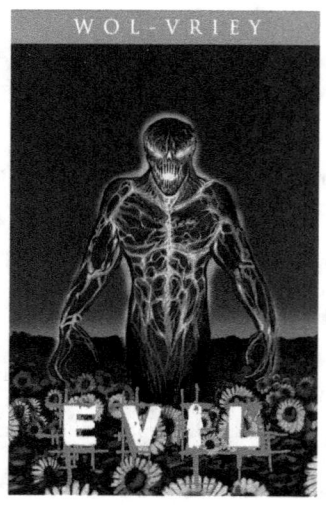

EVIL

The Evil began the week before Sylvia Stewart's 30th birthday.

Cathy Higgins died.

The Bargainer resurrected Cathy . . . for a price.

The price? Cathy's father Ronan had to plant some seeds for him.

But these were no ordinary seeds the Bargainer gave to Ronan Higgins. These were seeds from Hell: seeds which required human flesh as both soil and fertilizer.

And meanwhile, the unsuspecting Sylvia Stewart went ahead with the plans for her birthday party, which was to be held on Ronan Higgins' sunflower farm . . .

666

Ohio's State Route 666 stretches 14.7 miles between Zanesville and Dresden.

Most days, it's just a normal road with a funny name.

But for six minutes on the 6th of June each year, Route 666 becomes a gateway to somewhere else . . . a gateway to Hell.

Each year 13 unfortunates get trapped in the 666 underworld, with no way to get back home.

This year though, things are going to be very different. For one thing, there are currently a whole lot of turbulent human emotions at play in the underworld. And also . . . the psycho Al Gore is just about completing his collection of human heads.

And . . . what the hell is a church doing in Hell, of all places?

Burning Bulb
PUBLISHING